SEAN EDWARD

The Cartography Door

First published by Sley House Publishing 2023

Copyright © 2023 by Sean Edward

All rights reserved. No part of this publication may be reproduced, stored or transmitted in any form or by any means, electronic, mechanical, photocopying, recording, scanning, or otherwise without written permission from the publisher. It is illegal to copy this book, post it to a website, or distribute it by any other means without permission.

This novel is entirely a work of fiction. The names, characters and incidents portrayed in it are the work of the author's imagination. Any resemblance to actual persons, living or dead, events or localities is entirely coincidental.

First edition

ISBN: 978-1-957941-86-8

Cover art by Kristina Osborn Truborn Design

This book was professionally typeset on Reedsy.
Find out more at reedsy.com

Acknowledgement

To the wizard
To the Alchemist
To my queen and to my prince

Part 32 A: The Meaning of Books

"What are you writing?" asked Charon, not looking back from the bow of the boat.

Sarah let the pen nib slide from her last mark, across the entire page, before looking up. "Nothing, really." She closed the book, titled *Bound is the Dreaming Hand* in gold calligraphy, and placed it in the boat beside her.

She watched the boatman's back as he pushed the small, knife-shaped vessel along. Although his body was shrouded in a swarm of restless crow feathers and buzzing magpies that left the characteristics of his shape dismantled, Sarah still imagined the outline of a man beneath. A tall, imperious gargoyle of a man, but a man, nonetheless.

Sarah smiled.

They floated on the Acheron, a wide river whose deep waters stained the shore a vellum black. She had been here before and its poignant dye had left her fingertips coloured as well, but the ominous tunnel above and the dark endless night below—none of it stuck to her soul. She was certain she was finally on the right path.

The creaking of the wooden oar and the space it left in the water's berth filled the little spots in between Sarah's fingers with a sense of light. She beamed with what looked like the end of a long night, leaving a daydream fray to spill out from wherever darkness was usually found to be growing. When she noticed that she was smiling, her expression grew ever larger and she turned away from the boatman to watch the murky water roll away.

"You know, now's the time," spoke Charon in a voice that was like old coal.

"Time for what?"

The boat made a pleasant lapping sound as it rocked and the water pressed against its side. "Time for smiling like that, as it only gets darker from here, child."

"I know."

"Good."

Sarah closed her eyes and let the breeze braid all the little things into her hair. They were trinkets for her time, and a reminder how none was spent unearned. Her smile settled into a lazy grin; the world she knew was finally slipping away behind her.

"Oh! I almost forgot." Sarah reached into her flowered-dress pockets and grabbed the two coins. She held them for a minute in her hand, hanging between owning them and giving them up, their existence the shore between the water and land. They were heavy. The shore was heavy. It reminded her of her father and what was said in so many words.

The coins lead to the Cartography Door.

His voice burned. Sarah inspected the mirrored wasp embossment that graced each coin, its wild wings and stinger still trying to free themselves. His voice was nectar.

"Here you go." Sarah offered them up to the swirling of birds.

"Eh?" Charon's smooth laminar flow turned like so many glass shards across an icy path. He chuckled and turned back to the water and his oar, putting a free hand up in refusal. "You still don't get it, do you?"

Sarah's chest was that last breath of a fire before it smoked out; she let that cinder engorge her vision. "Can't you lead me to the Cartography Door? Where are we going if we are not going there?"

"So small, so insignificant." Charon chattered his teeth behind the storm of birds that circled his body in a constant wash of greying fabrics. "Of course I can, and I am. The coins are for the door, though, not me! Trade, equivalent exchange—it is not I who needs the currency, but the door that requires gain to transfer your place."

Sucking her bottom lip in so that her upper lip made a curtain for her teeth, Sarah waited with her mouth as the wallflower, scared to upset the dance on the water. She cleared her throat. She scratched with an uneasy hand at the fabric of her dress near her knees. She watched without focus as the red-veined river washed by, disinterested in whether it was she, or it, that was moving.

A vapour formed above the boatman's head; he steamed. The birds became frantic and hot at the top, spilling in and out of their pattern, crashing into each other as their effervescent nature increased and swelled above the chaos. Then the cloud, fierce and swollen and angry, pushed down on Charon's head. If shoulders were known, they dodged the rocket of feathers and let the boatman's angry expression compress under the pressure.

Charon's mass of ravens and magpies turned from the bow, and his head, creeping on the aged gears of his neck, exposed itself in the madness. Those empty sockets never felt more like angry mothers than when Charon spoke this time. "Didn't your father leave you a book or a journal? *That* journal, even?" And he pointed to the place where the tattered, leather-bound journal rested in her lap. "Does that one have no answers?"

Sarah swallowed. "I don't know… maybe." She picked up the book and opened it somewhere in the middle, where the book was most balanced in her hands.

Part I: Segments of its Fractal

The first few images, the first lines and the paths they crossed… they were always the trickiest. It was a lot like writing a book. The plot and characters would connect themselves together in time, the climactic fight scene, the villain, the kidnapped maiden… it would all—build itself eventually, but the first few lines… They were the hardest to puzzle together.

Sarah could see it in her head. The breaking glass where the tentacles spilled out and made origami of the air. A thick tar pouring from fissures in the sides of the tendrils where the glass had made clean but careless chasms of its flesh. Sound. Such an ominous sound. A sound that could only be imagined, something like a burning animal farm, a screeching sound that turned into a guttural growl that invaded Sarah's veins and turned her blue and cold.

Sarah reached out to touch the refracted mirror of her eyes, spilling the dream's memory out in reverse to her sense of sight. Its surface was marred—though you couldn't tell— and when she pulled back her digit, a black liquid, soot and iron, dragged itself out like a pinched sugar well.

"They appeared again, the tentacles and the Beast," said Sarah.

"Hmm." Dr. Pillapatti was not yet taking notes: she was listening with her eyes cast aside, readying the picture of Sarah's dream, practicing her neutral grey scale, when the noise escaped her throat. "That's happened several times now in the last few months."

Sarah tilted her head. "Has it? I have trouble keeping track." She looked away from the office and into the details of her dream, producing brass and key as the images played in her head. "In the dream it's all very clear, but I get… caught… in the time dilation, when I wake." It was strange, to translate her dreams, like reading one language and deciphering it in real time to another but with practice, and after clearing the murk of the first few images, Sarah could do it in her sleep.

"Have you checked your dream journal lately, read it over?"

"No, not lately."

"My memory says there's an increase in these dramatic episodes with the beast," continued Dr. Pillapatti.

Sarah chewed at her lip, trying to strip away the balm that she had applied there that morning on her way to her therapist's office. Trying to pull the flavour of her sleep from the fabric of her tongue. Trying to catch the last hints of her lucidity, so that she could taste the familiarity of its place just one more time while she was supposed to be awake. "I guess there are more," she said, with lemonade in her smile, the sour of the beast mixing with the sweetness of her sleep as she pondered the timeline in question. "They're in fully mapped dreams as well. Dreams that should have been without secrets, and have been like that for a long time." The words came out saccharin—"Dreamscapes that I thought were safe"—then souring again.

Dr. Pillapatti nodded her head. "I'm sorry that's happening, I know how important the sanctity of your dreams are." She breathed in. "Did you happen to see any more of it this time?"

Shaking her head as her voice trailed off, "No," Sarah answered, "just the tentacles," as her focus whorled back into the dream from this spot in her thoughts.

Splitting the old growth of their skin on the glass shards of the window, the tendrils barked while Sarah's body was splattered in the ichor that sprayed from the gashes on the creature's wounded arms.

Her body lit with shaking all over as an overwhelming static moved from her shocked heart to her rushed knees, while the tar-soaked tentacles whipped at her feet and drove her mad as she ran along a path between the buildings.

The black slimy arms followed, as they had every time they met, and Sarah knew she had to leave. She dashed along the path she'd run and wrote and mapped so many times before, moving along it with confidence of its shape even in this dark, without breaking a wrong step and twisting her knee. But she ran with hot flashes and blunt needles jabbing her body too; she ran with a belly full of knives put there by the entity as it cut ulcers in the soft tissue. She ran with a cold spike at her back from the beast who laid puddles of maere in the ground as it tore the landscape into trenches behind them.

"Did you choose to run, or were you not lucid?"

"No, I was lucid." Sarah looked down at the unchanged generic carpet on the ground. The red specks on its grey-wash fabric swirled and tried to jump out from their matrix while Sarah stared. Sympathizing, she lifted her feet from the ground, freeing the dots beneath her soles with the simple act of crossing her legs.

"Then why not choose to escape in a different way? Something more practical or effective, say, flying, for example?" Dr. Pillapatti had placed her elbow on her thighs and put a knuckle to her chin.

"Is flying really all that practical?" Sarah leaned her head into mocking and the doctor shrugged. "You already know I can't fly in my dreams."

"Yes. But the beast's more consistent appearance has raised a flag for me. This is a large change in what has been normally a very predictable dream schedule. One that you were more comfortable with than you are now."

Pillapatti's words became heavy stones in Sarah's thoughts. Tired from wanting to sleep, she was unable to lift them, and instead, she buried them deeper. "I guess."

"So now would be a good time to review. We should discuss some of the nuts and bolts again, and check for inconsistencies." Dr. Pillapatti smiled. "So." She raised her eyebrows. "I thought if a person was lucid, they could do whatever they wanted in a dream? I thought it was a perk."

"No." Sarah shuffled beneath the question and its weight. "Lucidity is more like a pact. An agreement between the dreamworld and me. I cannot do whatever I want but I am aware that it's a dream."

"How are you sure that it's a lucid dream? In a night terror you're highly alert or aware." Dr. Pillapatti readied her pen for an important note: Sarah could tell by the way the light came through the window behind the doctor's chair and struck her pen so that its tip illuminated.

"Yes. But in a night terror I have no control, I'm only aware of what's happening around me. When I'm lucid, when I'm in my tunnel too, I can choose to come or go. With no special effort, I can operate my body and make decisions in a safe place." Sarah was churning her head with the conversation, as if her thoughts were swirling as she spoke. "The environments themselves are predetermined, though. I can't manipulate them, but they rarely change either, and even if they do change, it's usually only colours or patterns… which is kind of a good thing."

"Why's that? Why is it important that the landscapes don't change?"

"If they're always the same, I always know where things are."

Dr. Pillapatti lowered her eyes to match the shadows gathering beneath Sarah's. "The beast must be troubling, then. It seems to be wherever it pleases."

Sarah didn't blink. "Outside of the tunnels, it has a lot of freedom. And I'm finding it more and more difficult to navigate my dream's surroundings with the thought of it clouding the back of my head."

The deluge of tentacles chased her through the varying fractal moments, calling behind her with its torn oil-slick voice, "Names to be given, names to be got!" The words cut at Sarah's spine as she tracked an overgrown path that exited into a small canyon made of passing carriages from her memories and temporary buildings from her head.

"So that seems important, doesn't it, Sarah? What it says as you're running." Dr. Pillapatti's pen was bouncing from the page to her mouth. "What do those words mean to you?"

The carpet's small red specks had floated away and it was just dust in the sunlight that stayed.

"I hadn't really thought about it much. Most of the beings in my dreams have a series of things they might say that are always repetitive but are usually… nonsensical… if anything is said at all." The denim scrunching up between Sarah's fingers felt warm, a scratching warm like sun-soaked sand, and it made her insides feel less frantic. "Sometimes it's different, but usually not."

"Characters or beings that you meet in your dreams tend to just repeat random strings of words?"

Sarah nodded. "Even my echo has a tendency to bounce back at me in gibberish."

"I wonder how that plays into the way you understand or don't understand the people around you." Dr. Pillapatti took a few more notes. "We should circle back to that, after you're done recollecting."

"Is it important?"

"I think so." The doctor smiled and the fabric in Sarah's fingers bunched up like a muscle.

Wooden padding slapped beneath Sarah's feet as the office slipped again into the background of her thought. The pressure of her steps dragged a cold muddy water out with them as she ran across the pond's floating dock; it cooled her toes and sent her chest into a tight coil of muscle. The water and its secrets were always there beneath the moon that often turned blue or red or an off grey, always in a crescent above the small body of water. Above the dock. Dark, segmented as the centipede in its unwavering forms.

Her white converse sneakers, ever the perfectly clean, valiant knights, carried her like stallions across the boards, while white clouds of dust from the spores on the monster's arms swarmed and smeared the air into a thick paste that settled on the nape of her neck. When the beast's breath lay its hand flat on her back, the paste condensed and her spine was thick with it. "Names to be got," it called again, garbage hot, summer warm.

The end of the dock was nearing as the smog from the beast's weather-making arms rolled in further and wrapped Sarah and the pond in an opaque haze. Sarah's body cried faint in the blindness as her heart stretched its own arms and pressed against the bony cage, trying to explode her chest so that she might stop and turn away, but the fear and her familiarity of the terrain carried her on. Instead, she barreled head-first into the maw of the tentacles' storm and where the light had seemed thinnest, the dock ended, and she let it take her to the compass rose.

She didn't jump, or throw her arms, or try to brace against the impact of water. Instead, Sarah fell forward in the way a stone pillar might, or as a tree would, letting her body become enveloped in the cocoon that was this body of water—of course, even prepared, it knocked white into her torso when she slapped against its surface. Concrescence, where two rivers meet.

Below the water, her eyes took to the silhouettes of the objects beneath, took form. In the liquid all around her lay a jungle of moss-eaten toys and books that grew black over the brown silt bed, and small, strange fish hid in large translucent plants. A door was embedded in the sand beneath her, like it always was, right where she had mapped it years ago, its hardware clear as bird-speak in the air.

More notes, and the words 'consistent' and 'escape' could be heard under the hushing voice of the pen nib. "We've talked about these before too, I know." Dr. Pillapatti locked Sarah's eyes in a hot brass stare. "The doors aren't just doors, right? You call them dream gates?"

Sarah nodded.

"Can you tell me more about the door's appearance and function?"

Turning her head and scratching her cheek, Sarah feigned to shake the tree of its apples. She spoke in an automated manner. "None of the doors look the same. Some are wood, others are metal. They come in different colours and fittings and work just like any door; I open them and they lead to another place."

"Have they changed in any way?"

"No. They don't ever change. I can always expect them to look the same. To be in and go to the same places."

Dr. Pillapatti nodded. "And they all lead to the tunnels, right?"

"Or from the tunnel to another dream."

Sarah reached out and grabbed the brass knob attached to the peeled back greening panels of the door. She propped two feet against the frame and pulled the entrance open just as the beast broke the water above her head. Shivering under the spectre of its hands about to reach her neck, just as it closed on her, she was drawn through the rotted frame by the vacuum it created. Sarah and the water and the tiny fish that swam in the current beside them—all of them with eyes so wide and terrified of being swallowed that all the moments became smooth orbs—all of them, in that moment, torn from the liquid of the pond, were released. Their chests concave, their heads feverish from the threat by beast and claw. Their bodies beyond the frame and door where tentacles could not reach.

Over the entombing rush of water and excitement as she poured into the tunnel below, Sarah could hear the howling of the beast, its bellow a throaty noise that gored the soft innards of her chest, a spot in her where hunger worshipped fear and chewed her to pieces even in the wake of escape.

"Can it follow you into the tunnel?" Dr. Pillapatti was still knee deep in words and meanings, always trying to pull Sarah back to an agreed upon reality from the dream.

"It hasn't yet." Sarah shook her head into the office. "Nothing any bigger than myself seems to be able to get inside." Pulling at her cheek, she tried to recollect everything she'd ever seen in the tunnel. "Some things, like plants and insects, small animals… tend to come and go, but they're rare, and the beast doesn't have that ability, thankfully… I guess I'm the largest thing that can go through the gate." Sarah blinked several times, switching back and forth between her realities.

"Is the tunnel a haven from the beast, then?"

Whatever stone was in Sarah's chest, that question split it with a hammer and some of her words were stuttered by the cracks. "My dreams had always been the haven—from everything—but it seems I'm getting pushed further and further from their perimeter lately…" Sarah slipped away in the question, unaware that her concern had washed up on her face like seaweed.

Seeing the confusion welling up in her patient, Dr. Pillapatti interrupted the train of thought. "Are you scared to go there, to your dreams then?"

Sarah's words snapped into the present.

"No—but I worry sometimes that I may not make it back." But her eyes were far away spheres, studying some other form.

Dr. Pillapatti cocked her head. "You're worried you may not make it back to the real world?"

Sarah turned away from all the things that worried her to scan the plain beige walls of the office. They were flat and seemed smooth, but were filled with orifices that you could make out when you looked past their flat and smooth. She wondered what would make such holes. "Back to my dreams," she said while she pictured a worm, eyeless and hungry.

Pen scribbles.

No space existed in the measurements between the doorway and the concrete floor that met Sarah on the other side. She lay herself into its embrace and accepted the friendship of its surface, one whose structure punctured and stole all the oxygen in her lungs when she landed in its arms, turning everything black for as long as the fall had lasted.

The impact, despite being conscious of it, sent a cry for respiration to reverberate down the acoustics of the tunnel's walls, leaving Sarah gasping on the floor in a puddle, begging for the brief moment of black to come back. As she lay there, floundering, experiencing the ins and outs of consciousness that came from moving between dreams and falling from ponds onto concrete slabs, she deconstructed the base sensations that flowed over her in waves. The sore palms. Battered hips and knees. Eyes clenched tight and throbbing in pace with her laboured breathing, a vivid reminder of the anxiety that tried to mask itself in exhaustion. The anxiety. The fear that still crept around in the bruised belly of her thoughts.

Focus stolen again, snap-stick awake. "I think it's weird that I feel pain in my dreams." Sarah's tongue was earnest with the soaking wet statement. "Don't you?"

Dr. Pillapatti turned her mouth one way and her eyes the other. "Some essays have suggested that tactile sensation in a dream is more likely a psychosomatic experience rather than an objective reaction."

"Yes, it's a dream." Sarah flattened her lips before she brightened again. "But this is a thorough sensation, one that throbs and lasts after the fact. Doesn't that come off strange, whether it's subjective or not?"

Dr. Pillapatti dedicated a moment to ingesting the question. "No. I don't think it's strange." She elaborated on the taste, "I think it's all related to something else, which just happens to be your normal. The important question is, are you comfortable with experiencing a sensation like that in your dream? What if it was a pleasurable sensation instead, would you think it strange?"

Sarah pondered that. "Maybe not."

"Patients in a recent study were documented as saying they had pleasurable sensations during a lucid dream… Does knowing that other people have those feelings make you feel better?"

The thought continued to badger. "What if my experiences had lasting effects that persisted after I woke up?"

Dr. Pillapatti bit at her lip. "I think your waking dreams require a level of careful consideration as well, but it's minimal, unless they've gotten worse since we last spoke."

Somewhere, Sarah's thoughts were all in order, but here, the memories placed past in present and the future slipped into obscurity; she was suddenly off guard.

"Have your waking dreams gotten worse, Sarah?" She persisted.

Sputtering again, Sarah fell through the cracks of the question and could only answer the way a sewer grate might, with a secret undertow beneath its calm veneer.

"No."

More pen scratches on the paper. "Okay, then. Please continue."

Once the essence of the place beneath her dream had entered her lungs, the moment relaxed and the oxygen in Sarah's exhalation rolled into the shape of moons, leaving a temporary geometry in the surface of the air. Letting her arms down to rest beside her proved the passing of fear. Only time could pass now, and it did. Sarah waited, closing her eyes and keeping balance amongst the repetition of waves. She waited and practiced breathing.

When the curves were dry, she took a minute to observe the tunnel, ensuring its unchanged form.

Arching brick walls that stood in stacks of poor manners sat all around her, as they always had. She scanned over each individual brick that was each one actually a book, spine out. Wherever Sarah had stood, today or any other, every title of every book was masked in an untranslatable nonsense, a slurry of letters and symbols without meaning; the clandestine titles ran for miles in the maze beneath her dreams.

It all looked the same as it had the day before, and every day before that.

"Where is the tunnel, exactly?"

Sarah turned back to Dr. Pillapatti, dry of answers without further docking.

"Let me rephrase that. Is the tunnel inside another dream?"

"No, I don't think so. Sometimes it's below or beside, or even above a dream, but it's an entirely different place. Every once in a while, I get scared that it may not be there anymore but it always, in some way, is there."

"Let's picture it. You are in a dream you've been to before and you head to a door, you know where it is. You open the door and walk into the tunnel, you walk a couple steps, find another door and you walk through that into a different dream—how do you know the place in between the two dreams isn't just another dream?" Dr. Pillapatti's silhouette glowed from the light shining in behind her and Sarah wondered if she knew how dark the shade was.

"For one, I don't recognize the landscape of the tunnel from any real-world place."

As Dr. Pillapatti breathed in, the light penetrated her back, briefly, so that she stayed sitting up. "Dream theory suggests that every dreamscape is an amalgamation or replication of various real-world places, is that what you're suggesting?"

"Yes." Sarah had turned and was staring at the pores in the wall again; they too, were breathing, and their breath fell on Sarah's eyelashes. She blinked in the current of their silence. "And I don't recognize the tunnel."

"But is there anything else? Are the rules the same?"

"Yes."

"So do you know? There's no wrong answer, by the way." Dr. Pillapatti smiled.

Rolling her eyes away, Sarah tried to catch a place in between her head and her mouth that made sense to both of them. "Have you ever been lost? Like say, in a new city."

"Several times." Dr. Pillapatti smiled again.

"How do you know you're lost? Is it because you don't recognize anything?

Is it because you're certain you've never been there before?"

"Well… yes."

"Are you sure, in your conscious mind, that you've never, ever, been there before? Or do you feel it somewhere else, inside? Swelling up like a beached whale, just waiting for a gull to pop its side and burst the black out onto the beach."

Dr. Pillapatti continued to glow.

Sarah continued. "I know because I feel it, just like I know when I'm dreaming. I don't need to see that the books and clocks are illegible, I already know they are, whereas here, you always have to check what the book says… you always have to check what time it is on the clock."

Her feet found their royal throne of soles and Sarah stood in the tunnel. She looked down the walls and every thought or each brick was doused in a shadow from the swinging lights that had been tapped in above her. The perfect symmetric line of interrogation-room-style light followed the expanse of the hollow; it pulled Sarah forward, making her stand on slipped tiptoes that danced for balance in her shoes. Her eyes, even though they could run forever in the tunnels, never ran ahead of her here—but she was content in thinking that they could, ignoring that they started anywhere and ended at a room with a glass ceiling.

Plumes of condensing breath rose into Sarah's face as she stood there recollecting, making rain clouds of her chin, dripping sweet skin nectar onto the floor. The droplets stole the air currents inside her periphery, its sound poignant as it bounced from her flesh, drew her attention to the ground where the herringbone stonework waded out into her unending musings, out into the endless hall, covered in the dust of footprints collected in other places she had come and gone.

Electric light continued to sway in the breathing room of her space, and Sarah sent her conflicted feet on. She took direction with the arc of the door, calling it North despite the lack of magnetism here, and she followed the lanterns, little eyes on bait that were spaced out evenly, a full body in between each.

"The next door is Building Space." Sarah hung a fingernail on her lip as she spoke to herself. "Then the field, then the junction east and west... and further junctions..." Her voice trailed off in the gloom of tunnel whispers, unable to hold her notes as she thought of the expanse and its long winding form.

Sarah slowed to look at the lacquer of another door's finish, inset in a concave wall. A black marble frame held a tattered, rotting door made from driftwood and slathered with honey. Her eyes followed its silver hardware as she passed. "Yes, definitely the dreamscape of building spaces behind that door."

"You've memorized a lot of the tunnel."

"I've had to. I don't like walking into new dreams unless I'm in the right headspace. If I spend all night in the tunnel, I wake up exhausted... more so than I do already... so I tend to check in through doors I've been to a lot."

The penned notes that scratched the paper felt like plastic knitting needles on cardboard, and it bothered Sarah's teeth. Dr. Pillapatti froze to watch the reaction before she asked, "Then, how do you visit new dreams?"

"I often wake up in new dreams but, the more I practice... the more often I wake up in places I know."

"How long have you been practicing again, Sarah?"

Sarah felt a stone behind her eyes, sweating in the heat of her thoughts and pushing small wells up into her eyelids. She turned her head to shake it from its place.

"Is something wrong?"

Sarah gulped, swallowed the stone. "Nothing." She looked at Dr. Pillapatti, but the view was shaken. "I've been going there since it happened."

Dr. Pillapatti leaned back. "It?" Her eyes became soft. "It's hard, but sometimes it's good to refer to an experience like that with plain and obvious language."

Sarah shook her head.

"Would you like to talk about your father?" An oddly painted smile followed more scratching.

But Sarah continued with the dream, the safety of its cradle beneath her again.

As the curtains rose and exposed the floor's persisting constructs, something changed: a small silhouette came into view on the surface of the ground. Sarah's eyes engaged it immediately; a peculiar anomaly in the consistently uniform design caused her to slow, pacing her steps with careful concern as she closed in, a hundred feet from the object on the floor.

"You weren't here yesterday," she said, an unknown taste percolating on the puzzled conversation of her tongue. "An oncoming paradox?" Sarah shuffled closer to the object's position and noticed it was moving, flapping its large black wings on the ground.

Feet halted again, thirty feet from a bird, a raven who started to tap a coin in its beak against the floor. Sarah, half turning the page, was wary of the paper cut that was already forming on her finger.

Synchronized gears stuttered then smoothed as the raven dropped the coin, spread out the iridescent tapestry of its flight and hopped backwards, bowing, presenting the gold coin like a crown to royalty.

Perplexed, Sarah walked towards it but something else below her feet lumbered with heavy steps in the same direction. Vibrations underneath her were suddenly flinging themselves upwards against the floor while she moved across the tiles that separated her from below. In-between each of her dropping tread, a thunder wave of similar steps intruded on her from beneath, and it jarred the bird who spread its black hands and made shadow puppet flight into the dark.

"Why was your immediate thought to head towards the coin if you were so skeptical from the start?" Dr. Pillapatti asked.

Sarah placed her tongue between her eye tooth and molar and sucked, attempting to draw the meaning out through her gums. "Sorry?"

The doctor continued. "You said that you saw the coin and the raven and you were wary of them. Why did you keep going if your initial reaction was fear?"

Sarah let her throat smoke the words while the coals churned. "I'm not sure."

Dr. Pillapatti raised her eyebrows. "Could you have lost control, as if you were slipping into a night terror?"

"It was something else." Sarah flashed between the two places, struggling to maneuver as which one was in her head seemed uncertain… except the coin. It stayed permanent in both memory and vision. "It was the coin." Her heart pushed at the image of the gold, and she felt her chakras shake. "I was drawn to the coin. As if I had been missing it the whole time."

"Could the coin represent something you miss from your waking life?"

Sarah remained silent.

"What could it represent?"

Sarah felt a weight on her back, and she wanted to tuck into the mass. Ball up under the gravity. "I don't know yet." Her words were frail lace in the heat of the office.

"Okay." Dr. Pillapatti made a knowing expression that was not overbearing, but motherly. "My clocks never run out of time for you, Sarah." She scribbled more notes.

Meanwhile, the tunnel shook, the lanterns hung from the galley swung with the waves as dirt took the place of the air and shots of soil pierced the interlocking stone above her head. The huge footsteps beneath her were causing the tunnel's structure to rumble as if to cave in as they followed her, threatening to end its infinity as they moved, too, towards the coin.

Two steps away, and a brick fell from the ceiling. It grazed Sarah's shoulder as she ran, and the abrasive stone lifted the skin from her flesh. Her body tilted sideways and her eyes almost caught the corner of the wall as she wobbled, but her vision did not stumble; it stayed darted on the gold on the floor. Falling forward instead, she grasped the coin's embossed surface.

As her face ran hot against the ground that tried to break her eyes now held tight, her body slid across the stone and pulled fractals of skin from the tops of her hands where a needle, or a stinger, from the coin stabbed the inside of her palm. When it pierced her skin, a door flashed in her mind.

A door in her head, brief before it disappeared, as she continued tumbling and dropped the coin.

"Another door? Inside your head, inside your dream… inside your head?"

Sarah flashed a smile. "I guess."

"Caused by a needle or something on the coin's surface?"

Sarah nodded.

"Was it another dream gate?"

Sarah massaged her left temple with her hand, trying to force the fingers in, as if to turn a dial back to look at the image of the door. "I don't think I've seen it before. It was a glossy black thing with golden gilding." Sarah squinted her eyes. "Two slots where a lock should be, a symbol… I can't see it."

"You'll have to check your notes."

Sarah nodded and Dr. Pillapatti wrote something down.

In all the commotion, Sarah heard the fabric stutter of pinions working the gait of their swing. She caught sight of the raven laying its wings out in a martyr's attempt to protect a cross. It swept down across the refuge of Sarah's arms and passed to cover the coin with its fall.

She and the raven collected eyes in that moment, as the dirt from the ceiling rained in thin pillars and the world below made hard questions of the sanity of the tunnel. They made eyes and the raven wrapped its talons around the coin, lifted its hollow-boned, hallowed body into the air, and flew away.

Along with it, the crashing feet that were below her gave chase down the tunnel, away from her. Leaving Sarah alone beneath the swinging lights.

Sarah paused and blinked a few times.

Dr. Pillapatti flashed her teeth. "And then?"

The air that escaped Sarah's lungs was the same that hung in the hall of every show that ended long ago. Her words, the only thing aside from dust. "And then… I woke up."

Part 2: When Children Begin to Wake Quietly

Cotton brushed the early filaments of unbrushed teeth, causing Sarah to grimace at the distaste in her disposition. Every morning she woke with the felt-like growth gently sweeping the surface of her ivories, sending a chill to her head. The strange sensation of filling cavities. She turned her head away and rolled onto the thick of her back, away from the pillow she used as a muzzle, jammed against the light reflecting from her wall.

Spots wavered in and out from the corners of her closed eyes, indicating the presence of her warmth, conscious thoughts bound to the physical realm. Thoughts like clocks or toothpaste or Mother's wooden picture frames and dust in another room, the taste of pollen still thick on her brain. The unconscious self sneezed, and its blessing opened Sarah's eyes to the sunlight, whose strong hands had already drawn back the curtains in her room.

Brilliant and blunt, the sun pressed Sarah; she squeezed her hand to mitigate the early wake effect. In her grasp, she held an emptiness, not there before. The spot where her fingertips should have touched the palm was spotless and she thought, for a moment, only of the coin.

But such moments from the dream realm would all soon slip away in the one star, the day's only glory. She sighed; the hours of the day were the only place in which what she wanted was always furthest away.

"Sarah?" called the hen-pluck voice from Mother's tongue, the final indicator that her dreams were gone.

Olive green paint from the walls cracked and splashed and sprayed across her vision as her eyes drew across the room. Over the brass rails of her daybed, through the shadows not hiding in the room and beyond the escape of untamed mountainous sheets over to the doorway, was Edna.

Her mother, whose red lips parted in famous portrait smiles, a poet neither happy nor sad. Her mother, standing tall against the frame, half in the hallway and half in the room.

"Are you awake?" she asked. Her voice, a light crisp microphone stutter, a smooth hankering for jam.

"I am now," Sarah replied. No emotion or snide in her mouth, just bits of cotton from her pillowcase.

"You didn't wake up with a start this morning?"

Sarah lay motionless, the effects of the question unnoticed.

"Maybe the night terrors are finally calming down?" Perfectly plucked eyebrows pushed the skin of her forehead into a tell of hand, the trick of makeup's age slipping through the cracks of her visage.

"I guess," replied Sarah, her eyes darting to the well-placed pillow on her wall. "They seem to be getting better."

"Good." Edna nodded, turned, and headed back down the hall. "I'll be downstairs, my love."

The door now an empty space, Sarah found her eyes wandering to the stucco ceiling with its thousands of miniature mountains, all careening slowly towards a single fixture in the centre of its tundra, a brass-ringed light with crystal dome. Nothing special. Just the witch tool she woke to every morning.

Sarah cocked her head to look closer at the glass's tells when a swelling, a sudden storm full with hot metal pierced the flesh of her neck and shoulder, sending her body into a single, painful spasm.

Sitting up, her hands flashed out and pulled back the thin skin nightgown she wore to study the pale paper surfaces of her body. Scanning the landscape, she ignored the pointed and delicate and white for a place on her shoulder that was dark and tender, purpled sore. A thick puddle of bruise was hung on her body, pulsing and throbbing the way you'd expect a felled wish to remain calm.

Sarah clasped it with her right palm and let her eyes feel about the textured surface for the reason of her battered arm.

Small hints of snail work flickered at her eyelids while Sarah's hands worked little memories of children's games to flatten out from pyramids into paper.

The ink on the tunnel's wall.

The cacophony of tentacles inside the dream.

The falling brick.

A coin that drew her focus.

She let go of her arm and reached under her bed, feeling around for where she left the book. The journal and its ink.

Strange artifacts coursed through Sarah's fingertips as she grasped it. She rolled into a cross-legged position, dragged the book from its hiding spot and placed it into the crook of her thighs. She looked down on the perverted mouths of socks both thigh and knee high, thirsty for the knowledge she would bestow, well-wishers and demons, her thoughts thick water to the porous skin of wood. On the cover, the handwritten title screamed out at her as it always had.

Bound is the Dreaming Hand.

Still-warming hands that had been cold from deadened sleep cut their amphibious skin on the pages as Sarah opened its contents, waking them without a kiss, startling them to life with a sharpened purge. Her enslaved and fearful digits flicked through the lined paper whose margins bulged with scattered writings and images blurring in the hastened pilgrimage of her blood. Ochre. Sanguine colour seeping into the border of each corner, passing the fanning hands above.

She stopped on a page, mostly blank aside from two words that dug like fingers in the earth at her depth. It read **"Dear Sarah,"** in red Garamond text, but there was nothing else. She sighed and flipped the pages again, ignoring the curious images that she often portrayed in playwright manners and jumped ahead to another random page in the book. In large yet tight-knit letters it read, "If I were Sleeping Beauty, I'd have a sign that said no kisses, I'm dreaming, and you'll ruin it."

A small place on Sarah's face where the sun could not touch her was still angled in the dark; there, she was most obvious.

Fleeing, she flipped the pages again until the most recent words crackled as they fell from the middle. Sarah adjusted the rushing pen that had come alongside the bound folio and tapped at the top of the page: 'Dream log, day 781.'

Like the falling images in her head, the writing slurred and curved out into a Russian cursive, fast swooping letters that all seemed to merge into and signify only one—but had several meanings that she could translate later.

Entered dreamscape of the machete man.

Greyed portables.

Rolling grassland in Auburn night sky.

The beast appeared again.

Again, I did not look at it.

Only saw its prying arms.

Ran to the pond door and jumped inside the tunnel.

When inside, the beast could not follow.

I walked, considered going further to explore more doors but saw something on the ground, a bird with a coin in its beak.

When running to it, the beast, it almost... like it might have broken in. It seemed. I was scared. The bird dropped the coin and I ran to collect it but there was something on the coin that stung my palm and I dropped it. There was a door in my head where the coin stung me. Black and gold with a symbol on top.

Sarah tapped the page where it said symbol.

A circle, inside a square, inside a triangle, inside a circle, burnt into the wood.

When I opened my eyes, the bird had come back and was leaving with the coin. The beast seemed to follow it.

A throbbing sensation reached out to her again from her shoulder bone. An old story from a grey-haired man, one that constantly poked holes in your own path, synchronicity from teachers on the forks of tongues.

Brick had fallen from the ceiling and struck my arm.

Severe bruising where it had hit me.

Not sure how.

Maybe I hit the wall again while sleeping.

...

After warming the nib of her pen at the top of the page with infinite spirals, Sarah added a note to the bottom.

Dr. Pillapatti would think my bruises are not from the brick in the tunnel...

She snapped the book closed and held the pen tight to its spine. Reaching over, she rolled it down her bedside, back to where she had found it.

The thick vanilla plant blossoms that her sheets had become muddled up around her in slow moving waves as Sarah opted to start a treasure hunt in the sea of fabrics that she sat upon. She rubbed her shoulder again while the thought of it stung her one more time, then she checked her palm where she had been stung, the thought of it rubbing her wrong again. "Maybe it's here?" she said aloud as the shadows of the water's surface splashed against the white backdrop of her mattress. Sarah searched excitedly through the pillows and tides of earlier nights with eyes peeled back on orange rind, fingers spry from the taste of citrus. Hopes high as the fruit tree bearings.

But a short time beneath such small spaces passed in an instant and Sarah rolled back onto her knees, spine straight, her arms laid beside her. There was nothing in the bed.

"Nothing." She threw both hands down in a dramatic slump and looked around her room again.

Nothing out of place.

No coin.

Agitated, she peered back over at her shoulder, at the inkblot there that had spilled onto her skin the previous night. To her, its Rorschach image was simple; with only a strange philosophy, devoid of material, Sarah's truth was a fantasy to Dr. Pillapatti, and it had no power to break the wall.

Falling with the sighing of her chest, Sarah let out an underwater wail. A quiet truth. An unheard cry like that of the netted urchin before she swung her feet over the side of her bed and rose on the window's cold side.

Her arms stretched up and Sarah touched empyrean's ceiling, behaviours of the woken gods. Her nightgown, fallen down on the shadows of demons who've long since left the Viking hall, brushed the spectre of a smile away from praying feet. Sarah yawned. She dropped her hands again and stood for a moment in the centre of the room, breathing the compass rose's projections before somnolence scratched at her eyes.

Instead of cupping her palms and rubbing away the excrement of dreams, she bent down again and reached into the open cabinet of the black, obelisk-shaped nightstand beside the bed. She grabbed a mason jar from the nightstand's belly. Daring, the jar managed to slip and Sarah doubled down to catch it before it hit the ground. Her eyes wide, she stood back up and stared at the glass body and its metal lid. She held it to her face and inspected its half-filled contents. White grain. Sand. Dust. She shook the material, and its smooth action reminded her of the movement of gold in pan.

Gentle hands pressed and popped the lever top of the jar and Sarah rolled back the lid. The smell was pastel press on her lip; she could rarely shake the scent during the day, but she'd gotten used to it, its sticky perfume a catalyst to her waking.

The jar sat into her hip with her left hand while she rubbed the product from her eyes with a dexterous right. The sleep rolled from her lids into the crease between her cheek and nose, where she caught it with her pointer finger, rolled it further to the cheek's bone and plucked it from the landslide of dreams. She operated the other eye, combining the sleep materials together and making a mixed ball of gunk in her tear duct. Tweezing fingers pulled it back out. When Sarah looked at it, it reminded her of wet sand.

She raised the mason jar and dropped the fresh-plucked material into its belly, where it would mix and dry with the other grains of sleep that she had collected. Securing the lid, she threw the jar back into the cabinet of her nightstand before looking towards her open door.

Morning smelled good from upstairs: cinnamon and syrup had elevated themselves beyond the maple wood banister and the Sri Lankan rugs that scaled the steps beneath them. Sarah perked in interest for the taste that might inspire her below. She pulled on her white rabbit slippers and headed down the familiar hall outside her bedroom, not speculating on any subtle changes that may have interacted with the pink-and-white pinstriped walls, covered in pictures of clocks and red balls. Instead, she walked, zombie-minded, down the stairs, through the black marble entrance way that held the honey-coloured door and silver hardware, and into the kitchen at the back of the house. Near the forefront of her mind.

"Coffee?" asked Sarah as she entered the kitchen, shielding her eyes from the light that bounced from the blue cabinets' finishes.

Her mother stood in front of the kitchen sink, her back turned to her as it often was, so that she might look across the open concept dining area, over the grand dining table and into the yard from the huge bay windows collecting fog. Edna cleared her throat and turned around, leaning back into the countertop, a smile on her confiscated face.

"Good morning," said Edna.

"Good morning, Mom." Sarah stood on the white tile floor just inside the kitchen. Her mother's smile had her leaning back into the frame of the entrance.

Both crossed their feet. Casual pause.

The stove to Edna's left took over Sarah's perception just as the bronze kettle on its surface began to yawn, its slumber disturbed by the fire in its belly, its piercing morning call filling the room with steam and froth and sound. The warm air pulled Sarah's disposition into a tight, ill-prepared smile as Edna raised an eyebrow to answer a question lacking in etiquette, lacking in tact.

Both bodies uncrossed their feet and paused with casual smirks on their faces while the kettle escalated to a scream.

"I'll get i—"

Edna stopped Sarah short of saving herself. "Oh, don't worry yourself, darling," she said with a disapproving tongue. "I'll just get it for you."

"Sorry." Sarah blew on her fingertips, to try to relieve the heat of the passive scolding while her mother's expression turned to smug satisfaction

Aging hands worked the modern knobs on the stove before moving the kettle to the counter where a percolator was set, waiting. A helping of coffee beans inside it—ground the prior night, their scent, which filled the chimney, who let the aroma out into the sky—sat quietly waiting to be mixed with water to satisfy the morning sacrifice.

Edna removed the percolator's lid and poured the water so that the steam bathed everything in heat. She returned the top, pressed the plunger down and stirred the Turkish mud into a fury of soil, morning brush, and golden sand. The colour: dark, long-standing like the woods through the window that Sarah stared at until she was reminded again of the coin, its smooth gold surface hiding a storm below the needle point it left in her hand.

She grasped at her injured palm, shook her head, and deflected back to the coffee, her neutral, her calm. She hoped its caffeinated water might flush the images of the coin from her head.

Or maybe she hoped it wouldn't.

Liquid slate poured from the jar into a turquoise cup, and was then pre-sented—with hesitation—to Sarah, who accepted the coffee with humbled breath and jovial lips but she worried, behind her eyes, that the coffee's colour might be too bright. She nodded, distracted by the white as she took the portents.

However, when the warmth touched her hands, she breathed in, a habit practiced for millennia. Mantra. Om. Welcomed Buddhist to the temple of the lamb. The weighted bags behind her eyes softened. And the coin, reminded of day, began to leave her most forward thoughts.

"Thank you," said Sarah as her cheeks pushed her eyes into half-buried gold.

"You're welcome," returned Edna as Sarah slipped by her, passing the light marble countertops to fill in the other aspects of her morning rituals: to stand near the window, embrace the condensate on their glass panes and look into the forest that blurred the lines of an early season's frost.

Sarah rounded the corner of the dining table with its thirteen chairs, or twelve... she stood beside the radiator's warming coil and breathed in the aroma from the black night brew in her hand. The cup's porcelain lip found its way to paler tones and Sarah sipped as she stared out from the frame of water that had snapped against the glass pane in the white window frame. In front of her, the late growth strawberries from planters set above the window fell from their dripping stems and dipped their red ink onto the cool glass. Looking closer, each seed was a single coin that couldn't last forever, even if the season ran later than it should have.

Sarah's eyes passed the blurry visions of the drunken fruit and currency, continuing on beyond a thin blanket of frost that stuck to the darkening grass in a flavour of plaid pumpkin senses that thickened as it stretched into the forest at the back of the yard.

Entranced by the everyday, Sarah entered the woods in her mind.

The water from her cup boiled itself down into a rain cycle that washed her fluttering eyelashes as she walked the pine tree canopy. From below the leaves, she dodged the light and ride the shadows that shone brighter the further she moved from the sun.

It made her shiver, somewhere between elation and calm.

Her eyes so heavy underwater.

The coffee making its way to her stomach.

She smiled, and every vision was undone in its presence.

"Good?" asked Edna from behind her.

"Very." Sarah brought her thoughts forward again, letting the light into the heart of her pupil as she did.

"I know your psychologist said it helps you to leave… to leave uhhh…"

"The dream, Mom?" Her eyebrows raised.

"Yes. I still think you are too young, but she says it helps… I just wish you wouldn't drink it black."

Sarah sipped at her coffee again, its timid smoke blackening the subconscious parts of her thoughts. "Would you rather I drink it with a bunch of sugar and cream?"

"Better than you seeming so grown up," replied Edna.

"Drinking coffee makes me seem older than I am?" Her smile waxing at the quarter turn of her mouth where she feigned to turn towards her mother.

Edna smiled her own huge apron and full moon smile.

"It certainly doesn't remind me of your actual age." Edna poured coffee into a black cup for herself and mixed its contents with sugar from a bowl that sat on the countertop. "Only a young thing—speaking of your doctor, I didn't see you last night after the appointment. Did it go well?"

Something shook at the tree branches in the woods near the edge of Sarah's vision. Not turning to look, Sarah's eyes stayed the line between the kitchen and the view from the window, only registering the position of the blur in the trees. A shadow. A dark movement in the green and brown backdrop of a breathing forest.

"Sarah?"

Distracted, Sarah replied in a quiet, half spent voice. "Yes, Mom?"

Edna sighed and continued talking. "What are your plans today, then? Do you have any?"

Her reflection wavering in the shadow's archetype… dancing in the winter glass beside the image of the tree that had shook, Sarah turned the image to that of herself and she said nothing.

"Sarah?" persisted her mom, looking up from the cup on the counter.

Her mother's words were like a slow station in Sarah's train of thought, something to disregard before it sped away behind her. She checked her travel map in her hands and answered only herself. "Oh, I'll probably… just take a walk in the woods." She turned and smiled. "It's gorgeous out."

Part 3: Simple Branches

Here in every footstep lived a thousand tiny things that would otherwise not exist. A trace, a breadcrumb, a place where with certainty, one can assume something has been but no longer is; like the pushed-down grasses of a doe's bed remind us that at one point, nature slept here no longer.

When in the city or the house, where the floorboards meet underfoot, no mar or mark is left in the hard-pressed polish of hardwood, especially when mothers sweep and mop behind the muddy foot. There is no reminder there that you were once standing in a spot, existing in a way, and drinking tea. For the in-between traces disappear. But in the forest, it isn't for days or months or years that your imprint is lost to the overgrowth or weather.

Sometimes you leave a mark forever.

And always your mark will forever change the value of growth.

It was in those marks that Sarah found solace. She found a state of being that was neither here nor there and she could watch it. She could press a sample of her foot into the ground, come back another night, and still feel its liminal effect.

When her feet reached out and grounded, Sarah found a comfort like her tunnel. For every imprint left was a reminder that the imprint was there and so was the person, even if they were gone. Or they were somewhere else within the in-between.

Wandering the same winding trail she so often travelled on her own, Sarah's body warmed to familiarity and footprints even in the cool air of the wet snow. Her taut strings loosening to unfurl, she let her mind to her feet's work and turned to the shy green lace headdresses of the trees above her, lining up in shoreline patterns to never touch despite the room in the sky. In a book somewhere, she had read the term 'crown shyness' and wondered if the effect had anything to do with the footprints she left behind.

Below the dome-shaped cupola of trees, the trail ran aground when a shadow line from the leaves appeared and fell off into sunlight. Sarah walked into the light and stopped to sun herself in a rare break in the crowns. She breathed, letting her pale cheeks turn a rosy red in the wine-drunk sun as it cooled apples for her mouth, tasting cider-sweet as she breathed out. The trees, sitting centre starshine, breathed in her exhaled breath and then breathed her back out, stirring the atmospheric mixture of humans and the places they stood.

It was calm until the coffee inside her finally rested, and faded out. She rubbed her empty belly, aware of the rain-worn peak and with its antithesis, the desire to be back in bed returned. In want of sleep, the coin's shapely image appeared again, reminding Sarah that it wasn't laying in her hand. She looked down and felt its desire swelling and pushing at the back of her eyes.

"No," she said, beneath a sigh. "This is a good place and—" she tasted the salt on her lip with a nervous tooth and looked back up "—I am quite fine."

To stifle the growth in her chest, Sarah squeezed her eyes and fists tight, pushing the green into her ears and plugging them from the ambient noise of the woods. She counted to ten and the growth subsided. As she relaxed, opened her eyes again, she found that the timber's din had been replaced now with a melody, a smooth river stone heartbeat faraway that called at her chest.

There was no denying it; it drove her immediately from the well-known path off into the trees.

As each foot fell to a secret rhythm only whispering to her, a new path began to unfurl beneath the underbrush. A skinny prey path that wandered in a snaking wind with a long but recognizable pattern. It synchronized with her own pendulum swing and made aware the coming-to-awareness beat in the forest din. *The* heartbeat, not unlike the polished belly of a bass or cello, coaxing chords with the horsehair bow, playing to summon the wind inside chests. A lead along in grey hair at centre white.

And it was all around her suddenly.

The slip away: Sarah watched it in the changing colours of the leaves still on their branch, their red and yellow spirit melting on the line between soaking up the sun and feeding the ground. The mixture of the floor and the tree canopy puddling with spring rain and fall thaw. The quiet sounds of the wood and their growing melody of wood-string percussion.

Dipping and weaving, the thread of sound dragged the needle long until the light broke behind a line of trees and suddenly, only the slimmest trace of its illumination escaped a fortified horizon. Its sparse column of light—a reading glass in the burrows of thought—bounced from the left of the path to splash against the right. When Sarah turned to brace her hands for the wash of knowledge, she found that the wood's music was coming from beside her, in the form of a sapling that was pulled over into an arch. A circle stood out on its trunk.

The strange misshapen tree begged a misshapen question. "I've never seen you before?"

Arched over, the tree was just tall enough for Sarah to walk under, but yet, she felt that it loomed over her, ominous as it looked down. In return, Sarah looked down as well, to where a head of leaves should have been, had the tree ever stood upright. But no bushy crown or leaves or branches were visible at either end of the ouroboros sapling. Instead, each end was a powerful knot of roots in the ground, suggesting that neither end had been the end that started and instead, each was the end that had been felled.

"Did you grow from one side… or the other?" she asked herself and the tree, into the open space.

Her fingers ran along the tree's surface in search of braille on the thin bark. The trunk was soft, and wet with dew and fungus. So smooth that thoughts slid along its skin.

Is this tree here just for me?

It beckoned unlike anything.

At the centre of the bark, as mute fingers crossed over the circle etched in the wood, a metal pin reached out and pierced, fast, at the flesh.

Sarah squealed. "Ah!" Drawing the wounded finger back to inspect its throbbing red questions. Squinting, looking closely at the venom-bit digit, a glass-coloured nettle could be seen, buried in the grooves of Sarah's skin.

"Dammit." She breathed the word through her teeth while the thin metal of the object worked itself back and forth, aggravating the sensitive flesh at the finger's tip and sending tin snips through her body. *The littlest things,* thought Sarah and she placed the nettle between her teeth and chewed; it tasted like soured gold, and she spit the finger back out, swishing her cheeks and wondering how little she enjoyed playing the fool.

Then the taste fed her its purpose and the image of the coin returned. With it, the pain settled and a new draw appealed.

Looking through the arch of the tree, everything beyond it was a golden sheen.

The melody revived, along with the curious scenes of currency magnetised and soon she was through the entrance of the arched sapling and onto an arterial pathway that continued into the wood on the other side. The run was straight and unobstructed for as long as puffed cheeks could gather eyes. It moved over the hills and glades as the causeway took hold and Sarah became as a liquid in its presence, huffing and gasping as she moved.

The path soon became rich with porous dirt, and digging toes were inclined to ball the earth beneath its soles, hungry to taste the things that a heart desires. The path carried on further and became wide and flat from the constant barrage of footprints and tracks that she recognized as her own, made by her feet. Only questioning them long enough to realise she should be looking up; where the trees and plants and blurs of birds became a long straight line of time dilation.

The sound continued to call her, but it had no need. Desire was taking the place of urge. And soon to take desire's place was a wall.

Oh shit, a wall! thought Sarah, as she realised that her feet had separated from her thoughts.

A large dark lumber structure had emerged from the soil. On its bark tree facade, a slender shadow grew taller as Sarah's lack of control dragged her towards it, without remorse, without consideration, until the wall was only an arm's length away.

She tried hard to stop, but found only enough success that she stumbled forward under the speed of her run. The pull carried her on as she pitched over and somersaulted, turning into a ball that broke, collapsing against the wall, fracturing its surface and spilling wood bits and a girl into the clearing beyond.

"Dammit!"

Streams and colours spun for a moment while a scattered head tried to catch up to lost eyes. Despite the throbbing confusion, Sarah quickly tried to recover, to sit up in the same instant to survey the site, to check if anyone had been watching.

Once her reputation was confirmed intact, she took in the clearing beyond the wall. A circle made entirely of straightened hardwood trees, twenty feet across with a smoothed circle of dirt in the middle. Smooth and even all around—except where she had broken in; three trees there were felled.

A lone bird flapped its wings to fly away, startled to flee by Sarah's noise and shaking knees. The fabric sound of feathers emptied into the horizon and its absence was replaced by the lack of sound. Sarah stretched her neck until it popped, searching with bright ears for the melody that had led her here, but it had stopped.

"But where is this now?" she thought to herself.

A spot in the forest so unfamiliar that she found self at the centre of incognizance. Or sentience of nascent. *Was this the beginning?* She yearned to answer the question, but it was dispelled when a noise like a burp, a vacuum pressure pop, overwhelmed her thoughts.

Her chest became a scene of ink, and Sarah thought that anything could be written in stone but so many more things could come of paper and quill. So many monsters could be made of the page; she ached for the monsters she knew in her dreams, for they could only wait outside the tunnel, a place suddenly far away from here.

Across the clearing, a hole had appeared, ten feet across and dark as vellum black. Black like the movement beneath your skin in the dark when you see movement in the closet door. Shiver, cold spell, handle-in-the-bedroom dark.

Vomit tried to climb her throat when the earth shook and the hole—fathomless and unknown—opened so wide for a bellow, a wanton in the dirt like teeth on concrete grin.

Sarah was reminded then that her tunnel was always a sleep away. Sometimes too far. Sometimes. And she wanted her bed. She wanted sleep as she reflected into the chasm growing wider and hungrier, screaming as it moved across the clearing, daring, like all things that weren't a dream, to swallow Sarah whole.

She crawled backwards, trying to get out. She pushed herself into the line of trees that she had fallen through on the way in, and her frantic hands clamoured for the opening she had made with her head—but to her puzzlement, she discovered the trees had repaired themselves as she gawked. She turned a moment to see that the place she entered was filled again with a hard grain timber, impossible to scratch.

Again the ground wailed from a place in the deep of its bowels and Sarah pushed harder against the wall of trees, suffocating her spine the way a mousetrap might a rodent.

Her body, hot with fear, molded a posture into the malleable wood, a footprint of the moment. A long tradition in comfort. A turn of the head.

Sarah squealed.

On the surface, vibrations from a thousand scampering legs crawling up the hole's walls tickled Sarah's pinpricks. Her skin went taut as the howling got louder, her mouth, salivating, readied for the gut reaction of bile while a sense of doors that shouldn't be opened crept into her heart.

The sun. Aware. Dove into cover and all went dark.

The hole burst with a spiral of insects.

The sun. Aware. Left forever.

Into the sky, the hole spewed ashen wings, clouded eyes, and the buzzing teeth of larvae. The infinite calamity that was so many metal wings charged Sarah to clench her jaw. She broke the tongue from her throat and let the blood curdle in her mouth as a tower of bugs rose like a winged column into the air. Amoeba and bats, cells and hands, arachnids with eyes made of crawling legs. Everything beneath and above Sarah shook, and her carnation of visions vibrated in the heat of such waking.

Watching the tidal hellwave manifested something in Sarah; all the trees turned dark, rotting under the shade the insects brought.

The spiral howled again, and its noise echoed in her chest, shaking the dust from sleeping glands, churning the mind to chum for the engine of sharks. Soon she would be fed upon, she thought, and a fiery embrace engulfed her.

Rising, the swelling vortex of bugs and wings took all focus, and with heaven's forceps in its hands, it readied to pluck the lamb from God. It rose and grew and hungered before it stopped—only a moment—looming in the sky like a great black wire worm before it all reversed and the hole was inhaling everything back into it.

Eyes became plates of concern as Sarah felt the sudden pull of the moment, a pull at her chest. Marionette to a coffin of rest like a cross with strings, the hole was become a vacuum for everything, and its powerful sway sucked at the pitch of Sarah's lungs and her hair; all the woods around her swayed and bowed towards the awful negative force.

The treeline behind fell away and Sarah's feet dug ruts into the ground, where the suction dragged at her body. She tried, desperate with her splintering nails, to hold herself forward as the tower of bugs sucked into the ground, but its mass entangled her along with it and she fell onto her face and her eyes scraped through the mud. Tear ducts filled with soil. Crying dark spots of dirt. Garden fresh in her cheeks as the roses pulled themselves from the earth.

Sarah reached her arms out in a frantic bid but grabbed at nothing and the hole came on sudden and fast. She slid up to the lip of its opening, where she could look in. It was forever black and in that moment of her mortal acuity... she was wanted there.

She wanted for the coin.

For her bed.

The place between.

And instead of clinging to life, Sarah turned and looked again into the mouth that would feed of her.

—and she let go.

She stopped fighting and went with the drag, throwing herself over into the dark waves. Aware that there were likely rocks at the bottom, ready to crush her body in defiance of the night.

All night.

No sky.

Conscious self lost in her surrender to the hole as the empty vacuum pulled all woken self from the real… and only the carapace remained. Whole. Floating. Desert dark soul.

When Sarah awoke, the clearing was not so bare, and the ground was beneath her solid. No hole to be found.

She lay on the ground beside the path, her head thumping with sun-drunk dehydration. Her eyes hot and ready to leave, but the ground still beneath her in the wood. The ground still beneath her.

The ground. Still. Beneath her.

Part 4: Tastes of Something Strong

"So you had another episode?" asked Dr. Pillapatti, her smooth lips stretching the word 'episode' across the standard grey-and-red flecked carpet on the floor, over Sarah's incessant tapping foot, up her leg and straight into her belly.

Sarah breathed in from her belly button and spit the sounds back at her doctor. "Why call them episodes?" she asked.

Dr. Pillapatti waited, but Sarah only widened her eyes and tilted her head. "You're deflecting."

Sarah's eyes wandered around the room that never seemed to change. She stared at the polished auburn furniture that sat at odd lengths from the walls. She took in the lack of clutter on their tabletop surfaces, burying her pupils deep behind her eyes. She waited.

Dr. Pillapatti sighed but hid it within a short professional burst of air. "An episode is a brief dramatic moment between two choric songs… so said my high school drama teacher."

"So… the exciting part?"

Dr. Pillapatti laughed from her chakras, pieces of herself in question. "For some, yes." She rolled her shoulders up and leaned into her loss of control, and bobbed her chin with the syllables. "The exciting part."

"Why would we want to limit or control the most interesting moments? Why not let them run free?" Sarah straightened her own shoulders, rolling back from her doctor's lackadaisical stance.

"Because we haven't all agreed on that version of reality."

"What's wrong with my version?"

"It lacks lucidity with the pact."

Nothing hung itself onto the rolls of blue chalked wires that cut through the imaginary angles of the room.

Dr. Pillapatti continued. "Why don't we talk about the episode first?" exaggerating air quotations above her head around the word episode.

Rolling back into her chair, Sarah gestured as if she were an old cob pipe and stories were burdens of the tobacco's smoke. "I was in the woods again," she began as the light in the room dimmed, slipping away and bleeding the colours from the atmosphere with it.

"The woods behind your house, yes?" Dr. Pillapatti asked.

As the room filled with the loss of saturation, a colourless haze began to take over the walls.

"One and the same." She tilted her head back and her mouth curved into a bridge's yawn across water. "Those are the only woods." As she talked, the ceiling in the room became transparent, the haze increased in white blind. The office constructs all chipped away from themselves, drywall and molding breaking from their perches in packs of small chunks, floating away without chime from gravity's sway, disappearing out into the abyss where the ceiling had just been.

"Did you have your tea that morning?"

Water was pooling at Sarah's feet, its reflective moonlit surface tides carrying tatters and haze so that they bounced and reflected, lighting her cheeks with their prismatic effect. She squinted in the light of the question. "Tea?" The notion seemed odd. "I had my coffee." She did not look away from the empty roof as she spoke.

"I thought you had tea in the morning; your mother hates when you drink coffee—"

There was a scoff.

"Tea has more caffeine, anyway."

The walls had dismantled themselves completely as they talked, leaving only a small triangular patch standing beside the two women, creating a stage for their show. The thin triangle housed a lantern, the shadow of Sarah's gawking body, and a chair. Dr. Pillapatti's voice raked itself across the hot coals of a wet ocean's surface all around them, but it was distant. The office had become very far away from the drifting swells of thoughts.

"I drink coffee..." her voice distant. "I drank coffee that morning. Strawberries hung like lights kissed the window and left marks of fall. So I walked to the forest." Shadows of lumbering trunks convened in the background of the foreground of the mind. "In the forest there was a melody, it pulled my strings to an arcing tree beside the trail... there was a circle in the tree's bark." Sarah let the last word drag on a bit, watching the symbol in her head before Dr. Pillapatti broke her focus.

"It pulled you?" she asked.

"Yes." Sarah shook her head, returning. "Pulled me with its spell to the tree, and then I was through it, like a door." In Sarah's hand a knot was forming, made of two braids of hair from someone else's head. Long gone soils. No flowers growing. "On the other side I found a path leading to a clearing at the centre of the forest. A place I've never been before." The dirty blonde braids doubled in size, becoming two huge tugboat ropes in Sarah's hand, the weight pulling and threatening her tendons with snapping.

Eyebrows high. "And we thought you had been to every corner of that forest."

"So I thought." Sarah shook her head again. "Not there, though, not where the hole opened." The hair in her hands was bleeding cold red liquid from the hermetic bonding of its knots and her eyes backed away in the meditation of weaves. "It was so dark and loud and magnetic and you could hear all the earth beneath the open pit." Her doctor may have tried to intervene, but Sarah was gone in the image. "It shook my feet and my head as I stood in awe of hell's open mouth—and then the thing burst, like a pimple, spewing nightcrawlers and fleas from its throat." Her knuckles gave way to snow as she pushed to hold onto their wriggling bodies that she bent like spines. Bent like frayed bamboo trees. "I wanted to run at first, but when the hole took hold of me like the song had, and started pulling me to its centre with everything else... dragging me to the edge..." Sarah let a moment of soul exhale into the hearth and she looked absolutely nowhere. "I found that when I came to the edge of the hole—" she shook her head in disbelief. "I let go. I let it pull me all the way in."

The haze slipped away and the room returned. Sarah looked back down from the ceiling and settled on her doctor's gaze.

Dr. Pillapatti had made a crescent-shaped red imprint in the soft spot above her cheek, below her eye. Aware of the pressure once Sarah had stopped talking, she moved her finger away.

"Quite the day terror then? Are they getting closer?" She shook her head, and the bun on top of her head warbled in her professionalism.

"Maybe a dream. The dramatic place between reality. Something exciting—Dr..."

"Why do you think you let go?"

"What do you mean?"

"At the end, you said when you got to the edge of the hole, that you let go. Why do you think you did that?" Her shoulder rolled with the thought.

"I don't know."

"Think on it for a moment. Humour me."

Sarah let her head rest from the question and instead she spoke with the growing orb in her chest. It was warm and tasted of striped candy, and its answer hung on the tongue like sweets. "Just something inside of me said I could, said that it was safe."

"What happened after that?"

The draw in the room was neutral, indifferent, and deep in thought when Sarah deposited her answer into the void of human symbols. "Everything was fine."

Chapter One

Three years earlier.

"I realise this is your daughter, Mrs. Hadder, but for her sake, you have to stay strong." Dr. Pillapatti had resigned her human emotions to rot somewhere in her gut. It pained her as she spoke, but her face was impassive and the tickle that would drive her fingers to tap incessantly in the wall beside her was stoic, lost to the barrens like her emotions.

"What would you do?" cried Mrs. Hadder, her thoughts like obvious heated bubbles that would form on red hot pokers pouring from the corners of her eyes. She tried, with fingers swaddled in fevers, to corral the falling tears into a drenched handkerchief held by a shaking hand, but she couldn't contain her voice, and the tears rang out into the vacuum of the hospital hall. "If it was *your* daughter laying in a machine like that, struggling to breathe! Terrified!" Her sobs ventured off into corners and carried the smaller of her voices. "Unable to recognize who you are?"

The hallway had emptied while the two women spoke. Its pale blue walls, usually littered with pale green scrubbed doctors and nurses, was a long extension of bitter emotional support that had laid a clear contrast between its design and the conversation on its hue. Mrs. Hadder had cried all over it, and the assistance it was designed for had been washed away. Everyone who had been there or tried to enter after had felt the melt of colours and quickly fled or veered away from its space, afraid to look upon the translucent fear and pain that was holding thin discussion in its boundaries.

People used to pain, afraid to brunt it.

"I would likely be in the same state as you, standing here with someone like me, *reminding me* that I had to be strong."

Mrs. Hadder's deep drowned eyes lifted themselves from the hand of the undercurrent long enough to look at the sky. Her head and shoulders peeking above the horizon for just a moment, brought the cool reminder of air, and she sighed.

Dr. Pillapatti reached a hand out and placed it on bare shoulder. She let the tickle win, squeezed gently, and then sealed the emotion back up again where the pill bottle in her pocket would find it later.

The words then came from her chest in slow unmelodic chime. "You can't go to her like this. She's scared enough already. She needs brave people to pick her up."

Mrs. Hadder shook under the weight of well meaning and purpose. "I know." She let it push out from under the relief of pressure built. Her face went from red to pale white to rosy still.

"Then take a minute and breathe. Gather the strength of a mother and enter as if you are there to save her, not to watch her die."

Sobs filled in the spaces between prayers on another floor and together they rose far away from Mrs. Hadder's low vibrational trembles. She leaned, full-hearted, against the wall and dug her fingertips into the paint, trying with a desperate heart to draw in the sterile colour and make her facade a stone wall rather than a broken keep.

"You can do this" said Dr. Pillapatti. "For Sarah."

Mrs. Hadder lifted her head, shook her arms free from their shackles and nodded to the doctor. "For Sarah."

The door beckoned without hands and let its hinges quake in protest as Edna opened it, one tile at a time falling from this side of the room to the hallway beneath its swinging gate.

Dry air pushed its face against the glass and slid into Edna's lungs; as the door swung with it, she coughed under her throat in response, stifling the urge to gasp and sputter. She looked down at her converse sneaker tips as they tiptoed into the room beneath her careful gait: they made no sound, and no gym class would kick them out. Edna stared at them, passing tile after tile as the door had, as it closed, as she barred herself in and suckled the tears from her eyes, fighting the air for moisture, batting sideways at the onset of water's rise.

The floor was black and white. There was no grey between the territories it upheld—that Edna tried desperately to find.

A small stainless-steel turbine spun at the corner of the room; the noise drew attention from the floor to the sounds that such medicinal machinery made. A pump heaved wound spirals of nutrient water, a pillow lung slumped and expanded with the closed fist of regulated air… radar persisted somewhere, making echo-locational patterns of heartbeats that sounded closer to rail spikes than human behaviour. A bag full of liquid sloshed, unprovoked in its vacuum. The resonance of this air carried a stick into Edna's chest, travelled along her ribs and swaggered into her heart. Once there, it gave her pulmonary pump a hammer with the heavy end of the stick—square in the centre it hit—and Edna slouched at the pain and stopped, holding her fist to her teeth, daring to knock out her sobs from the place they found themselves squatting.

Eyes fell tight. Throat emptied liquor onto tongue, and Edna squeezed the whiskey sour to contort her face. Calamity vibes overtook her fingertips and sent paintings in a child's classroom to make delicate arrows all pointing to one place. But the distraction of self could not overtake and her ears, which should have been full of the sound of her own pulse, squeezed the volume of the air into ranges of the heart and filled her head with a pique blue masquerade. She shook her head in place while her body stayed swayed, and that's when the scrunching carried into the ballroom centre, holding up a swan-shaped mask, hiding nothing, exposing the ballet that she watched to be a drama of her family's.

Hold it together, she begged.

The grating, scrunching sound of fabric blending continued to expel its opera into the air.

Hold it together.

The mending of fingers sewing such seams into cricket legs kept her head awake when all she wanted were dreams.

Hold it together, for Sarah.

Edna chiseled her chin into a confidence by artists and started with a hose on the ground, black and spiraled with an internal steel structure. She followed it along its path of ants as it collected similar-shaped veins and collaborated into a snake pit of mating reptilians that coalesced on the same side of a hospital bed. They turned to a vineyard of thorns as they passed a humming electromagnetic machine and collected the wires of its computer resistance before angling across the lip of the bed. There it turned to a single arm of the stoned giant, gathering, finally, the stories of liquid tubes that dripped from the barren ceiling with iodized mineral solutions.

Once whole, the conglomeration reached behind the garments that shuffled beneath two mindless fingers and entered the body of the patient, turning Sarah's body into the soil in which the roots of the hospital tree grew. Feeders feeding her in reverse osmosis, mycelium collecting, sap depositing, all things breathing for her sake and survival.

Tree of life.

Emblem of death.

Receiver of both blades.

Edna's breath hid itself at the cacophony of metallic intervention: her daughter, unconscious, sitting upright in a cast half coffin. Two of her fingers working independent of her body, the rest of her being operated by the machines that cast their shadows into the hallway behind.

Again the hammer struck her heart, vibrating a gong instrument all through her body. Edna doubled over and fed tears to her gut while holding her belly cross-handed, and her mind, positioned at a step's pace away, trying desperately to save it from truth. She kneeled there, at her daughter's dreamed crucifixion, Mother Mary beneath a picture of the cross. But no amount of wine or flesh would reach out and touch her shoulder; Edna just fell to glass shatter in the hospital room, making heart incantations instead of praying for relief.

Quiet beeping machine.

Fingers ruffling sheets.

Tears.

An arrow pierced Edna's throat as she crouched beneath the wonder child. Its blade one word, and the shaft three others. "Mom, is that you?" struck the larynx, shutting it closed and forcing the spirits to impede and head back down to the grounded vein.

Edna lifted her head, shame crowned on her better head but the tears held back by words.

"Mom?"

Lips quivered beneath the tingle of the feathers above the shaft, slipping sideways in small waves and tender voices.

"Mom?" asked Sarah again, her eyes tiny splinter atoms.

Edna lifted her half heart up and sniffled back the last speartip. She moved to Sarah's interpretation of self beneath the benevolent benefactors of machine elves and placed a swollen hand beside an apple laying between the bedrail. She leaned on edges towards Sarah's call.

"Yes, my love. I am here." Edna held back the river's current with her tongue and her teeth and her lip.

The machine, bedside, huffed at slugs of tempered air and pushed Sarah's lungs into plaster dove wings, making her chest splinter and rise. Falling only on the flight of light from her devices, Sarah spoke in between the spreading of feathers, too tired to place pinions separate herself.

"Mom, can you hold my hand?"

Edna reached out and grasped the exposed two fingers that had earlier split the room in half. She placed them in her palms, swearing to take the brunt of stigmata's effects.

Two fingers on old, creviced hands. They were cold, like the lake. Shuttered subway car lights passed Edna's conscious eye and she saw nothing but the ice beyond the dock. She had to close her eyes to keep it all back.

Sarah spoke up. "Where's Dad?"

Eyelashes are no good in floods.

Part 5: The Wading Sick of Darkness

The ocean stood a mile from where the line was in the sand. A mile from where Sarah stood with her feet buried several inches below the washup. Where her toes wriggled in the substrate and teased the taste of skin to all the tiny crustaceans within the painted beach.

Heavy breath in through nose cleared the taste of sleep with bitter salted taffy. Hold.

Sarah let her eyes close and open as they pleased while she imbibed the sea smell. The fresh froth-churned waters bubbled up beneath her chin as micro fauna and phytoplankton made living bracers of her ankles, made liquid cuffs and left water marks on her skin.

The mindfulness bell rang somewhere and breath swirled out, orbiculating amongst the soft breeze, filling the gull's wings above her with altitude and power.

For miles, the sand strained its particulate hands through phase-shift colours in either side-to-side direction. Miles that might have one day run their length like Sarah had, not in full or actually, but indefinitely in its futility; far enough to know that here is where she was happiest on its palm to stay.

This is where the dream gate for this dream was, anyway, here in the nothing with its white expanse of impermanence behind and where only a small piece of driftwood marked the otherwise nonspecific place that ran beside a universe of ocean.

A universe of ocean in front of her.

A smile drawn like fire on her face.

A universe of ocean.

"Far better than the beach at home," she said as smooth slices of rock brine hit her nose like citrus. The taste stuck to her tongue as she looked across the water, its surface so glossy up close that she couldn't make out a reflection of herself staring back.

And when looking far away, only the reflection of cinnabar clouds that swirled like oxidized galvanic metal strips showed their form in the rippling aqua. No other shadow could darken the water from above. This was the perfect place to reflect because here, you couldn't so easily see yourself.

Further away, a gull dragged itself across the clouds, tailing below the horizon and swinging amongst the current felt. As its noisy wings dodged in and out of the clouds, the light fallen on the beach dimmed and brightened. There was no sun here; the only light on the beach came from the bright white wings of the gull—and as it flew westwards, out from vision's cusp, the sky darkened and the horizon beside the ocean began to turn black.

Sarah noticed her feet had gone dry and itched terribly. She looked down and found that the tide had gone out, that the sand around her feet had desiccated, leaving her small toes exposed to the tyranny of an arid breeze.

Large puff out. "Looks like the dream is up." She spoke to her toes, disgruntled as she pulled her two feet from the divots below her ankles. They left an imprint and Sarah smiled, knowing that the tide was out; her casting would last all evening.

Where the sky had turned black, the sound of hardened material, crackling, filled the silence.

"Where are those sneakers?" Sarah asked, her pace quickened by the thunder. Her spine pivoted back and forth inside the comfort of her hip until she stopped and her vision narrowed. "Ah!" she exclaimed, stepping three feet further towards an ocean that was slipping further away every time she blinked.

Amongst the rake-line symmetry left in the muddy sand from the water's snaking body, the white fabric backing of two Converse sneakers lay exposed a few feet from the imprints of her bare soles. The sneakers had been half buried beneath the silt and now, as the tide had released itself, they had become ripe for picking.

As feet made snowflakes of the ground, a shade drew in on Sarah's silhouette. The sky and terrain around her were slipping into a black fog as the gull, with its lantern arms, had all but disappeared beyond the confines of the dream, taking its irradiated feathers with it. Taking all the light of the beach in its wings.

This was nothing new, and Sarah was aware of the starless blanket's weight now covering her body and arms as its creases, like reading glasses, further shadowed her eyes. "Shit," she said under her breath, as the darkness pressed her to work faster. Her pupils darted back and forth across the beach, hoping for some semblance of the light to have persisted but it was darkening faster than it usually had. Her eyes worked harder as she hastened the lock and pick schema of a dream gate by the driftwood's arm. Her lips pulled back behind her sweating teeth as racing tendons scrambled towards the footwear and their key.

Sarah dug the shoes out from their sand bed and put them on quick with shaking hands whose fingers had become dust on glass, and slippery. She grabbed each lace while trying to commit to memory exactly where the driftwood would remain behind her, but hot, heavy lead was in every fingernail as she worked the shoe's laces.

The last celestial wisps of colour left the beach and the ground became black earthworm bed. No light. Dark finish. The lock vanished from sight.

"Shit," she gasped again as the final knot came together and her left hand faded beneath her crouching body. Sarah paused to stare at the ethereal skin that was disappearing before her struggling eyes, her arm turned into frayed spasms of energy, then particles of light, then a wave of sound that flowed away east, where it was swallowed into the abyssal black growing on the horizon. The sound of dream machinations, thunder, and rain collided on the ridge of that darkest darkness advancing.

The freeze of despair cooled her to shivering; the weather beast was coming, and Sarah would disappear inside it.

Under padded breaths, Sarah spoke. "That was fast." Her wide eyes stared into a storm now growing to the east, a great entourage of grey condensate matter stacking in on itself far away.

"It never comes this fast!" she remarked, her eyes blinking twice before her body began to move in reaction to prey. *"No, no, no!"* she thought. "I can't go to another dream this way!" She whimpered. *"Not again."*

A new light swelled in the sky, one that was fast replacing the gull's gentle rays from the opposite side with a purple cacophony of electrified radiance inside the chest of a sonorous storm of clay.

A harbinger of change in the atmosphere.

It was a dream cloud, a steward that arrived on theta waves and pelted the ground with complex crop circle shapes until the entire dreamscape became a melted chaos equation for which new dreams could spring. Sometimes good. Often not. Nightmares and terrors filled the cloud with rain.

The storm's tusks, like mandibles, shaped from cumulonimbus wings pointed out in front where it felt for reincarnation in the hail that it brought, ready to carry ephemeral bodies from their sleeping state into the flash bang of the next higher frequency wave. A dream-eating pachydermal tempest. Everything but rampage became black and helpless in its four-footed wake.

Sarah, now panicked, made tangled tracks in the substrate beneath her body with melting marbled feet. She fumbled madly backwards, fear-blind as she searched for the piece of driftwood that had been behind her but now could not be found.

The encroaching elephant was coming fast and violent. It tore the sky and terraces into pieces of charcoal-stained sores.

"Where is it?" Sarah turned and swept her hands back and forth in the sand behind her. Unable to procure the piece of timber, she cried.

The downpour was close now. Close enough that Sarah could make out the surface structure of the dreamscape beneath its falling rain melting away, like a pastel runoff under a steam engine of cloud break.

Her head filled with memories of lost places amongst the darker dreams she had explored. *Absent of keys and gates and safety...* the storm roared closer to her puffing, red-worn cheeks.

"I can't go to a new dream," she gasped. *Sound was deafening thunder on her bed-lust wiles.* "Not like this." *Tears streamed down her cheeks.*

It moved like light rays in stained glass portraits.

A shed tear filled the well, and Daniel came to face Sarah in her head. *The hermit. The Alchemist. The man by the river's bed whispered.* And woke her from the dream within.

Bloop A cold wet raindrop pierced Sarah and she opened her eyes, gritted her teeth, and began searching again, her hands without vision still managing to sweep the endless granules of sand.

"It's here, Sarah! Just find it!" she bellowed.

Capillaries on the flesh work surface of Sarah's swelled lungs blushed with swirls of sanguine artillery as her bronchial system overworked itself. She turned from the frantic drowning picture of her dream and was on all scattered fours in the sand, her body slipping in nothing, it scraped feverishly on the ground for the lost piece of driftwood.

The storm almost atop her head cracked a shatter stomp of lightning and the flare of embers briefly illuminated the piece of wood that stuck up from the sand. The flash was long enough for Sarah; she jumped on the phallic material, slid it over in her hands and triggered a hole to open beneath her body.

The rain cloud's children fell beside her head and pierced the echo as Sarah fell into the sinkhole, the piece of wood, tight in her hand.

She fell, and thick brick staircase steps drove themselves into her hips and chest. Sarah grunted as she rolled down a flight of mossy stairs, fractals of glass falling in behind her, the sinkhole covering itself up as she tumbled.

The storm cloud washing the world away above her was unable to send its swell of rain down with her. Only Sarah plummeted into the tunnels beneath her dreams, their dark spirals a comfort from the pachyderm and its raging storm.

A final step cracked like sunshine eggs and Sarah's ill-prepared body spasmed on their surface, causing a knee to brace and then give out beneath her uncontrolled weight, forcing the thin dangerous calcium cap to hurdle into the soft cartilage of her nose. Blood splattered the dark steps as she hit the bottom landing upside down, her white sneakers still wet and filled with sand, stood up above her blurry head.

"Ow…" Sarah seethed under her breath while growing roses filled her throat with thorns of flowers spent.

She was on her back at the bottom of the steps. A familiar light fixture swung above her head as she opened her battered eyes to the interior of the tunnel.

"A little close, I think." She winced while she pushed a finger into her ribs to try to adjust something that bit as she had spoken. Snakes in tattered falls writhed under the facets of her skin, shaded tracers, pythons amongst the blackening dawn. Purple eyes. Dark spots in the sun.

Sarah sat up onto her rear and lifted her bloodied shirt to expose the spreading ink on her chest. She poked it with a curious finger and immediately reared back from the pain of bruised pears. "Dammit!" Teeth tight and breath scathing, Sarah returned the fabric of her shirt, looking away as if the pain might stop with inattention.

"Why should it hurt in a dream…" she muttered to herself.

"If it isn't falling downstairs, it's the end of a dream and the rainstorm that eats it! And if it isn't a rainstorm… it's that damned beast from the other night!" She shook her head side to side with a slow incantation to calm the senses. "At least—down here—I am safe."

Grabbing hold of the familiar wall with its bookcase-style bricks that ran for miles of thicket-like woods through the tunnel, Sarah placed her bruises beneath her and rose to stand on her converse-stricken feet, the sneakers a soft reminder that she had crossed the barrier above.

She checked her body, ensuring it was opaque, milk skin. Thin mind, thick brim.

"Aha! See!" She tilted her head back and yelled at the tunnel's ceiling. "This is my territory!" Her finger was pointed with stern knuckles at the ground. "This place down here is mine entirely! Hmmm!"

Once satisfied, Sarah looked down and wiggled her toes inside her shoes. More interesting was the conical light directly above her head that showered a cool glow onto her body. The luminescence of the lantern and the folds of her shirt left strange shadows in the wrinkles of her blood-dyed clothes, which dragged her attention down to the floor where a small pool of water collected blood from her nose.

She wiped her nostril and it stung.

"Hrumph!"

Ignoring the blood on her finger, she looked back up the staircase that she had tumbled down with rapid-fire grace. It was inset in the tunnel's walls and its door was in the offset ceiling far above her head. Both the door and stairs were made with stones cut into rectangular slats, stacked side by side and fastened together with copper hinges. Between the spaces of slate, sand still trickled down from the beach above, ran across the stone and denied gravity to weave its way down the stairs, across the floor of the tunnel and make its way to the pool of blood beside her feet.

Its path, not unlike the timid vulture, although indirect, was hungry.

Raising only an eyebrow and avoiding miscalculated alarms, Sarah turned and walked in an English reading path along the tunnel, the titles of the books moving right to left as she sashayed, their spines traveling away from the sand as they fell further into the impermanent parts of her vision.

Familiarity dripped from Sarah's eyes, splashed against the back of her throat and dripped into her stomach. The unchanged view, the permanence of the tunnel, was quick to quell any lingering anxiety that huddled up inside her after almost being washed away in the rain. Her belly was warm with it, as bee pollen might be, and she walked with lighter, airy feet to the next known place in her subconscious schema, excited to find another dream, of her choosing, to wander into.

As feet fell, the brick path slapped against Sarah's rubberized soles and made a quiet reverberation of the air that brushed by her. Slips of old pages in the breeze from the wall's lining tickled at her nose. Their eloquent words brushed red cheeks and turned them down a cool pale note lower, abstaining from blush and caressing the flesh until it became blue, careless and cold.

With a Christmas-grade sweater of heat at her stomach and a room sweet with cool, walking temperature air, with the safe guarded good nature of the tunnel… with the knowledge that all things here were only her own, Sarah walked to the next line of dream gates with her head secure above her shoulders. Not an uncertain slouch in such a high-heeled stance of confidence.

"It's good to be home." The resonance of her chords sung themselves along the walls and woke up the green moss plants that filled the nooks in between the books of the tunnel. Aroused, the moss stuck its long filaments out into the air in search of particulate matter to ingest. Sarah smiled at them as she and their tiny tentacles coloured the tunnel with the catch of a spoken song.

Several jovial paces into the nightshade that was the aisle-way of gates, Sarah came to a spot where a wall popped up and positioned itself at a right angle in her path. A fork in the road propositioned her choices. Sarah stopped to take thought.

She looked up to where neurons might form in real time and tried to pluck them with thoughtful eyes from the space of nothing. "If the beach is behind me and a fork is in front… That means left is to… the carnival." Sarah bit her cheek and shivered before pointing right: "The place where I saw that beast the other day is this way… and then the junction." Teeth burst in her mouth with crescents at the word 'junction,' and she picked up her feet to skip down the right tunnel. The lights swung in beat above her.

As the spines of her thought continued pressing back into the wild behind her, Sarah's ears picked up a gentle padding of atmosphere. A flutter of fabric that swept helplessly for non-existent currents in the air.

Feet came to abrupt stops and Sarah planted her hips and looked, craning to see into the dank tunnel that swelled behind her. There was something in the far away, fluttering just far enough away to be too far to properly sight. Small, quiet—but obviously there.

Sarah clenched her left fist as her eyelids distended into cups of sensation. She strained to look into the dark where a small shadow approached at face height. A series of questions in the shape of images berated Sarah's mind, the thought first of the raven and the coin, then the tentacles of the beast and finally of the storm. All those things chipped away at the sanctity of her tunnel, and it made her teeth grind to mud.

But as the fluttering movement came closer, her clenched jaw loosened and was replaced with a quizzical mouth as a small yellow bird appeared from the haze.

The tiny aviator bounced against the walls, struggling to make feathers work the effort of its flight, its DaVinci mechanism corkscrewed and unfit for design. It twittered as frail, futile appendages worked in earnest to arrive.

The sense of the known had melted in the sound of the bird, uncovering the recently stored chakra in Sarah's stomach. But children are made there, and she couldn't help but feel needed as the delicate, struggling bird approached.

Sarah placed her hands out, making beds of her palms. Places to pray and rest. "Come, little bird, you can settle here. I won't hurt you."

Just shy of safety, the bird made a fast swing upwards, and its beak dove straight into the light fixture above, shattering the bulb and sending a cascade of electrical interference into the air. It lit shadows behind Sarah and made a puppet of her heart, exposing all two of its character traits.

"Oh!" Sarah gasped as the yellow fragment of life fell to the floor and lay twitching, pulsing with vectored fear and painful blinded sight.

Sarah moved forward, pushing through the tendrils of doubt and hesitance, splitting the fear off for the need to comfort the fear of others. Smaller, less powerful beings. She kneeled down in front of the bird. Tiny hollow bones poked out from around its shoulders and bled its yellow feathers a darker shade of red. Sarah brought her hands with slow care to meet the tiny death.

"A canary," she said.

She pushed small fingertips beneath the charred body and the bird struggled, but Sarah persisted, lifted it up onto her gentle hands.

The bird shivered, cold setting into the open wounds on its arms. Small flecks of sanguine blotted like acid into the air around them, particulates of life in the open wind, things spiders would hook to and float on for miles. The canary chirped and in its small beady eyes was the blue ocean's swell. Then plankton. Then coral reefs bleached white. Then open empty sand forever.

Blood stopped falling from the canary's gore. The small bird stopped fluttering in her hands. Its heart, however mechanical, failed.

Sarah's throat pulled at the flesh in the back of her head, and she felt tears take its place. She tried not to cry for the tiny pilot, but salt will always find the riverbed, and she wept a little for the canary.

"How did you even get down here?" she asked over thin tears while looking back and forth down the tunnel. "Things hardly ever make it down here." She brushed her cheeks with the back of her hand and sniffed back the snot in her nose.

Moving all at once, the moss in the walls shuddered, making a lash at the meditation bell and sounding a flash retreat into the protective crevices of the walls.

Mindful, like whiskers, Sarah stood up at the sudden alarm and looked down the tunnel the way the bird had come. A breeze was moving towards her and on it, something like a stale bog smelled in the currents.

The tunnel pulled itself out from her, its strange loop unbreaking, breaking the confidence so often crowned. Sarah stepped down from her throne, apprehensive but more so curious. Something was out of place, and she had to walk forward into the lantern's stretching line of lights, to find what might leave a bird in hand.

Thin and nearly weightless, the canary's corpse rocked to the unsteady rhythm of her cautious feet. Wishing to be invisible, Sarah made her way with heavy soles towards the next doorframe. A familiar door that had been above her head a few nights prior. One that held back a huge pond whose silt held trinkets from her childhood. She sighed, heavy with the thought of what was held back, and continued on towards a growing, trickling sound.

Down the tunnel's floors, a widening stream of slow-moving, tannin-black water stained Sarah's white shoes with a yellow like cigarette tar. She lifted her sodden feet and the water squelched in protest at her desire to inspect it. She made a sour face.

"What the hell is this?" A deluge ran through the floor. As she moved further, it pooled in various undulations and made strange, eye-shaped water forms that grew slimy bubbles, black microfauna, and salamanders with forked tongues and bellies of fire.

Further in, her tracks got thicker and the sounds of trickling liquid got louder. Sarah arrived at the door in the ceiling, whose black walnut finish and brass hardware she had fallen through the other night. She looked up at it and shuddered, reminded of the dream where the beast had taken chase so she had to dive into the pond with this dream gate at its bottom. She checked, though, diligent, inspecting the wooden boards that were fastened hard with the metal work of a locksmith. No water was dripping from the frame or the boards, not even the keyhole in the doorknob.

No, instead the noise was in front of her.

Several paces forward, a black spot in the tunnel ceiling loomed, its dark outline sprinkled with the dust of chimney sweeps standing in hearths, bristles bristling. It looked as though something had broken through: book bricks were on the ground, lanterns were missing from the ceiling, the bricks so penetrated that the stars from her dream above it shone into the tunnel.

Gawking, Sarah walked closer towards the open spot in the earth where the water must have poured in hard and fast at some point, although now it only trickled. She stopped to watch the liquids, now working their way down the walls without any need to rush, leaving white stains on the books' warping spines. Her eyes became blackboards where white chalk spelled out the names of childhood fears in big block letters. Sarah shivered as she looked over the mess in the tunnel's passage. The entire structure had caved in, and the carved liturgy of architecture lay in pieces. Beyond the collision spot, the tunnel picked up again, but it was littered as far as her eyes could see with a trail of sand and water and building debris.

It was here, in the face of turmoil, that Sarah knew the bird's purpose and she wished that she had taken the tunnel left instead of right. A hole in the ceiling of the tunnel was no metaphor—it would be taken at base value, a hole in her safety. Sarah shook at its mass. Then, a further axe to the box that held her heart, Sarah saw something standing on the far side of the tunnel.

In settling dust, panting in the shadows, a wriggling mass. It stole Sarah's chest and all her perspective shrunk into a single moment of panic. Sarah clasped the canary's body tight, absent of mind, and its fragile chest burst into gore and feathers. When she looked down to her bloodied palms, a golden coin lay there.

She was screaming.

The day's light cast on her morning face.

Known voices were bouncing around the room with witch-broom streamers bursting from their burning plumes. The fire kicked at Sarah's ears and she shot up, the pyres burning so bright in her mind.

Her mouth was open and her uvula rang like the woman on stage, horned and vicious, but there was no crowd. No orchestral strings. Only the familiar olive tree-fruit walls that hung like drapes from the heavens of her ceiling were present. Her daybed's polished brass handrails. The sleeping room was here. The tunnel was gone.

Sunlight painted itself with oil mixtures on the whitewall of her bedroom door. The hall behind. No footsteps. No breathing except her own.

Fingertips pressed at the cage of aspiring hearts, Sarah pressed a little harder as the pulsation, so quickened by design of dream, smouldered, smothered, died out in her reminded hands. Breath was short but calming; Sarah's chin swung in and out, less and less as all things relaxed. She pulled her blankets back to expose red-rashed legs hot from running, cooling in the partial breeze from winter that snuck between the poor gaskets of her window. Still stained like all the rest. Cherry-red sun spent.

Sarah swallowed a lump, and checked if she was still screaming. It seemed that she had stopped.

There was silence from the morning doves usually outside her walls. "Did my mother hear it?"

Sarah waited a moment longer, but no concerned feet came down the hall. A door, an outside door, closed in the kitchen, downstairs, far away from her room. Sarah relaxed and threw her fingers back so that her palm could rest against her chest. "Oh, thank goodness."

She checked her hands. There was no blood, only the cool kiss of the long-desired coin.

A few more meditative breaths and Sarah slunk back into the comfort of her bed sheets.

"I think it's time I saw Daniel."

Part 6: Hermeticism's Greatest Feat

"And who exactly is Daniel?" asked Dr. Pillapatti.

Sarah squinted.

Behind the doctor's bobbing black top bun was a set of chestnut roll curtains that were never let down and the sun was always behind her. Sarah could not help but find herself wanting night while she tried to think in all the sun crowns.

"Daniel's a hermit," said Sarah as she rolled a warm travel mug between her palms. Her knees nested at angles beneath her, the chair too comfortable to sit in.

"A hermit." Dr. Pillapatti smiled and her white blouse scrunched up around her shoulders when she leaned in. "Is there more?" The question rolled around untamed in the room. Two obelisk-shaped shadows stood at the doctor's feet, on the rug where she was bent over, pretending to rest on her clipboard, trying not to touch them.

Landmarks disappeared and reappeared in slow motion as Sarah blinked with slug-bathed teardrops, watching the sun crawl behind the doctor. The obelisks stretched further and further across the grey landscape of the floor. The furniture disassembled and then reconstituted before becoming unimportant, again and again. The light, very strong.

"Of course there's more." Sarah tried to focus. "It's hard to categorize him though." She looked down at her focal point mug.

"What did your mother send you with?"

"Same as always." Sarah swirled the mug, trying to stir her thoughts up inside of it.

"Tea, or coffee?"

"Tea," replied Sarah. "Same as always."

The obelisks' thin cancers stretched further across the floor as Dr. Pillapatti straightened in her chair, sitting back from the demand to cock her head to one side.

"Same as always?" Said Dr. Pillapatti.

The sun dissolved. Its core collapsed, its gaseous rings evanesced into the cosmos, the galaxy swallowed it up whole before the demiurge repeated, throwing it back up only to start the collapse again. The methodic mime of Sarah's eyelids. The coming of dawns and apotheosis. In every blink, Sarah crushed her world.

"Are you distracted?" Dr. Pillapatti asked.

"Yes. The shadows on the floor. Impermanence. That stuff." She replied with a feigned, cold disconcert. Like Sarah, the shadows that formed and unformed in the room existed in too many places at once for specific egos to notice them.

The doctor raised an eyebrow, and stars slipped behind its questioned stance. Sometimes Sarah wished that they didn't exist here, where only her ego had evolved to notice them.

"Tell me more about Daniel, please? I'd like to understand."

"You probably don't believe he exists." Sarah kept her eyes closed, dismantling the visiting universe in the doctor's office space while trying to balance the important plates.

"I'm sure he exists… I just question how real he is."

Air circulated in the room; Sarah could feel it push the thin strands of flyaway hairs, the ones unwilling to tie up with the rest, left to dance across her head before they fell and burst on her cheeks. She smirked, unwilling. The irony of shadows and speaking of Daniel not lost to her.

"I wonder that too," replied Sarah. One of the strands of hair, charged by her words, flung itself into the abyss of her mouth, wrapping itself around the subliminal poles and unconscious places between Sarah's teeth. Opening her eyes, she fished it out with a hooked finger.

"You wonder… how—real—Daniel is?"

"Yes," continued Sarah. "But not like that. Not like you're implying."

"What am I implying?" The doctor reached down to scratch her shin, and the obelisks jumped as she rolled forward.

Sarah pulled back, frowning at the reminder that comes at a limit.

The topography of the floor neither shrank nor lengthened. She thought of how her bed sheets were the perfect length.

"You're inferring that yes, Daniel exists, but only to me. As in, he's real but he may only be real in my head."

"You should get your doctorate."

Sarah disregarded the doctor's playful banter and continued. "Although my mind is not entirely made up on that, as either. I am also not sure which *real* Daniel could even be."

Dr. Pillapatti looked away and focused on a discoloured square space on the wall, that Sarah was certain she couldn't see.

Nothing was said for a moment.

Sarah blinked again and the world was on the edge of things.

"Why don't you tell me what you do know?" asked the doctor.

Long frays of the room's atmosphere piled up and condensed in Sarah's throat where it churned gravity; the heavy weight on her spine made Sarah wince as she lifted her head. The birth of more questions always left more shadows to creep up in between answering them.

As Sarah raised her eyes, the obelisks stretched with her vision and she could not meet Dr. Pillapatti head on—they had grown too large and the chairs fell into their shadows, throwing them into a stasis floating amongst the abyss. Along with all that was thrown and swallowed, Sarah let the exodus of air exhume itself from her lungs into the shadow of those pillars, and for a moment—she felt like she could dream—the visions existed within reason, within the dream. *The dreams. Where,* "I met Daniel in one of my dreams. The one where I killed the rabbit. In the glade, the green place. One of my oldest dreams."

Dr. Pillapatti crossed one leg over the other knee, shuffling to get comfortable in her chair. The room switched places.

"How long ago?"

"It was when I started dreamscaping."

"So, he is a very old friend?"

"The only one from my dreams."

The two chairs floated as drift ice might under the feet of esquimeaux clay. Pots full of snow, full of water, on snow… above the water. They skated. Blue darkness for miles beneath.

"Do you have no other friends in your dreams?"

Sarah bit down into her doctor's voice, clamping onto something so that she wouldn't fall into the infinitum below.

"None of the beings I dream of operate quite the way Daniel does."

The doctor furrowed her eyebrows and made deep shadowed lines on the soft muscle of her cheeks. Spots which fisherman desired for stew, where hooks catch most often and ruin the meat. Her mouth went thin at the thought of hulls eclipsing the moon and Sarah, looking for more semantics to grasp, recognized the facial movement.

"He's the only one that doesn't seem in a particular or obvious loop," continued Sarah, her fingers tight jaws. "All the other people appear right where they started each time, or where I left them last…" A flash of the broken tunnel swung at Sarah's mind and sent her head dizzying to the whale.

"Sarah?"

A great hole opened in Sarah's heart. From it, a thin broken hand reached for the surface and something tried to pull itself out. "No," replied Sarah, whispering to herself "there's nothing to say of the beast." [1] [2] [3]

Dr. Pillapatti stared at Sarah's emptied expression, went to write something on her pad but stopped short of the paper and put kindling in her heart. "So…" she ventured slowly, "Daniel is not on a loop like, say, the machete man or the person who takes cash at the cinema are?"

"Like them," said Sarah. "Just like Mother Life or Father Death by the cabin. Like the rabbit in the hole." Sarah stirred her mug again by swirling her hands, the steam from its small aperture orbiting within the tiny focused spot of her eyes and pinned her to the now, the caffeine a good tether in the cold. Her mind took a picture of the chemical structure and she continued.

"No, not Daniel. Sometimes he *is* sitting in the same spot, but only of his own volition. He is not on a reel like the others. He doesn't seem to circle."

"Where is *his* spot in the dream?"

"It's a little outside the glade, to the right of where I wake." The caffeine smell settled Sarah's head and she could reminisce with cucumber stalk clarity. "Back aways from the gate. I found a… domicile of sorts, covered in brambles and overhung by a willow tree, by the river, beyond the glade. Daniel sits in a wicker chair beside the water there, fishing… or sometimes he's in the shack singing or laughing… or sleeping." Feeling the weight hefted from her shoulders by the comfort of that dream, she sat up expectantly and checked her surroundings for a book. On a shelf to the left, she found some non-fiction titles, unfortunately plain to read.

She sighed thick smoke into the air. "Sometimes, he even dreams."

"Did you find him accidentally?"

"I wasn't searching for him, if that's what you mean. I had just started lucid dreaming and had only then become brave enough to travel outside the regular dreamscape. I was walking without purpose when I found the river and his house."

"I would like to clarify the history, if that's okay, Sarah?"

"How so?"

"I'm just curious which came first. Daniel or the dream gates?"

"No, Dr. Pillapatti." Sarah adjusted again in her seat. The walls of the room, under no direct orders of caffeine, had begun to slip again, crumbling and then blowing away like so many sands. Time indifferent.

Beneath the chairs, grass had started to grow, dandelions took the place of mundane patterns and rabbit holes sprang up in places where feet would stand ground and breathe. Sarah placed the coffee away and she ignored the legible book title. In the stain of dandelions on her skin, she breathed the ink of her *episode.*

"Daniel was the one who showed me that the dream gates exist," Sarah smiled. "He came hand-in-stone with the doors. Paths led from wondrous art." Warmth ran through her veins.

Dr. Pillapatti applied a series of thin lines from her pen to the pad of paper on her knee. Sarah marked the habit and made her own important lines on an invisible page before continuing.

"He said hello to me… and waved… when I first came over the embankment to the river, but he looked just as surprised to see me as I was to see another human acting so… human-ly."

Dr. Pillapatti lifted her pen close to the painted lips of her curious nature. She bared her ivory desire and tempted the edge of the pen's tip with her inquisitive saliva, drenching her tongue in languish, and she came close to biting, then blinked and tore the ink away from the wetted verge of her black cat questions. Professionalism took its place again and she queried, back straight, mouth thin. "Why do you think he was surprised to see you? He wasn't startled, was he?"

"No, he wasn't." Sarah looked down to the rolling green topography that continued underfoot. A white hare had breached the groundwork and wormed its way under clean shaven legs. Sarah ignored it. "I've already broken you," she whispered to the rabbit.

"What was that?" Dr. Pillapatti asked.

"I'm not entirely sure, but sometimes I feel like I may have walked into his dream… you know? And he just—wasn't expecting me… ever." Sarah looked up and made a weak smile for Dr. Pillapatti.

The doctor lifted her chest beneath her blouse and the grass blades all bent to her breath. "I've read that the landscapes and the people in your dreams are reimaginings of places and faces in your—" she fished for the word a moment before being satisfied with, *"physically conscious life.* Is Daniel someone you recognize in your day to day?"

"No. No one has a face like his. Not the scraggly cut of his shadowed chin, the set of his cheek bones like ocean wind. His black hair long, curly, ringlets in some places where it touches his back…" Sarah sighed. "His green eyes, so terribly sad."

The doctor raised a pheromone game. "Are you attracted to Daniel?"

Sarah thought outside for a moment, pieces of strange men formulating in her head. "No, I admire him though."

"Why is that?"

"Because he's not concerned about being uncertain."

"It probably took him a long time to get comfortable like that."

"I doubt it. He probably just woke up that way."

The tip of the doctor's pen tapped soundly against her chin. "What happened after you met him? Did you—or perhaps did he—say anything important?"

Sarah's eyes kept on the floor where the rabbit now moved through the grass. Swirling and curving with belly muscles, the small, ragged tail on its back marking the way like a scent trail, down the embankment, across the river and into the hole with a wooden door beside the sign. Sarah then looked at Dr. Pillapatti, hard metal slate stare. "I can't remember what was said, but soon after, he took me to the gate."

"The first dream gate you ever found?"

"I didn't find it, it was shown to me."

"Right, sorry. The first gate, though?"

"Yes, further down the river. A hole with a wooden door beside a sign marked 'Were Here.'"

"And you trusted him enough to enter an unfamiliar door?"

Sarah turned her bottom jaw slightly and let the top canine place in the bottom premolar on her right side. The motion tilted her head and caused her left eye to water. Not drip, but it drowned the pupil's brother. "No, but I was desperate to know more."

Sarah took another swig of the coffee in her hands. The smooth liquid washed the backside of her throat and fell into her belly, making warm the bath house tubs, and Sarah soon found no reason to continue wearing a towel. She smirked, one side of her lip curling up in the steam and moisture. As the heat rose, the cold fell off and tucked its tail, pulling the obelisks away with it.

I like the smaller font for a whisper - has it been consistent throuhout? (Note for me to check)

probably hasnt been used throughout lol

We'll leave it as a formatting issue for the end. Putting a pin in it.

Part 7: Enter the Solstice of Suns

"This is where the corner rounds, you know. And you think the road becomes straight again. But it could get real dark, very soon, Sarah," spoke Zara while his long thin beard bobbed up and down in time with his chin.

"How do you mean?" Sarah stood in the marketplace corner, where bits of night dust had remained for long, permanent hours. The sun was setting behind the small herbal shop, breaking the panes of glass where it entered in behind Zara and making the drying plants that hung from the ceiling come alive as shadow puppets. In the rustling, dancing leaves like hands, the night was just beginning to disperse from the fractal of day and the palm of mannequins; meanwhile, the day was finally coming to its end.

Zara closed his eyes and stroked his long-since grey beard, something stereotypical of those that may have more knowledge than those that come looking for its letters and words. He thought for a way to provide the information in a more succinct manner. Sarah could see the tribulation in the creases of his cheeks and eye sockets. "When the sun descends and the night comes upon us, the veil tends to thin just a little." He opened his eyes and looked beyond Sarah, beyond the bustling crowds of people far away in the marketplace centre, beyond where Sarah and he stood. He searched for a lexicon that fit the novelty and when the honey of its comb dripped, Zara spoke clearly overtop the noise of the humans' buzzing echoes behind them, their tiny voices slipping away into a spiral of infinitesimal nature under the power of his voice.

"And we think, now, things will become clearer… that because the light is away we can now ignore the ego's representation of the world around us. That we may no longer see so easily through the lenses of our conscience and instead, we will see without a lens at all."

Thin grey linoleum tiles that adhered to thin grey concrete slabs that had been hoisted onto thick grey stone pillars deep below the earth, shook. The slip of glue and friction's weight slid a few millimeters forward and pushed Sarah to lean in on an angle, eyes listening to the thoughts of a man of knowledge like Zara.

"But isn't that what happens…?" Sarah tried to pull the knowledge unwillingly from clenched thoughts. "When I sleep, when the sun dims, when I close my eyes, I am closer to the other realms, am I not?"

Clouding ethereal eyes looked down from the empyrean of thought and drove stakes into Sarah's preconceptions. "Yes," said Zara. "And no."

A man walked by the stand with his eyes down on the screen of his phone, and bumped Sarah from behind, his weight and elbow nudging her closer to Zara's stand, pushing her further into the row of herbs. Ginger pieces impressed themselves into Sarah's waistline as she leaned in further, unintentionally seasoned and perturbed.

"Sorry, sorry, young lady," said the man as his tie lay loose on his neck, an informal greeting of the distracted. He walked backwards a few steps, bowing high from the ground, his eyes finally relieved from the chamber that his cell phone provided. "I'm very sorry."

Sarah spared little of her looks as the man turned back around and went about the unpleasant business of a 'people,' she would say.

The new position, however, pressing up against the stand and closer than ever to Zara, was pleasant and Sarah settled to keep it close. She could smell the fresh tiger balm that had been mixed earlier by skilled hands hiding just inside the cover of the stand. Relaxed, she dropped her shoulders in hypnotism of the comforting smell and let her chest heave and roll.

"How do you mean, both yes and no?"

"All things are a dichotomy. As above, so below," spoke Zara.

"Yes, I know. But what is on each side of duality in this particular instance, and why is it important?"

There was a visible sigh in the black fabric of Zara's shirt, and he placed a small amount of thin beige roots into a paper bag while he spoke. "How well do you imagine the cat sees in the dark?"

"Naturally very well." Sarah stepped into the point before recognizing its reason.

"And how well do you see in the dark?"

"Not as well as a cat, I gather."

"Exactly—you are stepping into the cat's world and yet are made for that of civilized man."

Sarah scoffed.

Zara continued. "You're coming round the corner to the place you couldn't see from the other side of its bend. Which is promising... but, don't forget, you are not a cat and whether you've rounded the corner or not, the sun has gone down and you may not see the light for some time."

Zara handed over the brown paper bag, its contents weighing a point of impact on the bottom, where Sarah grabbed it.

"Do you know how to imbibe the root?"

"If I tell you I do, you'll still tell me how to anyway," replied Sarah.

"The job of the shaman is to drown his patrons, but I always worry that one may not quite survive the lack of air."

Both parties stared quietly at the other until Sarah sighed and began to recite what she had read of Silene Capensis.

"The Zulus would often just rip off small chunks of root, chew them to pulp and then swallow. Before bed. On an empty stomach."

Zara closed his eyes, smiled, and nodded with his expression far away from the counter at which he stood. His blind image pressed for more from Sarah.

She inhaled the air around the stand and continued. "The Xhosa, however, seemed to treat the plant with a lot more... respect." Sarah tilted her head as if moving the thoughts from one side of her brain to the other, their meanings jumbling up on the way. "It was documented that they would have long ceremonies where the participants would not eat or drink for a couple days, then they would grind the root up and make a cold frothing tea. In it, they would bathe themselves and maybe some animals that they would eat later. They would drink enough of the froth that they might get sick and throw up—" Sarah pulled her head back and set her neck at an awkward angle, "—like a... surreal kind of *dream* party."

Zara continued to nod, delighted with her footnotes.

"So they would drink a bunch of tea over two or three days and then fall into a comatose state. Sleeping and having lucid dreams for nights on end. Pretty wild stuff."

"Yes," replied Zara, elated with the information. "And why exactly do these wonderful peoples take the root?"

"To dream, of course." Sarah enunciated each syllable, trying to avoid the facts she already knew well.

"Yes, but what's important to the dream?"

A pod of air escaped her nose in a light puff and gave away her position. Before Zara could cross his weighted arms to scale her response, Sarah continued. "Ancestors. Many, if not all, of the Congolese tribes have a deep-seated respect and appreciation for their ancestors. Dreams are believed to be a place where a passed relative could meet you and impart wisdom and advice. Shamans would often provide the root so that their peoples may dream, reunite with family, receive blessings or advice... maybe even gather some knowledge of the future."

"Good." Zara clapped two time-stained hands together and rubbed his palms until cookies fell out from the creases of his fortunate smile. "And you will make cold tea. Find a forked stick in the wood. Grind five hundred milligrams of root with the mortar and pestle I provided you, then pour the powder into water and stir with the branch until it froths. Drink the froth until you are full, then discard the water. You may vomit, but it is not necessary." Zara's eyes dropped to level the field between them. "Do you understand?"

"Yes. Thank you, friend."

Sarah reached her hand out for the bag. "One last thing, youngling," said Zara in time with the pivot of steps.

Sarah let an elevator of breath test the floors on her spine. The lobby and penthouse, loud compounds of description.

"What will you do if you need to leave?" asked Zara.

"I was just prepari—"

"The dream, child." Zara tilted his head to the same five o'clock that had become his beard.

"Oh! That's easy."

"I just like to make sure… these are tumultuous waters, even for selkies like yourself."

"I just fall asleep, Zara, in the dream."

The old man smiled wider to expose the white of his soul before closing his mouth and providing a final stern warning. "Be careful, Sarah. This is far more powerful than the royal Red Reishis, alright?"

"Yes, Zara. I am aware."

He smiled again and handed over the paper bag, its contents heavy as gold.

Chapter Two

It was fire.

Those soft white sphere moments where the skin has charred and the nerves separate from flesh—those were fire. A healthy mind lets go and blankets its red blood to preserve the oxygen but in doing so mutates the stream, and dimethyltryptamine is given taste. That interspersed feeling takes over—the stream to transcend the self-—and the soul is given a final assurance so that even the unenlightened may enter the bardo. Those last few inspirational moments in the empty space, when her diaphragm gave out… Was fire for her lungs as they readied to burst the soft white sphere of her perception.

After that moment, everything had changed.

After her bronchial tubes had been used to crucify the last cawing raven who carried her soul in its carnivorous beak. Following the moment when the pulled-tight membrane had been broken on the hammer's back and burst, allowing the book-paper flesh to expose and pour like sand into Sarah's body cavity. Succeeding the immeasurable pain of the universe's inattentiveness to her whimper, the single wisp of breath burnt out among the cold of the universe's flesh.

Beyond that was the threshold to the stewards of her karma.

The karma is better best.

There is, was, and after all that, on the opposite side of normally locked doorways, another sleeping body that Sarah looked upon. Dressed and bathed as she was. Decorated with an ornate and purposeful membrane… the placenta still attached and feeding the egregore of wanting to live. So much like her, she thought.

Sarah watched the body enter a ship of timber slats, inundated with barnacles and lamprey eels that sucked the blood from filamentous gills. Already the monsters fed from hers—or karma's new human deposit. Sarah then watched the ship turn to float away, its seventeen days of demons clawing at its back where the name—Bardo—written on the back in illegible, nondescript letters, faded away into a long dark canal of some woman who seemed perfect from another angle.

Something came over Sarah when the ship left. She realised that something might be very wrong. Why was the ship without her, why was she not gone?

Sarah gripped her hand tightly onto the wooden frame of an open doorway in the midst of the abyss. It cracked and splintered beneath her tendrils, and the small pieces became little glass bottles, ones she had often seen hung with twine from withered apple trees as spirit collectors. Sarah squeezed more, more and more until the portion of frame beneath her hand collapsed into a pulp and the doorway screamed from the pressure.

And then it was quiet. And all she could do was to watch the spot where the ship had disappeared full into nothing while the demon world swirled into chaos beneath her. Not sure why she was there but knowing something was amiss, and that she was somehow misplaced, the mold now grew beneath her hands.

Carpenter ants would be coming, she thought.

Then the door came. Finally the frame she sat within tired, and it let its door begin a slow, languorous ritual in closing. It creaked on its hinges, begging for the soft latch of its mechanism while Sarah panicked and pressed her hand into its wooden boards. She held fast, trying to push against the fathomless, to keep the door open. The door must stay open, she thought, and pictures of the ship and the coin rattled through her head.

"No, wait!" she screamed, falling further behind the closing door. "I'll go with it! I'll follow the ship!"

The door pressed back and Sarah's lips touched the vapours of the carpenter's stain. Her shoulder strained, her body cried out and she gritted her teeth, but still the door continued to close. Pushing its flat, unreasoning will against her waning strain. It pushed until her toes slipped from the threshold and she hung from the doorway.

Fire came again, setting ablaze Sarah's left fingers as the door tried to fit against the frame. Sarah herself now dangled from the doorway, her whole body flung out into the abyss while that one dug hand stayed hooked into the wood, slowly compressing, being crushed beneath the press of the door. Her knuckles burned, the tendons felt as glass and she cried out as her fingers finally snapped off and she tumbled out into the Stygian void.

Sarah. Cried. Out.

She cried out for the metal of the smith's body, as it had been shipped out in the boat named Bardo. And in here, in the falling, spiralling nothing, there was nothing. And Sarah fell into it crying.

Part 8: Walking Sticks Roll

Outside of the marketplace was a human kind of chaos. Streetcars laden with people crashed by the sidewalk on their electric glides, fumbling with metallic wheel noises that vibrated teeth and chattered away the quieter sounds. Smokey cars with cigar-toting drivers waddled by, bicycles, streetlights and painted yellow lines all filled the mind with a screwdriver's acoustics.

The sidewalk was little better. Shop windows were filled with bright, swirling, offensive signs that had been created to entice the coin-operated man, but they only induced vomit with their white static noise. Garbage cans spilled out into the footpaths, obnoxious birds flew overhead, and the crowds, a flowing bedlam of people pushed and pressed and moved all in one direction like a king rat, fat and hungry in the sewer storm.

The whole thing made Sarah sick, and she turned her collar up to the cold and wet. In the swell of people, a man in a long green fleece jacket bumped her as he passed. He didn't turn to acknowledge her, he simply responded autonomously that he was 'sorry' as he continued to worm his way by, distracted with a sea of concrete slabs that turned to pebbles beneath him.

Persisting against the grain proved that the swim of fish heads was only in front, moving in direct opposition to Sarah. She struggled against them as inside, her anxiety boiled, sent a red steam that rose from under the shelter of her coat to spill into the clouds, forcing a swathe of clean white coins to fall from the sky. Their flakes were thick with words like so many consonants spoken too close together and soon they carpeted the city in their mirth and misery.

Sarah tucked her head down even more, picking up her pace as the snowflakes melted on her kettle, all finishes referred to as—

"Black," she shuddered at the thought of their fashions.

Another person wandered into her shoulder; she didn't look up and they did not apologize. A thin green fabric swept the snow as she watched their shoes pass her by. "Only a couple more blocks to the cemetery," she whispered to herself. "The dead could not come soon enough today."

Beneath persistent feet that dared to forge a breadcrumb path, the landscape, once steep and endless, leveled off into a finite court that ended at a line of wrought iron fencing. The crenelated wall, poking out from a thick grassy knoll, was just the marker required to slow the people's sounds and as it appeared ahead, the flow of people petered off.

"Oh, thank god," Sarah muttered to herself. The people had stopped altogether and once she was beside the cemetery, Sarah could feel their tight grip on her shoulder waning as a mane of limp yellow growth that popped out from the snow and ran alongside the railing reached out to her.

Sarah jumped over the wall and she landed heavily, neighbouring Mavis Grande, mother, daughter, etc.

"Hello! Hello." Sarah nodded to the tombstone and walked away, through the cemetery lines.

Snow did not fall in huge swathes from the sky. There was no heavy traffic breathing smog, or chalk-addled voices. There were only stones and in the distance, her sweet, tender forest loomed up, a huge dark bramble wall.

As if the trees were conscious, aware of a growing smile and waxing intentions, the forest wall swept its branch boughs back on their trunk-fastened hinges and made a door for shoulders that passed through. The interior branches reached out to grasp the city gum from her skin, dragging off the smog and leaving her smelling sweet with pollen. The aroma attracted fine mists that bled from forest hands and turned into swarms of gnats and butterfly wings. They wrapped Sarah in a strange, buzzing winter harvest that she took as greeting.

"Thank you," she said, curtseying on the far side. In response, the temporary passage pulled back into walls, making Sarah as much the woods as rabbits are when the folds of the jacket were enclosed, the busy world and its static noise locked out.

Beyond here, the forest sounds stretched out from the unfurled evergreen needles and drew a coffin of resonance through its hollowed stumps and crumbling bark.

Here, Sarah walked as if there were no others, even beyond the forest gate and its cemetery moat.

Here, she could walk as if she and the forest held a secret pact wherein each was simply and only concerned with the other.

"Ahhh." Forest air wafted by, slow and steady as the brook. A small stream of light needled between the branches and pinecone bodies' empty spaces to settle on Sarah's brow. A moment kept, breaking the light from warming the snow beneath her feet, compacting underneath, its wrapping paper scrunch bundling up in her ears.

The desire to push away from people disappeared, and the task set out for came back to focus.

"A forked stick is needed." Sarah presented the words to the forest, hoping that the temple priest would hear her prayer, lighten the bramble and bush and expose a trail to ornaments. She kept the intention hard and clear in her head, hopeful that the forest would pick her up, but it wasn't long before her feet's meditative rhythm in the virgin snow turned to a hypnosis, and Sarah fell into a trance.

Eyes closed; and instead of a path appearing, a sense of direction through unawareness took hold.

Days later, or just mindless hours in the snow ahead—maybe seconds in the fractals turned to centuries—it was unknown; time did not penetrate the unfocused. The light that had been dripping in through the treetop's canopy now sat directly in line of the horizon, squeezing itself like an orange over a wire. Sarah had opened her eyes and it could have been another day. The movement of the sun was no tell, as it suggested little aside from passage; the length of that passage, how many times it had scrolled by could have been a trial of nights or hours.

Checking around for other markers of time, Sarah found she had wandered far enough that she had somehow crossed onto a known path and was looking through the familiar arch of a bent-over tree, a tree with roots dug up and a lack of arms buried in the snow. A gate through which she had travelled once before. One that now had a single forked stick lolling as bait as the tongue of its mouth.

Sarah's breath lay silent in her chest at the sight of it, waiting there for her. Her skin prickled and her mouth turned to sand—awkward and without rain-—as her thoughts whorled in the experiences felt before, laid beneath such liminal doors. She thought of the music that had dragged her to the great hole and how she had let it swallow her up. And then she wondered if the pact between her and the woods had continued beyond the portal she stood in front of now.

"Did the forest leave me here or has the king been usurped of his crown?"

"Humph." Sarah pursed her lips to one side. Her eyebrows, two sages, bowed in contemplation and placed her line of sight down on the bent-over tree. "I recognize you." And she couldn't tell what kind of excitement was boiling over inside of her heart.

She looked hard at the tree and focused in on the circle that was carved into its bark. "I know you rather well." The circle shape swirled inside itself, making Sarah's eyes sick as it pulled at her head from her stomach. It churned into spirals, found a frequency, and made a low hum of the forest floor.

Neck muscles pulled north and south, turning her tendons to stars as Sarah swept her line of sight back and forth along the trail she stood on, expecting some wildness to appear and push her through the tunnel.

But nothing, aside from a sense of familiarity that Sarah felt was misplaced, came in prayer or wild thought.

"I wonder if you're a trap?" She tried to place a mask on the familiarity she felt, but then bent over, grabbed the stick and waited, hunched inside the tree. Half bent in, half bent out, ensuring that nothing beyond the stick would ensnare her.

And nothing did.

"Quaint," she said and stood back up, wiggling the stick in her hand, twirling and testing its balance. "Perfect." She nodded and turned to leave.

But the stick was so light and easy in her hands. It held no weight. Carried no heft. Its value was too simple; it lacked frequency like the one that pooled at her feet, the hum. Then she rutted her heels and turned around, splashing mulch from the ground, lifting the low sound from the low bushes covered in snow so that it swirled around her. Her fingers wrapped the branch in yarn and the surface of it marred without effort. She looked up then, again at the ouroboros tree and remembered what the good doctor often tried to slow.

"Why not let it run free?" she heard herself say, and then she was passing through the tree, sound building like fog behind her.

The pulse's babble, however persistent, only filled the space behind her this time; it had no need to pull. It came unattached to resistance or concern, and although she wasn't entirely sure, every step now seemed more her own, the forest sound just a catalyst, a reminder.

Trees and sunshine passed by as fast as the rushing clouds above, leaving scattered shadows that joined the disjointed shadows from the branch-lined canopies. Time slid into a groove that rolled its curvature so smooth, footsteps felt like spheres and the path moved by, unobstructed beneath, until it came to the great barrier that it had halted at before.

The ring of trees that had been crashed into last time stood up again, rearing its face from the blur that came from things at one point faraway. It waited for pilgrims, leering down its nose, its trunks crossing like arms above a hole that had once been fallen through, then mended—and now, after time, rotted through again, the pillars at its sides withholding sand.

Sarah stopped to stare up at the furrowed brows of the trees looking down at her before glancing down again at the tiny stick in her hand. When she twirled it, the balance was all gone. She placed it now in her back pocket, inspected the old wound in the tree wall, then peered beyond it. Inside, the large insect-filled hole was still at the centre of the clearing, although now, it only heaved with a contemplative sort of silence.

Thick and swarming with the pulse, fog gathered up in cotton swabs behind Sarah. It crept into her ears and filled her head with pictures of the hole she had already drawn: the beetled black, the depth, the dawn, the long carried-on absence of noise. And she realised she had arrived at the bend. That she was without cat eyes, but the darkness followed on. The darkness stirred the visions inside her.

There was a crisp, fresh frost on the smooth plate ground that ran all the way to the giant black hole beyond the treeline. Underfoot, the frost was cool and the land sloped away from the trees. All things sliding to centre, to the gravity well, its dark surface as lulling as the sun.

Sarah thought—amongst her tangled head in knots with the hole—about the tree gate, how it had a circle marked in its bark and here, she would slide towards a hole. "Obvious," she stated.

And the hole remained obvious.

Unwilling to fight the angles, Sarah slid, flat-footed, towards the opening, only stopping within an inch of its pinnacle. She let her toes linger near the edge, daring herself to jump as she leaned over and looked into the faceless black below.

Every pistil bloomed to sweat as it burst from the ovum of Sarah's blossoming curiosity. She curled her fingers to make fists of courage at the rebellious toe that stepped out and dipped itself just beyond, hanging like a strawberry into the void.

She breathed in and held the breath. "So now what?" she said to the hole.

And it replied with a single, heavy pulse that resonated through the song that had already built in the fog around her.

"That's mad!" Sarah crumpled up the weak paper of her chin and it made a defiant ball beneath her lips.

The pulse called to her.

"Sure, it was fine last time but what's my security now?" She paced along the edge and left small cuts on her soles for water to get in.

Pulse.

Above her head, the sun moved in the sky and hung where it could illuminate the glinting mineral deposits wound through the interior of the hole. The length ran without a break, spiralling downwards out of focus until it broke into an infinitum of squares… excepting one spot, near to the point of being too far to see, where another tree, grown out like an arch, sat sideways from the wall, awaiting her commitment.

Really? thought Sarah, on episodic nature.

It pulsed again, all around her, but Sarah only gripped the loose fabric of her jeans, rolling it back and forth between sweating fingertips and gritting her teeth.

Become impatient, the hole sighed and began to turn itself smaller, shrinking from several feet across until it was just a manhole cover, unconcerned with the edge of things.

Sarah's eyes widened as she watched the hole recoil from the tip of her feet. "Hey, wait!" she shouted, watching the bend of the road slip away in front of her. She wanted nothing more than to taste the sun setting down and night carrying her on, so although her heart's valves were all open and she was flush as cards read sideways, "Okay?" She haggled for time. "Just, just wait. Let me get myself in check?" She would not let the possibility pass.

The hole, as if it understood, stopped shrinking and waited for Sarah to sit down. She swung her feet out into the open, dangling them for sharks with cuts on her legs, whimpering as they swirled and bled.

The hole pulsed again.

"Okay, okay," she muttered to the hole.

Sarah pumped her fists, trying to fortify the iron in her stall but her nails had dug so far that there was nothing left to mine; the blood in her palm would no longer draw, so the lip was bit and she found strength in that mineral bed. She closed her eyes and her heartbeat pummeled her ears; she turned her body so that her knees pointed down into the hole and vinegar flushed her veins so that she was shivering. She lifted herself in, gingerly touching around with her toes to find something craggy for climbing, and metal cinched her chest as something stuck like a ledge, something hard, yet slimy.

She tested it, pressing down with her weight while bits of her confidence broke off and jangled around like change in her belly, causing everything to shake. She sucked in a large swathe of breath and pictured a cat, nimble and sly; convinced, she put all her weight on the ledge, and it broke off.

At first, it felt as though she were not really moving, as if she were attached to balloons or had jumped into a tunnel filled with loose sand so that she sank into not breathing. But as her body turned forward and she got a sense of the tunnel ribs changing from a pulse, to a burst, to a seizure of movement; her senses alerted to the fire and the choice of not breathing became a lack of air. A white period overtook her, the blood in her feet went numb and gravity wells rolled through her, buoyed like a wave lifting her stomach, then her liver and then lungs.

She tried to scream… but a knot, like a sailor's, was pushed from her pelvis up to her tongue and tied her voice up with its string.

The archway of the other tree was coming on; Sarah passed through its tight grip to the wall, nearly skinning the needle thin and before she could gawk at the close call, everything halted.

Like a tethered ball, Sarah's body hit the end of a rope. The jolting movement grasped her like cold steel and her stomach piled up into her lungs as the tunnel wall piled up at her knees. She tried breathing in but the air, its structure like ground cinder block, was impossible to inhale. Her vision had continued to lurch forward, forgetting its ties before it, too, stopped and sprang back to a neck that had become a brick wall for all sensation to crash against.

Sarah prayed on her scuffed knees with her hands clasped in front and her eyes hung down. Eyes that inspected a craggy surface filled with moss and granite tops. Eyes surprised to find the focus no longer attached to a moving helix coil. They were distrustful, and so Sarah leaned back so that she was an archway herself, looking backwards at the tree that had flown by, now stationary.

Gravity had… turned. On the far side of the arched-over tree, the world had spun clockwise ninety degrees. The wall of the tunnel was now the floor and the infinite streaming had stopped, turning an endless bottom into a long tunnel with a green haze at the far end. No air screamed by with jagged teeth, no rushing sense or lack or rolling numbness. Just the tunnel in its own strange, self-discovery.

Waiting to get a sense of which way was up—as forward was suddenly no longer down—Sarah became aware that her ears were filled with a fluid that had collected at the backside of her head. Now the water whorled in its grace, no longer spinning. It turned her stomach and she turned her head down to throw up but, confused, looked only forward; the vomit fell in bubbles down the skim of her chin before melting into the zipper of her jacket and closing her in.

She coughed, then stood, brushing the vomit from her shirt. "Okay," she announced, entirely unassured, and then nodded to herself. "Okay," she said again, her heavy lips pulling at the awe. "This is just fine." The bottom of the hole was now in front of her, and it warbled as movement pressed against the holes in her vision.

When she turned around to look again at the bent-over sapling, it was no longer up and down but rather side to side, proper. Sarah bent to press her head through the opening while holding the branch with her right hand. She found that on the other side, up was still up, the drop was vertical—not left or right and horizontal—and there was a wind that pushed the top of her head like a cloud.

Turning 'round inside the archway, she caught a glimpse of a square carved into the bark of the arch. Sarah swirled out in the lines. "Puzzling," and she stepped back into the horizontal plane from the vertical one on the other side.

The rest of the tunnel bevelled out, gradually expanding until it stopped, opened up into another clearing. There, the faded tips of a pine tree forest filled its far end. Their trunks had pushed thick roots into the frostbitten ground, but the ground was perpendicular to the tunnel; they appeared to grow towards the tunnel, horizontally from a cliffside, rather than growing straight up. Their branches lay parallel, instead of plumb. And the entire forest bent towards the ground of the tunnel, grovelling or praying, as old gods would to older.

Sarah exited into the snow-burdened terrain and looked up, still expecting sky, but found the trees that grew higher up simply grew further across until their teeth touched the lip of a wall headed up from the opening of the tunnel's mouth. Light fell down in splatters between the thick wash of trees but there was nothing that could be seen beyond that.

And in front, only trees and snow. Sarah stumbled forward, her feet sinking like hot lead into fresh cotton purge as she moved towards the trees. She staggered under the weight of the snow on the tops of her feet that fell from above but didn't bother to look up anymore; she was overcome with the madness of it, trying to make sense of the horizontal forest. Baffled, she stared at treetops that had been flipped from their position just as she had been from hers.

As her eyes rolled in closer, the trees became a strange array of entanglement that only the birds or the squirrels might have understood. The flat, ink-drawn canopy curled and knotted its thin worm carved paths until the needles were labyrinth walls and only an acorn could pass the doors.

Sarah reached out to touch the closest turret on the moated castle, and when she did, she found the pattern. The conical spurs of the bursting coniferous blooms became snowflakes and in the drawn, Sarah found the geometry of the forest. She pushed her arms in and began to part it slowly for the rest of her body.

Not quite equipped like a bird with a beak, Sarah arms were made to spot ink by the thin needles on which she intruded. Her arms swelled with tiny red bubbles and as the branches thickened closer to their roots, they left long striations across her face and hands that would later smell like old sap. She closed her eyes and pressed onto the rootbed, which now sat upright instead of long down, and she came face to face with an avalanche of snow that had fallen, landed on an angle next to the tree trunk's base. Forty-five, roof-lined slip.

She sighed and looked up for answers. "Now what?"

Her ear ticked and the pulse called again above her, somewhere in the horizontal forest. She bit her lip, sighed again, and began to climb sideways, through the trees: a snake in search of apple seeds.

One leg stepped up onto a trunk then another, all positioned like ladder rungs as Sarah climbed to the clubhouse in her vision before stopping ten feet or so from the ground. "There better be a reason for this," she called up in front, sounding the bugle that ran the foxes' tails into dens and mother's hearts. "Honestly!" She looked around, presenting her hunting song to all omnipresent.

A chunk of snow fell from a branch somewhere ahead and made a puddle of her surprised face. "Pfft," Sarah coughed, then spit up the fine needles of bush art that had collected in the tundra's snow as it fell. "Come on!" she howled into the thicket, turning her head up to view what manner she would have shaken fists at, when something wrapped around her foot. She looked down into the bramble and nettles of brandy-wound vines that her warning body had once climbed through, and found the vines were climbing her as well.

Skinny-knotted plant tentacles wound around her ankles like arms, wiry and irate, making sunburnt grapes of her skin. Her eyes turned to large droplets where pools would collect in that moment and her right shoulder shifted over as her body was pulled hard. Another vine had nestled itself into her clavicle and chewed into the soft spot of her breast, its watery form nestling in.

Heart beating in alarm, Sarah had found herself in an incline forest, strung up with so many threads of hair.

A branch broke beneath her, letting her left leg slip out to dangle like meat. Another tendril came from the left, ensnaring her other leg and shoulder, cranking her hard in a clockwork rotation. "Hey!" The vines shook her and pulled, spreading her limbs out into vast constellations in the small concern of her sky before threading her into a cigar. "Hey!" she cried again, her tiny heart an overwound clock, ticking down to a darkening hour. Her feeble arms, weak second hands amongst the daunting face. Her struggle, real against the watchmaker's hands.

A carousel of branches fell past as the ceramic ponies in her cheeks swelled and jostled forward, exhausted and puffing with air as they fought to free themselves of the trees. Twigs snapped, boughs bowed, branches turned and churned and pulled as wintered-over cocoons fell and embedded themselves in the pileup below. Further the branches wrapped around Sarah, covering most of her skin and ears in a complete metamorphosis. They pulled tight, and soon she couldn't see.

In her head, Sarah felt the pulse of her heart, the bounce of her breath returning to closing lips as the tendrils continued to snake about her body. She was bound in an underwater cave as the tide poured in, a tirade of force and salt and ominous black water. In a matter of less than seconds she had been fully cocooned.

In her chest, she cried for sanctuary but she was so small and her hands were too weak to pray. The tears she shed could not press beyond the envelope of the trees and instead, she filled her own heart with water and began to drown as her breath leaked away.

Her pulse slowed. Her head drifted. Her tense body fell like a flat chord against a mute symphony beneath the waves, her voice just chatter amongst the tide.

Red overcame and she knew death was cometh… a circle of light appeared in the images of her mind, a melancholy thing, a play of sickles and bones. Sarah looked upon the void that would take her soul and in that moment, staring into the pupil, she held an epiphany of her heart as she gave up and surrendered to the cold.

Her soul knew there was an empty part after the exhale, and it spoke to her. Change is always painful, but pain is forever a marker of change. The lack of breath responded to her saccharin words and Sarah, having accepted death, relaxed. Immediately, the vines seemed less tight.

Although she couldn't speak or move, Sarah was, and had been, and would be again. Quiet enough now in her experience of death, she heard the pulse.

Sarah heard the forest's heartbeat; it spoke her into trust and faith and revered hands. So she calmed her heart and let the pulse of the woods control the flow. She gave in, just as she had at the peak of hole.

When Sarah awoke again, laying on the forest path, every dream had been a butterfly and everything was well.

Part 9: What Will the River Feed

Dark lines from the shadow's berth cut Sarah's hands from their wrists and made stumps of her long, thin arms. They had become plain, uncomplicated things and she considered then a life without them. An existence in which she would not be required to stitch the day to the night, where it would unfold by itself, untethered and without her involvement. Her hands were hot in comparison to the room, cold and sterile as they rested on her thighs.

It was an odd night, one where sleep's stake hadn't been driven by a hammer. Instead, it parted skin with gravity, slow into her heart behind ribs.

Her finger twitched and static electricity drove through the rough fabric of her jeans to hint at a generator inside; she pondered further: what do phantom pains feel like? Do the electrified spectres keep one up at night the way stratified thoughts do now?

Will children by the railroad track ever sleep?

A thin flash in the corner of her eye grabbed her attention. Her thoughts, pulled away from hands, dissipated into the smooth polish of fresh dusted floorboards. A shadow, or a trick of the light, had moused across the floor and run under her dresser's legs like so many fingers on stockings. Sarah focused in on the spot, an arrowtip huntress ceaseless in the chase.

And she waited...

But nothing came of it, no sound or scurry from the spot where the small shadow had been. No movement or evocation of movement persisted beneath the dresser where the illusion—or fault of the eye—had been.

Unconvinced but practical, Sarah lifted her hands back into existence from the void and checked the hair at the side of her head for flyaways and loose threads. She found no cut strings had fallen from the bun on the top of her head; it signified that nothing had dropped from her head into her field of sight. She sighed, still unsatisfied with the answer.

Making a line of her mouth like the gap of a cartoon clam, Sarah pushed her pondering expression up into a crinkle beneath her left eye and stared at the spot where there was nothing, where often nothing would turn into something. She waited in slow hot breaths.

Nothing continued.

"Ugh!" She rolled the half word from her mouth, following the rotation of her eyes from the floor to the ceiling before hanging her pointer finger in the air, a lazy gun directed at the dresser.

Breathing in, she prepared to say something to the nothing but only stopped, gaped and snorted before getting up on her feet. "This better be nothing," she said behind glossy lips while she searched for pearls in diver's hands. *"Because I know, if I turn away, this will turn into something."* It always did.

Across the creaking floorboards that she walked, swathes of unseen particles were pushed up from between the gaps, mixing with the air so that Sarah could breathe downwind. She stood in front of the dresser. Under the room's missing lights, the dresser's paint looked like cracked ivory in its fortune. She inspected the facade like a poacher, hungry for something to sink her teeth into that was long dead and couldn't bite back.

Following the well-thought lines on her Victorian furniture as she bent into a crouch, she let her hot jeans mate with the cold floor in gradual steps. Kneeling, she placed one real hand on the dresser top, set weight on her wrist and placed one real hand on the floor, leaning down to peer beneath the veil of her dresser's legs where the questionable had passed. Where there was, likely, nothing. *But maybe a mouse could have left droppings for her lungs.* The thought of something arriving, too coffee-strong.

The dark beneath the dresser breathed out as Sarah got close; she could smell the dust she had stirred with her footsteps and the musk from long veneered cedar wood. Her eyes got close. She laid her head on the floor and breathed frost into the empty place beneath the dresser and above the floor, and it lit the void for a moment…

Nothing was there in the blue.

Letting the expression on her face slide, Sarah relaxed enough that she could replace it with shock as a phantom pain kicked in; her hand slipped from the dresser's top and she fell over, sideways, on the floor. The sudden thud left the image of a rabbit in her head, and she had to focus back beneath the dresser, blinking her eyes, turning her neck, to confirm that still, nothing was there. It wasn't. *Or was.*

Trying to place all her thoughts beneath her, she got back up and crossed to her nightstand, beside the bed. She checked that the mason jar's lid was tight before pushing it aside to retrieve a polished granite mortar and pestle. As she cupped its cool veneer, Zara's warning played the lines of her palms like a fortune vinyl record.

"Just five hundred milligrams. Use carefully, of course." She spoke with a mocked stance beneath her tongue. "What would using more do? I'd hate to think what would happen if I used more." Sarah spoke into the dark and a future memory played somewhere on a gramophone in her head. "Maybe I could just stay there," she said with brows furrowed.

A pulpy lump, like something small and metallic hitting a soft piece of wood, or a swallow in the throat, sounded from the closet as Sarah spoke aloud. A line divided her head when she looked to the sound, to the closet doors that now creaked in old horror movies with Nosferatu feet on ancient grains of wood back and forth. Right to left. Cameras and actors. She shook her head and the noise stopped and she was the script. Or the pen.

Swallowing the same pulp and lump pushed Sarah to repeating thoughts. *If only I were dreaming, at least there the little wisps of nothing, doing something they shouldn't, would make sense.* It was becoming all too often, in her waking state, that things that shouldn't be there… often were.

Eyes drew to where the gumball finish of the mortar had started to sweat in Sarah's hands, warm from thoughts and shaking knees. She felt sticky and put the bowl down to clear her palms of sugar on the sheets. She rubbed her eyes into a glaze and then returned to the nightstand, where she acquired the brown paper bag from the marketplace.

Holding it up to the moonlight, the contents barked as they were shaken up and down, the crunching sound of low-growing coniferous shrubs under inches of thick-packed snow filled the space around her head. Mouth of the knight singing to the dragon's head, Sarah reached inside the bag and pulled out a single stump of root. She held this up to the moonlight too, inspecting the knotted, mole-eyed surface.

"Silene Capensis," she said, making drawn mechanical lead of her mouth. "I wonder what other corners you might help me to light…" Her breath was ringlets of air that chided the tunnels of her vision into mines. She spoke then, in flooded coal. "I wonder how much farther there is to go…"

On a scale pulled from the endless pit of her nightstand, Sarah weighed out a chunk. '0.052g' flashed on the LED screen, its green background marking the black numerals with precision. Sarah placed her hand back into the bag and grabbed another solid piece of root. In her hand, it was heavy, and her hesitation tried to place it back in there but… now she was scared, now that she had it, she was scared to put it down.

Again Sarah placed the flora on the scale; the black lines read '1.12g' on the green display. She put on her kabuki mask and played along with the non-fiction play. Then she placed the root chunks into her mortar, sat down cross legged on her bed and began to grind.

Spore-print flecks drifted upwards from the crucible's centre as the plant was milled into a powder; it flashed, goldmine in the moonlight, and when drawn into chests smelled like jasmine-soaked banana. Sarah's eyes glided into a gilded crescent of half-slip slumber as she worked and soon the process became meditation. Soon it was like sleeping or slumber and the room was a haze as she calmed and churned the pestle. The smell, the visions, the carving sound of plant into air turned her soft. Clay even.

When the instrument felt light, Sarah inspected the powder and found it now ground to bathing dust. She grabbed a glass of water from her bedside. She poured the root into her fountain of drawn dreams and again, from that deep well of contents in her nightstand, she produced the forked stick and began to stir her alchemic mixture into a frothy top-like plume spot plundered from the choked stems of dandelions.

When a bubbly formation began to expose itself on the top of the water, Sarah peeked, bird-beaked, down and drew the lightest fluff into her mouth. It was root-dry, earthy-wet and left a smooth bark embedded in the flesh of her gums. She continued to stir while her eyes watered the flowers growing on her fertile lips.

Her hands pummelled another round of froth, ignoring the long work of clocks and again, Sarah swept up a conglomerate of root particulate and flavoured dirt, sucking it back like a fist. As she drank the second round, her stomach began to swell and her eyes, creasing at the weight of her belly, caught a familiar flash at the dresser's edge.

Sarah waited, side-eyed on her bed. *I know something that isn't there is there.* She thought, uncertain of what to make of the visions in her waking.

But nothing stirred and she returned to drinking.

Four rounds of soil foam in her stomach, and Sarah was feeling full and tired and excited when the flash sparked her peripheries again, firing the neurons in stop motion. She ceased to drink and her pupils, like eagles, scoured the floor near the dresser for a rodent or insect or tentacle's spine. Maybe a sliver of dream.

She was, for the sake of her sanity, afraid that another episode might occur here in her bedroom, although she spoke to herself as if they were foreign and still undefined.

Then a scratching noise perforated the stilled room and a small, white-bodied rabbit slipped out from beneath the dresser. It stopped frozen once in the eyeliner of talons. Quiet. Squishing its teeth as if vegetation grew in its gums and roots filled its ears. It was Leporidae gravity, pink-eyed, long-legged gravity, and Sarah was wide-eyed and leg-locked as it appeared.

Their gazes tangled.

Not unlike the taste of strawberries, Sarah sat, mouth full, almost bursting like the bust of an imperfect mannequin, unwilling to swallow. Neither mammal moved for a moment.

Sarah failed: she swallowed.

Only another rabbit slipped out from beneath the dresser.

This one, twice the size, but same of colour and demeanour. Quiet. Waiting. Beady-eyed.

Oh, dreams would make sense of you two, she thought.

Speaking low, she acknowledged the collapsing of their reality. "What are you two doing here?"

Nothing was mentioned.

"I'm almost certain you belong to a dream."

Swinging her feet over the edge of her bed, Sarah primed her body to move, to step quietly and inspect the rabbits further. But she felt individual fibres on her soles when she placed her feet down, not a flat wood floor at all, and she quickly retracted.

Fearful that things had slipped further than she anticipated, Sarah bent over, and looked down. Her eyes turned to iced ponds; her floor had been covered in flora. Individual blades of grass.

Floorboards in individual isles had slid aside and tucked away into the encapsulating barriers of the room, exposing beneath them a green field of dreamscape growing from black roots. Grinding her forehead into thick water ripples, Sarah let her thoughts run for a minute before querying the obvious: "Am I… I'm already asleep. Aren't I?"

She looked back to her nightstand, its contents as always full of sleds and reindeer, and jammed her hands inside. *Just a quick test then.* Her fingers moved freely to find the dream journal's cover. She pulled it out and opened it on her lap while her hands worked with speed to flip through the butterfly wing pages, back and forth, looking for Waldo in the liquid language that now poured, like hot honey, from the pages and dripped into her lap, making a reflective pool in her legs.

Sarah looked down into it, the language that bled from the book into her crossed legs, and saw it had made a tar pit that bubbled just once. Babble in the babel, puddle and pages.

"This book is full of a nonsensical language," Sarah said with a light turned on behind her.

She looked away, staring with absent sight into the room.

"It is a dream then…" Her voice echoed inside her head.

She looked back down at the cup of silene capensis froth. It had fallen at some point and its contents were spilled out across her bed, laying a brickwork path across her sheets into the wall beside her.

Quick to follow along the liquid path, she reached out to touch it: the place where the silene capensis tracked to the wall, where the path had painted itself… Sarah let her finger graze the wall and it wasn't solid, it rippled—and her positions stretched out in thick circular lengths of plasma from where she was.

"That… is a smooth transition," she remarked, pulling her finger back and testing it on her tongue. She watched the reverberation of her curiosity wander up the wall and across the ceiling, and then straining her neck, she watched it disappear into the light fixture's silhouette as it slipped into the stratosphere of sunshine now above.

Sarah squinted, putting the empty side of her palm above her eyes, shielding the biggest things from the sun.

"When you stare at the sun, your shadow is at its longest," she said to herself.

Arcing with lightning, she flattened her line of sight and looked forward across the room—now a wide glade—skating rink gloss across the thin membrane of grass tips touching a breeze now fountaining in from behind her. She looked back, and the wall had ceased its existence entirely; a brick path stretched out in proper dimension from her bed, and her bed became the only remnant left of her waking.

Lost in the familiar structure, Sarah's focus was hard pressed to be dislodged when the squeaking began, its trumpet at the base of Sarah's neck; it crawled like an insect behind her jaw and nipped the interior of her ear. She pulled away from awe and looked to where the rabbits—now a trilogy of furry bodies—were making primitive noises as they foraged the microcosm of the field. Their fat tiny bodies, swelling and growing with plant nectar, soon overwhelmed the stumpy legs that held them upright. As they suffocated the grass below their bellies, the rabbits squeaked even louder, filling the plane with a scratching resonance like so many fingers of pines on the falling off of dried leaves.

Sarah closed her eyes and grimaced.

A popping sound levelled her nasal cavities and she wished she could sneeze.

The squeaking paused and a wet overcoat slapped onto the pleasant warmth of the sun.

Then the squeaking continued.

Sarah shuddered and swung her feet off the side of her bed again. *Horrible dream.* She stepped down onto the green, warm from sunshine, and let the inside of her toes be molested by the moving blades of grass. Her spine curved as she reached under the bed, barely removing her white converse sneakers before the frame and mattress crumbled into a heap of mulch. As she put them on and tied the laces, the remainder of her bed decomposed, feeding the grass where it grew thickest and all the dreamscape fed the rabbits in her head.

Another car windshield pop came from behind her, she was back, seated though, and the glass only scared her enough that her shoulders juttered; she wasn't covered in sandblast crush.

"The rabbit enters the loop… " Sarah sighed and talked aloud while she continued to tie her shoes, to cover up the squeaking behind her.

Squeaking, then pop.

Squeaking, then pop.

With one knee down and one knee up, halfway between gods and ascension, Sarah closed her eyes to let the sun bask her body in blankets. She stood, inhaled the fabric-fresh breeze and turned to walk diagonally from the rabbits to the closest far side of the glade.

Her primitive senses picked up the rabbits' nibbling; her eyes traced it from the shrinking grass that was always growing and her unconscious-inside-the-ego's-realm forced her to glance right at the moment that the three rabbits quivering bodies exploded, spreading across the ground like a strawberry under foot. Teeth marks that left striations on the ground. Fluffy tails like unspooled clumps of yarn covered with mucus and bile and blood.

Sarah winced and made a growl of her mouth as she watched, disturbed and disgusted. The crater of gore where the rodents had been creased at the centre, turned back, and breached an egg. The egg cracked and three rabbits birthed onto the fertile ground… and started eating.

Grass like ingrown hairs.

A fury of fists pummeled Sarah from her toes to the top of her head. She shivered, closed her eyes and kept walking, passing the trio of rabbits now and again, popping and squeaking under the weight of their gluttonous divinity.

She crossed the field to a perimeter hump which encircled the dreamscape, stepped over it not breathing, and walked into a self-generating atmosphere and greenscape on the other side. A humming—from a bird's throat but a human's song—took over the airwaves around Sarah's head and she descended into a steep shale valley encrusted with sand, a slow moving river cradled and its babbling mixed with the familiar melody that overtook the sound of the rabbits exploding in the glade behind her.

Part 10: A Hermit Makes No Sound

s the scent and air of the river valley entered through her open pores, Sarah's feet lightened. She walked down the sliding shale rock of the river's decline, and as she, neared the bottom of the slope, it turned onto a skipped shoreline made of black granite bottle tops, and—before noticing the long-discarded masses of hair from mermaids left skinned in the shallows—she smiled. Just as the priestess she was, she felt white and sacred amongst the familiar terrain.

The riverbed she walked was lined with willow trees. Their roots, like delicate spiders, wove into the crumbling detritus mosaic of the rock walls from which she had descended. They, like her gilded-alabaster body, hung onto their pedestals simply by the awareness of the plane or its environment. Trees in Daniel's valley were always above the letter's watermark. Their branches, stuffed with fabric-leafed spectres, drew only from the river surface, and although it coloured their bark an ocherous blond like the backside translucency of the crayfish that picked the shoals clean, they never succumbed to the weight of their status or colours.

Sarah's foot was absorbed into the calloused white sands of the river, becoming a morphing amalgamation of its constitute, the two confluent bodies of water becoming one as she entered its ankle-high clear-topped liquid. Gliding through the shallow river with her hair a thousand metres long, and trenching its underlayers for the red clay deep below the hewn surface, the sand clots haemorrhaged in the substrate of thin water. As she changed the water, it became florid with the blood of the land, its red clay dyeing the surface: all the sandbanks, a cherubic cinnabar.

Further down the stream's low, slow path of winding segmented earthworm, a shed or a shack came into view. From the building, a ramshackle tune sounded, its vibrato between a harmonica and that of the harpy to her ears. The sound occupied the valley's steep, angular sides and only rushed out from the incline to meet Sarah when her heartbeat sounded in its proximity, when she palpitated. And when the tune matched her rhythm and her blood coursed like water, she heard it every time she stepped—but only between the non-existent.

"Daniel," Sarah called out with a hooked relief pulling at the corner of her mouth.

She walked higher above the water that deepened while the sound from the growing shed became quieter, as if it whispered only when she was near. As it subdued, the melody rustled the tin-patch shingles on the roof, some ribbed, some rusted, some yellow, none the colour of tin, if that was anything other than gun metal, and turned the whole house to quivering like the feather tail of a hunting arrow. The entire shack trembled from top to bottom, its thin walls concave and falling in with the weight of sky that hung in the reflection of its various, ill-scattered windows. The shaking wound its way right into the ground through the wooden stilt pillars that held it several feet from flooding and there, the vibrato waded into the water, stirring the sand bed into frequency generations.

Making a soft ripple of her own, Sarah came to the dock in gong fashion but gilded-gown poise. As she entered the perimeter, several low-swimming mermaids were spooked, and swam away with small, tenuous flashes into their hovels and crab homes made where reeds grew close to the shore. The stirring of their tailfins signalled a windchime under the dock, and the singing emanating from the house stopped entirely.

Sarah looked at her wet converses, lifted each one further from the water she was walking on, and shook them off as she stepped up onto the rotted driftwood pier outside the fallen-down house. She looked up as a spot of sunshine that travelled through the willow boughs of a great tree behind the shanty hit her square in the forehead; it radiated from that spot and the entire territory shone brightly from her starlight tiara. The tree, decorated in hung glass bottles, grew its aching ribcage body overtop the house, bent at the sternum as it sucked itself inwards towards Sarah's luminescence, only cutting short when a gold mine voice scouted across the dock from the shack's front door.

"Sarah!" it exclaimed. "Good dream walker!"

Letting the sunshine slide from her head to her throat, she smiled and returned the call. "Daniel! Well dream caller! Missed friend..." She tilted her head and shot a mischievous eye in his direction—"long talker."

Daniel pointed a torn brown leather stockman hat down on his expression, causing a raucous of black hair to bounce out the back and cutting his face into two distinct grins. "Sarah, lost friend... short listener." He smiled large behind a shadow that wavered by his brightening face.

Sarah smiled in return and walked lightly across the dock into his opening arms. They embraced like dogs do. Coffee cups to fingers charmed. Eyes to morning. Friends at dawn. They squeezed each other with rosary bead hands and held the soft prayer of palms for a moment before stepping back from each other to inspect for scars or weather.

"I haven't seen you in some space, good friend," started Daniel. "I'm glad to see you walking my dock again."

Containing no mirth and instead allowing the iridescent chasm to open from her mouth, Sarah radiated. "I'm glad to be back on your dock; long have I dreamt of dreaming you."

Daniel laughed and brought deep tar from the mine pit that his throat had slendered, wiping it from his gleeful eye in a single black tear. He put his hand on Sarah's shoulder, the thick wooden paw of a pickaxe shaping her clavicle, and he looked straight into her whole, the ink of his lungs dripping on her chest. "Long have I been awake of your dreams." He elevated his eyebrows and turned his spine, raising a hand at the same time, palm up, to underpin two wicker chairs set beside his house. Behind the tree, the sunlight penetrated all the little holes of the chairs and burst individual swarms of ants into smoke-laden drifts that ascended back through the holes, leaving a rain-slick cloud above his home's social places.

"Come, sit beneath my rain and have conversation. I'm sure you're here for more than standing could contain."

"I do have questions," said Sarah.

"And when don't you?" asked Daniel.

Settling into the chairs was warm basilisk skin; wicker had a funny scent and a strange comfort to it. Sarah had forgotten the sense of it beneath her, here. Once she felt presence in its grasp, she looked across to where Daniel snipped the hanging string of glass bottles swaying on the Willow tree's branches. "So, how have you been, friend?" he asked on his tippy toes.

"Strange to some, as usual."

"Oh, that I suspected. How do you *do* though?"

"Just fine. Just fine."

Daniel approached, setting two clanking glass bottles on a wicker table between the chairs before sitting down across from her. "Just fine, is that right?" As the light rain haze that drizzled down from the gathering smoke cloud above them, the bottles began to fill. Sarah's clothes refused to get wet, but the bottles refused to stay dry; the liquid, as Daniel spoke, turned a translucent sky blue.

Sarah nodded, her teeth showing only her spine.

"So, haven't seen you in forever. You pop up on my dock looking frazzled and drawn, and you're fine. Just fine."

"I don't look frazzled," Sarah said with a gasp. She looked down at her clothes, wiped her jeans and then checked her hair for flyaways. "I look just fine, I'm sure."

Daniel paused for a second and let his face hang open before answering. "Ah, your hair is a thousand miles long and your clothes are clean—but frazzled isn't just in the shape of things. It's often in the eyes."

Sarah wriggled uncomfortably before Daniel continued: "and in the shoes."

"My shoes?" Sarah looked down. The rain had decided to wet her white sneakers, and coloured them a drab grey, something an old grandmother would choose of a sheep for mittens in desperate cold. Puddle grey. Lint and dead mold. "That's just the colour of the ground."

"And your eyes?" asked Daniel.

"I can't see them. How would I know?"

"You think I would lie?" he asked.

"I don't think you would lie," she grinned. "I just can't prove you right, is all."

Sarah pulled at the tendon that stretched her ankle and raised her foot so that only her heel bevelled the ground beneath her. She looked up into the sky and still, the rain from the raincloud dared not soak her hair or face. It just fell, glass shards in zero space.

She sighed.

"Is your mother still aware that you come here?" asked Daniel.

Slinking her neck onto the back of the wicker chair allowed Sarah to hang her head back further, to look deeper into the cloud. "She doesn't often hear me scream anymore." The rain drops plunked into the bottles beside her and sent her eardrums to lull. Sarah sighed again. "I moved my bed so that I can muffle my mornings into a pillow."

Daniel smirked. "I wonder, why do we scream when we wake up?"

"Children scream when they wake," answered Sarah.

Reaching long from his chair, Daniel grasped one of the now full bottles and brought it to his lips. He tilted and drank the liquid, the colour of seagrass, and let the contents swirl in his mouth. Churning his jaw like a penguin's throat, raw and raspy. "There's a saying that says: newborns should be close to their grandparents, for they have something to teach and to tell them."

Sarah sat back up. "What's that?"

"I don't know. I imagine something about here." Daniel leaned back while balancing the bottle on his thigh and letting his whole stance slide into his belly, the water again turning blue. "Grandparents are, by design, close to death, and children… they've likely just come from there. I'm sure they have something to share about the journey that their grandparents will soon embark upon." Daniel crossed his hands behind his head and hummed to himself.

A twitch started in Sarah's right—or third—eye and it swindled the sight from before her. Attempting to focus, she pivoted her neck naturally for a swan and questioned the motive of old friends. "The hell does that have to do with screaming when we wake up?"

Daniel stopped humming, paused, and then spoke. "Well, I can only think of two places that I know of for sure." Daniel unfurled one hand and left it palm up in the rain, not filling, "Here, and—" he unfurled his other hand, palm up, and it began to fill with clear liquid from the raincloud, "—not here. I imagine one of them is death."

"Which one is which?" said Sarah.

"Good question. I guess it depends on if you are you… or you are me. In either case, I would assume that children come from here or there and they probably miss one or the other a great deal." Sarah leaned in, and a drop of water nicked her cheek. She touched it; it was green. Daniel continued. "When they sleep, all warm in their beds, they visit here. And it is most comforting as it's the place they came from before being born, presumably. And when they wake, they wake with a start because it is not here, and they cry, for they find no comfort in being there."

"Are you saying that babies cry because they miss being dead?"

Daniel let a swarm of thick black knee slaps fall from his mouth and fill the chairs with distortion. "I guess that's what I'm saying, but I don't think it's what I meant," he said under strain of voice.

Sarah chuckled in her throat. ""Well, what do you mean, then?"

""I mean to say that, when children stop waking up crying… it's because they've stopped dreaming…"" Daniel closed his eyes and again leaned back. ""And my goodness, is that sad." The water in his bottle had turned black, and he placed it back on the table without lifting his head or looking back.

Piece by elegant piece, the river flowed by the two silent figures in wicker chairs. From somewhere beyond reason it spawned and swam backwards from its birth, filtering itself through rockface and dirt, collecting nothing, settling everything as it drifted by them. Through mermaid gills. Through seabird feathers. Through space and into the rain, it flowed around Sarah as she sat quietly, in a wicker chair beside an apparition. Or a friend.

"Do you think I'm the apparition?" asked Sarah.

"That's what you've come here for, questions of triviality?"

Her nose itched and she scrunched it up as if to make a wish come true. "No, I was just thinking."

"About what, this conversation has already been had." Daniel lurched forward and let his face glisten with smooth river rain.

"Yes, but it was never concluded," said Sarah.

"What things do conclude?"

"Are you the dreamer, or am I…?"

Daniel sighed and reached for the bottle again, its liquid now a pale yellow.

"Just humour me," persisted Sarah.

Daniel spoke with the bottle on his lip, before gulping back a wine-blue liquid. "Why does it matter?"

"Something has started following me, Daniel. Something here wanders around freely in the manner that you do, and it chases me."

An eyebrow pinned high as he listened, the liquid escorted his stomach towards his head.

"And I wonder if it's a dream or not."

"Why ask me then?" said Daniel, turning the bottle from his mouth and wiping a sapphire drip from his lip. "I've no idea what's real or not… especially here, of all places."

"I'm having a lot of trouble too… deciphering what's real or not anymore, that is."

"Is this place any more real than anywhere else?"

"It's beginning to feel like there's no barrier."

"Maybe there never was." Daniel sat back in his chair again, content to listen to the sky cloud opening further as the world of condensation crisped the outer layer of his skin, making him permeable only to liquid, protected from all other things.

"I'm worried—the other night, a brick fell from my tunnel and hit my shoulder, and when I woke up, it had left a mark on my skin."

"Hmmm."

"It fell, it fell when this beast—this monstrous thing that had been chasing me through my dreamscape—had shaken it loose as it stomped around beneath the tunnel… shaking it from another dream."

"Very concerning," Daniel nodded.

"Then, later, when I came back to my tunnel, the ceiling had been caved in… as if the beast had collapsed it and come through."

"These things do happen."

"No they don't!" exclaimed Sarah. She stood from her seat and slapped Daniel on the knee, at which he jumped and sat forward. "I don't think you're taking my situation very seriously," she plied.

The bottles both turned white, and Daniel looked Sarah straight on. "I take it very seriously." Then he relaxed. "But I'm not sure what you expect of me, my friend."

"Guidance!" shot Sarah, throwing her hands into the clouds; when she swung them back down to confirm her statement, water from the rain splashed across the ground and sprayed Daniel's chin with liquid. "Help… brainstorming," Sarah stuttered. "Some kind of… *something*."

"Well, what does it look like?" asked Daniel.

"I don't know. I've never really seen it."

"Has it ever grabbed you?"

"No, I've encountered it only a few times and I've made it to my tunnel before it grabbed me."

"Sounds like a dream."

"I don't think it is."

"It seems you are more settled than I on the subject, then."

Daniel leaned back again, letting the paper of his arms fold like origami to melt behind the weather of his wicker chair.

Sarah pouted, crossed her legs, and looked sideways to the river. In her mind, she walked along its surface, passing Daniel's small home, beyond the trees and shale valley walls to a door with black writing she couldn't understand. Its tall licorice-wood planks stretched from beneath the ground to above its curved frame, exiting and entering, empyrean, through the plane cut of a woodcarver's hands.

Still half in the images she had made in her head, Sarah asked, "Did you make the doors, Daniel?"

He scoffed. "The dream gates? No, I didn't make them."

"How did you know the dream gate was there, when you first showed me?"

Daniel chuckled in a way that only an inside joke could sound. "Only when you came did I know, Sarah."

"That means you are a dream," sighed Sarah.

Daniel lolled his clock-gear head, shaking the information into sober thought. "Yet, only when I showed you did you see, and if I were a dream, my knowledge is yours and you would have known of the gate before I showed you—but you didn't."

Looking for something neutral to do with her hands, Sarah opted to place one on her hip and the other beneath her chin to suggest she was ingesting the new information. Inside, though, she simply crossed them and pouted, not certain of how to proceed. Even the bottles, clear and translucent, were impossible to read. "You know, I only come here when you do," started Daniel. "The rest of the time I am free to, or am commanded to, dream my own dreams." He curved his neck the way a curious bird might and pondered, "What powers you must hold in your hands... I wonder, Sarah." He sat up and his bottles turned yellow. "What else is there? I'm sure there's something about this beast that is consistent beyond not knowing what it looks like and its chasing you in your dreams," he asked.

"My house, too!" Sarah blurted as the thoughts in her head gave way to sudden images. "I think it's in my closet."

Daniel waited.

Placing her finger to her lip, Sarah tried to massage the words from her head through oral stimuli. Her eyes went blank as she queried the question Daniel presented.

Impatient, he pried. "Come, there must be something of more value than that?"

In his question, Sarah saw the coin. "Of course! Duh, the coin." She felt flabbergasted by her own incompetence.

"The coin?"

"Yes. There's a coin. A bird was carrying it in its beak in the tunnel when the beast tried to come through."

"And…?"

"Well, when the bird left with the coin, the beast followed it too."

"What's on the coin?" asked Daniel.

"It's gold, and it has a wasp embossed on its finish."

Daniel pushed a squall of blue air from his lungs and creaked his chair, purposefully, as if the lines of thought were the joints squeaking. "Well, there is a river here, and a river there. And in both places, it is called the Acheron. Funny enough, you'd need a coin to get across it."

"The Acheron, like the river Styx." Sarah tipped back into the arcing support of the chair, letting her spine bend to its framework and her mind wander in the wooded thoughts.

"Well, they are two different rivers, but the lore stands that you'd need a coin to cross," said Daniel, looking elsewhere, existing outside of conversation.

Sarah said aloud again, but to herself more than for the sake of conference, "The river Styx. The river you cross into the afterlife." The words hung in her throat on an old nail, itching and burning as she suckled on observation.

Overhearing her talking to herself, Daniel replied, unguarded. "No, I don't know how to get there, though."

Sarah scrunched up her face but did not reply.

As they sat with bundles of wheat in their mouths, chewing the gluten paste into gum as the sun above them swelled and churned in jawbone stutters. It distended in the centre, and the expansion began to warm the air beside the river, while currents like rain overtook the air and water. Soon a breeze, then a wind, then a gale, drove up on the side of the house, hugging it and increasing palmed hands on the other side.

The wind pushed at Sarah's eyelashes, pressing them against her eyelids and drawing thin tears to bulb and bloom at their corners. She blinked and looked up, the raincloud above them dismantling, wool coming apart in sheers to splash among the fields. Opening his eyes, the cloud dispersed and left sunshine to crawl across Daniel's face in so many worm-like muscles.

"Oh," he remarked. "Looks like more of your strength, Sarah, pushing in from the East."

"You know that's not me," she said with plain glass mirroring her eyes. "I can't control the weather here."

Mustangs' hooves bucked more at the riders and an endoubled press of wind kicked Sarah's hair back. She placed a palm up in front of her. "Looks like, not even the dream root can't stop the storm fronts from coming."

"What's that?"

"I'm using another herb—I was hoping it could help reduce the push from other dreams," said Sarah, staring beyond Daniel into the horizon where clouds stacked like children's hands, placing snowman torsos on snowman thoughts.

"I guess nothing controls your dreams?"

Sarah bit at her lower lip, trying with temptation to ignore Daniel's Luciferian tongue. But his words were like bamboo slivers.

She rose and tried to keep the conversation outside of emotion. "We haven't even agreed on whose dream this may be."

Wind blocks echoed between them.

"You know, I was satisfied when you came. You've only just been satisfied now," he replied.

Daniel was smiling when Sarah looked down to throw a shade of expression on his face.

Thunder shook the soundscape apart and pulled the birds from the trees on their strings. Avian silhouettes overtook the river tops and drove all the crustaceans to hide with mermaid fins in their hollowed-out dens. In turn, the ground became sunken, as all the air from beneath Sarah's feet was inhaled and held in burrowed lungs.

"I still don't think the storm fronts are my choice, you know." Her eyes fluttered and her hands kept back nothing of the wind.

Daniel shrugged. Behind him, a tidal splash of sheeted sky fabric had driven into unshapen coastal rocks and thrown itselfs high into the skyreach. There, the centre turned green as hung water doubled in size and spectrated light into shards of jade and juniper seed. The wind pushed harder and soon the clouds were moving towards where she stood and he sat. Behind the storm cloud, a wall of hail pixelated the ground, chewing the landscape into pieces of nothing.

"Storm's coming, Sarah."

""Yes, I see it," she replied with shoulders sunken by air.

Slinking further into his lackadaisical slide, Daniel smiled wide and closed his eyes beneath the shadow of a cloud now encroaching the tidy island of his home. "Our meeting, then, it's coming to an end, yes?"

"Sadly, it seems. Lest we get thrown to the same, seemingly random dream from here." Sarah bent down and tightened the laces on her shoes.

"Aha! I don't think we could have such luck unless you willed it."

Sarah stood up as small notes of hail began to tap a melody on the tin roof of Daniel's house. "Where will you go now that a dream storm is coming?" asked Sarah.

"Oh, I'll let it take me." He looked at his bottles, a royal purple reflecting the bubbles that danced from his mouth, shying away into the pull of the storm's breeze. "Who knows, maybe there's another Sarah who needs me elsewhere."

"I doubt you're needed much elsewhere." She let the words crash from her chest and stumble into the air.

Daniel smiled further into the corners of his cheek, wave marks beneath the ocean on his sand-laden skin.

Sarah giggled. "It was nice seeing you."

"It was nice to see you too, friend."

Sarah turned.

"Come again soon." His voice followed her as Sarah dropped her foot onto the ground and ran towards the nearest dream gate.

The storm tearing the world apart behind her heels left pieces of unheard sound, on which to speculate forever.

She would see Daniel again, she was certain.

Part 11: Where the Wanderers Breathe

A petticoat of air hugged Sarah's waistline before it departed, brushing her face like a winded scarf as she closed the flat-planed white wood of the dream gate's door. She looked down at where the breeze had held her, half expecting some apparition of self to be holding the curves of her hips, but it was just the ghost of her dream, long departing from the seam of light that disappeared between the jams of the door as she pressed.

Like the dark now trapped within the frame, Sarah let out a vocalised relief while she hung her head and cracked her neck, letting the door hold her up as she gathered herself somewhere between out there and the tunnel.

Behind her, the path of cone-shaded lights sighed as the pressure of the storm outside diminished, its remnants exhausting through some unknown means. Out through portholes, into swamps or through the crevices of roots into swaying trees… through Sarah's navel as she breathed from her lower lung. Beyond the scope of meditation, the tunnel always breathed such storms and passed them at the reminder of a bell.

It rang.

And Sarah closed her eyes to lift her head so that she wouldn't pass through anything so quickly.

Checking her body, one step at a time mentally noting the position of self, Sarah squished her feet in the little patch of mud that lay in front of what was the first door in the tunnel. It would leave spots on her sneakers that her shoe tongues would lap up, sweet receptors full of greed and silt and muck. It left spots on the bottoms of her jeans.

Ignoring the irrevocable stain of beginnings, Sarah operated the depth of her tunnel as it laid itself out before her.

"Been a long time since I was here last," she said as the light from the lamps drew the reflection of the tunnel wall into her mind, a reticulatingwormskin sheen in front of her. She had to step back and press herself into the alcove of the door to wrestle with the idea of all the knowledge of her dreams there before her.

"And what would I do with it, now that I'm here?"

The tunnel returned her question with a gust of cool air.

Sarah breathed with a heavy fist when the air touched her face. She clenched her hands and flexed her throat, pushing the drip of saliva that hung at her Adam down into her belly, preparing herself as the tunnel moaned. She turned her head to the door to avoid the dust and a wave of heat—like a wall of sand—that hit her straining body.

When she closed the dream gate, it pushed all the air in the tunnel forward; after travelling its length, it came crashing back like a wave. It always did, returning with a chasmic bass that pushed at putty skin, sending ripples back in half-dried glue. The sudden rush pressed Sarah forward into the door and she knocked her head against its wood, rapping the brass with the knuckle of her tooth.

The bell rang again, and Sarah relaxed; the wind died into a slow current of gentle air.

"Someone should really fix that," she breathed again, turning around and stepping forward into the tunnel. "I should fix that."

A trample of mud spilled out from the threshold at the door but cleared within a few lengths of quick sneakers where it turned to a dirty red brick. The sound of feet had filled the tunnel space as the walls at the beginning were still smooth, slick and tidy as glass below the years of dust. But slowly, the echoes dampened as book titles and covers began to form striations in the wall. Intermittent. Here and there at first, words and play as irregular patterns.

Sarah laid her fingertips against the tunnel's curvature and dragged the lures behind her as she walked, leaving a clean, raked line in the dust. Where she groomed the walls, more book spines grew from the ruts she left behind. Saplings, at first, that quickly grew into the hardback stories that comprised the long lines of inscrutable tomes already starting to populate the tunnel walls.

Stopping, Sarah turned to watch the titles grow as her eyes watered them. Left. Right. Slender. She blinked, a passive cat, and waited to see if the words that grew made any sense at all… but only nonsensical arrangements of letters protruded from the new batch of pus, as always. She frowned, turned forward again, and continued on.

When Sarah approached the first branch—go right into the tunnel wall or continue on up front?—she stopped again to look up. Scratched into the masonry above, were an arrow pointing forward and a series of circles with a rectangle beneath them. She puckered her lips, placing a single digit like a lover in front of her breath, and then fought with a firm hand that was leading her to the branch to the right.

"I'm already here, now…" She sighed. "Without any answers." She thinned her lips before carrying on. "So. What dream should I take in next?"

As she stood, awkwardly aware of how strange it would look to no one passing by, a heat began to boil in her belly. "Do I go straight?" She pointed further down the tunnel while her visions drew her images to the right.

"Or go right?"

Somewhere, the anxiety of another moment turned her stomach to rise, and her body shivered from the cooled sweat that dripped into the open. Looking down the branching path, in her head she saw a familiar door at its end.

Her stomach therein boiled further, pushing out a line of words without connections.

Finding no sequence, she moaned and scrunched her face into papier maché shapes, while her eyes clawed their way to the ceiling, where another etching lay. A crude scratching that depicted a wolf or a dog with two circles in its mouth. Above that, an arrow pointed down the path to the right. Sarah, whose face was now blue and bloodied with twisted-up emotions, experienced a series of flashbacks in her head. A long path, a bloodied ground, and the tongues of two people lolled out in the dirt.

Shaking with black and white images, she placed her hands against the wall to try to push herself away from the right, but a magnetism exuded its finesse onto her strings and Sarah found herself stepping towards the branch in the tunnel. The images in her head turned to hands which begged her with finger rolls and welcome palms. But the images of those tongues still shook Sarah so that she filled the tunnel with dry blood to drown in the taste.

"No." The word fell from her, letting loose to the ground and turning her teeth red from pressure. "No!" Sarah spat again, and she pushed herself away from the wall and barrelled down the straight path, running in drunken falls. Desperate and aware that the walls might pull themselves from their frames to chase her.

As if creeping backwards, the walls further in were populated with more titles of further illegible works that would someday dictate all such dreams, or already had. On all the titles, a dust hung on their print from so long ago that someone had passed. Before read and now scrambled into tea leaves. Told information lost to fortune telling cups.

When the branch in the tunnel had fully been engulfed by her movement forward, Sarah relaxed and thought of the places ahead, realising she had not been here in some time. "It might be nice to revisit them," she said, biting her nail and looking away from the endless tunnel that tried to peer into her own thoughts. All she could muster was, "I really do talk to myself a lot." And the words echoed into the vastness around her, turning upside down and returning unkempt.

"e olyoltmtl taa D feklsyolira."

As she walked, there caught in the corners of her eyes, the titles on the books she thought made sense but, before she could catch them, they disguised themselves in a nameless root and lexicon again: something indecipherable in a dream when glanced at. Sarah edged the letters of those words with a goldsilk pen, and even then, they were worthless. Somewhere along the path she would give up on learning language and, when the lampshades aligned their out of sync swinging, Sarah did, and continued walking: less thinking.

The bricks continued for thousands of bricks. The lamps as well carried on their monotonous swinging, falling out of sync and then back in, then out again, repetitive spectrums of white stinging the tunnel's corners. For some time, it was necessary to walk with a hand above the spotted side of her half-lit face. When her heart couldn't keep blood there, the tingling dragged her one hand down and then lifted the other up. Before long, it seemed as though both arms might detach and find a floor to shade rather than a fickle woman to bother.

Dream time, thought Sarah. *It dragged.* It was passing without notice on the colour of Sarah's shoes. When once they were splattered with mud, they soon became spotless white soles without any loss of traction, ever, without slowing or burdening themselves, but Sarah's eyes required attention. After pace on pace of blank film, her eyes had to be held open with fingers as the unchanging scenery around her persisted in not changing. She felt the tunnel ceiling weighing on her head, and she felt like laying down to sleep as she stumbled through the nonstop nothing that resided in this part, the long of the tunnel.

It was when a black frame lifted itself into Sarah's vision, like a vignette, that the sombre weight doubled and she lurched forward, stumbling on the tips of her feet. Overwhelmed, clumsy and tired, Sarah fought back the desire to sit down by gnawing at her lips. It worked until the skin became so raw and dry that she had to lick the agitated tissue, which, in turn, convinced the dry air of the tunnel to seep further into her chewed flesh. Aggravated, Sarah wiped at her lips with fingers that were slim coals on fire. Smoke rose from the combustion, settled soot into her eyes and soon she was rubbing them.

When her eyes opened, she was home.

"Shit." Sarah spent the word under her breath and started to blink, pushing at the soft backing of her eyes to will herself back into the dream. Away from her room.

Retreat.

The arms that had considered abandoning her before now stood straight out at her sides and the tips attempted to press the sides of the tunnel out. She looked around. Her eyes were still heavy but they widened at the touch of sunlight from the swinging lamps, their glow blaring at her pupils and turning them into giant pits of light. Sarah let the cool air from her room escape her chest and enter the tunnel. Relieved, she let her guards lay back on the corners of her hips and without notice, she again closed her eyes.

Only a blink turned into a long sort of rest and Sarah awoke to the synthetic fibers of her sheets winding up her body like a cocoon of lost sleep. The pillow she had planted on the wall was keeping her from screaming into the hall, and she chomped down with angry jaws to avoid the shock of electrocution.

"Oh!" she moaned into the pillow while her eyelashes drowned in the desire to be covered with sleep again. "I just want to dream." She covered her iris from the light and chewed her teeth until she lost all sight of trains and thought.

Cotton turned and pearls beaded witness until Sarah, opening her eyes again, found herself back in the tunnel.

No longer filtered by a pillow, the air escaped her lungs with slips of freedom scraping at her lips. Sarah grabbed at her heart with a cliff-bound palm, trying to hold her breath up inside the panic of waking, dreaming and waking.

Dreaming.

The black frame on her vision cleared, and her heartbeat slowed to adagio while the wavelength frequencies steadied back into the dreaming state.

"Close," she muttered, then continued in the tunnel.

Time passed outside the dream in slow motion as it did inside the dream, motion slow.

Several attempts in dreaming later, she found herself running towards a glint of colour, an oasis she spied amongst the monochrome path, that had appeared in the tunnel before her. Arriving in time with the birds who would take in the sweet nectar of such bare fruit, Sarah found herself in front of three doors amongst a desert of grey; containing her hunger was impossible. Sarah's bicuspids, ever indicators of the corners of her mouth, grew arms and lifted her lips far into the creases of her eyes as she sighed in the break of the tunnel to her right.

Three doors, the trifecta entrance, embedded in the wall.

Left, centre, right.

Green, red, yellow.

Three, one, two.

All three doors a shade of garden growth.

All three doors a reflection of the lucid jump.

All three doors to one.

Breathing heavy under the weight of her joy, Sarah murmured to herself. "Finally."

It came back after she had caught her breath. "linaFyl."

Sarah giggled.

All three entrances were arched doors with white wooden framing and brass knockers of no distinctive pattern. The left was painted flat green with one single flat board, the centre, red, and the right was yellow. All three stages of the fruiting blossom. Above each door was a series of scratches that when stared at number the doors—one, two three—with clean vertical lines.

Reaching her hand out, Sarah collected the knocker of the left door in her right hand, and delivered it three times to the brass plate beneath.

The tunnel perked up and returned a knocked noise that echoed once.

She tapped the knocker of the right door twice and the tunnel kicked back three times, causing her to smirk beneath a wide grin.

The centre knocker felt warm in her palm; it glowed beneath her fist when enclosed and Sarah imposed on it, striking it twice.

The tunnel did not return her call—instead, all three doors opened at once.

Sarah did not hesitate.

Stepping into the milk of the galaxy, she let her body fall into its glass. Becoming a tall drink of cosmos, entering a dream from a place that only spirits can, she was complete in such moments of hydration.

Chapter Three

Dark wine waves. It was always grey at the lake outside the cottage where Homer called the sea home. It was grey, and the water was merlot. Sarah's eyes reflected silver ingots in the trees and were taken by the sense of clay, unformed, formed, heated, cold. Long sunless days in fall when they were supposed to have been hearthstone and warm.

Dean looked back at her with his wide, polished stone eyes that refused to change, even dug amongst the sunken treasure sitting on the plank of his arm. He held her hand gently, but was pulling at the string that guided the puppets back at the cabin, and Sarah was forced to stumble along. Drunk, or tired, the edges of materials fuzzy and blended in pixels, unfinished. All light, none from above, seemed scattered when it touched their gathered palms.

There was a rush in their step, their soft feet an exposition of their hard thoughts, as the skin was punctured like fish on stuck-out slivers from sunburnt boards. The whole plankway rocked its carriage arms as it matched pace with the two moving bodies, gaits like boughs in nursery rhyme babble. As all the timber swayed, it itched the tips of the hardwood nails and the oscillation pushed their hammered heads out, turning all the dock to a bed of them on which only the spiritually conquered could walk. One foot after the other, on top the water.

Sarah stumbled and the length of arm that was pulling her suddenly shortened, causing her to fall. Her knee struck the dock, then she turned and her shoulder fell on a nailhead that sent stone to hot rivets along her body. Everything swirled as if the palette of watercolours had dropped, smearing her sense of vision into a whirlwind of colours that all collected at the floor. Sarah sat up to a kneel and held her bleeding shoulder. Her body's hot plasma spilled across the wood, collecting with the streaks of paint and making a sensation of her purging throat.

Dean's hand was sharp where it touched her back, stroked her spine, surprising her sense of comfort in the act of relationships built with water and characteristics like concern and kindness. She could hear his voice somewhere where the halo remained static, unwilling to bow its head to the divine, and it sounded real. The vowels, enough to draw the words "are you alright," or "come on, let's hurry," bounced around in Sarah's chest before she looked back up into his cold stare, the impatient stones unwilling to wait for enough pressure to compress them into diamonds.

Dean was still mouthing something.

Even now.

The words were formed, unformed, heated, cold and worried.

A wooden cross with tuning strings attached pulled back, and Sarah dragged herself up from her placebo child on the ground. When standing, hooked arm and two sizes too small, the wind found itself whirling around her ears and neck, caressing the strange place where she felt uncomfortable, a dip, a clavicle; it was stunning, the amount of venom in the small glade near her shoulder, above her breast. She looked over and it was Dean's hand again, its tight fingers digging the church steeple, his beak arching forward, his wings curled in and his gargoyle stance forward, protecting something behind from the demons in front.

"Why are we rushing?" Sarah leaned forward and took a half step while trying to cover her shoulder from the atmosphere. "My shoulder, it—it hurts, can't w—"

Dean's grasp tightened and pulled the guidewires more. The bridge arches, ready to fall in and collapse, moved with the tension and Sarah stumbled forward again, coughing or slouching or trying half-hearted to stop and lick the wound.

The teetering dock ended in a hexagonal platform with a bench. In the summer, birds would wait there and chatter while hatchlings swam in the water. Pike and muskies dangerously close to webbed toes would sharpen their gnarled teeth on the driftwood and stir the sand bed into a flurry of mud and water. The silt would rise. Baby birds, yellow and white and fragile, would often slip beneath the stew of tusk and murk into carps' bellies, mother bird continuing to click and eat from the hands of predatory farmers on the dock, all the while. Sarah focused on the place for balance and was suddenly aware of all its stars.

As they approached, the bench's scratched-in-blood-pen writing appeared. Little hearts with initials in them, a doodle of a scarecrow. Some memoriam. It took Sarah's gaze and the force with which Dean turned her around was lost to the haze of letters and numbers, so clear and vivid in the cut surface of painted pine.

"Sarah." The words were faint images of themselves, photographs of someone saying something. Lost, inscrutable in the definitive lines of hieroglyphs.

"Sarah." Again, that sound. She turned to see Dean penetrating the thin sphere of vapour that surrounded her face. His face was monochrome, his expression noir, his voice mimed until he shook her.

It wasn't hard, but enough to let the sound in. "Sarah!" he cried. "Sarah, are you listening?"

"Where's Mom?" Again she was distracted, and looked around at the cottage and its yard.

Dean's face morphed into a swirl of oil paints as he shook her again, and the lighthouse looked upon her tiny ship. At her solid eye. His eyes burned through the inky storm, daring to melt with the fire that was his passion. He was fire, his irises bright red, his name shifting to David's but his eyes rejecting the change. His eyes, such polished stone, set ablaze.

"Sarah!" he cried. ""It's time!"

Sarah looked away, scared that the burn would cause her to ignite, that she might immolate right there on the dock and scorch her name into the bench while David watched

She looked for Mom.

She looked for Dad.

Only David remained—and he slapped her.

It wasn't hard, again: just enough to gain her attention, and his words were liquid gases. "Sarah, it's just me here. No one else. It's time."

"Time for what?"

"The dream. You have to wake up!" And he shook her again.

Four feet in various-coloured converse sneakers were not moving, but the entirety of the dock swayed as if possessed by water. It sloshed the fluid beneath them and around them, causing an electric disturbance that had Sarah's hair reaching above the crown on her head, entangling it and suffocating the gem at its centre, causing light to stray from the middle of her garden fair.

She reached up to adjust it, but David grabbed her hand and pulled her grasp away by the wrist, strangling her arm's neck.

"Don't touch it," he said.

He had placed it there some time ago, while drinking coffee and talking about tea. While he smoked tobacco and fell to his knees in light of her. Sarah, crown bearer.

They stood there, the lake an angry pencil-sketched picture, the cottage behind them cold, the trees stretching bare limbs out into the old electric sky. Sarah, looking quiet and harmed and regal. David, penetrating the skin of her armour. The dock, a final barrier between two worlds, where one might meditate, or provide oblation, or dance… accomplishing all things at once.

"Where's Dad?" asked Sarah, looking down at her white shoes on the black midnight dock.

David curled his fingers around her. "He's right here and he agrees." His voice sounded scrabbled, all mixed up like the pieces of tones were churning in a vase.

Shoes slipped away into streaks of wet paper as Sarah dragged her gaze away into the sky and the topography around her. "I don't see him." And she turned back to find that piece of wire had pulled the coil apart and Dustin had endured the drag.

But his polished stone eyes had withstood. They grew bright, and the heat they emitted clawed at Sarah's neck; she couldn't talk under the pressure of temperature, and she coughed and looked away. "It doesn't matter what you see," he said, his tongue a hasty mess of slurred vowels. "You have to wake up now—it's time to dream."

Dustin flipped her arm so that the veins pointed up and her palm, exposed, darted behind her delicate fingers, trying to hide. Without looking, he brought a thin rectangular blade down from the holy mountain. Sarah became a fountain.

It was warm then, Sarah's body, her one hand especially. She could make out a blip of the sun clawing its earnest obsession through the thick dust web of the sky. It was dawn but no birds were singing as Dustin wrapped his arms around her and they fell from the side of the dock, only one of them breathing in before the drop.

The water became ice, its surface especially.

Shocked into tranquility, Sarah took in what thin slips of information she could as they cut her fingers like paper. The dock, from below, was a black, crisp-lined shape without individual features, getting farther away as the temperature dropped, the undertow catching both sets of toes and pulling her deeper into the substrate below. The sky was even further now and no longer had a sense of being above her; instead, the membrane of surface water had turned hard and polished itself marble, obscuring the directions with reflections when pressed. Dustin, however, did not fall away and when Sarah pushed, he pulled tighter, squeezing a thin red fabric line to string out behind them.

Leaning back, Sarah looked at him and it was strange, it was like a mermaid had overtaken him and now, he was dragging the siren of his heart to the bottom of the sea for feasting.

Then his visage thinned, bleeding away in the bubbles that escaped from their clothes. Dustin pulled all the scraps from his face, tearing the skin off from what always remained, to expose the bone, to expose her father beneath, lost in the decision of a clock face, those damned polished stone eyes always rejecting the change.

Her father's grasp, once taut, had now loosened its heat and Sarah's chest was, in turn, taking on the colour of the lake.

Her shoulders shook and the last remnants of warmth exploded with mercury into the water separating them.

A space.

In between, a clear drawn bubble of gelatin air escaped from her father's mouth. Sarah breathed it in and was overtaken by the image before her again, the air lifted and her father lolled back, letting the water expose his collapsing throat. His clenched hand, reduced to a weak grip, let go altogether and Sarah reached out to grab him in return, revealing the shape of their thoughts, refusing to break her clutched, idyllic pictures.

In tune.

The cold of the lake mounted them on a sapphire rock in its black, bleak, silent underwater. A trail of them, a trail of memories in the red yarn of her heart, fell out of her wrist behind her as they descended.

A trail of ochre.

For a lifetime, they fell further into the abyss as Sarah clutched her father's hand and slowed their descent on strings of her heart. But the pressure, the weight of collapse, snapped his sternum in half and his chest collided with the skin, leaving a cracked mountain of points and jagged corners that pulled Sarah in, so that she might be closer in his death.

She pulled him up and hugged him so that her body fit inside the broken hollow of his.

Amidst the submerged noises that had never surfaced between them, she felt all the air empty from his fallen-in lungs escape into the atmosphere when his larynx finally gave up. Sarah breathed no more of him, refusing to grasp no threads—she only leaned out to look at him once more. His curving spine presented a message from the cycle of his ghost.

And Sarah released her grip.

Letting him go into the frost layer, where he sank as if it were bottomless.

His long-gone eyes, desperate for companionship.

Sarah found everything but her cheeks to be dry in the liquid all around her.

The tip of her father's sinking shadow brushed against Sarah's skin as she rose towards the surface, free of all that cement and ready for air.

She tried not to look back at him.

As she fought to climb the water column, her atmosphere slowing, Sarah's heart pumped empty space into her veins. She began to feel pale against the dark blue backdrop, her head floating further from her like she was on a string or there was a balloon tied to her wrist. She kicked and the dock seemed closer, the sky, not so far away. She kicked with tired feet and her body waxed lighter while an oval shadow framed the dimming focus of her gaze.

A thin aqueous sheen, the surface, came in the form of a glass ceiling as Sarah approached the apex of her dream or—dying.

But it was solid.

She hit the surface and it was stone.

Iced over, blocked with tomes she couldn't read. Sarah blinked, then pressed her glass hands against the impenetrable sky and more red fabric spilled from her. The shadow frame on her vision engulfed more of her escape and her heart felt further and further away as her head slipped into another atmosphere. Then another. Then another until she stopped and closed her eyes.

Then Sarah could not help but to… slip out of time.

And she fell.

For no amount of human scale, she fell.

And without her, the lake and its water stopped existing.

She was then inside a tunnel, beyond the nothing where a blinding light appeared. It pierced the armour on Sarah's chest, pressing its sharpened spear into her heart, making her aware: everything is golden here.

With legs folded in Jupiter's shape, Sarah broke the barrier and slipped into a cosmogony of self.

Clouds appeared around her and began to pass her by. Now, she was falling from the sky and in harmony, all the stars in the background lengthened into points. A trail of thick black smoke that rose from a faraway ground was getting close; it enveloped Sarah and she wore it like perfume. Beneath her, a topography of treetop canopies pulled back their labia to expose a log cabin in the brush. The lonely cabin.

Sarah looked upon it and its black wood entered her like she did the forest, uncomfortable but familiar. A needle. A hole.

The last lonely cabin in Sarah's dreams.

Blocks of wood toed in ballet slippers, Sarah touched down in the clearing around the cabin. At her presence, the soil turned dark and rich and black-pearled. Once fed again by her touch, the forest closed its open canopy, hiding its treasure within a pine needle shell.

The cabin waited there. Quiet, hushed, its timber planks a black moss brush, its white moulding, a birch tree's blush. The windows' hallowed hazy glass were impenetrable to her view.

The door, red.

The red entered Sarah too, and she was shook amongst the colours.

In the door's spectrum, Death was stood a man. He split wood for the hearth with his hand like a scimitar, like an axe. Sarah knew him when she interrupted his task, she knew him by face and name and touch. When they shared eyes, his shadow walked straight through her flesh and Sarah could feel the call of her bones in his quiet silhouette.

"What be you here?" he asked, his voice a clouded ash with fire for its breath. The woodcutter asked and his eyes shone white from the hallow of his hands. He looked through her with the direction of his shadow, beyond her culture and its swine and saw Sarah, stripped of all those materials. His eyes undressing.

Sarah mute in the splendour.

When she did not answer, he approached and swung his hand to cut her throat. But the motion was slow. It stopped altogether.

Sarah lifted the tatters of her ego's clothes and dressed herself in front of what some would call 'inevitable.' The picture of the scimitar against its grain was frozen. Sarah reached out and held Death's hand, then turned its blade back, and like the beak is to the egg, pierced his chest instead.

And so Death fell amongst the earth that she had turned black, and more darkness flowed from his mouth to lay upon the black.

The door of the lonely cabin opened.

Red.

Red grain.

And *she* stood there. Life—the crone stood there in the doorway, the host. The hag who moved the wood to its fire and marked the sky with smoke. She looked upon Death and smeared the soot into her hair before she came unto Sarah with arms outstretched. With skin wrinkled. Grey hair and grey eyes and wisdom. With clever hands ready to sew the fabrics that would bind the story of her hearts. She came to embrace Sarah, to consummate her soul with the smoke that still stuck to both of their clothes and Sarah knew her by her eyes, full of colour.

When Life came close, the cold of Sarah's bones rose and she hugged the old woman one more time before she broke the crone's throat with her elbow, spilling more black upon the black upon the black.

Bodies, quick to rot and worming.

Both heads remained a moment before, too, returning to the mouths of maggots as Sarah looked on them as if she were the goddess of the insect. Her wings crystal and her legs many, she cleaned her front appendages with golden saliva, watching as the flesh of the faces turned to the skull of the bone, turned to soil, turned to spagyric mist which she breathed in. Her throat coated black with earthen detritus.

Before the quiet could settle in, a trail behind the lonely cabin called to her and she left the clearing in the woods. Walking feet like mechanisms, the story came and a narrator beyond life and death remained, moving Sarah's hands and feet and chest. The narrator read her story to the trail and suddenly she was fast upon the path behind the last of the lonely cabins.

Compelled to move in uncontrolled blurred steps that stripped her peripheral view of its focus, churning all the linings of trees into sideways sticks.

She moved for aeons in the collapsing matrix of the trees and learned every name of the Druids' alphabet therein.

Ailum for elm. Reach it and be deep.

When it was lost in the nature of memory, Sarah stopped abruptly and was turned to see the space she had made.

There beneath the tops of fly agaric gills, the sweet final drips of sap from the elm had ascended and froze in stilts. The sap, like spore filament traps, stood unmoved on the log for which the deliverance mushroom grew. Stasis of all blood, come from the bark, half chewed, its flesh the pulp of the log lay half buried in swamp and yellow lily pad bloom.

Sarah watched it there, the rotted husk of the forest trees. Of Ailum. And it spoke no words; instead, it lifted its head and its trunk become the body of a wolf and its head became hell.

Cerberus.

Underfae.

The head of the wolf turned to Sarah, its pelt without eyes, its ears stood back; its mouth wide, it shone its many teeth and tongue. There in its throat lay the head of the woodcutter and the hag.

Death and life. There, it was done.

When Sarah awoke, she was in a field of wheat.

To her right was the burning cross.

To her left, a trident of seven spears.

Beyond that was the road. Both ways forever, she stood at its centre.

Nothing said, for it was long.

Part 12: The Show Of Hands

*I*t always took a moment for the dream to catch up, thought Sarah.

She had passed through the three doors in the tunnel and entered a familiar auditorium in a cinema from a single door. On the far side, everything was a temporary blur of colours and lights across a series of glass walls that blinded her. Sight-drunk yet excited, Sarah stumbled into a crowd of people that flowed like mechanisms. One touched her arm and she turned abruptly only to be pushed by another that knocked the balance from her legs.

Damnit, Sarah whispered to her better self. Despite the resonance of the prior dreamscape and the obvious truth of this being a dream, she still felt a glow of heat swell up around the tips of her ears as her cheeks turned a barometric embarrass, and she wondered if everyone was looking at her. But when she turned around, the people were still blurs and their judgemental faces could not pierce her skin.

Stretching her arms out for protection and stability, Sarah stepped back and connected with the comforting flat white paint of a wall. She pressed her body up against it and waited for the sticky colours to subside. As she did, her ears overflowed with the electric liquid of human noises coming from all around her. The cinema was a static hum of complex circuitry, full of people who left footprints in binary patterns on the floor. The same people that were always here, geometric and smothered in silver silicate wire, as they'd always been.

But she wasn't here for their familiarity. "Word to screen is always worth it," she said to herself. Beyond the people, there was something valuable that she hungered for, and it meant mentally pushing through the crush of the atmosphere and the pink of her eyes.

Sarah waited patiently, hanging onto the idea of what was coming while her dream swirled around her. Scratching her plastic fingers on the wood that carried light in bodied trails from the door she had entered. As the noise peaked, Sarah counted its final moments in the air until it landed on her sneakers, slapping against her heels and fraying out in front of her to match the silhouette cast.

Breathe out, and the halls pushed with her chest. Control.

Mindful, she thought.

Once tidy, sighted and intact, Sarah let her hand from the wall. She studied the math of the flowing dream-people walking in laminar streams in front of her until she found a gap that smoothed through the crowd. She stepped out.

There were small bundles of people scattered throughout the wide hall, huddled around garbage fires, or wandering, or in single podium lines standing out front of black entrances, taking up the spaces where normally feet would fall. Sarah wove around them and counted in algorithms, distracting herself with the patterns; every nine steps were six lights and three posters between the closed doors of the hall. Her body worked in method with the effort even though the posters on the walls did not.

At the end of the hall, the cinema opened into a grand ballroom filled with patrons who sat cross-legged or lay down beneath a ceiling that would have taken days to return their echoes and eyes. Their bodies loosely resembled the architecture of the rest of the room, which stretched its giant, black, empty torso out into several other halls. At the centre, the only freestanding structure in the cinema, a large circular desk, held the ticket booth.

"I called ahead," said Sarah hastily to the man behind the desk. She couldn't hold her honey back, and it pressed her words out in fast wings and legs.

"Oh yes," said a red-clad and silver-buttoned boy. "Sarah, right? I have you down for six fifteen." *Yes, yes, I know. Now hurry.* "You'll have to wait—I'll come get you when the room is open." He was operating a series of black walnut levers that, in strange coordination, allowed a clean vapour to pressurise somewhere in the ceiling.

"Thank you." Sarah was beyond impatient; all the necessary steps always egged at her but what was coming, she enjoyed enough to make cake.

Agitated but conforming, Sarah backed away from the young man, paced in a circle, then doubled back twice in succession to his position before sitting nearby, with a group of distracted listeners on the ground. She ignored the familiar music playing in the cinema… but tapped her foot, calling out the mutinous memory of her muscles.

Three, two, one—she counted.

The young woman she sat beside, her face riddled with metal brackets and her eyes deep painted chasms, turned towards Sarah and asked, "Hey, what are you doing here?" She rested one hand on her right-angled knee and hung her eyes low and glossy.

Sarah recognized her from somewhere else in the real world, but could never pinpoint it. Nor did it matter—she was here for the screen; its blank canvas was calling her.

"Just here to work on my book," she sighed, reading the same sentence over and over and over again.

"Cool, what's it about?" asked the girl.

"It's about a dream." The end of the last word carried away from Sarah's chest, like Japanese licorice, thin and stretched.

"Can I see it?" The sugar candy snapped back at Sarah from her mouth, but she didn't return the favour. Instead, she turned away, though the girl continued chatting.

The boy in his red vest stepped up behind her, a lantern swinging from his arm. He smiled aqua blue. "Your room is ready." He bent down and offered a well-timed hand to Sarah.

"Perfect." Sarah provided her own hand and stood up.

"Can I come?" asked the girl, unfurling herself beside Sarah.

"Of course." *It didn't matter. There were a thousand different answers in the dragged out and half beaten farm animal of the cinema's dream. In all of them, the girl grieved over her dead horse.* Sarah sighed, but no one asked what was wrong as all three of them left the main heart, wandering into one of its arteries, blood pumping cold blue thought.

Outside the cinema door was the same hall as every other, coming from the same ballroom that they all did, but here, the door was where the only *other* door in the whole dream had stood. It was tall and arched at the top, and it stank of rot from its water-eaten wood. Its lacquer was a thin white paint left to crack and disembark in wounded salt lines that left deep gashes at their long-resisted gnashing from the changing of the norm.

Sarah felt movement in her stomach. It relished those crevices in the door's levels of final finishes where Sarah waited, while the bellhop and her 'new friend' discussed the theatre's rules. She listened like she had the music… at the back of her skull, well known and useless, staring into the dark spots between the pulled-back fabric where the ends of insects were found to form. Waiting, her ribbons about to tear with the excitement of a present popping forth.

Then, the door creaked open. As the pressure adjusted, the room's air rushed out and Sarah breathed in the fumes of its photoshop development, her eyes rolled into the shapes of tiered balloons, and she stepped into a place of true lucidity.

"The Telling Room," announced the boy. "This is where gladiators come to feel overwhelmed: the amphitheatre of the dreaming soul." The movement in Sarah's stomach turned to surging pressure in her heart and her fingertips left static resonance wherever they pointed.

Always in bloom of the Telling Room.

Everything was matte black and covered in a tight honeycomb foam that came without corners, allowing the room to stretch up and out far beyond the borders of its spatial limits. Trying to focus on the expanse was pointless and instead, Sarah walked to a middle line and looked across the rows of chairs that rose in steady washes out to a foggy sea, away from a small landing on which she stood, small before a huge screen. There she breathed and swelled and observed.

From the tiny markings of her position, Sarah worked at random to choose a place of camp. Counting inwards from the outside ten seats in, she sent herself up a flight of stairs, seven stories all in bounding thunder.

Then she squeezed along an aisle sideways before fitting herself into a chair. Seated dead centre, unintentional, the screen on the wall in front of her overtook all sensation of naked feelings and she gawked at its raw, blank canvas, bare of her thought and ready to accept it.

Between unobserved breaths, everything found its way out of Sarah's focus. The black of the screen bore into her like a huge and stunning pupil, the great sensing object of a giant squid, feeding in dark water. It penetrated her with gnashing beak and stripped her with needle-lined throat below the clouds of a red horizon sky. Sarah was scared and naked beneath the knowing of such eyes. Such delight in vore, incubi and hunter. It made her quiver, excited to be sat beneath an absolute.

Teeth showed, excited to reflect what the screen would bare.

Heart showed, elated to pulse in rhythm with the sonorous mirror show.

Footsteps beside Sarah's head drew her focus and she looked to the left: there, the girl and boy were approaching. He held a tablet at his left hip. The girl sat, and the boy handed Sarah the small screen from his hands. She accepted it, nodding, feeling for the stylus beneath, smiling and nodding more when she produced it from its tiny pen-shaped sheath.

"Thank you," said the girl. The red vest departed, and Sarah turned to the tablet and did not wait to scribe on its thin window surface as she burned inside with a phonographic image, sprayed with ink and long settled in a glass case, broken. The stylus in her hand swung across the small screen in her lap and attempted to make no sense of its operation. The words instead became free. They did what they desired best.

"It's beautiful," said the girl beside Sarah, a girl that she didn't bother answering as her wrists operated an engraving of her own heart.

Sarah's eyes rolled into white and that was where the senseless led letters. She typed:

bopmo sw ltirho sad' eir er duahcrnd sgnfeinehtn ywtbehyni bhhsooh t nrelvcne itsts saih

eoaeepeupopmesfntdue a t .r tiom.te tcdna o frsswwrms eansafwsd meaaree nhtolt re h auomrgthaidre, h sorhuyonh a ee f melioe ficeetddsebseyumrmt ei.a em hah sfne slites ee uhao o

And her nonsensical words swept across the tablet. As Sarah's lazy wrist swam across their constructs, she struck the words' positions, unhindered in moving on to each next consonant or vowel, and the words broke apart under her blind movements. They effervesced into tiny drain-wash bubbles that floated out into the theatre's haunt, stuck to the movie screen and produced tin sheets that rippled.

The words became images, became motion pictures… became art.

The girl beside her gasped again.

On the screen, Sarah's mother clipped at roses from a red garden at the front of her house. The images washed into a bronze hue.

A man walked onto the screen from the left, and he smiled.

Sarah smiled back from her chair, and her heart rose to a single-coloured spectrum of gold.

For a brief moment, she wasn't concerned. She didn't think about her doctor or the weight of dreams or the worth of gold. She just rested, watching her father interact in a way that was wonderful.

Then she turned to write more, but when she asked her hands for cursive, they would not move any further, and the screen began to pixelate into a clutter of letters and slurs.

Sarah grunted, trying to regain control of her lashed wrists but it proved pointless. The sensation in her heart was deteriorating from gold to a pale yellow shade that soon sank into the black, just as the screen.

"What's wrong?" asked the girl. *That was out of character.*

A mumble of unaligned needles on the seamstresses' carriage caused a bundle of thread to jumble in Sarah's throat. Her frozen hands couldn't grasp the thread, to pull it free, and she began to choke. Though her feet kicked from inside her skin, her shoes didn't move. She shook her brain, but her head ignored her, instead it tilted the column back and forced her gaze up, to the screen which had become a tar pit of molasses. It groaned and it stretched as something beneath its surface pushed against its back.

Sarah found herself unable to blink so much as move as splashes of oil, thick and bulbous, reached out from the screen towards her: their filaments like insects in a haze. Thousands of spore-like arms with ballpoint heads full of metal grasped for the frozen person that was Sarah.

Her heart stammered amongst the charm of their heads and she felt her bones begin to quake.

The cesspool of reaching oil, mad with a sort of hunger, turned into a horde of tentacles that slid further across the air like fat needles. Sarah tried to move again but only drops of steam slid down her throat, hitting her belly and causing the water to rise to the back of her eyes where her face streamed with fear.

Immobilized in panic, she could only watch and listen as the screen squirmed; as a moan from the other side coaxed the earth into spitting worms from its ground. The sound filled Sarah, turning her blood into scimitars that cut her insides away.

One of the tentacles curled up above Sarah's head, producing a flesh-soaked lantern that exposed her motionless body to the inspection of its murky green tint.

The girl beside her screamed then, but her voice muffled under the shadows of more tentacles scaling the walls. She shot up and began to run along the aisle, but a tendril grabbed her ankle. As she fell, it kicked back hard and her body made a pendulum, her head slamming against the floor as the noise from her mouth abruptly stopped. The tentacle lifted her limp body upside down and hung her close to the front of the theatre, where the sense of a mire was becoming something else.

More rippling, and then a great maw cast itself in black-sooted resin from the surface of the screen. It distended from the fabric, huge-barbed and gnarled teeth, an under-bit jaw with no flesh to hide its bone. It grew from the oculus of the tentacles and birthed itself into the room, crying, screaming and ready to feast. Ready for naming.

"Names to be given," it spoke as it unhinged its jaw.

Sarah squeezed her stomach into a knot and throw-up bubbled in her throat. She tried to swallow it whole, but she could barely breathe.

The mouth of the beast rose on its bodies of snakes and rolled up the aisles towards the mouse Sarah had become. Driven by its salivating and starving teeth; even the prey could tell it was ready to plate her body.

"Names to be got." The words rumbled like a rolling steel cylinder. Words so close that Sarah could smell the ink of their print.

Sliding along the ground, its jaw reached Sarah's sneakers and its breath found its way between the fabric of her skin; filling the textile of her clothes with steam that left a gasoline resin. Sarah thought of lighting it, of burning up right there, but her hands, her limbs—she still couldn't move her body.

Hunger opened its mandible, retracting bones and sinews so that it was large enough to dwarf Sarah's body. Muscles worked the tendons like cranks and the beast's mouth, on the tip of its violence, lifted itself face to fate with Sarah. She tried to look away but a drop of saliva formed on one of its fangs; the rabbit is a curious prey: Sarah's reflection in the median that would court her body to its throat kept her staring at her death. Her everything screamed in that moment and the unlatched teeth of a serpent began their slow descent into fullness.

Thunder crashed from behind the screen, the noise overwhelming even its low breath; screaming caused the beast to jar in motion and it recoiled, snapping short of Sarah's nose.

Everything became white, unholy, and a flashing strobe.

Suddenly under control, Sarah's eyes blinked and the room stuttered out in seconds as the lightning that had crashed through the roof of the theatre split the timber, and everything that had been holding up began to fall around them.

Colour returned to the conal shapes, turning positions foreseeable. The beast was now frothing and thrashing beneath a dream cloud that had formed and stormed into the cinema behind it. Rain pounded the material of the dream that encircled them, corroding and unmaking the structures of the realm. Deconstructing the beast, tearing the screen apart, turning essence into melted pastel puddles on a nothing of somewhat floor.

It was all being pulled apart.

Thunder crashed again and Sarah watched the curtain of rain pick apart the beast's jaw and tentacles as it sloshed back and forth in its pool of spilt oil, everything behind it slowly turning into a fog, the beast turning into a puddle that would melt away into another dream.

The rain overtook the seats.

Overtook the screaming.

Overtook Sarah and her feet and she disappeared into that which hadn't been formed yet.

Part 13: Storm Water

On the far side of any storm, there is an echo. Whether it be remnants cast from broken trees about the ground, puddles laid like bear traps, the half memorised tail of a rainbow's crossing… or the humidity. It resonates—the storm—always after it's passed.

Humidity is the most often scanned-over echo from a storm, but it's the most consistent. The rain, although stopped, hangs in the air as if strung there for decoration, continuing to soak the cut hides and tattered dresses of the woodland princesses who had run to hide from the thunder that was crashing.

A dream storm is no different. It resonates and leaves all its prey marked with wet and the echo's wet continues to sodden them.

On the far side of the dreamstorm, after the blink of its chaos, Sarah squirmed frantically, hugged by the hot wet that was its afterbirth. And as she could not see, the flashbang tumult from inside the storm having blinded her until all the colours had melted into white, she panicked in the thick drench, certain it was the belly of the beast.

Being eaten was the same fear as being hugged unwanted and she was all over trembling that she might suffocate. It wasn't until the sharp shapes that dug stone carvings into her shins, that pressed and almost pierced the soft belly of palms, only pushed and did not bite or chew, that Sarah realised she was not ate or eaten. She was just a blind fish, plucked from a normal dream and cast on the rocky shore of a new world by the claws of another bear.

Now, a different fear overwhelmed her in the humid sky. Uncertainty now plagued her weary, deaf-and-blind sensations. Bewildered, she tried to stumble away from the new. Her head, full of webbings, uncoloured things, and the constant perturbation at her skin. Close shaves, knuckled everything. She fell down two or three times, trying to run from the emotion that nothing was an existent comfort, and many small stones burst her flesh and bled out so that she screamed, light and airy. When finally she was full of so many shoreline holes that the humidity had gotten in and slowed her, she stopped and simply whimpered in her blindness.

Sarah rolled herself onto her side to let her muscles rest, and to take some of the weight from the cracking shin splints she bore. With her one cheek face up, hair splayed out like sunshine behind her, a light caressed the paler paper of her thinned-out face. She breathed, and some of the frozen shatter from the storm left Sarah's body.

Little olfactory sensors began to work. They took in jasper wood, not gasoline. Forest smells, near mountainscapes and under sunshine. Perfumed nature filled her nose and opened her airways, allowing the pressure to equalise, pulling the weight from the back of her eyes so that sight slowly returned.

First pale, then blue, splendorous Solis broke into sky above. No theatre ceiling tiles were being thrown down in the wake of a dreaming storm. Muscles worked by little hands dragged the tendons into operation and Sarah unfurled herself from the ground, sat up and let the slivers out of her heart.

She was on a hillside, somewhere above a network of pine trees scattered among a dark sphagnum moss ground. It was daytime; she sat in a small gravel pool of crushed stone. Sarah looked around but there was nothing else, just a clean, hilly expanse below a thin pulled-out cloud.

"Holy." Sarah braced a plume of flyaways with her hand as she collected and positioned her crown. "That was… something." Appalachian swirls whirled up her jacket and threw more threads of her hair into a messy, beaded headdress. She could not contain them all and instead, let go and her hair became the fluid movement that carried up from the sail below her hill.

She brushed some dust from her pants and stood for a better view, trying to situate the new dream within her list of maps, but couldn't place her position on the hillside, nor recognize anything around her for miles. She checked landmarks like huge cedar trees, but they turned into ashes. Well-sculpted rocks took form as unshapen masses. A river or a stream would turn into a ravine or a creek, and all the shadows pulled up into nothing, painting the picture of a dream she had never dreamed before.

A thick bulbous cloud rolled overhead, and Sarah ducked, fearful of anything as the new surroundings made her timid, mousy and fleeted. The sudden jump pulled a string somewhere from her back and she thought again of the beast thrashing through the cinema screen. It made her feet light and she decided to move as, even though it was unlikely, the beast could be close.

All the way down the hill, Sarah left flat white shoe prints for foxes to follow. Small flora bushes lay thin under her wandering toes and she fell forwards often, feet catching knolls and hands finding nothing to grasp. Below her was a dale that rose into another hill, its peak grown in with a mushroom-top pinnacle of various foliage, a small forest of tree bark encampment that looked like a campout for surveillance, and Sarah pressed to climb its camouflaged stand.

But as she walked, clear globules of saline began to wrestle with her lashes, obscuring the fine pointillism of the canvas for which she had entered.

Whiskers on her cheeks flicked back and forth, free after being pulled taught from the exodus of her mouse hole, her better senses trying to place how well her head would fit into further entrances or which way the wind blew. Her eyes followed suit—darting in under wet pinnacles, playing balance in shadows and lightness, trying to grasp the better mark of stars not visible in the sky—but there was nothing there to practice cartography with. No constellation above the wayfinding boat and sail and warm water current lines.

Images of the beast, manifesting from the dark in the cinema screen, dissolved in Sarah's pixelated head, but it left room for the obvious. Her mind was blank. All the images she took in as she walked were etched there now. In the present. None of them were being pulled up from previous dreams.

She felt hot.

Then, strange. Cold. Freezing. Full with spider legs up and down her spline.

Catapulted into sudden vision, Sarah became aware she had marched all the way down the hill and now stood at the cusp of the stream that ran through the dale's meridian. It had appeared shallow from afar, but once her toe had tipped into the point of its edges, all black fell in and Sarah was above nothing. Her head had crashed into the water's surface and she was falling deep below the river where her breath was far away.

There was nothing else beneath her feet after the line in the sand gave way, and when Sarah kicked her blind toes for floorboards in the dark, nothing came, and she pencil-dove further into the blue. She kicked again, but her feet made no sense so she tried to hold her breath, but a sea of liquid made every part of her porous, her flesh absorbing the deep, and she sank even lower.

Inches of blue liquid became miles of blue torrent… and then black.

Even though she knew she would drown, her lungs kept begging and opening for air, taking in only water. Water became cement and cement formed its structure, and Sarah became a part of her own fortification. She tried to scream but it was just drowning, and her eyes churned a stainwash red that bled out into the veins of the rock, like chum into a nursing shark's mouth.

She was dying.

But it's a dream, someone's voice called in the back of her head.

Stop trying, she thought.

You'll wake up soon, he said, from above the water.

Her chest was ready to rupture. *You're in your bed.* Extremities, thin spools of soaked clothes in the cold. *You aren't really dying.* Head, a pocket of helium in a hot room. *It's fine.* Her heart being slowly cast in gold silk iron.

Sarah's eyes closed and she looked inside, inside the inside, and the cells in her body died.

Golden light arrived.

The field, with the barn and the cross and the…

…the man in a boat, holding out his hand.

A hand pulling at her dress.

Someone tugged at the cuff of her clothes and the nape of her neck. Hefting her from the water.

Water taking over the effort of her ears, a rush of upward motion dissolving the farm and the field.

Sarah opened her eyes, but her pillow wasn't there; instead, she was lifted, her body being dragged up from the mire. The golden light became a full sun, and she turned her face to its rays.

"There, now you're okay."

He patted her back, his hand calloused and hollow.

"No need to thank me." His voice, its timbre like a low drum, sent a pulse into Sarah's throat and she coughed up a minnow. It flew away like a seed.

Sarah watched the small fish struggle, its little fins in the currents of the dale, using simple motions of vision like a mechanical iris to follow its bumbling flight pattern away. She blinked; clouds above her kept strafing and dragging out the waterlogged haze, so she wiped the corners of her eyes with tissues from her pocket. Not soaked. Not wet. Not damp or frayed. Then she breathed and turned, under full control, to look in the horse's mouth.

——

The man smiled back into coffins. His mouth a thin blade, and his eyes those polished stones, refuting any kind of weather. "I knew you'd be okay," he said.

And all the water in Sara's body drained at that moment, leaving her sunburnt and parched on the beach where she had drowned. "Daddy?" she heard herself say, seeing the man shift and fray like cotton pulled fresh from the plant.

"You have to find the Cartography Door, Sarah. It's the only way for you to stay." The words slipped from his serpent tongue, entered her empty corpse and filled her stomach with MacIntosh apples. All bodies of knowledge in the shape of the cross.

Then, as Sarah sat with her legs out and her ass soaking the riverside, her head a complete loss, her father got up, turned, and phased out of existence.

Halfway up the hill opposite that which she had descended, he reappeared, walking in scattered fractals.

Hot cider saturated her veins and Sarah sprang up to leaf them, letting her muscles boil the sugar to the top. She ran, tripping over stones and stumbling over tapestries of fallen logs, trying to test the distance between her and her father. He stood with his back turned and his mane catching the debris of a rotting sky, matted nature, flowing seams. As Sarah got close, her finger reaching out to grasp the saplings growing in between them, he turned and his polished-stone eyes stopped her in her tracks before he disappeared again, then again reappeared at the top of the hill, smiling, his hair still a filter for the trees.

An impartial regulation of physical states took hold of Sarah as she placed her following sprint. For all the embodiment of movement, she was held and stretched over slow time. Her skin and self became a plasticine effigy drawn out over a matrix of collapsing realities, as if raked into an ellipsis by marble-chipped hands as she was slow motion and space-evident as she ran.

It was almost never, before she reached the top of the hill, where a forest shaped like a mushroom grew and her father sat like high noon. When she reached him, again he disappeared, this time without an image to follow, and Sarah sat at the edge, alone.

Exasperated lungs pushed on her stomach until she purged the remnants of her lunch and slung herself forward on the top of the new summit overlooking a chasm. The timid sun at her back, a breeze in her hair, chunks of vomit on her shoes. She placed her hands on her knees, cantilevering the shape of exhaust, holding herself where a sweater could not warm her arms and let look a symbol of planets, a cosmos of effort. Human-involved stars and a horoscope of yarn: when Sarah finally retracted and pulled the thread, it was apparent that her father had been gone for hours and only the small patch of trees remained.

The trees at the summit were lush with old growth and riddled with woodpecker beaks. It smelled like Chippewa stories around the fire, smoke long distorted and floating up with the sage. Sarah paced in and out from the mythological brush, her body a body of fables and fact; she walked from one side of the tree line to the other, only exposing herself long enough that she couldn't look back.

On the far side of the trees, she noticed a place to hide that overlooked a dropoff cliff and the rest of the dream's landscape.

Hopeful that Daddy might appear again, Sarah sidled up behind the rocky hiding spot and peeked over its edge into the wilderness of her uncharted dreamscape. Her focus stretched beyond its capacity, trying to incorporate its enormity and all the masses of form. She found herself at the verge of a massive valley, filled with a coniferous rainforest of haze and roots and green-spooled canopies. She gasped and half stood before she became aware of a scene unfolding beneath the cliff.

Fast dropped the hammer, and Sarah thinned out into a clandestine crouch. She hid entirely behind the shadows, armed ready, and then popped only an eyeball above the rock. New dreams and dreamscapes, new manifestations of entities caused cautious actions, and Sarah was quick to raise the collar on her noir detective coat when she caught the glimpse of radio villains in the waves.

A small gathering had corralled a huge iron cauldron on another plateau, far below and across from her little summit. The people bowed and heaved oblations of giant garden flowers into red bubbling water inside the pot, stewing above a pyre of burning dolls. They chanted and danced while a tempo of licked blades fell around their ceremony of carnal sounds, each one of them screaming, teeth bucking back from open mouths while painted chips of their skin slipped off to wander the telling of the wind.

Sarah tucked back into her hovel, laying her spine straight against the rock. She rubbed her legs, wrestling with a strange welling of emotions when flakes of black, peeling from the skin of the screaming chants, began to rain down on her secluded hill. Ashen splays of fresh-curled wood from planing tools dropped all around her, a flurry from the volcano's hobby mouth. One landed on Sarah's lip, and it was her first cigarette for the hundredth time, cancerous. She rubbed it away, smearing the black facade of men across her face.

Pulling her hair back, she leaned over and spit the charcoal from her mouth. It polished a pebble beneath her feet, glistening now from the sun, man and saliva fresh from Sarah's teeth. "Gross," she said, turning back to look where her jittering spine had lay, and peeked above the cusp of her rock again.

The dancers, surrounding their boiling soup, had all peeled to red as their skin dropped away, leaving them patchy apes as they danced and swayed. The pot, a human wide and a halfling tall, now rocked back and forth on its uneven base above the heat of the pyre. It sloshed, throwing hot red water that coiled in koi tails and splashed the people dancing 'round. They screamed louder, their noise now beside Sarah, piercing her ear drum and making everything clear: hard static. She cupped her ears. Squinted. The pot and its worshippers only got louder.

"Fuck this," said Sarah, smooth stitches winding up and down her spine. She turned around to head back towards the forest, but pivoted into stone. A huge, endlessly tall barrier of fortress, blank slate, had risen up where the trees had been, and its girth encompassed the hill. Sarah now stood at the tower wall on a sliver of land, with nothing but a sheer drop and the screaming of man behind her... and the temperature rose. The fire grew beneath the pot and cast her shadow on the tower wall, her traced image a reminder that even her spirit was small beneath the heavens and their titan rock upon the hill.

Beside Sarah's graphite-sketched silhouette were the shadows of the men on the plateau behind her, and their pot and their gifts of blood, and all their noise. They knew her now and their focus squeezed the hollow bird bone ribs in Sarah's chest, compacting her blood and adding pressure to the follicles of her skin. She shuddered, hallowed fits beneath her wavering strength as she watched the men grow tall and their burning fire grow hotter and stronger, the pot for which it spurred growing even bigger than them all; and now, its flat top broke into a spear. The level plane of the pot's cutout image was interrupted by a vine that rose high into the air, curling into a hook at the top.

At the flex of its apex, she made out the shape of suckers: a tentacle rising from the sacrifice of man.

Sarah's heart found that step you take in your dream—the one that startles you awake when your brain is convinced it's falling—and she dove back down behind the rock, covering her mouth, her voice crawling like a crab up into her throat and pushing its seashell-covered legs out between the gaps in her hands, clawing at her cheeks and leaving scars of her fear.

"Names." A cavalcade of dark tonal shapes filled the valley, its voice lifting the black of it, into the sky. Sarah watched as clouds of coal tar filled in the space above her head before letting loose the consonants from its ink mine voice. The words fell over everything, covering her and her shoes in layers of bitumen, foul and unrefined.

"Names!" it cried again, and the men all around it screamed and painted their bodies black again.

From an unmarked ship, a captain plumbed the depth of the valley and all that returned was the beast. Ubiquitous and crawling its unshapen form into Sarah's ears, it left her position pathless with the fear of coming aground a real happening, whose ship was taking water on whose land.

Sarah swallowed back the saltwater crustacean.

"Names!" it roared, and Sarah lay down and closed her eyes. Her body turned into a leftover statue from Pompeii's vision of Rome, and she held close the little bit of warmth left from life inside a home.

"Names!" It howled. And Sarah could track the wet footpath of tentacles slithering through the basin below her hill, scuttling and mucking its mucous-covered body through the path dens of wolves and deer. The men screamed and jumped behind it, their bodies a mass of oil on the sacrifice hill.

"Quiet," Sarah said to herself. "Slow. Have to leave, position yourself sideways, find the image of your body outside of sleep." Her eyes, tight with dried ravines, squeezed as she tried to picture herself in bed, far away from the new dream and the crawling tentacles of the beast.

Rocks crashed into the valley below. "Names!" It was close now, tearing at the patch of grass behind the rock. Its worshippers boiling into a gelatinous puddle of fire dancing descant, its feeding arms rising high above the chorus.

Find your body, Sarah. She rolled back and forth and turned neonate on her ribs, pulling her knees in tight, gripping circular with the cusp of her arms.

And she saw herself, quiet and alone in her room.

There it is.

Sarah smelled the warmth of her blanket, the slow stoke fire of self while one slept. Her blanket fibres dammed the diver of her breath.

The dream, gone.

...Thank goodness for that.

Part 14: Surmised Recollection

Numbfingered sunlight scratched at the window, its mute assertion thumbing away at the white trim paint, parting invisible creases to read the story behind the pane. Someone's story of tired legs. Someone's story of stolen shoes. Someone's story of stewarded Delta waves cresting alabaster peaks as all its tellers set sail—away—into a dusty sky.

Sarah's ship, sailed or sailing.

She, the master of a land haul dinghy sitting coastal, islands on the horizon unrecognizable.

There were no other sounds in the room aside from the light trying to find its way in, which Sarah would bask in later. For now, she let her piano wires stretch, slipping all melody out of tension and allowing her somnolent state to find its own, calmed ascension. She curled her fingers into the pillow that lay pushed against the wall, then pressed her face deep into its spilled cotton centre until her ears were covered and the sound of sunlight slipped away, replacing it with her own pulse. Steady… constant.

Sarah let her pupils search for luminescence in the darkness of her meringue bedding, its thick sugary features that of whipping hands. When nothing but black and air bubbles filled the neuron tunnels of her sensation, Sarah's archetypes replaced it with images of the dream state passed; she took a moment to reflect on lucidity before sitting up and winding taut the tuning pins of her morning waltz.

Once her melody found its cadence, Sarah sat stalwart in the warm morning presence of observation, as it had so intended.

As Sarah sat, her nightstand echoed shadows that pulsated on the side of her bed. The cavern of its presence grew along the sheets, reached out and grabbed her hand to drag back to its shrinking body, reminding her to ravage its cavity, for proclivity's sake. Sarah agreed, and took her jar from inside the open womb.

Dust from her eyes laid eggs on her fingers and from that the polyps of her sleep grew. Sarah brushed them off into the mason jar and they fell into embryos of culture, the new children mixing with old. Sarah replaced the lid and watched the polyps budding in the morning light, their jellyfish arms soon to spread amongst a sea of granular charms.

The jar was placed back in the cupboard, and Sarah extracted her journal.

Bound is the Dreaming Hand.

She opened the book at random and found it read, "Dear Sarah," but nothing else.

She flipped to an empty page and started to write.

Dream entry A46

500mg of silene capensis

Very powerful, but desired effects not experienced.

Further trials required.

Birth into the dream very visceral.

Entered, as requested, the rabbit dream. No change.

Visited Daniel, discussed the beast and the nature of things... he was unhelpful mostly however, the gold coin is something I should follow. We both agree.

Entered the tunnel, visited the cinema dream only to experience something new there. Sleep paralysis inside a dream...

Then the beast came.

Then a dream storm ended things and I slipped into a new place.

Daddy was there. He told me to find the Cartography Door, it is the only way to stay." Then he disappeared.

The new dreamscape is unrecognizable; however, once in a high position, it looks like a lot of the dreams could be seen from there, but I was interrupted by—

"Sarah." A low woodcut voice broke her train of thought.

"Hey, you awake?" he asked, his words like scallions inflaming her tear ducts. She felt swollen in the face, her cheeks inflating, creasing the aspect of her vision, its horizon pushing all the words on her page up into a bunch of cryptic nonsense. It quickly fell into a puddle at the bottom of her journal page.

Sarah turned to the doorway, where the voice had broken in and unsettled the contour of her face.

"The gold coins will point you in the door's direction, Sarah," said her father. "The coins."

Sarah wasn't breathing.

She was screaming into her pillow as she woke in her bed.

Fabric stained in sweat.

Body, a sudden impact.

Recoil, the position of robin eggs as those polished stone eyes fell into her.

Sarah took the breath that broke up the time in her dream, and she sat up. "Hhhh, shit." Darkness cut her sentence in half as the greed of the window moon counted all the blessings of the sleeping, taxing those that wake in her domain with letters.

"Jjjjjj that was sssssssss." She put her hand down as a tether, ensuring that it was the heavy side of a ballooned string and her journal made presence in her palm, its oak body still hard after being pulled and prepped to hold the ornery presentation. Spinal column turned in such a way that only a lamp could, or a lighthouse, its keepers always the shade that designated land from sea in presence of the radiant. Sarah shone the light over the cover of her journal, usually housed under beds or into cupboards and picked it up, her prescient hand acting in root networks to connect an old tree to that of nutrients.

Its timeline flipped open to the last entry.

Sarah read the words inside her head, every letter forming a precisely clouded déjà-vu.

Dream Entry A46

500mg of silene capensis.

Part 15: Mom Discusses Glue

The house was full of cider fog as Sarah fell one step at a time down the stairs into the main hall. She dragged her shoulder across the front door, picking up flakes of honey as she did, reversing bees in action as she trudged along. A picture on the wall beside the door, mirroring another on the other side of the portal, hooked her evening wear and tore a piece of lace remembrance off, leaving the textile forever on the corner where she jogged, its level always tipped to hang a jar, incorrectly on the wall.

"Sarah?" asked Edna, her voice filled with smoke and her head a fire detector. "Sarah? You're awake… you don't look awake."

Grey in matted fabric unwashed for days, combed through with dust or rock, Sarah's dismal bunny slippers slaved not hopped along the white tile beneath their fur as she groaned into existence in Edna's kitchen. The slippers left black streaks behind her and somewhere in the house you could hear the gypsy's call for baiting bets. Her hair, a ribbon fallen off and tangled in a creek. Her eyes, half asleep. Sarah rubbed them as she walked past Edna, towards the last supper table that overhung the garden wall.

"Good morning, Mom." The greeting was a baby bird fallen from the nest, its sticky, featherless body warbling on hot concrete. Edna stared at it, at the words, at the flightless bird coughed up on the floor, and her heart was all blue jays, little blips of colour in the white snow blankets of trees. Edna put her hand on her chest and let it sing.

"Sarah, you poor thing. You look terrible." Edna, become a silver age movie as she glided across the tile to her daughter, now sitting in a chair and looking out the window. Edna placed a hand on fledgling cheeks—they were cold, and she turned her daughter's face to inspect the damage of the long night's half rest.

She stroked the cool coal of Sarah's cheek and then placed one thumb and two fingers on her chin, holding her like a Fabergé egg. "Long night, my love?"

"Longer," replied Sarah.

Fingerprints perspiring glue, mother swept her adhesion along the fine cracks of Sarah's face, sealing the remnants of moonlight in and painting her a white spectre for the day. All wounds unhealed but put away with the med kit. Edna dragged a thin epoxy wisp with her as she dropped off the corner of Sarah's mask, turned and headed back to the bronze kettle on the stove. It had started rumbling, the spirit of its animus no longer cold. "I'll get your cider ready," said Edna to the path of mothers in front of her as she placed the still glue-struck hand on the kettle and lifted it away, finally breaking the thread.

Sarah couldn't place the words that jumbled up in the air with so many other steams and smells. She couldn't grasp them from the kitchen atmosphere, nor pluck their wings and make them miss migration with the other butterflies, but she understood her mother's intentions and smiled: having faith in a mother's path.

While the cider poured its gold into her porcelain mug, Sarah turned away to gaze at what made sense to her. The candy-dotted window that overhung the backyard was again frosty. Sarah left more untranslatable words in the mist that had formed on its glass; she reached out to line them with gold gilding but they still lay dormant in their inscrutable sleep. "Thank you, Mom." She didn't turn as the cider made its imprint on the table beside her, a ring of unshapen wood. She didn't flinch when Edna placed her hand on her head and brushed her hair with loving fingers, parting her spirit into braids and ringlets... Sarah just waited for the night to disappear from her heart as she watched the forest breathe on the other side of the window.

In the corners of the windows, strawberries still hung from their planters, high above Sarah's head. Their long, frostbitten vines curled and kissed the siding of the house and swung random ampersands out into the window from where the red blots of fruit tinted glass fractals with their pregnancy. Every fertilized flower frozen from winter's abstaining, a rebellious marker of life beyond the cycle of seasons. Even if their fetuses lay quiet, all springs and falls come with time.

Sarah grabbed the cider in her cold hands, pieces of her ribboned skin falling on the floor where she would be swept up later. She took a sip, and the warm substance wove down her body like the braids Edna was tying into her hair. Hopefully, mother spring would place flowers in the boughs. As Sarah sipped, the strawberries took on shadows in the glass, growing, as if the sun had filled them with contractions and their static bodies were preparing to burst with seeds.

She watched them double in size. Then triple. Sarah turned her head sideways, trying to make sense of gigantism—her braids would part off-centre when she looked later in the mirror. The strawberries, now off from centre of the forest middle, had climbed across the glass and overtook all focus, wandering or not… and they grew ever larger, covering the view with their dark red labour, sucking the kitchen of all its ill-gained light, hiding the tying knots of string on Sarah's stretch of moonwash hair.

Cold porcelain hands reached out, their surface marred from teeth and cracked with the poured form of its maker, and grasped Sarah's lips in glaze. They bowed at her summit of vapour, turning their heads down and, making a ramp of their arms, rolled out the amber crisp liquid of cherried trees. Sarah's throat greedily accepted their oblation and every microbe was washed down. Blinking at the heat of her creation, she churned her head again, a sour twist of neck let the strawberries fall from grace.

When she turned back, the enormity of spotted vines had curled back in cessation. The window again let in light, the forest behind its veneer, breathing. The warm cup of cider breathing below Sarah's nose. She was full of apples, all without cores or poison. No writing on their flesh. Nothing to be exchanged for their consumption.

"Sarah?" asked Edna. "Are you okay?"

Press pause. Catch up. Which fact is reality's maker? "What do you know about the coins to cross the River Acheron?"

"Sorry?"

"Something I heard."

"The river Acheron… you mean the coins for the boatman?" The unfinished braid in Edna's fingers unravelled itself, skittering across Sarah's head and trying to dive for and hide in her ear.

Sarah nodded, slow. Her skin, red dye on a violin bow. "Yeah… for the boatman?"

"Mmhmm," replied Edna. "I don't know much, just what I remember from school."

Excited, Sarah let the words jump from her mouth. "What do you remember?"

She could feel her mother's face scrunch up in thought. "The Romans used to place them in someone's pocket after they died so that their soul could pay the boatman into the underworld…" She paused. "If you had no coins, you would be stuck on the shore." Edna spoke while struggling to wrangle the loose threads on her daughter's sunshine crown. "That's a strange thing to ask, even for you."

"A magpie I saw was carrying around a coin with a wasp on it, I think."

"A magpie?"

"Yes, it was tapping the coin with its beak, trying to get my attention." Sarah fumbled with her cup while trying to explain her question, but the locked cage being built around her head made it impossible to sip cider and have respectable conversation.

"A magpie?" Edna asked again.

Soft dimples made spots where once Sarah had tried to sew buttons into her face, so she could cover or uncover her smile. Mother had taken them out while she had slept and now she bent over to inspect their long torn threads as Sarah's face cinched itself up with imaginary fabrics fastened.

"Yes." Sarah was now choking on her four-point attachments. "A magpie." She coughed out, trying not to let the small clouds of heat that would turn her eyes into curved delicatessens jump from her mouth. The little puffs of heat carried minute gases of laughter. "A magpie was… tapping it."

"A magpie," repeated Edna.

"Yes, dammit! Sometimes they trade stuff for food, shiny stuff, it's a real thing." Sarah frumped in her chair and crossed her arms, a child attempting stage performances for laughs.

"So you wake in a daze, stumble downstairs barely saying anything, and then out from thin air comes these odd questions about currency delivered by birds?"

The chortles dampened only by stubborn hands still managed to craft Sarah's face into a thin smile.

Edna continued to braid, knotting her thoughts into Sarah's hair.

"Well?" asked Sarah. "Is that all you know about it, then? All the information you have on bird-delivered coins?"

Edna spat out a few choice guffaws, and Sarah followed, lightened by the rare sound of her mother not worried. When they stopped, Mother sighed a relaxed tone that hid behind her nose.

"Yes, unfortunately. That's the depth of my knowledge."

"That's too bad," returned Sarah, still beaming below the needle stitch patterns of her mother's hands.

"Maybe it was just a dream, Sarah," said Edna, without thought.

Shoulders found weight below words like these and the smile dripped from Sarah's face into her lap. Under her hushed cheeks she spoke to herself. "I don't know what is, sometimes."

Catching a glimpse falling in the reflection of the forest, Edna squeezed Sarah's drooping shoulders and let her own confidence fall in line. She flicked her teeth and leaned in to hug her daughter. "I'm sorry, Sarah. That just slipped out… it was mean, but it wasn't meant to be."

Sarah patted her mother's worry all again. "I know, Mom."

Edna sighed into Sarah's back, placing her cheek where the warmth of her breath had prepared her sweater. "I'm sorry." Her breath seeped further into Sarah's chest, purifying itself in the filtered folds of her daughter's, venturing to further notes. "Why do you go there anyway, Sarah?"

"Go where?"

"The tunnels…?"

She thought for a moment. "I don't know. I guess I like to see how far I can go."

"How far have you actually gone?"

Respirating, Sarah took every syllable from those words and drove them further into the depths of her sandbed. Shovels extended, dug, buried. Someone had marked it on a map and ate the ink of the paper thick. It all became treasure. Mystery. Myth. Sarah read the story back and the red of her lips seeped through the pages. Rose at first. Rouge. Then pink… and then faded. Only the reflection of the window caught every hue of the peacock's feathers. "All the way to the end."

Edna's weight shifted. "What do you mean, the end?"

She ingested more pirates and their flags and tried her best to translate the jolly roger to such naval fleets. "I entered the tunnels at the start of their… everything. The entrance, I guess."

Edna turned her head again and this time rested her ear a little left of centre. And listened.

"I haven't seen everything in between, but I've been to a place at the far end where the tunnel stops at a yellow door; after that there's an auditorium… and there's nowhere else to go. There's no exit, just the one yellow door back to the rest of the tunnel." Sarah's heartbeat slowed into a smooth-raked sand. Every pebble dispersed, every line smooth, every hand gone from the undetermined ripple.

"Is there anything there at all?"

Air.

"Yes," said Sarah.

"What is it?"

A single black opal burst from the petals of its silica void. It grew, stretched, and bloomed into a pool of water on the ceiling of Sarah's thoughts. She had stepped beyond the yellow door, and stood in the auditorium. Again. Looking up, the murky blue looked back, split by the silhouette of a woman.

"Persephone," whispered Sarah. "A pool of water in the ceiling. There's a woman floating there. I call her Persephone."

Part 16: Weights For Nodding Eyes

"What does the space in between a dream storm look like?" Dr. Pillapatti asked.

Small parcels of used air delivered themselves back to trees and Sarah thought, nestled high atop the question. "It's hard to explain."

"Try me."

Sarah let the taut part of her forehead shrivel up with the spectres of language and lexicons considered natural for people. "If you took a mirror and placed it, finish forward, in front of a perfectly painted gloss white wall… the space there is what it feels like between dreams."

"So… the reverberation of a smooth image?" alluded Dr. Pillapatti.

This is why Sarah kept coming back. That, and her mother's mental state seemed to circle the doctor like a sewer grate. Dr. Pillapatti was always willing to try, even if the concepts were lost to her, not yet described in her Freudian notes and lectures.

"It's a place that should be the perfect image of its own light, but instead, it's blinded in the dark."

The doctor nodded and scribbled on her pad. "And these storms, they are another way for you to move from dream to dream."

"An unintentional and undesirable way, yes."

"Was it undesirable to leave the dream at that point?"

Sarah let the side of her lip write in calligraphy the many ways in which she was divided over such a question. "No, of course not. It just isn't the way I would have chosen to leave."

Dr. Pillapatti pushed her notepad into her belly and leaned over, squishing her chest up into a fatherly talk in hiding. "But you had no choice."

Flat white shoes scuffed the carpet below Sarah's dinner table, a single child reciting family sitcom endings on a dock made of briny wood. "I would have woken up."

"Would you like to talk about the sleep paralysis inside your dream?"

The wooden boards creaked with salt-jammed knuckles and folds of hands. Sarah tried to listen to the wisdom of docks long boarded while she drowned out the dinner table talk. Already the sunlight that was omnipresent in Pillapatti's office—the beams of light that passed a curtain never closed and splayed out in every direction once they crossed the bun and hair pins on the doctor's head—was dying, as the grey of remembrance and the desire of truth melted away the manifested placeholders. Offices, tables, chairs, and their shadows.

"Sarah?" Again Dr. Pillapatti's voice crossed the strange translucent veil of Sarah's mind.

"Yes." Sarah stood on the rocking dock's structure, bending her heart to match the current below her knees.

"Would you like to discuss your paralysis?"

"No."

Eyes were floodlights on boats, dead in the water. "Whether you appreciate it or not, it sounds like the storm was a good thing. It whisked you away from a place you're not yet comfortable even discussing, let alone experiencing."

"Yes."

"Sometimes it's good to relinquish a little control." The doctor made a small cube shape between her thumb and pointer finger before sitting back and pulling out her notepad again. "What happened after the storm, where did you go?"

Wind picked up from the east side of Sarah's saltwater lake and it pushed the image of Dr. Pillapatti into a spray of mineral matter. She flew away, her calcified form to occupy some other place. For now, only voice remained, and it was just Sarah on a dock, the end of which was marked with knife wounds and the imprints of watching birds.

"Somewhere I've never been."

"That's interesting."

Each toe chased a bruised heel, one board at a time, as Sarah walked and swooned the sea beneath her wayward feet. When the currents came to love her, a shaking began in her head, and soon her whole body was ready to leave. "I don't like to just pop into a new dream. Not without some warning."

"Everyone else does."

"Everyone else has some control in their regular lives."

"Do you feel helpless when you're awake?"

The motion inside her corporeal suit came to climax; Sarah achieved her apex and left the body sleeve. She exited the top of her head and rolled around, face to face with herself. Her body closed its eyes on the dock and she let herself dream inside the thought of her dream. "Everyone does, but they feel even more helpless here, inside the dream, where I am most in control."

"Here in the dream? You're in my office, Sarah, this isn't a dream."

"How do I know?" Sarah's body shivered as the wind blew frays of hair into her face. She, in her astral plane, reached out and brushed the hair aside, letting the corporeal being stay inside. "My dad was there," she continued. "He was there in the new dream."

"You saw him?"

"Yes. He was many other men at first, but I always knew it was him."

"He was other men?"

"Sometimes."

"And how did you know the other men were him?"

Dr. Pillapatti's voice drifted farther away, and a fog engulfed the dock, its structure the tongue of a god; god, the form of vapour, incapable of reaching out.

"His stone eyes—they all had his eyes." Sarah looked at herself and the mist was a glass that rose between her and her body. All things wavered in the presence of nature, scattered fragments of light through the fuselage of crystal smoke.

"How did it make you feel, seeing him?"

Sarah's body opened its eyes and its mouth. The fog became a storm of wasps. She reached out and tried to pet the fear from her own cheek. Wiping a single tear with a non-corporeal thumb, it passed through her body, which dripped with tears she, herself, could not touch. "It made me feel the same way I felt on the dock… "

"Scared?"

Sarah blinked and nothing had changed. "Helpless."

Still the sun dumped fluorescent crayon wax onto the sheen of the walls. The shadows behind the tables and chairs were so tight betwixt the void that they could not exist between, so that they compressed and black sprayed out in penumbra fountains across the same wall to Sarah's right. Which way was the sun facing? When it stayed, it turned everything bent straight towards her again… the shape of light not existing pierced the places on her body they touched.

Dr. Pillapatti leaned closer again, her shadow hooked to a carriage, dragged out and filling the space between them with night. Fabric mouths of carpet yawned, the floor fell asleep, Sarah didn't watch. She was the moon, just a reflection of things.

"I can only imagine how futile it must have felt. You trusted your father."

"I didn't."

"You didn't what? Trust your father?" Dr. Pillapatti asked, turning her head and letting the light further embrace Sarah's eyes, further skymarks for the moths that swam in the murk of her guidance.

"No. I trusted him before but when I left the cabin… something was different."

"What was it?"

"It was like he was an entirely different person."

One of the winged pollinator's stench flowers and ladies of the night escaped the bubble of gloom that was shaped like Dr. Pillapatti's blouse and head. It took currents from heated mouths and rose into Sarah's glazed field of vision. She watched it there, burning into ashes in the light.

"Often, in our dreams, just as in real life, we assign different bodies and names to people we are close with, but who have done harm to us. I would associate this with the idea of protecting the original image of the person, the pristine and crystal-clear vessel that we viewed them as, by encoding them with a new identity, and that identity becoming foreign altogether.

'When you experienced that feeling on the dock, you were likely defending your father from his actions—but eventually this idea, this facade, it will fail, and the bones of truth will surface from underneath.'

Once all was eviscerated, only the light remained, and that too… dwindled.

"Maybe it will help to discuss the events that led up to it. I think that's part of the reason you are here, isn't it?" continued Dr. Pillapatti.

"You mean, I'm here for reasons other than my episodes?"

"I think your episodes are related. They are certainly important… road marks in your path, but I don't think they are the source of your coming here, no."

Looking down, Sarah found the shadows were formulating shapes again, turning from blobs of people into straight three-dimensional objects. Flat rectangles. Domed rivet heads. Water. Water in the shape of a lake… depth meant dimension. Dimensions were related all to shape… dimensions of depth below the lake.

Sarah blinked but the boards kept slapping the rubber of her sole.

"Can you remember what happened before the dock?"

Dust compacted the breath of her nose and plugged her sinuses. It blocked her ears. Suddenly, Sarah could hear nothing, not even the waves lapping against the timber frame of her personal pier. She turned right, all the way behind and saw the cabin that they had visited last summer. Snow had heaved bundles of weather onto its roof, and it bowed in wherever the walls weren't holding it. Every action led to more snow on the weakest places of its smile.

Sarah stared as the mouth of the cabin pressed further and further into splitting from the weight of the sky… until it broke in half and exposed the inner workings of the structure. A honeycomb of bees inside. *"If God isn't an obsessive compulsive, then why is every honeycomb perfect?"*

"Sorry, Sarah?"

"No. I can't remember."

Dr. Pillapatti reached out and Sarah's shoulder became the lever that broke the floodgate's seal and she burst further into the foam of her vision as the doctor spoke. "Talking about it doesn't raise it from the dead. You have nothing to fear, Sarah… Sometimes we have to go back to fix it and that can be difficult, but it won't hurt you again. It can't. It ended that day."

"No." All wings swarming like weather. "I don't think it has ended," said Sarah. "I think it's just resting, like the cicada might."

"You don't think it's over?" Dr. Pillapatti asked.

"No, it feels like it's just sleeping."

Sarah moved like a pulled thread, her arms ready to remove themselves from the seams that dragged them to her torso as she was turned around and tethered further onto the dock. Stumbling in the misaligned boards she fell, and where her knee split, she bit her lip hard, lip-syncing every step she stumbled on in the forest's dead above the water.

"That's an interesting statement, coming from you."

"Why is that? Is it because my dreams are strange to you?" asked Sarah absentmindedly.

"I don't think their deviation from what you consider normal is of any real importance to me Sarah; I think you're overly critical of them, though. You even display some pareidolia… I don't mean that as a negative statement by the way, but rather something you should chew on."

Blood filled the organ of her mouth and soon it was a pool for blue jays to wash the sky from their feathers. Sarah's head became a weight of worlds; she tried to mumble as her father picked her up and dragged her further along the pier but the water, the cabin, they were both full of the things her bird bath was not and she was scared they might steal it.

Dr. Pillapatti's blouse made the subtle pulse of a diaphragm. "You know your father was very sick and I think he did some things that you're still not sure how to feel about. To take some of the pressure off, I think you end up focusing on your dreams."

Sarah's capillaries distended at the smell of sap from the pulp of the dock as it sprayed up around them running. The timber, thick with waterlogged pores, could not breathe and instead, the wood became rotted with barnacles and mold and memories of both that extruded when compressed, attempting to lull the oxygen in, only further drowning the submerged pathways of long-stopped growth.

"And because you focus so hard on your dreams, they spill over into your daily life."

Sarah blinked once or twice, just so it would seem as though she were here. "Doesn't that make them more than dreams?"

"It makes them episodes, as we've so poorly named them. Experiences that you find more interesting, and therefore more distracting, than your real life."

The cabin moved forward on the dock as they struggled in reverse time, back and forth in sequences of a state of mind. Sarah squeezed her father's hand behind her and the door of the cabin opened, its red door, red inside, took her body greedily, ready for the cobwebs to be pulled from its frame of motionless chronology.

"Would you rather I focus on drowning?" asked Sarah.

"Not focus, you shouldn't laser in on anything like that. But it's good to air it out a bit. Talk about it. You said you don't think it's over. Why is that?"

Spinning, the internal characteristics of the cabin were lost to elliptical shapes, a delicate leap from the toe and a smooth transition of her feet to the floor made an experience like smoothed crude oil. *"Look! My dress, it has pockets!"* She mouthed the words or spoke them, pending where she stood in existence.

"Because he showed up in my dream and because… I think he did it for reasons other than being sick."

"What reasons are those?"

Her pockets full, Sarah weighed a thousand pounds of steel and the rafters bent in strain to the weight of the floor beneath them *"Do not lose them!"* He said, responsibility the shape of snow.

"I'm still trying to figure it out."

"Okay, that's a route we can discuss more. But do you think trying to understand your father's intentions will help you feel better? Or worse?

Do you think you'll fully ever be certain of them? It might always be just a question."

His shadow leaned in close and the words came like ghosts. *"You have to find the Cartography Door; the coins point the way."*

"I think something went wrong and he's trying to tell me something." The words came with wire that tugged at Sarah's stomach as she pulled them out, gagging.

"Is *he* trying to tell you something or is *your* subconscious trying?"

The roof broke. Everything became wood splinters and snow. Soon, Sarah couldn't tell the difference and the moment passed.

"You know we have more than one subconscious?" asked Sarah, blinking back into the room with so few doors.

"And that's a derailment." Dr. Pillapatti leaned back from her position so close to the skin of the fleece, its golden sheen dying to show the reflection of the sleeping lamb that reflected only Sarah, chewing again on the blood of her flowing lips.

"There's another, further away. In our dreams," Sarah said, watching the shadows beneath them as though they were circling wasps.

"Are you talking about dream yoga?"

"Is dream yoga where you meditate inside a dream?" Sarah cocked her head to mimic the sensibilities of a clock.

"In so many words, I believe it is…" The doctor made a thin soup of her smile.

"Probably then."

"Why don't you tone it down tonight, Sarah? If you can. Maybe try to steer your focus to relax for the afternoon. Your mom said you looked tired. Like you haven't been sleeping." Dr. Pillapatti looked at the notes she had made on her pad, holding them away from her as if they were hot. "You should go on a short walk, maybe in a park. Away from the woods, though." She smiled. "Maybe take some time and do some yoga or meditate. Just not dream yoga." She wrote a few more things on her notepad and looked back up. "A day or two without diving deep, maybe? Get some sunshine and when you come back, we can talk more about your subconscious."

Part 17: Lines are often Territories Long

*I*n every meditation, the spirit's body will always enter in the same manner, aware of its volume or not.

Sarah grasped at her chest with the grip of her breath upon the luminescence of the golden light behind her eyes. Its heralding washed over her feet with thick fabric silk brushes. In its arrival, it was time and Sarah stepped into an ocean of her own movement. Where it ended was uncertain, but it always started the same way, just as it did for every other.

Sarah lay, floating face-up in the pool's water. She breathed in, held, breathed out, counting the seconds and adjusting the time until she was breathing the entire world out and only herself in. She kept pace with her fingers, closed her eyes and that golden light heralded a voice in her vision. Far back in the tunnel in her head, further than always and always there; the luminance drew architectural lines—invisible and white in her dark—in long delicate pulls that coaxed the suture from her heart. Sarah stopped grimacing and the muscles on her forehead relaxed, unfurrowing like so many rabbits, sharpening the dials that tuned in her inner focus. Straight obedient lines in the dark.

A bird called from a nearby tree and its call interrupted the aisles of introspection. The lines on her head shambled forward from the dusting sand, but she drew patience inward again and released the disturbance from her thoughts.

But again the bird called. The golden light faded and white broke a horizon line on her vision, forcing her eyes open at the onset of dawn.

She blinked.

The world, aware of her again.

The pool water felt warm as its smoking aura rose into the cold air above her. The part that stayed liquid hugged her muscles tight as if a towel had been strained for rug making, drawn taut on the loom. She was the loom and the fabric. God was the fabric and the loom. Invisible hands pulled her feet and dragged her body upright in the deep end where the smooth cashmere water stretched out forever—from sun to sun, like rain could. Sarah floated, with the front of her face, the shine of her eyes and teeth and throat just above the water line. From here, only the sky was found, and the tops of trees. The tip of the water. Nothing else.

Dusk was falling and the clouds above her head were still heavy with daylight, satiated in sunset's colours, a glowing pastel drawn out by the knife of the artist. They stretched their thin strands of misty broken fleece across the sky and dipped their fingers into the trees where their hands refracted between the leaves and the birch bark surrounding her pool. The speckled summer bounced from nature to nurture beneath the baggy eyes of Sarah's sleep-guarded face. She looked for the bird. It was impossible to see; it may not have even existed.

Again, she closed her eyes.

She rolled her head back further, letting her ears slip beneath the gentle ripple-back from which she'd entered. Memories of herself sloshed against the softening lines of her face, her expression fading into the palace of her mind. The water drew itself in to nurture her nature and blind the sensations of a body's definitive experience by muting everything through the deprivation of her senses.

Golden light returned and brightened as she sank lower into the liquid, just a nose of breath above its mercurial finish. Sarah's hair splayed out as ink behind her, its experience of the mental image turning the single strands of lace into machine-pinstripe colourations that designed themselves along a sloping perspective that pulled her backwards.

She was falling backwards in her head. Experiencing the change in perception, a fluid movement from physical plane into astral realm where she had come to be. Fourth dimensional preposition, the cosmic relevance of Sarah slipping out of time.

Time: no eater of death here.

Muscles continued to loosen from the grip of tendons whose flesh was made of men. Fabric on clothing no longer touching skin. Toes like loose ornaments above a carpeted floor.

Sarah was the root of a plant and her head became the flower as she entered the subconscious.

Here, her lips—once taut—became students and slipped into a rhythmic chanting of breath.

Breath, a deep beast in the dim.

Its breath so thick that the atmosphere inside her head turned negative and her ears plugged.

No more birds, at all.

Just the chest locked away, far away with treasure. Seeding the inner with its breath.

Just the light and the sound now. Sarah's shoulders dipped and rose with endless thoughts, without weight. All of them, the same. All of them, words that made the tunnel in her head where the golden light remained. Feet caught the undertow and slowly, nothing remained on the surface as Sarah slipped completely into her immersion.

The bitter fall air, the pool and its mediums disappeared completely.

Time: no eater of death here.

Sarah's non-corporeal body broke the membrane of the 'real' world's outer rim and she descended into the place in her head. Perception was a state of mind and this, not normally tangible place, was real.

She descended at a gentle pace, one foot pointed downwards, the other angled beneath hips in such a way to make the number four in her legs, Jupiter falling into the sublime reality of her life.

Subconscious.

Clouds passed as Sarah fell into herself. The surface below her was concave from the other side. White and black and tribal, natural geometric design. Amazonians ingesting ayahuasca plant patterns. The world slowly came into blurry view; she extended beyond the state of vision, and arrived. Sarah's sole touched the ground and she stepped out into what was considered the map, a network reimaging of the numeral path inside her meditation. The fractal realm or the spiritual migration. Seasonal. White blank place, as in canvas.

"One single colour from a million plants in bloom," Sarah said as she looked across the images that she'd created unintentionally. To herself, unintentional. To herself, that which was, the driver who speaks to the voice... Likely the field of wheat was intentional as it flipped the earlier grey scale buildings upside down and the topography vanished and reimagined as the crop.

Focused.

Farm.

Eyes pressed of ink impressed the reading of the farm back to Sarah's mind, right side up. Not upside down. She maintained focus, picked apart the particles of sand from the gravel and the rock. From the mineral and the vitamin. From the sacrificial lamb who strays amongst the fields of crops. Its white body, a dodgy suspect in the golden sprouts that invaded the corners of her mind.

Sarah, the rock bed that feds the mycelium who had stretched and engulfed the vision of ti—

A turned square of light blasted at Sarah's thin umbilical cord introspection. It was followed by a hot red burst that opened her eyes and severed the internal link.

Her crop turned to black, and the white city turned to clouds, turned to golden light. Pulled like the loose strand, all her inside thought turned to nothing. Above her internal sky, the white light of day kicked like sand in her eye and the soft membrane of her vision gelled over quickly and hardened. Rubbing away the sting of day, another practice in self-mutilation.

Her teeth showed as she grimaced. Thin lines in the tendons on her cheeks. Unnoticeable unless under layers of varnish.

Black camouflage splotches took form between the breeches of light in the trees that returned. Sarah was back in the pool, head tilted back, still mostly underwater. But eyes open. Breath returned to obvious. Something noticed in the rear of her head. There was a stinging remainder on her forehead where something had hit her, and she reached for it with her claw. A knife. A hand-turned hand that touched a soft spot on her head above her right eye. Whatever hit her left no mark. It no longer hurt.

The sting slipped away faster than it appeared. Assuming time moves one way.

It probably never did.

The pain. It probably never hurt.

It just surprised her.

Muscles contracted and Sarah straightened her spine out, lifting her head above the water enough that her chin sent a ripple of mute voice across the surface's skim, soon to bounce back. The skin of water, connected to the edge of the pool.

Vision of this reality returned and the blotchy shadows, like those that newborns see, formed into Greek statues in front of her. Sarah reached for the buttocks of a form called Goliath, before preconception tackled her and she was just in the pool,

under the trees beneath the sun,

where a bird called,

somewhere.

A bird called.

Sarah looked to her right. On the fence that surrounded the pool, it was high noon and a bird wore a shadow from the brim of its brow, across its eyes, leaving only the gleam that comes from water that reflects the light of day. Sarah connected pupils with the bird, a raven or a crow that looked down—she was not sure the difference between a raven or a crow. Or a magpie, but understood it has something to do with a pinion.

Now she wasn't sure.

Black metal sheen that directed green from the grass and blue from the water sparked, and gleamed under the bird's wing from its feathers, as it ruffled its coat of flying on the wooden wall. The magpie stared hard at Sarah, as if expecting something from her while its small talons carved the timber into thrones where kings sit and die. Its eyes were black, or perhaps she couldn't make out the colour in the haze, drawn from the pool beneath her eyes. Chlorine increased, and ascended if the acid wasn't right.

The acid wasn't right.

Sarah's eyes.

Small gears from toyshop bodies of miniature mechanics cranked the raven... the crow... the corvidae's neck to turn sideways, the bird questioning what is seen. Beckoning Sarah to see something. It was well known.

"Did you hit me... little flying machine?"

The magpie shuffled sideways along the wooden posts, as if demanding. Already exhausted of all its patience.

Sarah looked around, she stood up above the water and then peered down into the clear murk of the pool. Something circular shimmered beside Sarah's feet and the sirens became jealous of shiny things, splashing the water with more violence, hoping to cloak the shining object in the ripples of their fins. Sarah ignored them and reached down into the pool.

Forcing her face beneath the water and stretching her arms into spirals, she collected a tiny disc from the bottom, its golden glow echoing the curiosity of Sarah's wonder side, the child, the scavenger, the coin collector inside.

Drawing back up, the air felt cold compared to before. In Sarah's hand, the heavy plunder was warm.

"Are you the same bird?" she asked under her breath. "Is this the coin from before?" Sarah presented the small coin, in-between the ledges of fingerprint on her thumb and pointer finger to the bird on the fence.

Little carving feet again shuffled across the planks of wood. Corvidae said nothing, but was surely, possibly, maybe not understood. It cocked its head again to tell the time.

"It has to be." Sarah drew the coin closer to her eyes and squinted, her small vernacular of vision tracing the outline of its surface. Both sides of the pocketwatch-sized disc were imprinted with a familiar winged insect. The top and bottom of a wasp, respectively on the top and bottom, or side-to-side of the coin. "As if the bug were used when casting," marked Sarah, dreaming sadly of the poor soul, captured and emblazoned on the coin. The spirit of a nectar collector, a carnivore, a pollinator caught in a monetary transaction of power. Its stinger was likely still throbbing as the metal had been poured.

Sarah flipped it back and forth a few times in her hand. As the thin circular metal slid unfettered in thought, its edge caught her pink skin and the tender tissue of her eggshell envelope split open, spilling blood onto the surface of the coin.

'gasp'

Short bursts of air filled the small scared flesh of her lungs as Sarah battled with the sensory winding of her pain.

Teeth were taut.

Lips turned to lace, thinning in the grimace of her smile.

Hot flashes of amber in her blood.

But Sarah did not release the coin even though pain did not release her readily. Instead she bit her tongue and let her pupils dilate, a vision of the door flashing in their senses. Then she turned the coin, exposing a sharp stinger still throbbing beneath the poured metal.

She looked up to the bird for understanding, but another bird called somewhere. The corvidae nodded at Sarah, lifting its thirteen feathered wings above its head in an arc, forming a church wall halo above its shoulders. The sun burst through the centre of the bird's folded arms and illuminated the coin's surface, which reflected light into Sarah's eyes. She turned for a moment to shield herself from the blind visage of faith, and when she turned back, the sound of the magpie flapping its wings was already trimming beyond the birch trees and clouds that smeared across the sky.

Questions asked.

Staring dumbfounded into the spheres above her head, Sarah grappled with the fragile glass shards that made up her reality. She folded the coin into her palm and placed the stung finger in her mouth to suckle at her comfort, but no blood touched her lips or tongue. Pulling the finger back out, she looked to where the stinger had stuck her, in the centre of her pointer finger. At the apex of the fingerprint's sand dunes and hedge maze's trim line.

Nothing was there.

No stinger.

No sting.

No blood.

No wound to hold onto.

The glass shattered above her head and fell, unceasing, to the membrane of water at her shoulders. She unfurled the remaining fingers that still encapsulated the coin.

There was nothing new on the bird's trinket. The wasp remained. Its stinger deep below the surface of the coin's finish.

Nothing had stung her. Or the stung was already gone but the image remained. The door of black with golden gilding and a symbol at its centre, a circle, in a square, in a triangle, in a circle.

Sarah sighed as she always had when the flashes occurred. When things not real bared their venomous teeth at the barb of the flower garden soiree in her hair. Her bow, too tight. Her braids in bunches beneath the empyrean. Her head tangled up in the aether of this place.

Her mind unsettled again by those moments that crossed over… *Am I on the edge of it?*

Folding her hands in slow patterns on looms, Sarah buried the coin in her fortunes and again closed her eyes, sank down, and slipped beneath the veil of the water. She left a soap scum on the surface that prevented water bugs from laying eggs or passing over her seventh chakra while she was transported to the other side. The best chance at finding the place where the wasp sting came from. Where the flashes burn themselves up from.

Where the water becomes the edge that she straddled in time.

Chapter Four

"Quick, Sarah, put these in your pockets!" Darius pushed the pockmarked golden obols past Sarah's outstretched arms, beyond the someday scars, pressing after the veins that swelled with toad venom into the empty and ragged pockets of her dress. *It has pockets*, she recalls saying as she swayed her tiny hips, with the protruding shape of a fist through the seams. Both sides. Both cheeks pushing cool with smiles.

But Darius wasn't happy; he was draped in a sheet that was stained with yellow sweat, as if the sunflowers on her dress had dyed his skin, as if he had rolled in her fabric and come out with his palms up asking for dirty water. Sarah had none to spare from the mirages that were fogging the corners of her eyes. "What are they?" she asked, her mouth now crooked, her expression frazzled.

"They're important. Tickets. Fare." He glanced at her with those polished eyes as his rough knuckles passed the seam in her pockets and pressed grit into her pores. She couldn't breathe through her skin there, and all the trepidation wept from his breath. "They will lead to the Cartography Door."

He raked his skin back along her sweet fruit flesh, pulling it back and exposing the seeds therein. Sarah winced but she knew it wasn't intended. It was just the mark of a carpenter. A boat maker. A man whose hands had strangled trees and twisted roots into chairs.

Placing his hands into his own pockets, he rummaged around with the cuff of his watch scraping his jeans into frays and sensitive filaments of time. She watched his fingers roll in and grasp something, pulling back the line hard, the finger hooks had ensnared a package. Light burst from his palm when he brought it forward; there in his hand were two more coins of similar fashion. One for each one.

"See?" he said, while the blades of his five o'clock shadow sliced falling beads of sweat into further fractions of time. "I have them, too." He nodded, as if in confirmation of their purpose, but Sarah choked on the smell of gold, and she coughed.

Blood splattered against the sheet over Darius' eyes.

He blinked the colour rose, pulled back the sheet and was anew again, his name changed to Drury but those polished stone eyes never changing

Then thin, clear water ran down the sheet and he kneeled, outstretched his arms and hugged Sarah.

He held her until she was red.

"It'll be okay. I promise."

"What'll I do with them?" asked Sarah.

Leaning back, then standing, Drury's shadow hung its coat on Sarah's effigy, burying her beneath its warmth and black. "Hold on to them. We will use them together. But if something happens—" he turned to look at the shape of the window in the cabin wall. It cut a square of bright winter light, the white that doubles up on the white and forces you to cut slits in the wood of your face, it cut that into the timber of the cabin and fell on his face. Sarah only caught that which slipped off the side and cut an angle of the shadow that covered her heart. Bathing her sunflowers in his eclipsing form. "If something happens, he will know exactly what to do. So don't worry. You won't need me when you get to him."

"Who?"

"The boatman, he'll know what to do."

Drury turned back and threw his talons into the rabbit of her shoulder strap arms. He shook her, not hard. "So *do not* lose them. Do you understand? It's very important." And his eyes were soft metal.

"Yes." Sarah's face was the drop of ink before it left the broken pen. She would stain anything from here on in.

"*Sarah?*" A voice came from outside the cabin. Faint and nimble, its mousey feet subtle on the spring of Drury's head.

Focus shifted from Drury's clenched jaw until the muscles wrenched Dawson's face into space and he was grinding aspects of grass and dirt beneath the white visage of molars. Sarah's pupils wandered up to the rafters. They were cypress and the wood was cedar, and it creaked under the weight of the voice.

Her shoulders bent and the room shook back and forth. "Sarah," pointed Dawson, his hard voice spilling old liquor smell into her face. "Are you paying attention?"

His irises had become fir branches, hidden amongst the polished stone, that would burn easily and leave little ash on the cabin's floor.

"Yes," said Sarah. "Sorry, but the roof was talking." Fir wood burns very long and leaves little chance of tracking.

"Never mind that." He didn't bother to look up, his head too level with the moments churning round the ground. "When we get out there, it's necessary that you follow me right to the end. It's going to be cold, and probably—" He swallowed an apple of arsenic; it budded and fruited in his cheeks. They were red, swollen, deer-food bait. "It's going to be scary." What was supposed to be the crisp skin on his tree's fruit kept crinkling, wrinkling up under his fiery eyes, as if the heat weren't candying them like it should have, but burning all the moisture out. Soon it would rain candy apple eyes. "But I'll be right there with you."

Those words reached inside Sarah and gripped her heart. They squeezed it and she wasn't sure if they were honest or not... not because she couldn't believe him, but because Sarah had dreams and sometimes they said what everyone else could not.

"*Sarah...*" The voice came again at the roof and when Sarah looked up, white was leaking in through the shingles. The roof was bowing in the middle, its inverted smile breaking the cabin's structure where all the points of architecture were left out.

Snow began to tumble in, its papercut features breaking the splinters of light and dark, spiralling the tones in the refraction of their white. Soon it was everywhere, and everything was frozen.

Dawson was motionless, frozen, not moving in sync with the falling, hand-carved remnants of sky.

The roof distended further, bulging in the centre, as if filling with the contents of Sarah's questions. She reached into her pockets; unable to move her feet, she fumbled with the coins in her hands, in her pockets, in her dress. *Look, it has pockets!* she remembered saying and the roof split like a peach, broken in the centre. The voice came through, all nectar. And pollen. And what bees turn peach-fruit flowers into, from vomit. *"Sarah, it ended here,"* she said.

Suddenly, it was Sarah's father who squeezed her shoulders again, his eyes flashing stones, all other images melting away. Above her, the roof is in one piece, light only entering from behind the man in front of her. "Sarah." His mouth is a strange shape, slowed-down vowels, cut-up syllables, punctuation too long in the face. "The Cartography Door—the coins will take you there. The one with the three shapes inside the circle."

Sarah looked through an empty and featureless field of fog at her father.

He continued, as a small gleam of sunshine broke a hole at the place where the space between his lips at the left side of his face met his cheek and drove into Sarah's mouth. "You know how you always wake up screaming. Cause you don't want to leave? Do you know?" Sarah nodded as the glazier set another layer of sheen across her eyes. "That's where we are going, Sarah. Where you belong. And the door, it's the only way to stay." He smiled.

Sarah smiled.

He stood straight up, and the glimpse of light disappeared in his purpose.

Grabbing Sarah's arm, he brought her to the door, on the other side of which was the dock.

On the other side of which, there was only potion.

Part 18: Sand for Parcels

Between the slats that moonlight's brushes had painted white, brick stacks of shadows compiled to saturate, leaving Sarah's sheets wet with dividing lines in her sleep. Not a peep from the crickets that stumbled in between the penumbra of her fabric, creased, shaping the lines of her breathing. They simply jumped, fell and rose between the shapes of her hips and breast and feet. All totemed atop one another before her head that lay awake, despite the resting of her body. Dichotomy, balance, nervousness steeped in the midnight hour.

Why can't I sleep? she wondered, laying perfectly still in the shape of snow angels made from cotton.

Slow demand on kneecap bind and hips swing. Sarah turned her body slowly from her back to her side, and hooked her arm beneath her neck, thin polyester between the folding limbs and skin.

Across her face laid the fence that sheep would jump while counting, made from a curtain of blinds curtailed. Sarah closed her eyes like gates, but the moonlight snuck like so many lemons onto her tongue, its sour bitter hiding in a gospel mouth now salivating, flooding the eyes and irises until they pushed her eyelids aside, desperate for air, letting in the full of the moon.

This time the demand came sharp; Sarah swung back to her back before the foam in her mattress even noticed she was gone, filling in the imprint with tiny hands long after the body had left it. Sarah's fists made themselves apparent, as tight as her eyes were not. Bloodshot. She summoned for bedtime sand and sweat, but instead, "Fuck! This sucks."

She spun again, this time away from the shutters. She pulled her sheets into a nautilus shell and tried to hide her softened self from the fleshed-out warmth of distant thunder, that rolled closer than sleep seemed to come.

And even closer still, a magnetic pull from the sky matted everything, covered all things and filled Sarah's closet with a frequency that began to hum in her head, a growling, as if something was denning inside. A great body that would spill out with red eyes and sharp teeth.

Strange scratching sounds followed the static dissonance of the storm. Outside, inside her head. In her room. In her closet. Strange scarring.

Sarah could hear its constant movement, cusping the line of reality, and she felt as though eyes were everywhere. The thunder came louder, followed by a fist of light that punched her window and shook the slats of shadows into vibrant, colourless flashing colours.

Sarah sat up, threw her hands skyward, then down and squeezed them into fists. Beneath the show of frustration, something crept beneath her facade as she pinned her sheets to the mattress with hands shaking and trembling. Another flash of light came; she squeezed even more tightly, ignoring that she'd lost feeling in her fingers as she strangled the neck of her bed.

Outside, the rain clouds gathered, full of ire, at the windows in her room. She raised her ears to the drowning noise that came along with it, sounding like many deformed bird legs marching across the lawn, screeching at the porch and siding. The storm puffed up its chest, flapped its wings and lifted its grotesque body up to Sarah's shudders to press its feathers against the glass. The ink from its quills bled, leaving streams of water that poured down the windowpanes.

The girl sat on the far side, patterns from the glass leaving scars on her cheeks. Her focus loosening as the scrawling plume of the storm beckoned her with draughts and current to rise and come forward. And although the closet breathed and lashed out with thin ribbons to fear, she did. She walked, balletic, across the floor to look out into the night that called from the treetops.

In the sky, a grey plume of mammatus clouds had formed from the scattered feathers of so many angry corvidae. The centre mass of the clouds puckering as it wheezed electric air. The cloud pulled air towards its centre, a forming, inhaling mouth that took breath for a fire it had yet to stoke as its edges turned to pleated crafts, formed upside down. Fields of wheat, beneath the hungry mouth bowed to the ravenous intake. Locust swarms that had been resting in the wheat now became thin lines of sleeping insects, being inhaled like smoke into the lungs above them, surrendered so as to inseminate the ovum in the storm's uterus. The clouds shivered with their pupae, then pulled back and burst another shattering noise into the night.

The boom of thunder shook the landscape of the sky, its breasted cartography mesmerizing, rolling with waves of low grass and high hill, then smashing against Sarah's window, shuddering the whole house back two steps. Sarah felt its presence in her chest. It echoed out, across her bed, into her room, and resonated in her closet.

She stepped back, and sat down again on her bed, laying her palms out for balance against the onslaught outside. Unconsciously, she tucked her head down low, to stay hidden beneath the howl of the squall, but her head perked right to a noise, something outside the storm and the windows and even the clawing from the closet. A low tinny growl that came from the nightstand beside her bed, where she hid the jar of sleeping sand.

She craned to find the displaced vocal chords of the tempest, reaching into the nightstand; she searched with her fingers and found the mason jar hidden in its temple. She lifted it from its place and held it aloft, trying to illuminate the inside of the jar in the darkness of the room.

The jar, still filled with a thousand nights worth of sleeping sand, echoed, chirruping, its frequency matched to the storm and her heart.

Another barrage of light pummeled the house and it lit the room long enough to reveal that the mason jar's lid was vibrating. Its tip-top screw-on stopper was warbling, reticulating its throat, calling from the tiny gaps that had abscessed the plates of metal protrusions and glass cavities on its head. The jar tried to fumble itself from her grip, to get closer to the floor and cry, but Sarah tightened her arms and bore its struggle.

The light from the storm dwindled again and abandoned a tall slender doorway in the recess of Sarah's left eye where knowledge could get in. It marooned her, alone with the jar and the closet that growled again, louder now, matching the shaking of the glass in her hands and warming her skin uncomfortably.

A loud single clap from the heavens barked. It pulled the fixation from Sarah's skin and instead called the rain, now coming in through the rafters, and dripping into her room where it began to fill pans and pots and random boots with swell water. Her closet too, seemed to fill, and pushed like a pregnant stomach against the double doors, fat and expanded with ocean as it cursed the handcrafted carpentry. It growled further then, deep into the low embrace of throats caught in sperm whale bellies.

Sarah's right eye disappeared completely as, de novo, a spear of light followed the thunder that came from her closet, or her mason jar, or the sky outside her window, piercing the exterior bricks so that they tumbled into her room. Luminescence cured her blindness, and Sarah looked further into the jar despite her fear of what might be inside. And she saw the sleeping sands were stirring.

With her left eye, the jar showed to her its destiny. She watched it crack open and black oil pulled itself from her sleeping sands, slipped down her forearms and entered the knotted umbilicus in her belly. There, she rotted and spewed black upon the earth like so many lanterns unburned in the cosmos.

There, her heart churned at what it witnessed, and she pulled away from the vision. Her right eye came back to view—she was without chakra or position and all things became unaligned— and that's when the beast spoke. "Names to be given." Fear overtook her chest.

Her closet entrance was now splitting and tearing as its pregnant contents grew and pressed like so many fingers in possessed skin. It started to call as it thudded, a balloon of liquid anger backing up and charging, over and over again against the portcullis walls. The noise became the storm and the storm took over her room with bright death.

The jar shook.

The door pressed, to its limits.

Sarah felt circular teeth carve out portals of her flesh. Light would burst from her soon. And she was all alone with the beast as it tried to free itself from possessions, leaving her motionless as its tentacles slipped out from under the door to hunt for her possession. It called from so many orifices, "Names to be got!"

She whimpered at their maws as the beast pushed the closet doors like elastics into the centre of the room. Thin membrane faces looked at Sarah and she backed away, she hid her head, placed the jar between her knees and covered her body with hands of feeble armour. She cried and the floor became an ink blotter of her heart and the faces kept pressing. Pressing and pushing and moving the furniture about the room. Her bedpost repositioned, her dresser scraped against the hardwood and the nightstand tipped over and all the contents of her dreams fell on the floor. The journal, her mortar and pestle...

And then something golden broke from the ink, heavy as it clattered against the floor.

Everything stopped moving when that golden noise touched the ground.

The room grew to shallows and Sarah lifted her eyes. The coin had fallen from her nightstand and now lay between her legs. The coin that the raven had given.

She reached for it, and the mason jar shook so wildly that it dared to break from her clasping legs while the door of the closet burst from its hinges and a dark miasmic cloud fell into the room.

The beast yelled and all its tentacles drove for the place between her thighs.

Sarah grabbed the coin before her body could be split into streamers of flesh by the foggy, rasping arms that spewed from her closet. Before the jaws of the beast could gnaw upon the raised edges of the coin. Before the jar broke and the ink spilled, Sarah clutched the coin and the storm...

Stopped.

The closet had its doors. The jar was not shaken from her arms. The floor was dry, and incense filled the room. Her sand was back to dreaming.

Sarah lowered herself back into the bed, clenching the jar and the coin to her chest.

She let herself catch her breath.

Part 19: Still Waking with a Start

"You look as though you haven't slept at all," said Edna, standing too tall and shaped like question after question in a line of heart-shaped cocoons.

Her elbow leaned against the counter beside the stove while she waited for the kettle to sing. Behind her, the cabinets shifted, opening and closing, dragging their wood into the open air for burning.

Sarah sat with her elbow on the kitchen table, waiting like the diligent night guard for tea that would soon come. She tapped the fingers of the other arm while her bed-bedraggled head tried to figure out if the table was slipping out from beneath her, or if she was falling off of it. She blinked hard in her thoughts, not at all nodding off but entirely unprepared to be awake. Her eyes were on the tea kettle; she couldn't wait for caffeine but her focus was a shift of colours through the prism glass.

"Are, are you there at all?" asked Edna, as a renegade line of saliva slipped down from Sarah's open mouth. Edna's mouth curved in the way a thief might as the drop touched the tabletop and turned the world bright red. "Sarah?" she asked, waving her little hands. "Sarah?" she asked again of her whitewash daughter, who stared blankly into nothing.

Under her fuzzy head, somewhere amongst the blurry static of morning's drag, Sarah felt cold growing through her arm. She tucked her head in for warmth, looked down at the woodgrain tabletop and found it had turned to ice, thick and marble-long with black liquorice saltwater content.

But ice.

Ice that was metres deep, that held canoes hostage while the polar bears sniffed out a rotten wound. While one hid amongst the drifts of snow. While gulls circle overhead, like vultures, aware that the stranded and wounded were already dead. Ice that you died on.

Sarah, seized back from the sudden hyperborean that had swelled beneath her, started to cull the heat in the room. When she did, the now-frozen string of saliva broke, and its frost shattered into a million expositions of the morning's steam.

Vapour filled the room.

The kettle was boiling; the air around it vibrated while Edna called again. So often, as she did every morning. "Sarah!"

"What?" said Sarah, her eyes two small pepper marks in a field sight far away.

"You were screaming again."

"I was?" She looked around as if the culprit could be someone else.

The kettle was bouncing and raging now on the stovetop, its feet bright red, and Sarah zeroed in on it.

"It's just the stove." She wiped her chin with her sleeve and left watermark traces on the fabric.

Edna grasped the black handle and moved the tea kettle from the stove, then began to rummage through the cupboards for a cup. "I don't think you slept at all, you know?" The open cabinet door into which she spoke was like the whale, hungry for Pinocchio's Geppetto.

Her palms were ethereal markers from the squiggles Sarah would soon find in her eyes, and she pushed them hard into the sockets, trying to rub the madness away by pushing the bright-coloured worms in. She squinted hard. Bit at her tongue and pressed harder into slow change cavities from birth. "No. I don't think I slept either... well maybe just there, just for a minute."

Releasing the pressure negative between the flat of her skin and the curve of her orbital bones drew Sarah's eyes to focus. Edna was now stirring the ochre liquid in a green cup on the light-polished finish of the countertop. Her digits, free space. Her eyes, lanterns focused on the wick of her daughter.

Dry tide sand was in Edna's mouth as she waded over to Sarah, slouched at the table, no dust mites between her and the ground.

Sarah looked up, Edna looked down, and she placed the cup between them.

"Thank you, Mom," said Sarah numbly, her lips still thawing.

"You're welcome."

The white apron turned away and polka-dots followed a swaying of hips as Edna headed back to the centre of the counters. She left no footprints as she walked, only a strange crossing of shadows on the ground where the sunrise hit her back and the fixtures encapsulated her red hair. She turned back once, centreed, and waited for her daughter to make claws in the soil of the day. A moment for cat's stretch, a silence for growth.

Sarah looked into the silhouette she left on the table, drawing the outline with her inner thoughts. She lifted the cup and drank the liquid, bathhouse-warm. Honey washed her throat of the rasp from when her voice had clawed its flesh lining. Ginger combed her stomach. Lemon pursed her lips as the alchemy of spices swarmed at her tongue and tried to sap the pollen from her papillae. All business, fighting for control of taste and sugars.

She inhaled, and the action drew more sense up while oxygen worked down. The sweet amalgamation crowded the cavities of her eyes and ears and nose. Soon she swam in the bathhouse and the fleshy tattoosdisappeared in the effervescent rise of heat and moisture. Her head, a warm stone from where the heat had risen, slowly became sapped of temperature, and all the house was her focus. No noise.

"Better?" asked Edna.

"Mmhmmm," Sarah replied.

"So then, what happened last night?"

"Hmmm?" Sarah mimicked drifting in and out of body.

"Last night. What happened?"

"You mean, in my sleep?"

"You didn't sleep, though." Edna shifted her chin towards her clavicle, where violins might rest.

"I don't know." Sarah continued to mime the actions of fatigue but she was well aware of the question, just biding for hands on the clock. "Maybe I did. It's hard to tell some nights." Sarah shrugged, playing off cool drifts from her shoulders. "I'm sure it's nothing."

Neither party looked at the other for fear a weather balloon might swallow them whole and drag them up to where the view was clear. Lucidity was for stars, and Sarah had enough of that at night, while Edna had enough of it in the mornings. They were human, and they craved obfuscation in the presence of the den mother. Wolves rarely understood the desires of their cubs, anyway. One scent always leads to another, but not every member of the pack searches for prey.

"What will you do today?" asked Edna, breaking the until-now-unnoticed, red-stained glass that Sarah was crafting for Mother to peer through, favouring weather talk instead.

Lifting the cup to her lips, Sarah pretended to think on the notion of where she might go. "Probably the woods again," she said without turning to look at the bay window behind her. "Get some fresh air." The house had become stagnant.

Part 20: Shaken Boughs Drop Gold

At the wooded boundary of her backyard, boughs laden with evergreen needles pulled back, and their hinging elbows, hung by strings reined taut, allowed a curtain of coniferous to swing back, revealing the entrances that others were not privy to. Sarah entered, knowing the gates by memory were accessible with a fluent language of keys, hers and hers only. Not even the rabbits—the king of enemies—could mimic the tumblers of such coppice locks.

Familiar trails parted legs and left long lines of dark-scratched ruts that ran on into a faded horizon. Sarah walked their crosshatched strips below the canopy of the forest, behind the world, with her collar still high but her buttons unbuttoned, the winter wind not ready to pass the trees stood as sentinels outside. Sarah sweat under her jacket, small drops of exertion pooling in the hollows of her folded clothes made a cavernous noise of her walking, even if she stood so tall as she had in the cold. The puddles were distracting as she walked, but warm enough that they had not frozen, and Sarah was left to carry the weight of her water.

As the trail wandered east—as it always had, toward the marketplace, in the same direction as Mecca—Sarah drove her gaze into the sun. Even with the matchstick formations of white birch trees in front of her, the light blared, leaving a huge line of crop circle markings scattered in her vision. She had to lift her arm and steer under the fabric of her sleeve, guiding the light into the left hand of her path.

The immediate danger of roots and deer droppings kept her eyes focused down as she walked into the blind the same way she stepped into the open arms of trees, with nails on her soles and a spine made to be untarnished, the trail beneath her an extension of her direction and not a place that steered her needs. With her eyes down and her arms up, the only perception left to the uncharted was her hearing, which buzzed with the growth of trees. Sarah listened to them talk in their long, deep voices, not at all like the shape of their leaves, rather, like the tendrils of their roots.

A knocking came from below her, the taproots burrowing further towards long dead scents for which they had need, sniffing about, locating nutrients and water, and then gulping them up, the opposite of animal chatter. She followed the same magnesium and iron, potassium and phosphorous… the nitrogen handed over from other trees—maybe the mother's—as it rolled up the roots and into the trunk. The trees breathed in, and when they breathed out the food kept traveling up through bugs and pulp, along the networks of bark and their maps from woodmaker gods, to the branches where a single bird tapped. Sarah raised her eyes.

In a paper scroll roll of curled papyrus and boreal deciduous, a wood-pecker stood, wrapped in the birch tree. He waited motionless, ten feet up and a good arm away, for Sarah to focus before he started tapping again. Driving his thin conical beak into the flesh of the tree, splitting its skin and pushing the pulp's clear cider out to the folds of the wound where he garnered the attention of the world, a magnificent tyrant, gifting the trees with the new spaces he'd form and the old spaces left by the beetles he tore from their limbs. A balancer of plates, a divider of things.

A line or a seam, like that found at the edge of two masses, as water meets beach.

"Hello, Mr. Corvidae," Sarah exclaimed and the bird stopped again.

It turned to face her, and its beak disappeared in the shadow of its feathers. It opened its mandible wide, displacing only a thin vein of light and exposing a red tongue in an otherwise black field of nothing specific. Waggling, the bird spat a beetle from its throat that fell, still slumbering, catching the iridescent colours of its shell in the carousel of its tumbling before it struck a branch and bounced into a wall of white.

Sarah stared where the beetle had collided with the wood, studying its transcendental journey from trunk, to belly, back to tree. The place it finally settled was beside a bent sapling, pulled into an arch with a circular carving on its bark. A gateway in the forest, familiar only to the fey and Sarah's journal.

The portal stared back at her like all ominous things of better writers. Bleak, shimmering, memorable, forgotten.

The woodpecker returned to its role as a reminder chimed, breaking Sarah from her stream of visceral surreality. She cupped her hand beneath the cloudless sky above her water-filled head and noticed she had been dripping from the unzipped part of her jacket. She looked over, but the woodpecker had gone, only the gate remained; nothing moved around it.

Dust, frozen in light beams that shot through the canopy of snow-laden branches, refused to move. Sarah squinted with Inuit glasses, then stepped, left-foot waltz that her right foot followed and back, copying the footsteps marked in the ground, strafing her vision side to side. But the dust was painted on a canvas of tall black lines and empty spaces; where she went, the eyes of the painting did not follow; they were caught in the stasis of art. A matrix of warped lines around the portal's welcome home sign.

Sarah sighed and reached for her single-strap pack, its military colours hidden against her coat. She flipped open its flap and produced a thermos, hot with red relief, and poured herself a dark roast. As it flowed, the air breathed cool onto its surface of black marching brigade. She sipped it and let it steep in her mouth before pouring it into her belly, where the caffeine was treated like gold, pedestals, virgins, paintings coveted by Spanish helms.

The stretched sapling bared its shape in colours that sunrays bounced off bubbles made, its tireless spine untangling. Sarah chewed her lip and sipped again, draining the embers of her fire into a boiler gone cold.

The portal remained, specks of chronological clouds still present.

The trees took her exhalation; the forest hung on her every word.

"I have to see Zara," she spoke to the wood. "And it's getting late." The sapling shuddered, letting small crystals spray dog fur water.

"I have to get there before the market closes," she pleaded.

The sapling grew and then shrunk.

She pointed towards the city. "Out there first."

A roll of old fossils relieved themselves as the sapling began to move, lengthening out its body before stretching back upright and casting a straight shadow that walked into the ruts of Sarah's path. Its dark side blue with fungus, its left, the sense of parasites unable to be plucked. It rose into the sunset, stood sentinel waiting for further orders from the führer.

"Next time, I promise." Sarah placed her hands on her hips, coffee splattering the ground and leaving Rorschachs in the snow. The forest sighed at the sight of ink on paper, a breeze that pushed the dust away and let the sun beam as it pleased.

A smirk crept to the side of Sarah's cheek and she broke the snow below her, turning to leave. "I'll be back." She spoke half to herself as she walked, parting with thick tracks of her boot in the butterflies of coffee.

On the other side, the forest broke and Sarah found herself buried in graves, then walking in ghosts and then under the colourful array of umbrellas and cloth spun canopies of the indoor marketplace. She was a radiant drop of fresh palettes in the morning atmosphere of the shops. Their logos and names stuck out with gilded edges; the gold of which, pressed and folded by sages, spelled out titles like 'Zosimos' Cupboards,' 'Clocks by Paracelsus' and 'Three Herbs of Hermes,' where Zara sat, neatly tucked beneath with his head down.

Sarah walked to his stall through a T-shaped aisle, layered in filtered sun through the dusty greenhouse windows above them. Sarah soaked it up; photosynthesizing changed her from pale to paler. Her fingers snipped rose buds for idolized mortician mothers. She even closed her eyes as she walked, unimpeded by crowds that were not there. In the early morning market, it was quiet, just Sarah and the sunshine and Zara's garden of herbaceous affair.

Warm sun, servant of the moon, fell harder while Sarah's eyes, remained shut, and praised her nightgowned body. Massaging the white milk of her skin and encouraging her blood to flow steady, as it did, her sinuses flared with pressure. She breathed in the scents of the hall: Zara's stall came on strong and stronger as she walked. Rhodalia Rosea permeated her skin, golden seal left bitter pockmarks in the fleshy centre of her tongue and Sarah coughed at the acid and a cool mint that caught her eye just in step of the stall. Sarah opened them wide, every flower turned to her in reflection of the warmth.

"Good morning, Zara."

The old man hopped, bent over half-stalled. He turned to look at Sarah sideways from just below the counter of his miniature shop. "Oh, Sarah." He stood back up, holding his back, his hand a makeshift cane of gnarled roots. "How are you?"

"I'm well. What's the smell? Mint? I've never smelt it so strong."

"Ah! It's my tea!" He beamed and lifted a white porcelain mug up into the light. "It's good for your stomach. You should try some."

Sarah smiled. "No, that's okay. I'm fine with coffee." She patted the single-strap sack at her shoulder. "Besides, I can get mint anywhere—you have better things to offer."

Zara puzzled his mouth and breathed out through concocted lips. He placed his mug beneath his waggling beard and stood back, his skin shifting into the array of his forest plant backdrop, all standing in ascension on teetered shelves at the rear of the stall becoming a camouflage of half raised eyes. Zara was a bartender of flowers, their pollen, the likes of which bees had drunk and vomited up in honeycomb patterns, sacrosanct. He knew the risk of their bumbled flying and he folded his arms in wait.

"What?" asked Sarah.

Huge squid oculi trimmed into flat plane dusters and the breath that pushed out from thin lips now filtered through the old man's beard, purified before touching tainted waters. Zara leaned further into his wall of scape-scale mosses and bulbs, flowering jettisoned shoots of green grass couples, palpitating yellow pistils in beds of red-rocked petals.

"What?" asked Sarah again, this time leaning forward to place her hands on the fresh wax table.

Zara turned his cheek to the right, his eyes not moving as he filled his preferred cooking flesh with a pocket of air. It was something to mull over in his mouth, despite the taste of sea, which he didn't like. "How far did you take it?"

"Why?"

"Because you are covered in bruises."

Sarah pulled her hands from the counter and touched her head where the brick had spent her thoughts, but the swelling was long gone; there was nothing there. "What do you mean, where?" She unhinged her hands and brushed the fabric of her sweater clean. Only spare particles of dust swirled out between the two unmoving objects.

"I told you it would get dark, I told you that you are no cat."

Sarah looked upon the old sage, his hand a pattern of oaths, his tongue, which only answered in riddles… his eyes, which only provided thoughts. Sarah returned no answer to his statement, she only waited to see him through. Zara continued when the shadows didn't move again. "It's like you still don't see anything at all."

Periscope head rolled down and into an interjection of little thought. "I'm not sure what I'm supposed to see."

"Yourself! You fool. Surely you can see that, child, it's written all over your face when you look in the mirror… have you looked in the mirror?" Zara lifted his tea to his mouth and slurped; his eyes did not move from Sarah and her curve.

Sarah shied back from the sudden outburst, its lines too drawn at centre for her to respond without some thought. Alas. "Not today, no."

"Do you remember the last time you did?"

"No." She looked around, the sun was not moving across the canopy of glass. Morning was not yet transgressing, and it made her anxious. She began to fidget in place, bobbing in short increments, up and down. Distracting herself with the gentle pull of her own anxiety.

"Maybe you should, we are most at danger of what we see, what we seek—seek and you will find what you project." Zara's steeples rang bells to match her movement but he stood to avoid signalling a sermon, drawing away from the counter and pulling his grasp from her neck. "I'm sorry, Sarah. I worry. I am a shaman, and my purpose is to let you drown, but I hate to watch you struggle." He reached for his tea again, and drank.

Sarah turned her position to smug and looked sideways at Zara as he strategically envied his mint. "Then you'll have to help me."

Either the tea or a spell of ego left the old man's mouth in a parted smile when he lowered his mug. He placed both palms flat against the table and leaned into the triangle's tip, eager to make the calculation of its angles. He breathed in and out once, quick, no successions. "With what or how, can I help?"

"Help me see further."

It rolled like barrels of wine out of his mouth, full bodied, swollen with tannins. His laugh was intoxicating: the flowers and the shelves giggled wherever Zara's body was not. "You cannot see where your two feet already stand and yet you want to go further?" Zara pretended to wipe a small tear from his eye. "You are a dangerously brave young one, I respect that."

"Well…" Sarah put her hands above her head to hold the weight of water and her storing of it. "Help me find a map then… to—to place where I am now?"

"A good man once said *the map is not the territory,* Sarah. You'd do well to remember it."

At this, Sarah opened her bag, produced the small thermos and poured the warm essence into the little travel cup of its lid. The stand filled with honeybee wings as the aroma of nectar travelled cold to hot; it tickled the better senses of Zara's keen scent.

"I thought you had coffee?" he asked.

Sarah cocked her head, "No, tea. Honey lemon. Helps me clear my head." She sipped from the corner of pollen, trying to mull it into honey in her mouth.

Responsibility took the place of Zara's teeth and he wandered back to where he had laughed. "I just think you need to slow down, be careful. Stuff like that. There's a lot in our dreams that are more than just dreams."

"I know." Sarah washed the flecks of antennae down with the nectar half-made. "I think I'm on the verge of something, though. Or someone else is… and I have to see it through. Lest the archetypes here are right and the archetypes there are just… well, imposed synchronicity."

His eyes turned to church steeples and Zara looked hard at the words that Sarah had chosen, as if they were moons and the tide was in speculation.

As she put her boat out to test the lunar phases, Daniel came to mind. "Do you know about a river here… that's also there, Zara? The one that the boatman travels?"

The boat crashed hard against Zara's shore. "You should be careful of such things." The table, where herbs were mixed with magic, had two grooves where Zara's elbows had shaped the conversation of every wayward seafarer. He decided to rest his arms aside from them. "Some believe that the gate to Hellmuth resides somewhere inside our dreams."

"Hellmuth?"

"Fenrir stalks a lonely path, and in his maw is the shape of rivers. A boatman sorts his daily catch, and sends them off, finally delivered."

"Fenrir? That's… another name for Hellmuth?"

"That is its name. Fenrir the Great Wolf lays at the edge of three paths and in his mouth, the gates to the afterlife reside."

An etching was solid lead in Sarah's head. So heavy it drove her teeth through the lining of her tongue and left her swallowing the taste of afterthought. She winced, coughed and looked past Zara into a collapsing wall. "And in there lies a boatman?"

"Yes." He nodded without thinking of it.

"That's who I can ask then." Sarah spoke quietly to herself.

"What is it, Sarah? Have you seen yourself?"

"No. But I think I know where I can." She looked hard at Zara. "I'll need more red Reishi. Please."

He turned to fill a brown bag beneath the table. "If you plan on mixing them, don't increase the Capensis dosage as well."

Part 21: Breathe Out Of Your Body

Tannins from the root still circled the pores of her tongue, the arenas of taste that battled the salt in her mouth left Sarah dry and thirsty for something aside from dirt and water. More than what the toadstool could amount. She was hungry for sleep, not just dreaming, and it edged her as she flicked a fat muscle against the plated roof of her mouth.

A canker was brewing there; she poked its red ridges and slapped its sore swollen protrusion, bled its leechy, tooth-lined oval mouth in an attempt to distract from her thoughts. But it was all scalpel-removed circulation and she placed her middle finger flat against the bridge of her nose, and rubbed.

Every sense was electric as she lay, the sheets spiralled constructs on her ankles, sweat drawing them closer so they would not break, her stomach growling. Outside, the wind pushed flat against the siding and the house breathed in from the bottom, out through the attic. Sarah felt its respiration, its airway presence. Every corner and wall. Every space between the vents and floorboards. All the worming reticulation of a giant swollen centipede scuttling through ovarian absences. She watched it.

In through the basement.

Out through the attic

In through the navel.

Out through the crown.

An unflinching constant, slowing the ground beneath.

A burning sensation at her ankle dragged at her focus and a sudden change in momentum pierced her skin. It was like the bite of an ant, a miniscule pinch that spread quickly across her shin, but when Sarah tried to ignore it, trying to convince her mind that she was asleep, it spread further still. It wasn't long before the itch had sprawled its shingle-like impression along her foot and up her thigh, inflaming the thin layer of meniscus with its lemon juice claws… dragging the smoothness of her thoughts into ripples.

Sarah had to break; she bounced up to scratch the itch. And she itched. And her nails were sharp and they broke the skin and all the stars let themselves in until she could find comfort in distension.

Then she lay back again.

Her eyes so open that she was an emptiness for her room.

Moonlight aggravated the brushing whiskers on her narrowing eyes, its beauty no good for man's chin, though Sarah could not grow a beard to hide,so she was forced to lap in the white and was she powerful? Tide-stricken island or Mariner, driving off the coastal line?

She was awake.

"Ugh."

Sarah took a Charlie Brown fall and shook her head, sat up, swung her feet off the bed and stepped to the window where all the evening's light drove in with hammer pin hands to keep her awake. She grabbed the chord that dragged the thin slats of plastic down, pulling hard on the mechanism so that the blind dropped. But it only fell halfway, then stuck, the veil exposed and shadowed in equal parts to blame. Her body stood vertically planed in an infuriating boundary of light—horizontal on her penumbra—and made a triangle in her room that could only grow further. When she looked back, her bed was still illuminated, exposed by the shape of the light falling in.

Eyes narrowed again.

She turned back to the window, now with fire for teeth, and she pulled the cord several times, shaking its geometric surface into a spasm of organic roots, attempting to remove it from its cogs and free the gears so it could fall flat and block the light. But still, the Pythagorean thing failed, now splaying across her bed in a huge square of white exposure.

"Fine!" marked Sarah, and she left the blind.

Her hard, flat feet traced themselves back to the bed, and Sarah rose to and sat on the light of her failure, cross-legged in the centre of its gleaming triumph.

Sarah moaned. "Just a moment of rest and dream." And she scratched at her scalp.

She looked outside; the moon hadn't moved in ages. Instead, it stayed as bright as it could in the centre of the western sky, pounding into her room, teasing Sarah's gritted teeth.

She took a large breath in, exhaled slow, steady, and fluid with persistence. She closed her eyes again and tried to manifest the next best thing. "If I can't fall asleep, I'll just leave," she whispered to herself.

On her right hand, she met her thumb with each finger, counting while she swelled and deflated with the same words she had given to the room. Their fuzzy black ink sticking to the nest of her skin, compacting and building until she couldn't—

Relax, she thought, and counted again.

Five in.

Two hold.

Seven out.

Seven in.

Three hold.

Nine out.

Massage the clay until it holds its shape. Spin the table. Wet the air. Smooth the silky, pottery skin.

Sarah continued to count until the action was her palm's muscle memory, its fortune no longer attached to the actions in her head where she now pictured herself behind her self, in front of her body. Dislocated so that she could align her chakras.

Each one was an important marker on the stairway's rise: root, sacral, solar plexus, heart, throat, third eye and crown. Each one was designated to a sacred nature of dye: red, orange, yellow, green, blue, purple, indigo.

Each position on the energy totem manifested inside the liminal realm she was experiencing. She reached out to touch each chakra so that it became a deep hole. Sarah then filled them all with the correctly-coloured inks and let them churn into tidal pools of energy. Soon the colours and holes all aligned; Sarah lay back, adjusted her head in minute degrees—calibrating the signal—and left her thoughts clear to frequency.

Sarah's spine sang gold. When aligned, its position was moksha, and divine.

A bell chimed. It echoed inside Sarah's chest and she felt a phase shift coming as her awareness disassembled. The plane of her reality fell away and the ringing shook her until she was ejected from the top of her head. She had become incorporeal, astrally projected.

Finally, the walls talked back to her.

"allFniy," they said.

Sarah's extension of herself, now her, smirked when the words she spoke answered back from the veil.

"erPfetc," she said, and it bounced back again. "Perfect."

Sarah looked down at herself, still sitting on the bed, whereas she was afloat. She slid down to the floor to inspect the room. The walls were intact, the roof still white, the moonlight continuing to project its triangle of nuisance from the window, gracing her meditating body in a sheet of reflected light.

Sarah's conscious self nodded.

The closet doors were closed. Her room door was ajar. Her nightstand glowed beside a collection of coffee cups askew on the floor. The journal still lay close by. She continued to scan the room, and when a pin of light pierced her focus, it swung back to the nightstand: it *was* glowing. Sarah floated in closer, and her spirit passed halfway through the bed while the rest of her lay in the thin of it.

From inside the nightstand, where no light could cut or grasp, a brightness emanated. Sarah drew closer and exposed the jar full of sleep. It glimmered, as if overwhelmed with glow bugs… all mating at once, their neons showering the jar with fluorescent green, its highlighter tone spreading in thin shapes out onto the floor below the bed.

Sarah reached out to try to collect the jar in her hand, but it passed right through—her hand was without body. Recoiling as fear roiled up her empty flesh—as if she might turn to stone and fall out of the ethereal to break into pebbles upon the floor—she grasped her hand with the other and looked wide-eyed back at the mason jar. But the glow was gone; it had disappeared in her short moment of inattention. Stopped when she turned for a second to the presence of her mind.

Jutting her head to the left, Sarah tried to peer at the jar from another facet, but it had stopped illuminating in all landscapes. She let her shoulders drop. The interior of the nightstand had turned black and she could no longer see, her cat eyes only those of humans.

A cloud of unknowing swirled in small spirals from the roof of her mouth before it left for the ceiling where it would form into a single drop and drip like sand in the morning. The yellow mark that it would leave would never be noticed.

Sarah turned away, back to her physical self that sat cross-legged on the bed. Breathing in and out. Circling herself, she inspected the body she possessed during the day, its skin so pale, the pockets of dust under its eyes so full of irritation… its hand, sore and chapped and dry from the dust or the constant washing. The aura of light around it faded and grey.

Subconscious emotions for self.

Hands not made of structures reached out and Sarah touched her body's face, caressing her cheek with feathered fingers that she couldn't feel herself. She would not wake but instead know some form of embrace as she waited for morning to dispel the reeking night.

The body breathed out of time when a tear welled on its cheek and Sarah shifted in and out from the moment. A static flicker of self, her experiences crystallized and carved and placed on a shelf for her to idolize while studying.

Sarah kept petting the cool of her own cheek, back and forth and up and down, drawing her fingers through the sand of the veil until she fell into a state of non-thought and a self-induced trance took over, a meditation inside the astral projection.

Nothing compelled her then and so Sarah dove into the reflection cast by the wall of sand.

Opposite the exit, she swam into the castle's mouth through the bottom of her spine, the root of the self. Unlike the possessor who would make its doorway mouse the crown, enfeebling the pineal gland and taking over the conscious realm, Sarah sought to continue her dislocation, to further herself from the tethers she found in her home.

To do so, she had to ascend to the manifested physical realm.

The inside of her body was a warm and open pool. She knew it well, and resisted floating face-up in the water; instead she climbed information cables that spilled across her body in so many tripped-over canisters of ink and veins and static wire ichor. Sarah crushed them to soot as she used them to climb. Breaking apart their envelopes as she rose, dismantling the brain from the body entirely and ascending the cavern of her body towards the final disconnect.

Sarah passed the heart, its beating the fan chop whistle. As she passed, she grasped fat handholds of arteries left by the passage of weather on the mountain of her spine, and she squeezed them off, too. Removing the cord that fed the mouth, she kept climbing as meanwhile the cutting of air slowed, and the treasure box, presented by the woodsman to the witch, slowly turned bare. Her heart, just another antiquity in the ascension of gods.

Beyond the throat was the lantern of her pineal gland. A thousand days of summer stored, so bright that she had to shield her blue eyes from the Egyptian dye, leaving Homer's sea a dark red wine to the readers behind her. Sarah climbed with one hand now. A triangle of many points past the back of her mouth where it stank like ginger and lemon. Where the honey would smooth the concrete of her voice. She passed it and dug her fingers into the soft corpuscle of her brain, fleshing it away as a parasite might.

Then she was the worm, and every piece she ate fell to decay as she fertilized the death she created behind her. Sarah tunneled far inside, navigating by the light of her pineal gland lighthouses, ensuring she crashed and dummied herself on the beach's sharp rocks. She climbed the shore and tore the mucus off, like the pregnant wasp does her wings to the fig's trapping petals.

Enter the flower.

Pollinate until spring.

Once all was removed, Sarah could extract the fresh juice of her pulp. She was no longer herself, possessed of body; she was simply a pilot in a new shuttle. The fuselage, her brain. The throttle, her spirit. The sky, her body imagined as a goddess ready to rain. Sarah drank of her fruit and would fall into the dream state from a different place. There, she pierced the membrane with the only defence she had left: her sharp and darting stinger.

Through the layers, past the flesh and fat, Sarah drove beyond the substrate of her cranium that fertilized the roots of her third eye to the final spherical diaphragm of her brain, separating thought from wave.

Sarah's spiritus hovered above the opaque, pearl-coloured veil accumulating all the lack of angles. Where would the graphite tip of the mason's compass prevail on perfect circular protrusions? It could not. All things fall off from the earth-sized ball… excepting Sarah's poison stinger.

She turned upright, pointed her thin ovipositor down and then drove it into the veil; burying it to the abdomen and passing the final mucous membrane inside her skull.

The sensation was smooth, a bed of soft paint below a water's surface. Sarah's appendage surpassed the silt and popped through on the far side. She squeezed her uterus and deposited the egg within a stream of toxins into the far side.

Sarah exited her spiritus, borne in the egg, and birthed herself into the dream.

Part 22: From No Other Mother

First, there was an egg, and in it Sarah was fertilized. Then she was the fetus, becometh the crow, and she pushed her eggshell hull apart from the inside with spindly legs and soft feathers. She pressed hard into pieces of porcelain paper that snapped off into huge sheets so that the light might let itself in and colour her wings with black motion sky. So that it might blind.

It was there that Sarah realised her renewed control while she lifted a wing to protect herself from the spears that fell from the sun. With her other appendage she continued to break away at her birth and soon the fissures of her shell turned into canyon shelves and the entirety of the ocean's reflection poured into the carapace… Sarah, the fledgling, drowning to air in the natural light.

She winced once or twice, retreating to the rear of the half-caved shell, fearful of what brought dreams and what realms she might befall. But the soft call of what she knew, the territory and its ever-giving arms, drove her to the front again and she kicked out of the shell, tumbling out from its armour into welcome.

Grass met the thin fluid-filled sac, within which she stretched and pierced it, letting in a tight stream of cold wind that flashed her like darts. The sudden change in temperature—hot to cool—touched her skin the way a stranger might, and she trembled in the opening air before rolling into a ball to protect what little heat remained. But the turf persisted, its bed of nails further lancing the paper layer until all her limbs spilled out and the membrane failed completely. Sarah huddled her arms in, suffocating her breast in her knees, shivering. The tepid air like glass, an agitation of bleach, turned her blue as the grass soaked up the amniotic fluid and turned a furious red.

One by one by one, Sarah adjusted her eyes to the sudden white that had risen up while she burned into this plane, taking in the shapes and fractals all around her from in between her shielding arms and legs, book spines and broken luggage, shatters of bricks. Releasing the shock, she let what was usually stagnant air circle her lips and dry them of the birth that had recently bled there. The air was freshening, and its rigid bite loosened from her flesh. Hand by foot by mouth and disease, her body released the squeeze and stretched itself out long. She lolled onto her back; the bright light diminished into a soft moon and a trail of stars like breadcrumb stories fell away into another day's horizon.

Images reported back to her flashed from black to colour and back again until they stabilized. Sarah sat up, sore from birth and needing time to collect herself, allowing all the joints to fit in place and all the pieces of sightline puzzles to extract, rearrange and settle.

When all came to, she was in the tunnel, standing where the ceiling had been broken through and the dreamscape that blurred above had poured like sand into her path. She watched as her head projected a reel of images: an enormous, venomous shadow with great rasping arms crashed its swollen body through the ceiling and laid waste to the ground before reeling away, although she wasn't quite sure in which direction. The images faded and she was at the centre of where the beast had landed, in a crater several feet deep and wide in the tunnel's path, now just a fracture site of tumbled bricks and ill-stacked book stacks scattered about.

Her path, which led away in both directions, seemed to remain, but this spot had been mutilated. The forest dream above had let its substrate fall into the tunnel where it wove amongst the deconstructed architecture like a river of black tar that carried all manner of rock worm and pebble beetle and gold flute with its long winding serpentine tail. Amongst the dirt that had rolled in, various outcrops and shelves made by the unexpected departure of frame and structure had settled and small foliage-bearing plants, low lying shrubs, had started growing. An ecosystem had fallen into her tunnel and made itself at home.

Quick, dusty wings passed Sarah's face and she found herself following a granite-coloured moth around the opening. It travelled on a brush-drawn current up along the rocks and bricks before rolling away into the tunnel's mouth, traveling from the birthplace without any thought of dying. Dust from its wings choked Sarah's throat and she swallowed hard while she thought again, on the beast, clambering through her tunnels.

Sarah looked down the tunnel opposite the moth, it was mouth dark and ominous. She turned and looked to see where the moth had led; it was the same black vacuum for a few feet, but the swinging ceiling lights lit thin halo wisps in the path further down.

"That way, I guess," she murmured to herself as she climbed out of the crater.

Digging and dragging her way up the mountainous crevice, a sudden realization scratched. Sarah's nipples were brushing against the soft dirt, her knees—uncovered—scraped sharp corners of blocks while her spine arched and reflected the moon's silver pull as she rose. She was naked in the tunnel, and it made her wonder if she had entered a dream or if it was a persisting projection of self.

At the summit Sarah pulled herself up so that she stood full-bodied sun from the hole. A bird or reptile chirped somewhere above the halo, its noise echoing down into the holds of books where it ran away into the paths. Sarah tried searching out the source, but it faded into the shadows. Lips pursed and eyes buried into the brows above their reach, she took a moment to think.

"Why am I naked?" she asked herself, looking over her mother's labour. Her slender body looked fine, no bruises or welts or cuts. Some minor raised red where a rock may have pressed her. A little blood. Oh! Her knee, one cut where she had climbed across a block. Sarah lifted her knees one by one, inspected their pinnacles for chips when she noticed the shoes on her feet, white converse sneakers, without a mar, not even a speck of dirt on their clean white soles. "Okay, at least I have my shoes on, just no clothes."

Sarah put her hands on her hips and the chirping returned, crisp and tinny and Sarah thought to cover herself with her hands.

Eyes like predation in the shadows weighed her worth. Sarah shivered; the salt prickle tongue of Canidae sentries dispatching the better part of comfort sent electric waves up her back and she walked backwards, further into the tunnel so that she was covered in shadows.

It chirped again there, and what sounded like rolled dice were several rocks breaking free as two green eyes appeared on the far side of the crater. Automated cameras thinned the shutter and Sarah's eyes focused on the intruder. The chirping by the window, the sight of cricket heads… a fox.

Two red triangles atop its skull, and a tail dipped in riverbank mud. It had popped up from behind a gathering of rock and tripped all its followers into the well below, each marble screaming the way a stone does as it fell, with glints of light from every balance spot shimmering when the floor came up to meet its tired body.

Sarah watched the rocks split into pieces. When she looked back up, the fox had slipped its smooth polished body further down the tunnel across from her, leaving behind it a spectral trail of rust-coloured paint that strung out like a ribbon from its tail. The motion of its path stayed upright, frozen pointillism blur.

Sarah held her breast hidden and her body's entrance guarded.

Silent night.

When only the sound of starlight bathed the opening of green and brown and rock into a buzzing of unspoken words, leaving her a body of bees, did she talk. "What would you like, Mr. Fox?" Sarah's voice warbled across the open pit.

The fox lifted its paw and licked.

"I have someone to visit who looks a lot like you, you know?" Sarah continued to fill the space with words, trying to hide herself in lexicon. "I believe they are in the direction behind me. You're not from there, are you?"

The fox stopped tasting the rocks with its nails and turned towards her. Its small black lined face disappeared into the gloom dark behind it so that the green of its eyes expanded into emerald charms.

"Strange that you're in here," Sarah said to herself, shuffling her feet and turning in a hundred dollars of dimes to inspect the tunnel behind her.

"Srtnri'ganett yeraoh uee h," said the tunnel.

Sarah shook the hair from her head then shuffled back again, clockwise, but the fox had already moved. Before she could follow the trail markings of its oil-spill body, it brushed by her leg in a blur of white and Sarah stumbled, exposed herself a moment and then stood upright again, quickly covering her naked body. Between her legs, an unfettered trail of red lay hung in the air and directed her to the fox, now sitting on the same side as her, in the shadows.

"Don't do that!" she gasped.

The fox looked back at her with marked dotted lines.

"You spooked me, Mr. Fox." Sarah bent over and brushed at her leg while managing to keep one arm over her breasts and one suspicious eye on the fox. But it was wet. It was wet where the fox had made its sly move and Sarah's focus waned to her hand where she found it had been cherry dipped, all her fingers capped in wet paint of the same colour as the fox; on her legs was a fresh line of it, painted by the fox's tail.

Demon-sly were the fox's eyes when she met them, his mouth curled, his teeth bare and shining in a lantern's light. The animal's haunches sunk and then sprang sideways as the small canid jumped and moved further away, into the lit part of the tunnel, leaving an archway of red dye at Sarah's waist height, a fabric of dust and time weighing nothing in the open air.

Sarah looked again at her fingers, recognizing them as no longer naked, then decided to step into the static resonance of the fox's tail. The paint it left draped across her in so many raindrop garnets. She spun and twirled and the red left sequins of currant, a ruby-spotted dress clung to her body. Sarah clothed herself in the carnivore's marks and found relief from the shine that night had left on her skin. She smiled, inspecting her newly acquired dress in the cusp of the first lit lantern in the path. She looked back to where the red fox trail was slowly vanishing, the longer it hung in the air, but as a dress it seemed to linger and hold.

Sarah checked again with the fox. "Thank you." Then all the remaining lights dimmed at once to an ominous lower glow.

The elements inside the bulbs of the lanterns strung down the hall had all shrunk from white to orange and were bleeding off into black, making a quiet, gaseous noise as the magic seeped from the glass enclosures. Sarah listened to them, their falling frequency turning into hard flat lines. She followed their cries as they passed her and headed to where the hole in the ceiling still lay. Grey light. It was still moonlight, the silver still cast on the new terrain in an eerie metallurgy that itself flickered in and out, slowly slipping into a dark spell as well. Beyond the opening, through the opposite tunnel, all the lantern lights were flickering a thin, vaporous green.

Something was shaking them. Sarah pressed her hand to the wall to find that the whole world was vibrating. She again thought of a sac, bulging with black, brackish arms that squiggled like rubber sounds; she winced and pulled her hand back so quick that the wall might've been red hot.

Above her, the lights failed all together, an absolute black pulling all the colour from Sarah's skin, leaving the tunnel a sea of impenetrable vellum dark. Hard breath into her hands followed and she gasped at the splinters that now travelled along her skin, penetrating her with nerve-tight lines and fever thoughts as she tried to adjust to the dark. Her mind focused on the sound of a wet tentacle, and she shook all over as her arms pushed out from her chest and back in with her ice-pulled heart.

Don't move, Sarah thought, even though she couldn't anyway.

Just give it a minute. She had no choice. She couldn't see a thing.

The thing moved above her, getting further away, which meant closing in. Sarah's pupils swelled and drowned themselves in the thick of the black, letting the darkness in so that soon small speckles of vision would reappear. Her eyes adjusted by manipulating a single source of coloured light in the tunnel around her: the red from the fox's tail. Its smear of melting paper crimson skin left a trail of breadcrumbs that illuminated everything around it. Once her eyes affixed to its gentle glow, she could make out the path below her and the grin of the fox, waiting with eyes around the bend.

Above her, sea sounds continued to move; wet with sand and slick-backed, the membranous aqueous sinking bottleneck ship skin caressed the ground as it slurried back and forth, searching. Sarah took tiny, quiet steps, trying not to garner its attention, but it moved in languorous movements, careful not to miss the sensing of preyed upon things. When a pebble popped out from under Sarah's shoe and knocked against the wall, the movement stopped above her, and a noise, something like a fat trunk sniffing out the floor, took over.

Shit, she thought as she gritted her teeth and chattered in her chest.

Reducing her voice to scant plucks of a harpsichord, she bent down and spoke to the fox while the moonlight behind her shuttled into further spasms of harkening dark. "Excuse me" she squeezed out while rolling the sides of her mouth down in a fearful grimace. The fox churned its head, listening. "I think you probably already know where I'm going. Do you think you can help me get there… to the door with the wolf etched on its tunnel wall? I don't think I can do it without your tail." The words stumbled off her tongue as she shook with ballbearing uncertainty. "And I really need to move fast, there's something after me." Sarah mouthed *'It's above us,'* while pointing a trembling hand upwards; the sniffing stopped as if it was aware she was talking about it.

'Maybe it heard us?' She wanted to cry as a small piece of soil trembled and fell from the ceiling above her head. The movement started again, back and forth, creating a seasick sound that lulled Sarah's stomach into green, and she knew the moment wasn't long before something would purge.

'Please,' she mouthed, as little spots of wet built up in her eyes.

More soil fell as the entity above them began to move with more than curiosity. It lumbered the way a bear might, caught on a smell, wading through shallow water. It tracked and headed for the hole in the ceiling behind Sarah, where the dream had opened up into the tunnel. As it did, the moonlight above jarred and stuttered into complete and perfect black.

Sarah's eyes adjusted further, and she could make out the fox's head clearly. It pointed up, following the movement of the thing above their heads, too. "Please, we have to hurry." She reached out, trying to show how empty her hands were, how in need they were of help; the small canid made something of a nod before it headed further down the tunnel, leaving its fleeting trail of illuminated rust behind it. Sarah followed. The fox tail rolled right, turning 'round a bend, and the open space behind them vanished.

Under the tail's red guise, the spines of the books in the walls all looked like they had been infected with a sudden fungus. Scaly raised rings with deep socket pores had emerged from the brick titles as they smeared by Sarah's vision. She had never seen the growth before, and wondered how long it had been metastasizing, how much had she missed with the lights on in her tunnels? Had the single-celled amoeba and viral structures always clung with their owl feet to all the corners and surfaces, to all the pages and dust covers? Trying to catch longer glimpses of the bacterial polyps under the red light was futile; the fox's movements were fast, and Sarah feared losing him if she slowed. The layers of growth would have to wait. *Or had they already?* The point of lanterns faded with each rouge mar.

The path rounded a bend in the tunnel. As Sarah ran, the curved wall patterned into a film reel end with tall black lines that staggered and then collected the further they neared the end of the negative. In between those scratched markings, she would lose sight of the fox's tail. Its red fur dampening and then blurring into the epileptic white and black bar design until her chest tightened like a dried rind.

Every time she lost sight of the tail, Sarah pictured an arm reaching up out of the dark to grab her heel. The red algae on the walls slipped from her thoughts as she remembered the reason for her running now. It made the fibres in her lungs fray and work. From the thumbing of the page, which made her sweat words, soon had her feet sloshing through ink that she made with her concern.

All of her senses had turned to her vision's loss while she moved; little of her could make out smells or tastes or things to touch in the hard fertile vapour of the tunnel, but in short moments in between, when neither of her feet were on the ground, she could make another distinct something else. Not in front and not the waltz of the fox's black stained feet but rather the unnatural slap of something more naturally inclined to the sea following behind at the same pace as the pointed dog nose that she tailed.

She pictured her closet doors shaking and a black world falling.

Sarah ran harder at that, almost catching the fox, who in turn, sped up as well.

Wet cold sneaking feet keeping up behind.

"N oeme gb eisavnt." A kind of frantic bass came over the tunnel, words picked up from a thrown tongue twisted until fat in the middle so that they were non-construct, but Sarah recognized them even coloured-pebble scattered. It was the Beast. The reverberation in its voice was a needle in her glass castle chest and it penetrated through the brick until she was alert to the points of enemies, tines sharp and nefarious.

In front of her, bricks were falling as a rumble through the floor enraged and threw fits into the walls and ceiling. Sarah counted them as they fell, matching it to each slipping step that pulled like a vacuum at her ears. The numbers passed by her head so fast and came so often that she became lightheaded, and her stomach turned.

The Beast was moving faster than her, and soon the wind that came whistling up from behind turned into a building of storms. Sarah kept her ears back but her eyes still front and in them, in the crude red light, she could see the fox had bent its ears back as well, hanging its head low, a noticeable change in the position of its tail. Flat and suspicious.

"Not long now," whispered Sarah, and the walls listened from the bottom of their elongated wells. The noise from behind echoed ahead again, a loud booming darkness bellowed, "etetbaos o ngm," turning Sarah's glass lungs into sand that filled her sickening stomach until she swelled. She rolled with her distended skin into a crawling of leeches that bedded her until she was pale white. White like cheeks that bit the mirror flesh.

Wicked witch. Stepmother. Beast in the mirror of fables trailing her, its steps getting closer.

Another turn to the left and the fox picked up its pace, stretching its tail out into a straight spine to cut the morphing breadcrumb line into a small, almost impossible trail that Sarah had to squint to make out. The tunnel passed even faster, the tentacles' gait increasing at her back. She let a rivulet of concern wet the slick of her back and it tightened her all around as a door passed on the right. A recognizable one that lifted her white just enough that she could gain track.

Here it is, remarked Sarah to herself as her muscles became coal-spent embers, drawing the skin in close, scolding her inside out for running so hard. *The hall is next.*

Sarah clamped down with steeled girder on her tongue as she and the fox made a close turn to the left at a branch. Her shoes squealed under her pivoting ankles as her body fought to steady itself and her heart hoped for breaking. Her hand dropped to the floor to make three points that tore the skin of her fingertips on the fresh-broken stone. The burning sensation was unmistakable but she wasn't distracted: she noted the wolf's head, clearly etched on the wall, a beacon that flashed her stomach from green to a softer yellow.

As they continued, also unmistaken was the sound of eyes that replaced suckers for tentacles as the beast rounded the corner fast behind them, the arms of which dragged out to catch fish, the sounds of which laid out behind it for miles as cephalopodic appendages squelched at the finish of a brick sea floor, dragging a huge body of water through a tunnel smaller than its form. Echoes of it for short miles in front. In Sarah's eyes, reverberating, drawing the one hard sense backwards, overwhelming but yet to overwhelm and she found herself caught between hope and teeth.

She trembled as a thin memory of a doorframe cut with silver hinges and obelisk plate locks surfaced. It would stand sentry at the end of the tunnel, awaiting a change for neverending guards, its secured house a shadow unknown to the Queen's best. In its presence flowed the red ripple, the wake of the fox's rust-coloured tail, and as the door came into view suddenly, very near… the size of the squid grew upon their rudders just as the door. Sarah checked back from the helm and when she doubled up again, the door had welcomed the fox without opening, as if it had phased through and only she now stood in the way of herself.

It came on fast, even with notes of its arrival in the far back of Sarah's mind and she had to brake on her heels to keep from smashing into pieces on the frame. Her hand, a fine rabbit, chased the hole after the fox and swung the door open. Late for time, she dove into the dream, passing the ochre panels of the unembellished portal door without moments and she follied over the fabric seam. The dream gate's threshold. Nascent to the wolf. Sarah's body tumbled into the dust of her own feet as the door swung like pickaxes behind her. It slammed, and something slammed into it after her, buckling the concrete forms that held Sarah's stomach aloft, causing her to finally vomit.

On an axis where skull meets totem, Sarah's muscles pulled to spin and the world inside the dream morphed right to centre and steadied on the door... but it had stood despite her failing. Its frame spit dust, and its doorknob rattled as the hinges barked rust. The cry of desperate teeth gnawed at the other side, but it remained. The door stood black and solid against the storm.

The Beast howled.

Scrambling backwards with teeth-shaped nails, Sarah chewed with her molars and climbed into her throat, eyes on the door, heart in the tunnel of her chest, until she found a low pine tree under whose boughs she shrank and hid, the way a pierced deer might stumble into the brush. Or the way the stud teaches its fawn to hide in the nests of a thrush. Sarah placed herself in the magician's sawing box and waited for the cuts to disappear.

The door shook a moment more.

Then stopped with a wailing of red orca mouths retreating from the glacier cusp. They would wait for her. But the seal pup stood on ice that could be shelved.

Pressure slowed.

The glacier would not melt.

Sarah lay back on her head. She startled there for some time until nausea passed and her wind died to a brush with death. Sarah opened her eyes again and took in the dream

with the wolf

and two heads.

Part 23: Under Foot

With eyes closed and her hands clasped on her chest, Sarah stayed under the tree, smelling the scent of pine until something gentle licked at her face. She shot up, bouncing to her hands and knees in expectation of some menace, but she found the red fox beside her, leaning back with one front paw hung frozen in the air.

She exhaled the flash of weight gripping at her chest. "It's just you."

The fox nudged forward again and sniffed where it had kissed her, then smiled, turned, and left.

"Thank you... little light. I appreciate it." Sarah waved in waxing moons—as is the fashion with foxes—before she rolled back over and checked her cheek with her right hand. Holly red had streaked her where the fox had last been.

Between the network of slow needles above her, a meniscus bulging with mute sunlight drew its water down on Sarah. It was noon; overcast stole the sky to grey and she reached out to touch it. Conifer hands fell in her face and she made tea with those that stole her tongue. It tasted bitter and it woke her from her slumber state beneath the tree, setting her to standing up.

Sarah stood on a deer path that worked its way into the woods. A rabbit-sized trampling of the low-lying plants trailed towards the dream gate one way, but led to her purpose if followed the other. She sighed as she looked down at deer hoof prints mixed with human hands and recognized the forest spirit's marks. It had journeyed through here long ago, yet still its tracks laid with the other ungulate points, unable to be washed away if it rained, if it ever rained. Sarah checked the clouds, grey matte pulled across the sky by antlers, and no water that wasn't bound could leave them. Following the sky north, away from the door, she fell into the horizon of trees and then back on the path.

She sighed again.

It was lonely in this spot, in this dream. Behind her there were too many things. And at the centre of her purpose lay the uncertain. This dream, before, had not been pleasant, and if it led anywhere at all, she didn't know.

Again Sarah closed her eyes and examined earlier moments. Her father's voice, the dreams and where they went… the wolf's head. Her eyes opened and she inspected the path again: imprints from converse sneakers laid back and forth, overtop of each other, unable to be washed in the rain. She pushed her foot forward and made another stamp of herself in the mud; she would check from the change layer but it wouldn't come.

As Sarah walked, she took note of the trees and their positions, the mother pine well known on her right. A tall elm without limbs, standing without light or growth in the centre of a clearing to her left… a sapling she had dragged from another dream and planted herself in early versions of sleep. Sarah stopped and inspected its tiny trunk; it hadn't grown at all, dwarfed by the Gaelic alphabet that surrounded.

With her pointer finger and thumb, she grasped one of the elm's hand-like leaves and tested its marriage. A breeze pressed the little leaves of the tree and on its hands were smoke that wove a black fabric into her nose. She recognized the smell of the cabin, the forest trunks that burned in its wood stove. The loneliness. Sarah got up and continued on, not looking back at the tree… the lonely path stole all her attention.

It was after so many shadows of pine that she came to the clearing in the wood where a huge circular pad of bent grass had been made. From the chimney of a small cabin at the far end, black feathers burst, as if a thousand magpies cooked in its hearth and Sarah could see it, in her head, from above.

The cabin waited for her. Quiet, hushed. Its timber planks a black moss brush, its white molding a birch tree's blush. The window's hallowed hazy glass impenetrable to her eyes.

The door.

Red.

From behind the cabin that stood so bold in the gold carven letters of storybooks, a man appeared, coming from the wood on the far side of the lonely path which continued into the forest. He carried an axe on his shoulder, beech tree handle in his dark hand, polished metal claw at its end. With his other arm he dragged a tree to the centre of the centre, where a circular ring had been burned from the bodies of other trees. He stood there and Death was his name, and Sarah knew him, for a thousand times he had met his end at her hand.

Splitting the vaginal lips of tree trunk hips where the path tapered and left itself unaware, Sarah bore herself upon the clearing. Death looked upon her; she knew him by touch. He split the wood as she just had and always they were the same.

"What be you here?" he asked in the same wood-charred voice he'd always had.

Nothing was said except his eyes passing through her and she felt it in her throat where the afterbirth had stuck, and she couldn't talk.

He approached and swung his axe without fear.

Every time he swung at her, the sensation was surreal. There was always a smooth black marble weight in her stomach that took all the upright ascension and dragged her voice into inaudible chords. There was always a slight crack in the placenta ooze that let a hair's breadth of breath pass her throat, like a muted scream. There was always a sense of mortality, but time would always slow down, and Sarah would catch his axe—every time in every dream of this dream—turning it inwards to split his belly where hers would not feel well.

And Death would fall. And angels would spew from his mouth. And every drop of blood was black ochre stained.

Before the cabin's red door opened, Sarah had looked up and steadied her feet. In the doorway, the woman named Life appeared, smoke still wet in her drowning hair.

Life, the hag, she looked at Death and then on Sarah as she had every other day before. In every recurring nightmare or dream, she saw Sarah the same way, smoothing the soot of her threads into the deep wrinkles of her skin like tears before she approached. Arms outstretched, ready to surrender or flame the paper fan again. Sarah wanted to call out to her, maybe to stop, but there was nothing in her belly that could be forced.

When she came to Sarah with the stethoscope in her eyes, Sarah cut her down too, with the axe. Chipping the shoulder where fathers might have left her and skimming into the place from where she could not speak. And the hag fell, and she lay beside Death as they had always shared the same bed in storybook lore.

Sarah had spent them both and they lay: the woodcutter and the hag.

Again the path called to her, but this time with a kulning melody from the other side of the cabin, from where Death had come. Sarah followed that cattle noise, waded around the back to continue on the path she always had in the dream, and the possessive spirit—which always took her—picked her puppet body up on its strings and began charging her across the lonely path behind the lonely cabin.

Sarah was powerless, willing to be, experiencing this dream the way most experience any dream: without control, under the direction of some other force.

In those movements in another's hand, she knew the names of the trees, although she could not speak their names out loud. *Ailum for Elm.* Reach it and be deep.

Then she was stopped and the dream turned her so that she looked at a puddle where the mushrooms had grown like trees and the rotted trees grew from the fly agaric seeds. There, she could talk again. "Here, it is here." And she used her voice like a weapon.

Om mani peme hung

A log floated to the water's surface.

Om mani peme hung

The log turned into that of the wolf's body.

Om mani peme hung

And the wolf then looked upon Sarah and opened its jaw.

Om mani peme hung

Inside the wolf's throat were the heads of the woodcutter and the hag. And they both gazed at Sarah as she chanted, and rolled their eyes to white in agreement as their skulls rattled with rocks and tongue.

Om mani peme hung

Om mani peme hung

Om mani pe— the strings that held Sarah then loosed themselves and vibrated away to the tune of her mantra, setting her free from her dream's possession.

For the first time in this dream, she stood on her own feet, in control, in the cold ground of the lonely path. In front of her stood a gate, the open mouth of the wolf ready as a doorway.

"Fenrir."

Slate by slate, the camera position fell into a stack of handpainted backdrops, all of them passing Sarah, the hand crank operator, as she inspected the landscape of the wolf. Its matted fur was brushed into lumps that held pockets of insect seed. Its tail was rough and bent, its legs skinny and gnarled. On its back was a great hunch where its shoulders met like sentries that held its thick, submarine neck aloft. And on its neck was a head, gargantuan and raw where the fur had matted until fallen off.

Huge empty eye sockets sat in its head, and inside them, a universe of meteors that lit massive forges of gold. The forges illuminated the long staircase of its snout, battered and hungry with scars and worms. And hung from its snout was the maw, the glorious gate for which Hellmuth had made its home. Hollowed teeth dyed a tarnished brass for hardware, gums burnt black and affixed like a frame. The tongue, a threshold, held back a golden fleece in which the heads of Life and Death were suspended.

Sarah would stand inside the mouth as it swallowed the woodcutter and hag, their skulls disappearing into a convulsion of red fleshy muscles and mucous stain. They fell away into the dark of Fenrir's throat and Sarah would recount it as the falling of stars in the dead of a mouth.

Something dripped on her ear; when she turned to look, she saw her hand spitting blood. She had placed her palm flat up and the other flat down so that the lion thorn pierced both hands as she stood, holding Hellmuth open, caressing the fight of the wolf.

But it was crumbling down on her, platelets of carrion-spiced flesh fell as she trembled under the jawed door's weight.

It stank.

Rot and black sand built a miasma around her as she dropped a knee and the jaws bore tighter. Sarah coughed at the smell in her nostril while the wolf broke down around her, turning from a canine gate into a stream of tunnels. The wolf's mouth disassembled as mycelium broke the roof's flesh, digging through, overwhelming the opening with root.

She coughed again, and this time she fell into the deconstruction, stumbling further into the path as gates fell around her. Spirit hands, alive in the saliva, grabbed at Sarah's shoes and pulled at her to come with them. She kicked and fought, struggling down the tongue towards the throat, uncertain of where else to go. A light appeared in front of her: the uvula, red and glowing with infected flesh.

As the wolf's torso crumbled under the weight of these huge fungal growths, crushing it in their tap root hands like a can, Sarah fell over and the throat took her like a lamb, swallowing her whole. The mast, sturdy and tall inside her broke, throwing its white canvas sail into the ocean. She fell into the sail, wet and dangerous with sea water, and it enclosed her, overlapping several times as the briny waves crashed in and she was a silent film's drowning.

Falling into the back of throats.

Blinking out into the dark of night.

In all that white, there was a solid blip of cosmos that consumed Sarah as she drained into an unconscious state. Her chin turned up, her head back as she continued to roll and be wrapped and soaked in saline and canvas. It all stuck to her slow-motion skin, and she looked like unfinished marble.

With diaphragm chisel and muscular hammer, Sarah was sculpted as she passed the first world gate to be deposited on the other side onto a bed of sand and thistle.

A root or an arm lifted her up by the ankle. It slapped her twice, dislodging the slag from her throat; Sarah coughed and puked herself awake, upside down, the acid reflux from her stomach dribbling into her nostrils as bile fell across her cheeks and painted her geisha white in the world beneath the wolf, upside down.

She panicked but didn't flail for the muscles, taut in her throat, kept her silent and still as the arm laid her down on her back, a virgin birth into the dead realm.

From prone to even more innocent, Sarah stood tiny in a cavern's mouth. Long and hollow, its roof ordained with carved arches that started very small but grew to enormous heights as Sarah's vision took her further where the red burrow opened into a ceaseless lakebed and amphitheatre that stretched on into darkness. She tried to step forward, to advance as the bleakness had, but something caught her throat. She grabbed at it, and found a wet cloth wound around her neck. She followed it down her body to find it part of a beautiful dress. Behind her, the dress caught halfway through the wall through which she had entered and it had encased her in holy robes. Sarah pulled at the gift, ripping the cord from a puckering hole that swelled with birthful pain, freeing herself and the placenta along with it which fell, fat and bloody onto the floor, splattering an ichor honeycomb with it.

She eyed the placenta, breathing there with its fish lungs out of water, the veiny structure of white flesh pillars upholding nothing as it fed nutrients to the place it fell on. Sarah's eyes followed it back along the fabric of the white dress and found it fed her navel.

Four fingers in a diamond tried to separate the chord from the belly button but it was for life and therefore clung without dignity to her intestines. She could sense the dehydration, the aspiration of the placenta that lay in front of her as its walls caved in from the weight of the atmosphere down here. She could see it turning grey, wasting away without the cover of bellies and, like an animal, something without reason came over her as she watched the thing, bloody and helpless, feed itself of dying. Diving to her hands and knees, circling the organ, Sarah readied for its meat.

With four fingers and her teeth, she tore apart the placenta, bursting its ventricles with her dental implants. Chewing the flesh down with molars and bicuspids. Tasting the scent of blood with her long snake tongue, she devoured the organ and her umbilical cord until all that was left was her covering. Her white dress.

Sarah stood and wiped the blood on her chest with both hands. The imprint made the shape of a bird, and she was reborn in death. And rebirth made her sick and she had to hold her breath by covering her navel, pretending not to vomit in her chest. When she did, she swallowed it back, found feet again in her purpose and walked further into the underground, holding her belly button. Protecting it from stitches that bled.

She stepped out from the small clearing where the root had admired her body so, and she walked towards the black sheen of a lake. There was no path to follow, only a series of arches that each led one to the next, between half-spherical antechambers, walled with red-veined roots that grew down from above. Every chamber opened one into the other, bubbling up like soapy water in the magician's hands. Each one successively growing larger from one to the next until meeting at the centre of Sarah's focal point. There, the space at the centre was astronomical. A cavity for Saturn's tooth left by skilled sculptures, its top half filled with black, the bottom, a lake coloured like no darkness ever had.

She felt an unfamiliar frequency all around her as she walked. A sense of thinning-out that was empowered as her dress scraped along the black slate ground, where splashes of sand had been laid in some winter long before. The train of her fabric left a trail of hooks in her swaying hips but echoed no sound, just trace. It made walking an uncomfortable thing as Sarah stumbled from one well to another, each one deeper and deeper with mud. Every single episode clouded and tied up with the vocalizations of the frequency that muted her footsteps like pockets where the world would normally fill with aether. Every one of them a raindrop with a history. Buzzing.

Trying to match the sinewave left Sarah beyond her wavelengths and she quickened her pace to the lake, hoping that it was a cloud to be passed. But the storm kept coming, filled with her voice, echoing back in miniscule facets of rain. It filled in around her feet, dragging at her with incubus fingers that wound their way up from the ground, personifying the sand into clutching claws, reaching for her thighs, for her privates, for her gown.

No. My navel! She screamed in her head and the noise of it doubled back

Sarah gaped at the sound of herself as it overwhelmed all thought, and a migraine of steel clamping on her sinuses had her vomiting from the strain, thick with blood and bile, dehydrated but wet enough to splat into the sand beside her shoes. When it scattered into the ground at her feet, the noise stopped, the hands ceased crawling, and all absorbed into the mud.

She stared at the spot, huge illustrated circles of puke left all things gained, now lost. Quiet all around. Under her dripping eyes and the spark of ember, Sarah straightened up and began to walk again, again towards the core of the cavern. The sound, now completely gone.

Arriving at the central threshold proved the grandiose nature of the chamber, the weight of eyes on its stretching planet of space. Sarah stood mute in the face of a god realm that stretched into fractal scapes, Iranian church vaults, long strides in the ochre wood. She looked up and out at first, noting the perimeters of the antechamber disappearing into the fade of its own dark sky, each knot of nothing tying everything together into a blind bind.

No red veins grew in the central chamber to illuminate the dark void as the other spaces had; instead, when she looked into the impenetrable lampblack of the water, the contrast was so great that the sky lit up as if it were white, leaving Sarah without shadow in the lack of reflection.

A portal of tears dripped an oil lacquer into a repressed image of childhoods kneeling in prayer. The back of her knees fell out behind her, and Sarah dropped further into the church pews of the chamber's unending walls and there she wept at the dark, letting her essence swell then disperse into oblivion.

Time did not move in any noted direction as she sat at the dark of the lake. Later she would think back that she may have never looked at the water to begin with, but she knew something had passed because the rowing came.

Flat wood oars paddled in the water's ripple, pushing the sheen of liquid with tidal inches against the beach's placement. Sarah watched it come.

Him come. A man in a boat with an oar that parted the inky water.

He rode upon a small canal boat, a skinny long thing made of ebony wood with a sharp curving hull like a scythe. He rode upon it as if the boat were a horse and he, the black rider.

Inside the flock of birds that stormed around him, his eyes shone out like lightning, keen on Sarah and the shore. The birds, unable to calm, made reverberations of the cave all around them, and Sarah's ears filled with their wing's feathers; she could feel the puddle of her soul muddy as the blackbird and yellow-beaked whirlwind descended.

From the chaos, his imperious form reached out a haggard, bony hand. He stood waiting and Sarah paused, unable to form thought until he wove his fingers up and down, grasping at the upturned air in beckon.

She stood to meet him with her shoulders and head drooped, with her eyes wide and the same chaotic bird sounds buzzing in her chest.

Him. He whose name was without calling and she called to him.

"I… I am here for your help. Charon." And she was as small as words before the stone.

The figure's fingers made a slick motion of pinky to pointer in rolling succession, a carpet unfurling, quick-step mantra. Then the hand returned to the bird storm and he said nothing.

"I am here as my father wanted. Here at the River of Acheron."

The boat slowed and beached beside Sarah.

On a painting, the artist would pour a line of white from above that separated the two entities, slowly filling a flipped pyramid until a barrier formed from the ground over Sarah's head. The white was obvious, thick and blurry of the image. It was in all intentions the authors required, splitting the space between her and Charon.

The stage backdrop's motion jutted into advance, engaging the lower jaw and stuttering out the atmosphere of the play. It creaked with lack of oil and played all the versions of artistry in as many ways as possible, to confuse the crowd and take away from the staggered start. Composers lifted, lights shied back to main, the actors all came to stage… but the rusted extension proved constant and dragged all things sideways.

"My father said you could help if there was an issue."

Again, a Jupiter eye opened in the swirl of cartilage and feather and the hand reached out again. Its long bony fingers, held together with crinkled tape, cracked all the joints as it settled to hang in the air, open to charity, the common plate of pastors.

Sarah looked beyond the long line requirements and tried to pierce the white barrier, then the barrier of Aves, but no movement nor stirring behind the many walls. Charon stood on his prow, unflinching, and Sarah could not see beyond the lack of such effervescent ego: it was just a blur of wings, a flock of gulls leaving the beach with a flurry of clattering shells ricocheting in the wind.

"I don't have both coins." The words came from Sarah much the same way poison might froth at the mouth, bubbling out of her to fall on the ground so she might inspect the failure of her stomach. "I only have one, but I… I'm not even sure what's supposed to happen with two."

The hand didn't move.

"Dad said you would know what to do."

A whole star aged in the silence before Charon broke the vacuum of its space. "I would know what to do?" Pitched like a hammer, his voice split Sarah's teeth in her head, each syllable a crack of the anvil that bleeds or is bled. "He said I would know what to do?" The end of each word dragged its chains through the dirt as the carriage pulled another king through the mud. "What to do about… what?" Hard consonants ended the way jaws might on tombstones in the dark.

Sarah shook at the cold of his voice but hid the shiver, digging her feet into the shore of the river, she stood tall. "About… about all of it."

The swirl of feathers halted and positioned itself as if an eyebrow had been raised before carrying on. "All of it?"

"I guess…" replied Sarah. "If you can?" She realised her confidence had been found short of her ankles.

"Let me get a look at you." Another socket for storms appeared in the confusion of feathers and in slow painful slugs, a white sphere birthed itself from the seam of an open sore. Bone cold and covered in fractures, as it exited it left a scar among the outer covering of wings that stretched and expelled with blood. The sphere grew and tilted up. As it did, it exposed its hollowed sockets, and nose and teeth and mouth. A skull pushed itself from the womb and on its crown, a halo shone of silver.

The skull peered into Sarah, its eyes nightmare-kept, the white goddess' pools of midnight. Gospel for Saturn. Covens of pitchforks and knives.

Sarah felt a chill in its eyes that was beyond the one in her body and bones. It froze her to the place she had been born, and in it, she had always been cold.

Charon's grin opened and fumes of green poured out as he spoke. "Ah... yes. Sarah, I presume, one of those that slipped the thorn and refused to feed the worm her blood, yes. I remember you."

"You do?"

"Of course." Charon's head rattled and it twisted in an uncomfortable fashion, as if its neck was on hinges and rods. "You let a coin go, you've misplaced your death and now, most of all, you're lost."

"I am... I am lost. Can you help me find my way?"

"Find the coin. Find your death. Find your way."

"But I don't even remember losing it in the first place."

"Ah." Charon let his teeth chatter and chomp. It gutted the light around their clearing and left rats' feet to fall from the mound of his maw. "You don't remember losing them at all? But it's why you stand on the shore and not in my boat... it's why the Beast chases you across the realms."

"The Beast? What do you know about the Beast?" Her eyes were halos on the brain.

"Simple humans, so much is beyond them." He swayed his head back and forth and continued chattering before speaking. "Don't you feel the good claw that the beast put between your beak? Now you can't clamp shut." The skull looked away, searching the perimeter of nothing and when only blackness continued did he resume. "By starting the crossing but leaving it incomplete, you've left a great space for your shadow... don't you see it? Opening up its own portals to access the realms and tunnels temporarily, stealing coins, daring to cross my rivers in search of deaths... These are all just equivalent exchange of course, whether it bothers this one or not… Coins are words for alchemy, no? Aren't they?"

"I don't know."

The boatman moaned. "You've started an exchange of two coins… obols to be exact, and only offered one obol in return, now there are two and each one has a potential to meet the Cartography Door, assuming one destroys the other." He smiled in the way a cadaver might. "A potential for either has been left ajar."

"What is the Cartography Door?"

"Hmmm, didn't your father tell you? It's *the* door."

Sarah swirled with the riddles while the boatman tapped his fingers on his oar.

"Can you take me to the Cartography Door? Dad said I had to find it."

Charon clamped his bony hand on the oar, leaving an imprint like hash marks for the dead, and he spoke with seething. "Coins lead to doors."

"Is that the coin the raven gave me?"

"Tricksters, ravens… up to no good, thieves to one side." He swung a rickety set of bones into spirals. "Don't you have any questions that don't answer themselves?"

Sarah thought while the birds whorled and then asked, "What if I gave the Beast the coin?" The boatman's jaw slammed shut and black poured from the spaces between his teeth. "To satisfy it, so that it leaves me alone."

Charon shook his skull. "Foolish, so little concern for your ties… if you did that, then you'll have lost for sure, and it will only come for the apple."

"An apple now?"

Charon leaned in close, and a miasma poured from his tongue, filling his eye sockets with vapour. "Death, Sarah. An apple is the knowledge of death. Give up the coin and you will show your belly. When you are exposed, the Beast will surely come for your guts."

Sarah swallowed a lump and turned her head. "Okay, what about the portals? Where is it opening its own portals?"

"From the same place you are," he answered.

"But it can't go… well, no." Sarah looked down, chewing her thoughts. "I can't go all the places it can, can I?"

"So many questions you humans have, nothing solved on your own, it's a wonder you ever make it anywhere at all." He chomped his bottom jaw only, letting it flap up and down with relentless mocking. "What's important is that you lost part of your ticket, and in doing so you've left a potential for yourself to take it. Shadows take the most space when under the faintest of light."

Sarah looked back up at the skull.

"You are now in the process of either becoming one or the other and both of you have equal rights, a dangerous position if you ask me because either one of you could finish it now and you both seem eager to." He made a crude smile and then began to retreat into his cover of birds.

Sarah placed a finger on her mouth and looked down as she thought. "This only seems to create more questions."

"Even the end of the book is too early for a human to grasp its meaning, I guess."

Charon returned his hand to the top of the oar, positioned above his other to rest, to steal back his peace before pushing with an unseen shoulder, to free the boat from the shore.

Sarah didn't look up, instead puzzling her own thoughts. "So I have to complete the exchange my father started? Could I just use another coin?"

"You don't have to do anything. If you could have, the Beast would have already."

"Well, why are there only two coins?" She looked up and found the boat moving away and her toes turned to frostbite.

Charon shook his head. "Equivalent exchange, Sarah. There's only one." Then he pushed again with his oar and the boat lurched backwards, falling away into the slick of the lake.

"What?" The boat was moving faster. "No, wait!" Sarah found herself barking at the boat. "Please! But if I have both coins, then what?"

"Then you'll have a choice." He pushed the oar again gently. "But the Cartography Door is the only way to stay."

"What does that mean!?"

The boat continued to move away, and Sarah found herself in pursuit. She splashed into the water, its cold like a spiny finger looping the corset of her skin, pulling her chest taut and forcing her heart to thin with contraction. She shrank in the shallow but pushed into the depth. "Please! I have more questions! My father, do you know wh—" the bottom of the lake dropped off in a smooth glass sliding, and she was up to her mouth full of throat in the black water. The sudden shot of Baphomet's breath at her tonsils pulled them right off and left her breath so breathless she could not afford to swim, and she sank.

Sarah was feverish at the water surface, but it was so cold. She tried to scream out again but the boat was gone or the surface too dark or the knife in her veins too sharp to just cut; it severed her tendons from worth and the water rushed in further on her as the white dress clung and weighed and pulled.

Last hand straight up, positioned as in cathedrals touching god, Sarah hung, vertical in the water, sinking down, bubbles carved with soapstone spilling from her mouth. The white dress, an anchor, her body slender in the cold drowning bleak again.

The surface was ice anew and she could feel her father leave the clutch of her hand in the empty palm of the boatman.

Part 24: Must Be Dreams

All that was left sacrosanct was the river of oil that passed through the surface of the coffee, from one end of the cup to the other. Leftover blood from the caffeine beans? Soap scum in the bottom of the cup? Fluoride maybe, from the water, chlorinated… fluoridated? Or a reminder that the only sacred things are those that divide us, these are the things without question of what they are, for they are the formation of the line or its wording of the question.

Why am I divided?

Why is it that I don't know which side of the black bean water it is that I reside on?

Why am I still in the middle?

Edna had left a spoon in Sarah's coffee, its metal finish unfollowed as it disappeared into the black surface depths. Lifting it proved nothing: it slipped any residue as it broke the water's tension at the surface, returning with wild diver's eyes that give you the bends. It was as quickly aware as it wasn't when back in the coffee. Sarah stirred the flat mixture, no cream or sugar or milk; she never had, that's why the spoon was so clean, and she couldn't figure out why it was there.

"Mom?" Her voice was someone else's when she talked to her mother. She loved her, but her mother did not, or she did, or she loved herself. What was the sense of things in the discordance of wealth?

"Yes?" Edna turned from the stove, where she always had been in every chapter before, stirring something, unaware of its presence. Fiddling with the shape of her shadow, cast by the light of the overhead fan in the sheen of the induction range. Edna wouldn't smile there, with her red lipstick all worn off years ago.

Sarah stirred the spoon again, lifting unseen silt from the bottom of her cup. It would surface though, add to the oil, make the division a little wider without anyone the wiser. "You left me the spoon?"

Her lipstickless mouth smoothed out to the right, pulling her cheek on the left and leaving her in a choice of cards. "So you can take the bag out?"

"What bag?" Sarah asked as she looked down into the split surface.

"The tea bag." Edna spoke from far away.

Floating where the oil slick had been was now a mesh bag filled with herbs, tied to a string, with a small paper tag hanging down the side of the cup. Sarah tilted her spoon back and released the bag's essence from its steam-trap mouth deflating on the surface, all the air escaping with it and heading for the window... the red window, tinted strawberry.

"Oh, right." Sarah's voice was not her own but she went back to drinking her tea without sugar or milk, or cream.

It was warm in her belly and it made all the cold feet go away.

"Some mornings, I swear," huffed Edna.

A pause then came between the rising sunlight outside and the scattered silhouettes of empty vines from the windowsill. Everything was silent, dust particles still life frame bottled. Sarah wanted to twitch or shiver as someone walked over her grave. But she didn't; one foot was already there in the morning calm and silence.

Edna turned again from her conversation with her daughter to look once more at the stove top. A brass kettle on its surface, the handle varying colours in the heat. Steam disappearing into an overhead fan that wasn't on. The chimney just the right length so that everything pulled into its effect, from the basement to the sky to somewhere else.

Sarah turned too, to the woods.

Everything outside pulled at the string tied to the kite that was her chest. Always so full of air. Always stuck in hungry trees. The language of leaves beckoning her sense to loose itself from small, unattuned and childish hands. Ones that ran when a parent would turn. Ones turned over by nuns and slapped red. Her hands, hot and beaten.

Why so many variations of things? Sarah wondered as she looked at the coniferous trees blowing one way and the deciduous another. The branches spinning and twisting in slow, heavy-handed wind left all the leaves spiralling from their stems; manic things, desperate to be upright and collect sun, turned brown as she watched. Brown with fall. Brown with winter. Then green again as the light hit just right and they turned their bellies up to hold oysters and collect favourite rocks.

Sarah sipped again at her tea, and it brought her back to the kitchen where she breathed in the swell of its spell. The resonance it brought from memories far away, in the room beside and above and outside of it. The kitchen, the only place Mom seemed to be. The tidings, filling up the onset space of Sarah's thoughts. She sipped again and decluttered with the scent of lemon ginger, mint too, maybe, juniper berries. When she set down the cup, it was heavy like her eyes.

Edna's ear twitched at the flat sound of the dismissed cup on the table where Sarah sat, and she decided to confront the gold seam that ran a streak through her pottery, head-on. Without turning, she asked her daughter, "So… how was your night?"

Sarah rolled her eyes up to where her mother stood, hung over the stove with so much weight tied to her chest. Waiting for more that never came, her answer walked with braces on its legs. "It didn't go as planned, if that's what you mean."

Turning from the flat induction magnet, mother looked sideways at daughter from between her hanging arms, setting her half-mask expression on her bicep and hiding the words with her elbow. "You go in with a plan?" The question was graffiti written on the underside of the train car, paint in a place that only the paid hands would see.

"Sometimes."

"What was the plan this time?"

"I don't know."

Edna slid backwards with cold hands on a hot stove that screeched as the temperatures despaired, and she stood up into the opposite of monks, questions for the unfaithful in golden robes. "You had a plan, but you don't know what it was?" She walked over to sit at the table in front of Sarah, who played with the paper tag on her tea, flicking it with distracted fingers so that it swung as a metronome between the two shades of green in the room. "Or did you forget it when you got there?"

"No. It was more like… I thought I had an idea of what I was doing but I don't think I had a layout… exactly," replied Sarah.

"Ah. So, you knew what you wanted but weren't sure how you would get it."

There was cold in Sarah's eyes; it scratched at the surface of the glass and left a frostbite scar she couldn't quite shrug off, leaving her staring in strange directions. Down, to the side, eyelids bundled up like sled drivers burying the black in her eyes. Following the trails that wind directed and the Moon's positions suggested. Sarah wandered about the room before returning to Edna and the ice-capped whale.

"Did you know what you wanted?" asked Edna.

"I wanted to know more."

Sarah pushed at the carcass, cold and half-chewed by Greenland sharks, their bodies centuries old, the carcass just as many. "I tried to do something that Dad said I should do… something he told me was important."

Long and sharp, a tooth scribed a line across the surface of the cetacean's skin and it split, dumping black flesh into the ocean, stirring the hunger of the slow moving fish further. Beside the ice break where the insides collected, every word is a sharp jawline pushed beyond the maw of its keeper.

Sarah watched the predators on her mother's belly and turned her lip in solitude with water's process. "I'm sorry."

"No. No, please." Edna let the rest fall into their mouths and turned to her daughter in famine, grasping one hand in the other. "It just surprised me." She looked past Sarah. "Dr. Pillapatti said it would come up eventually—I just…" Edna smiled, and cracks from years of bad luck mirrors were strewn across her face as she put herself together, missing pieces and all. "What did he ask you to do?"

"It didn't work."

"Oh."

"So it doesn't matter."

Edna sighed in a way that cooled the tea.

Sarah let her hands rest in Mother's as she asked her, "Why do you think he did it?"

"I don't think he was well." All flows into water and every ghost will bathe in milk for their skin's purest colour.

Sarah pulled her hand from Edna's cupped palm. "That's what everyone says."

Edna sighed again and something metal fell from her eye, piercing the tabletop behind her hand. The noise reverberated in the house's ribs, beating in tandem with the heart of the home, pulsing with the sequence inside her tears. Hands curled into fists and lips turned under teeth as the pace of the noise increased and soon the room was nothing but full and Edna scratched at the table where her hand was a fist beside the tears she bled for sharks.

Sarah reached out again.

Honey lemon tea. With ginger.

"He talked a lot," Edna began. "He talked a lot about your dreams. He was probably more interested in them than even you are now. We fought endlessly about it." Edna's look at Sarah was a wall of reflections. "About your dreams, that is—he said that you wanted to live there.

"I tried… I tried to convince him that it was normal for little kids to think in fantasies, but it wasn't something we should encourage—not in the way he encouraged it, anyway."

Sarah's brows furrowed up into multiple thoughts but only one spilled out. "How did he encourage it?"

"He would take you into the woods and fill your head with stuff he read on the internet." Everywhere, Edna's foot was tapping, her knee shaking, nervous nerves ululating at the hip where a child once sat expelled into the ground through shoes. And Sarah felt the vibrations all the way through her as they pushed her closer and closer to the edge for which she needed peaking. "He kept telling you there was something to it, like you had stumbled on a treasure that none of the world knew about. He made the dreams and the gates in the woods so much more important than the daytime that you became obsessed too, as obsessed as a man who spent his days and nights on the computer looking for portals and myths and magic… for—" Edna threw her one hand in the air and watched the space where a ball would've been, expecting some memento to appear and Sarah saw it too, the spot was a sphere that was missing— "for obols and Hellmuths and where the hell they all were in the real world!" Edna's voice rose into a network of black roots that grew from her feet and spread across the floor. They slipped across the tile, bit the grout and nuzzled into the corners beneath countertops, spreading a grape wine seed that replaced the penumbra of every object with a thirsty knot. "It just pushed you further and further into a fantasy, a really dangerous fantasy and for what? Was it for you, Sarah?"

"Mom?" Sarah squirmed beneath the falling sky and its fragile counterpart the ground.

"He was looking for a way out, too and it turned out to be dangerous!"

"Mom?" Sarah squeezed her mother's hand, just enough that her heart knew, and the roots receded.

"Sorry." Edna swallowed the next few lines of expression and forced a smile. "It's just, you know, I'm worried 'cause you keep looking, too. In the woods and in your dreams…" She feigned a smile.

"I'm not just looking for a way out…" The coin and all the tentacles in her tunnels reached out as she spoke. "I'm looking because something is looking for me."

A kind of bewildered knowledge overtook the room and Edna leaned in close, as if something might be listening, like she was at a door but something black was on the other side. "So, run?" she finally said, so small in her voice.

"I did that already."

Edna looked at the door as if it might break open right then and lowered her voice to the worms. "It almost killed you last time."

"I think it's still trying to kill me. I have to finish whatever's been started…"

They met eyes and a polish covered all the white and cream and green and black, leaving colour and shadow all the same clear-coat gloss. "Your father said something similar to me just before it all happened." She looked with molten lead. "I trusted him to protect you, and it's hard for me to lend that trust out any further…" She looked with pin cushions. "I can't help but see your father in those eyes… somehow even now it's still got a hold of my trust."

Sarah squeezed her mother's hand again. "Now it's me you're trusting, Mom, with *my* life." And she smiled.

Edna's lip quaked, and that was seed sown. All the tendrils in the room slowed and moved to their darkness while a light descended upon thought.

"Did you say obols?" Sarah asked.

Edna nodded. "Yeah, whatever the hell those are anyway." Happy to move away from graves. "The *right* obols and where they were found. That talk was always at the kitchen table."

"The right obols?"

Both parties took in a long breath.

"He said you could buy your way in… but it had to be right."

Sarah was suddenly full of scarabs. "Did Dad ever say where they actually were? I need to know where they are."

Edna thought about the question, skillfully turning it over in the furrows of her soil before letting out an exasperated puff of gasp. "Yeah, he did. It's why he bought this house… it backs onto the right forest."

Part 25: A Trail of Gates

From inside the backyard, where in the summer, dandelions grown were brewed for tea; where zucchini stalks waned, their fresh flowers pulled from the vines for frying; where soil, rich with waste for feeding, was churned and tilled and planted, Sarah parted the snow melt with her boots. Around her the fruits and green were unpicked herbs and brown shoots, they stood deaf-mute, unable to pronounce the vowels of the season. She passed them with her collar high, her eyes on nothing but the dark green pines of the forest in front of her as it broke, turned to ocean parts and welcomed the tide.

She took a path, known only to her as it had worn in the same treads of her boots for days; no other pattern split the traction of her toes.

And she mumbled to herself, her head turned to steam and wires. "The right coins?" she said as the thin hand of snow made bridges for her feet across the soil. "Where in the whole world could the right coins be?" She spoke, belittling her query. "Why, in the forest, of course." Upwards inflection. "Why else would he move us here but for some surreal line of dreams?" Sarah ducked her head beneath a low branch; when she slowed beneath it, something had changed. "Only Dad…" Her voice trailed off.

In the skirt of snow that had banked the pencil-dipped stippling beneath, a visual oddity had occurred: a separation growing between all the layers of things. An eight-bit, two-dimensional plane had opened, splitting the physical textures that normally met. She bent over to get a closer look beneath the spreading layers and found the snow was now floating several millimeters above the ground, no longer sitting on it at all.

Questions like: 'where was the coin' and 'how far does gold grow,' became small.

Pupils turned microscopes with lenses several shades of inquisition deep, flicked one after the other under the strain of the space between. The two solids under examination—the snow and the ground—were expanding, pushing themselves apart like two metals from similar spheres.

The query pulled Sarah's skin taut along her scimitar-shaped strain to the point that micro-fissures opened like mouths on her skin. Sarah's sweat swelled and poured into little cracks in her envelope, and it stung, and she reared back to scratch at the agitation, allowing all the forest to settle under the cones of her vision. Red. Green. Blue. A lower dimension where nothing was touching any longer.

Slowly, the purpose for her visit was misplaced and Sarah focused on the dwindling constructs of her reality. She wondered if this was another episode or something more serious, a dislocation from the ground?

Every layer of molecule had come apart, expanded like an exploded diagram. Sarah opened her eyes to the snow-laden topography of her wood, where the trees and bark were separate, the needles and stems apart, the snow and ground divided… individual particulates of frostbitten hands. The symbols and sigils that made up the lay of the letter of the land were as printed on glass blocks and split into fragmented, divergent strands.

Sarah rubbed her eyes, even pinched her soft skin, growling at her own stupidity when the welt cried back at her.

But the dissection of things remained. They hovered in distinct entities apart from each other, carrying shadows on metal tethers that hung beneath their bodies like pulled-back layers of skin.

A fog rolled from Sarah, breath billowing from her gaped mouth. In the wind's current, rudders and sails, her breath split its atom open right in front of her, exposing the makeup of the flat and cornerless. It wandered to her right, where a great ash tree stood with its branches flung tall and heaving into the torsos of demiurges, its thick amber bark running lengthwise, in contrast to the fall. She stepped off the path, walked up to the tree, and wrapped her hand around the bark, a completely disparate entity from the pale pulp beneath. She pulled it back like a door to expose the tree's naked flesh to the soft of the sun. When she tilted her head and looked up, Sarah could see all the way to the sky.

Everything remained floating apart. The berries from their stems, the stems from their trunks, the trunks from the ground. The ground, all different planes, diverse frequencies, layers of alive and no longer interfering. Static. Resonant. Sarah put her arms out to collect radio channels and steady herself while she made circles and spun, letting all the layers of air splash along her fingers. Then, pigeoned home, she stepped back to the path for a sense of direction, trying to piece together the pieces not together. *Where is the forest taking me now?*

A bent-over tree appeared to the left. Sarah dropped her arms and her shoulders fell without the weight of wings. "Oh." The word fell from her mouth in a bubble of blue ink. "It's you." The pulled-over sapling with the circle mark, the beginning of other paths.

"Of course it's you." She pointed at the tree gate's centre, its innards a thin haze of potential liquid.

"You know, you're kind of like bad liquor, you pop up when some people might think they need it most but… I know I'll wake up on the floor after a visit with you."

Sarah began pacing in front of the tree, breaking apart grades of air as she walked. In her head she pictured herself drinking a thick, amber liquid that turned to tea, then to mushrooms and Sarah remembered Zara's beautiful teeth spelling a story for her.

"But…" and she hummed while scratching what men would hide with beards from the new moon. "You could be one of three," she whispered to herself. "Zara said there were three *gates*."

And in the gates in her head, there were coins, and they were plentiful.

She half-crouched to surprise the tree, knees bent, arms out. "The coins? Do you know anything about them?"

The tree refused to answer, so Sarah stood slowly, placing her hands in her pockets to puzzle the interior of her jeans and thighs, weighing her thoughts.

As she played at sections of fabric, a buzz entered her ear. An electric worm in the anterior of a wood string, a twelve-string guitar. A pulse. It entered her from the gate and it pulled the anchor weight of her boat below the water, where she could see the air. Where she might watch herself drown from beneath. "Ah, the dreaded piper of my forest." She scrunched her upper lip into a clamshell, hiding the dirt of a pearl in her mouth, an inquisitive thing.

"So…" She dragged the word through the snow and mud with a tipped foot on the ground. "Maybe you have a coin?"

The pulse grew stronger.

"And that's what I'm to believe?" As she said the words, a disc fell into her palm inside her jeans, and she turned a temperature that matched the snow. Without looking down, she extracted the currency, held it aloft in the air, and presented it to the tree gate. "This coin—" she shook her head. "Only this one."

She leaned in close and her focus switched to the coin. Its sharp wasp, embossed forever in a tangle of gold. A small, insignificant being dragged into some chaotic mess. She felt for the little insect as it squirmed and squealed, being buried beneath the constructs of something bigger than itself. "The coin for Charon, Charon for the Cartography Door." Her eyes hung in unused door knockers.

The weight of gold—so many pounds of flesh in her hand—overpowered her and she let her arm fall down, revealing the tree in the background again. It was glowing, a yellow jellyfish in the dark sea. When Sarah lifted the coin again in front of her face, closer to the tree, the light increased, agitated by the salt on her face.

She sighed. "Of course."

Placing the coin back in her pocket, Sarah spent no further time investigating and she walked through the gate, brushing an oil paint of the world on the other side, long to dry, expensive to buy, but the medium of any great piece.

Chapter Five

So little do parents know of a child's sleep, the constant arriving and departing of conscious waves swollen in the unguarded bedroom. Shadows under the bed, hands at the windows and eyes in the closet: small mementos from the journey of little feet on hallowed ground. Even amongst the stuffed animals and blankets clung to with fire beneath, footprints of dirt are left on the soles of feet, tracks from the bed to the edge or ridge or cliff leading both away and to, from. Not every print a small foot like a mammal's. Not every trip back carried out by the child alone. Not every dream simply a mixture of the food scraps and daily adventures in the woods; in most of them, those dreams, we are truly chased by demons. Children, the mediums between two worlds.

After not nodding off into so many visions of introspection, small-legged jump over squatting body from the book to the lullaby to the bed, after so many feigned eyelashes closed to connect the mouth of flower petals as if the light had gone away, Sarah lay awake. Her eyes collected fragments of light that bounced in from beneath her door and across the sheen of teddy bear eyes, pouring the room into a smooth marble slate. Are both those things the same? Sarah was the contrast and she lay there shedding light and sculpting the room, listening without hearing to the conversation in another place.

They were talking on the first floor. Sarah tried to ignore it, to fall into a slumber, but the thought of so many masks and tongues with sharp teeth sticking out from behind every facade kept her up. Kept her from the loop that they said *she so recently had come from.*

"She must spend more time with her grandparents," they would say, and she would ask why; and only in books would it be told that she and they came from and were going to the same place. But they lied. The transition had been a smear like honey in the glass of her eyes, now collecting light from the hall; and it came on every night.

Sarah thought of the places where her feet would step and the world would crumble underneath them, and she felt like the needle that connected the hem.

So many mouths with voices that sounded like the things she had done in previous lives. Why were children only aware of resonance? Why is it that children blow out candles when they still have yet to collect all the realm of their physical breath, spirits in the ghouled chest? Sarah lay awake and respirated in that questions. Those question. sdrawkcaB again.

Silhouettes: shelves filled with dolls, a shape like a toy chest. The armoire. A rocking chair where Mom used to feed the bottle—but no longer—but still the chair hadn't been moved. The chair moved: another spirit in the room. She barely glanced at it, a small thing with a kabuki mask painted red with white stripes. It was harmless, she could tell, by the position of its tail between its legs. She turned over and faced the wall, which was white. Which held her shadow; the light came from behind her. and cast her shadow on the wall and she stared at it, desiring the sleep they had promised before bed.

Refreshing. Chromatic. Smooth.

But it was like the pillows and comforter, all slumped together on Sarah's arching body, reflected in the shadow on the wall. A lump. Something so hard to swallow without the sugar they so often promised.

The impish thing, the small spirit, shook the chair as it left through the closet and Sarah didn't turn to watch it. There would be more; the night could not be through, as she hadn't entered that place and she couldn't. Too many mouths in her room just yet. Hungry for her, she swore. If only she didn't wake up, they may never prey upon her.

"She keeps asking about it."

Small slips of the ears downstairs weave past the dormancy of the floor.

The words remind Sarah that she knows she's not meant to be where she is now. Or at least—

"Where else should she be?"

It was Dad again, claiming the things that Sarah had said during the day, those etchings marked in such wet clay that both parents could skew their meaning and shape. Sarah just wanted to be free of the teeth at the side of her bed, and either sleep's embrace of them or a doctor's pad would dismantle them, either or would suffice. Of course heaven, when it did come, was always nice.

"You shouldn't joke, that's our daughter."

"I'm not joking."

"I don't think it should even be discussed."

"It's just talk. Sarah talks about it, we should, too."

It was impossible to differentiate the two voices as they both said the same thing. Impossible as the planks that had swelled and bent and splintered under so many paths of toddling feet, strained the tones of all their water, and the tones came up flat. Sarah turned in her bed so that her ear wasn't pointed at the drain; she rolled to her back again where the ceiling was staining, where that one time it had rained so hard that the closet had flooded and days later, after it had been repaired, that yellow stain appeared.

When pressed, Dad had said that water takes the path of least resistance. Before the ceiling had given way above the closet, a rivulet of rain had swum the banks of her room from the attic and found this pathway least resistive. *Then why didn't the water come through here?* And Dad had said it probably had tried, but sometimes things don't always end up as they should. He said it was better this way, there was a lot of rain, you could have drowned. He laughed after that.

Seventeen mattresses, and still the voices jumbled themselves through the floor and her cotton pads to float Sarah's head as if they were a pillow. In their voices, so stagnant with constant refreshment of their own pooled water, Sarah churned, in the sea of thick words that saturated the fabric of her bed and made everything sticky, sweaty, salt so dry that it itched her skin and marred her as she turned, leaving marks on her arms as she turned, that she swore weren't there in the morning. But the armbands would come off, and Sarah would turn and turn again.

"I didn't start these conversations."

"Are you sure?"

"Of course."

Violent end of a blade of grass tipped itself at Sarah's arm, a rash for allergens to green, fresh cut. She turned to scratch and see what had pressed her; a moth had flown down to rest on the bed. Yellow and black. Not orange. Patterns like dried riverbeds where the earth had been red clay and the men hadn't dug it yet from the well of mermaids. Instead they just lay there naked, like this moth that pressed its proboscis into Sarah's arm, searching for the pollen at her centre, intubating the spirit from alarm.

The bed sheets shifted as Sarah got up; enough being told in muffled talk and enough being drained from her pores by the imaginary, real-life moth. Sarah shooed it with her hand and it disappeared into the other dark parts of her room. Fluttering away to where it didn't exist, probably the closet; its threshold; a beach; a place where two places meet; where children were happiest. The in-betweens.

Down the hall where the paper curled from years of smoke from a fire years ago, little feet cuffed with unicorn slippers slipped unnoticed to the stairs. There, unsocked feet would dock and prepare to embark on an adult theme, questions and answers that young ears would never hear. Children should be seen not heard, but perched here, they would hear, unseen, for the truth was, parents always believed those that were not, were already asleep.

"She came to me again yesterday. She asked why the small monsters keep appearing in her room at night and I said they weren't real."

"That's good."

"Then she said when she goes to sleep they are there too but they are normal in her dreams."

"Okay."

"And she says, *I*, as in herself, *must be normal there too.*"

"Okay. Then what did you say?"

Lack of words filled a cornered and unwilling mouth, a tongue in teeth, ill-desired to lie.

"What did you say when she said that?"

"What am I supposed to say?"

"That you love her, and she *is* normal! Oh! And I don't know maybe, that normal is *here*!"

"But what's the difference?"

"What do you mean?"

"We don't know anything about dreams, really."

Sarah could imagine her mother's mouth turn up at the statement as if she were barb-hooked at the corner of her gums.

"I'm pretty sure we know they aren't real and that your daughter should be reassured that *here* is real and that she should be here. And that we are here. And we love her…"

Sarah could picture her father cowering under the weight of her mother's fish.

"What did you say?"

"I said maybe *you* are." The voice trailed off into the sort of ghost that might wear sheets.

As Sarah crouched at the top of the stairs with her toes curled over the lip for a sense of balance, her hands glued to the black wrought iron banister, her ears trained to the living room below, a Gaussian blur caught the corner of her eye. On the far side of the hall, a spectre floated, half-balled, half-flat on the bottom, a sphere wearing a bread bag for cover.

It didn't move or have a face, and was without any colour that would fit a person's palette of paint. Just a hand-sized spectre, floating in Sarah's peripheral. When it didn't move when looked at dead-on, she turned back to listen to her parents, ignoring the un-red non-herring.

"For fuck's sakes."

"What?"

"Jesus, we are trying to get through this together in a way that ensures our daughter feels safe when she's awake."

"But she doesn't."

"I know that! That's why we have to make it safe for her. Telling her that she might belong elsewhere is not reassuring."

If all the lights were on downstairs, the blind wouldn't have known it.

"It just feels like I'm lying to her."

"How is it a lie?"

"It feels like gaslighting, like I'm just ignoring her feelings and forcing her to believe that she has things backwards."

"She does have things backwards."

The rails under Sarah's hands grew hot and she chafed at them with Indian burns and pink bellies. They squelched under the wet of her focus and blurred out everything not within the focal point of her eyes. Except the spectre. It grew when she pressed her head against the railings, trying to get closer to her father and the spilling black of her mother's stuffing.

"Not for her, she doesn't. The dreams are more real to her than this is. She feels safer there, so why should I make her feel otherwise? What, what, because more time passes here."

Then it was tight beside her, the featureless levitator. Sarah turned to look at the smooth finish of what would be a face if there were a body. It was close, finger-width close, and now it felt under shade as it stayed with a lack of pigment on its skin that left a sheen, a polish, a greasy mirror image that reflected Sarah's own fishhooked face. She shifted under the weight of her perplexity, now encroaching on her earlier lack of concern; that's what made for shade. For shadow. For sparse expanse of light in the hall amongst all the night-drawn darkness.

"Because she *is* here... do you not hear yourself?"

Her eyes went wide apart in her reflection on the spectre, as if she were astonished and although she was, it was the spectre growing larger that forced her image to mutate and distend. It waxed as the conversation waxed on downstairs. Sized of Sarah's head, then her body, then her skin and flesh were pressing through the spaces in the bars as she tried to pour herself into the place she least wanted to be while this fruitful ghost flooded the cavity of her house.

"I hear myself fine. Do you not hear *yourself*? You're trying to convince her that the way she feels is wrong and if she can't feel any other way she needs to pretend."

"What? That's not what I'm saying."

"Yes, it is!"

Touch flat on both sides, the wall behind and the Sarah in front. The spectre had ripened in the hall and swelled to an infinite size as Sarah squirmed under its belly, suffocating in its bland, slime-mold form. Her parents' voices muffled out under its ballooning sourdough fabric. Sarah kneaded at it to get out, kneading it and it grew, rising so that all of it was all that filled her known.

It was black inside. And there was no noise and Sarah couldn't breathe.

So she screamed.

And the spectre exploded red at her voice.

"Sarah?"

She could hear again, and it was her father pounding up the stairs in between her own heavy breathing and screaming.

"Sarah! What happened?"

He was shaking her, small twig under the supervision of children, bending beyond its need. Sarah opened her eyes in the forceful gutter wailing of her father's hands and the entire hall was painted in blood. Pulpy, warm, intestinal blood covered everything. It was curled up in Sarah's clothes and wrinkled the ceiling with rows and rows of ripple pattern gore.

"What's wrong, Sarah?" Her father asked, holding her. "Is it another dream?"

Part 26: Beyond the Gates of Wings

Everything felt purple from the taste of blueberries, bruised when falling from high bush trees, tumbled to the nitrogen-rich ground to turn to seed. Everything was purple from Sarah's head to her knees, but her shins, most plush of all, screamed purple from the roots and stones and stumps she had stumbled through when crossing the circle of trees that held the hole. She thwacked and thumped those shins again on the cusps of jutted out rock from the hole's tunnel wall as she jumped and fell through the second gate. She had bled them, like juices, like the berries they so resembled; she had bled them for the wine of her presumed feast on the vertical protrusions of pines that came from the incline forest, half upside down, growing so that *their* fruits had less distance to fall.

Sarah rubbed her purple shins as she rested for a moment from the upwards crawl, in a safe space in the sideways forest, and she grimaced, red with the blush of hands too early to pluck the fruit of spring. Her chest heaved in and out, her heart making imprints on its skin in the shape of ribs; everything ached and throbbed while her body protested amongst the ladder-ring tree trunks, too many to count the years of their lineage while Sarah counted the laps her head was swimming, heavy with water and uncertain of which way was up and out.

When she caught hold of nothing, Sarah reached again to press on, but found that the brushes of needles had collapsed in. They stabbed her palms, left her bleeding, and she pulled back to eat the wealth of their pointed labour, which was a soured red current on her broken skin. She sucked her teeth in argument with the trees, but they would not give in.

"Shit," she exclaimed quietly, and sat down into the groove of a fir tree trunk beneath her. In its woody arm's rest she would be forced to give in, and it wasn't long before she leaned back to the protest in her bones and muscles, angry with the shape of discolouration. She nestled into the branches and sticks around her and started counting her fingertip mantras, chanting words to keep the cold from setting in, certain that the forest would guide her once the pulse picked up again.

High frequency waves penetrated the meniscus and grew a song inside her. Sarah continued her counting while the waves lifted up the flesh and hung it higher in the sky, that birds might pick at it, that it might seed itself and deliver germination to the wildflowers that grew in long meadows where spirits are aware of freedom... freedom's pearl in the mantra of her hands. Sarah counted, and in her numbers, she heard movement in the trees around her.

At first it was light: rustling acorns, fissures appearing in bark. But as she continued, her valleys of ochre settling, the machinations of her blouse relaxing in the subtle waves of higher founding, the noise surrounding her increased and the vines surfaced from the recesses of their hallowed trees. They wrapped around her ankles and wrists, ribboning the skin into long lashes of red-present dress. Sarah, in the present but lost to the clock that set its hands to tendrils.

The vines wove themselves into her skin from the places they grasped, rasping and penetrating with their fiddleheads. They punctured Sarah's surface and sewed a fabric of closing in. Cocoon. Chrysalis. Pupae within. Sarah counted, relaxing, giving in as the forest made a nest of her body for caterpillars to feed until spring. For eggs to hatch. For new exposure to begin.

One, two, three... Sarah made notes of every rosary in her hand and it played a melody to match the pulse in her ear, the woods explaining that every thorn has a purpose that both refuses and begs to be put in the paws of feline kings. Deep in the black pads of a predator, where a mouse might be dinner or a crown might be handled in the ways of old kingdoms, where man was but a nervous pilgrim.

It became dark. Sarah closed her eyes, blocking out no more of the night than what had already settled in her mind. Observation clears the sky of constellations; fortunes are for gods, but Sarah did not pray in the black of their shadows. She was above them, in the higher frequency of the pines. One. Two. Three. She ascended beyond the patterns of her fingers.

One.

Two.

Three.

Inside of her was the connection to everything else that crawled, hunched over, in search of sunlight.

After a long journey through the moonless current of a lonely sea, a dot appeared in her vision. Far away. A bright white object, growing. Her feet found traction with the help of lift and objects moving, her body cut along the crescent shapes of tidal waves, travelling closer to the ball of light, expanding where the pineal gland must be releasing chemicals to protect the red blood cells. Ripening. Distending. Overwhelming sight, the light at the far end of her travel grew to immense size and blinding strength, heat stretched beyond the cool grip of ice, a welcoming sensation in the night.

But the pulse was behind, and Sarah stopped.

Seek and you will find what you project.

She decided to move in opposition to the light.

Slowed dramatic pace accompanied the static place. Sarah halted in her own stasis, a fugue state where all the understanding of self dissipated and she left her in its void, staring at a light and longing for what was behind her, while a cold dust orbited the moment. While a body searched the empty husks of satellites in the frost. While she waited for the motion to reveal itself and her position to be exposed.

A hand reached out and grabbed her shoulder, finally here in a place where decay would not come. Machine bolt and nut its grasp, or like a bear hibernating in a cave suddenly awash in dreams of chase, it was tight, crisp and jagged. It cut along the underside of glacier walls and peeled her skin beneath it. The paw pulled hard, a fast bandaid motion that spun her around in the void so that the stars were behind her, but Sarah cast no shadow and the spectre that held her was illuminated in perfect, unobstructed light.

An eagle's head, cast from metal, sat upon the shoulders of a tall, lean woman. Its eyes were two great polished blue stones set into the jewelry of a predatory bird. Sarah washed her skin in them, and the rest of her was thrown in the fjord's icy waters to sink. And she sank in those eyes. For days. The bottom of the ocean never came to rescue her from the fall, the light from behind her shimmering on the glass ceiling of the world.

'Come.' The spirit gestured with a free hand that swung out on thin black tendons, no muscle or bone or skin, just the long tendrils of action from where an inkspot landed on the tissue of its shoulder. *Come*, it gestured with its hips and its eyes, both spiralling, hypnotising as it turned its hourglass shape away, allowing the glass that was its back to shine in the light that Sarah could not imbibe or shoulder. It took her hand and then walked, dragging Sarah's schoolgirl skirt along the tongues of boys through the dark. Sarah followed, watching the skirt of worms that was its legs manipulate the lack of earth beneath their black, muscular bodies.

They walked, and Sarah decomposed slowly. She watched the hand that held the hand of the spirit in front of her turn transparent and then rip in some places, peel and fall off in others. Somehow the bird kept hold of a hand no longer there and although Sarah's skin and flesh and feet and hair all fell away as they travelled through the dark night, somehow she continued to be pulled along, her shed of body just a marker for when she found the path again. Her lack of corporeal religion, a basis for all faith to begin. They wandered forever in space without stars, until the light behind her faded into nothing and her body was just a projection. Her intention became the way of existence.

Do not seek and you will become the intention.

When nothing remained, they appeared on the porch of the final gate. A stone slab had been laid down to float in front of a bent-over tree in a blanket of nothing, a triangle marked on its bark. The porch had a welcome mat that read upside down and Sarah felt aware of home. The tree stood there, both ends buried in nothing, just the roots, growing from each resolution, hanging in the eternal space. The spirit turned and looked at Sarah.

'Here,' was all it said.

A cluster of gas and speech floated in the Bardo of Sarah's thoughts, staring into the place where the entrance would be while she waited for her body to follow the markers, to return. She waited patiently, in honour of the ouroboros as her bones took place and the nerves reattached and her flesh become real. She still held the hand of her guide, and they shared gestures of pressure when she took her first steps towards the gate.

Sarah feigned a smile.

The spirit did nothing.

The welcome mat was like grass, grounding Sarah as she brushed her bare feet against it before walking through the gate. No one waved goodbye.

Part 27: Persephone

The other side, as all things always were for Sarah, was a tunnel. Two feet in, no feet out, acceptance of movement was the ballet of a dress, which streamed out behind her as in front; the press of her rhapsody breathed on in the walls of her tunnel.

A gentle clicking noise flung a snare roll at Sarah's back and she turned to find the gate had become a wooden door at the end of the tunnel, and the door had closed. Sterling silver, somehow tarnished green, plated the furnishing of the yellow-painted door; where a knocker should have been was an emblem of a snake eating itself and Sarah breathed, the tail of her mouth falling to the ground. She checked the knob; it opened, but there was only wall behind it now. She looked at the ground where her tail end had fallen onto the threshold, and the floor was an unmistakable herringbone stone.

Blinking in quick flashes, attempting to reposition or locate her environment, Sarah inquired her surroundings. Lanterns were strung from the ceiling in one long row of triangles: they stretched on along a hall made of books, stacked spine-out. Upon close inspection, each title simply read, 'End.'

"Wait. This is my tunnel," Sarah spoke, only to herself. "Hey!" She turned back again to the open door and swung a fist at the flat rock wall behind it, turning her knuckles into a sharp springy pain that left her vibrating. "Hey!" she yelled again, too overwhelmed to attend to her wounded hand. "Hey! This is *my* tunnel! I've already been here before..." She pummeled at the wall, turning her fists white, then red, then black from blood and force.

"There's supposed to be coins here, or something! Something other than the stupid tunnel!"

She slumped, her head against the wall, turning slowly to rest her back as she sat on the floor, a blank stare filling her chest with a lack of weight as purpose took to fleeting.

Sighing, Sarah looked around again. Placing the book ends together, she cocked her head, staring at the wall beside her. "Why can I read these titles?"

Turning appled with a questioning eye, she stood for a close inspection of the books that lined the hall. Each one a molded or faded colonial colour, red or blue, Sarah imagined their faces faded to the brown beneath their fabric jackets, the letters standing out on water-lined cliffs. E-N-D in Garamond, Times New Roman, various gothic architects. Each one with the same title, never faltering like so many titles in the entirety of the rest of her tunnels, all of them turning to scribbles and illegible hieroglyphics, excepting these. None so strange as read writing.

Sarah watched the letters for a long time, long enough that her legs got bored and her feet started into a slow amble down the tunnel.

When the yellow door had turned into a hazy ball of white, the letters that spelled out the titles started to jumble. Sarah noticed it on a black-bound book with red letters first. When she got close, the individual letters transformed, turning their flat lines into curves and making spaces where there were no obligations before. It happened to all the titles eventually, some turning numeric, some a language she couldn't read, others just a jumble of illegible symbols carved into wood where someone might have been, impossible to tell whose initials were pushed into the heart.

Sarah took a step back from the black book, and read a couple titles back, all the same 'end.' But when she moved forward, beyond the coffee-stiff book, all of them scattered into digital clocks in analogue dreams: completely inscrutable.

Finding some solace in the familiar, she paid little to less notice of the rest of the books and continued on through her tunnel, under dreams, into well-known territory, where she would map this oddity later.

Soon, a thin rivulet of water stretched its membrane down the centre of her path, and she walked through its cold shallow hands washing what was left of the debris on her toes. It filtered through her, leaving a black slick of earth that deconstructed in the water as its particulates dispersed like so many glass shards from a broken bottle. The tiny waterway ran clear, then muddy, then clear, and Sarah felt the air lift with the purity of its baptism across her path; cleanliness was all it took.

As she continued to be sanctified and sanitized in what was becoming a slow running brook, the tunnel walls grew around her. The number of bricks multiplied, and they stacked like undigested snake bellies all around her, each one more full than the last and each one further expanding the size of the tunnel as it sat, food drunk in the wall. They led a trail of reptilian slender that opened into a massive unhinged jaw, an archway, wide and booming. The expanse of it, forty feet across, was lip-lined on both sides as it rose in a black stone ridge that led into a single pachyderm head. An enormous beast, a keystone that held the archway up in its carved mammoth tusks.

In the opening, it was only black. A thick velvet curtain hung like a ghost from the jaw of the elephant-shaped centre stone, leaving all things unnoted beyond and before it. The stream, shrunken in the mass of the elephant and its void, flowed out from beneath the black, so clandestine in its motion that you couldn't see how it passed.

Sarah stopped short of the inkblot veneer suspended from the keystone. Her feet, cold and wet. Her vision, overtaken with a bold charcoal void that absorbed everything but the gleam of her eyes. Her chances of reflection impossible in the flat, penetrating map to a starless sky. And she felt the desire to press on, to continue mapping the uncharted.

She placed her left hand, palm out, against the clean liquid surface of the curtain. When her skin met the plane of wood, she pushed her grain against it and the dark stain parted, flickering the match of frequencies before dispersing, like the mud of the water, filtered out.

Past the fallen cloak of the star-seamed curtain and beyond the white elephant gate, Sarah entered the body of a dwelling that she had been to often, but could never quite place. She breathed in the familiar area and once her cheeks deflated, stepped beyond where the wall had once existed and into the open arms of the auditorium, a place she recognized as the end, where a vast glass ceiling above her, neverended.

Water turned to thin ice crunched under Sarah's feet as she stepped into the wide-open room beneath a dome. She spread her hands out and spun her body slowly above the liquid that covered the floor, each pass in her circling turning the constellations of her hair into a blurred image of the moving universe, an unmappable swirl of the stars from above as she tilted her head, closed her eyes and continued to swing.

She felt a pressure here. As if the cold water painted in the cupola's dome had stolen the weight of gas to balance equilibrium with a sky, unseen above. Sarah's head was squeezed as the internal expansion gripped her sinuses, squeezing them to ring with bright red wire. She had experienced this in this room before, and had learned to adjust it: she turned even faster, spinning and stomping her feet as the room rotated around her. The tension became confused, started to slip out from her splayed fingertips, encouraging Sarah to spin even harder.

The water, coerced and rising, rode up through Sarah's well of body and effervesced out the tips of her fingers, leaving a waterfall of mist and bubbles to cloak her spinning form. She was a steam god and as she descended, she breathed the vapour of her labour into her chest and sinus and head… and the swelling stopped. The fleeting pressure of the room balanced with the sensations in her being and all that remained was the cold.

A thin shale of ice from the pond that broke in her drift.

Sarah let her heart rate slow to a drip and she yawned in the aching cavern of the auditorium, stretching her arms, her hips, and then, setting one atop the other she made a statement in the clear. "Another place I've already been." Her eyes bulged. Unimpressed, she slumped a little.

Filling the room now that her dance with pressure was done was the lurid sound of water, like a thoughtful raincloud far away. The shallow reservoir below her did not leave a large space for impact and Sarah followed the noise with ease to a hole in the ice only a few feet from where she was standing. There, offset from centre, a fine cylinder of liquid poured itself up to the cupola. It was falling from the image above her head. "Persephone," she said, as she brought her gaze up to the cupola, where there was an ocean of sky.

Smooth and polished to a linear reflection, a concave glass ceiling glimmered back at her. Small sparks from the layer of snow beneath her feet created a halo of her own image that was lost in the shine. The ceiling shone in only the way that the moon does, mirroring light from the other side of the earth. It gleamed Egyptian blue, its crack from where the water fell invisible in its spectrum of hues.

"Persephone," she said again, looking now to where a woman was floating in the absence of space. Floating in a dream in the centre of the sea in the ceiling. Asleep or drowned in the liquid, Persephone waited, laid out like stasis weight, with her back to Sarah and her sleeping eyes pointed away.

"You know, it's funny I'm here. I was just thinking about you the other day." Sarah spoke at the image. "I thought you were the end of my dream tunnels—but I was wrong. They actually keep going through this wall to another door that leads to the forest behind my house." Sarah looked back at where the curtain had been, where now another wall stood, pathless. "Of course," Sarah sighed. "Were you aware of that, Persephone?"

The silhouette behind the slow gap movements of her thin, white dress, flowing in the gentle current, didn't answer. The woman's body didn't stir or speak to Sarah's question; it laid there, corporeal, thoughts astral, body just asleep. A centrepiece to thought.

"I was just as speechless," remarked Sarah as her lungs pushed at their handmade cages of skin, trying to pull the essence of the quiet, floating woman into her chest. A body like Sarah's, able to sit with unrest, couldn't. She didn't. No matter how much air she breathed in and held, her skin was still a slate rock painted blue. She made fists beside her hips and tried with diligence to outlast the breath count of the floating woman… but the poetry on her lips rose and she let the air out, pretending to avoid the times she had counted.

"Hmm." She said nothing, but meant every word of it. Curling her mouth into a pocket of misplaced thought, she turned from the body and looked back about the auditorium walls and tunnel passages. The drowned, never ceasing its quiet on the canopy above.

Sarah checked the entirety of the auditorium. The walls were all the same, all leading up into the cupola of water hidden behind glass. At the far end, the door she would have normally come in through was a narrow metal opening, painted white and trimmed in black. She remembered the first time she pushed through and found Persephone. It was then that she had realised the end of things didn't always settle for conclusions and that she was now coming close to being left in a vex with other curses.

"I don't suppose you'd know where to find an obol, would you?" she asked, turning her head only sideways enough that the water she had pushed wouldn't catch her good side. "I am looking for one in particular."

It was the word particular, Sarah would later think, that hid the noise that would have had her running. Likely. Maybe not. But Sarah didn't turn her head all the way; she stayed hovered, half listening to the floor and the other half, her own head, while a layer of hands pulled at the glass ceiling. Digging into the opposite side of birds in the sand, the fingers fleshed out crystals that had merged and formed… breaking them apart so that a fissure, a scenic ship in its decanter, broke across the centreline of the bottle that held the storm back. It wasn't until the rain began to fall that she repositioned her head to find the source of thunder staring at her from the ceiling: the woman, her face hidden behind a steam of boiled water, was ripping the roof in half.

So many snow-lined fjords in Lego pieces shattered across the smooth laminar surface, turning it into a hard-slip glacier, splitting where the water escaped as if pushed by the seals and sharks so hungry for pups beneath the splintering walls. Sarah's hands didn't move from their soft pulpy fists before the glass had broken into rain droplets and the sea fell like a mirror onto her head, there was barely time for her to change to great big sad black discs that hunger would never catch—or never cared to notice—as it slipped its rows of teeth around her grey-printed cower.

She was underwater, gasping before the light could tell her not to close her eyes, and the water was pumping with a fist of energy into the back of her throat. It broke her larynx there, forcing the cold across it to sing a siren before pulling the cords from its box. Sarah would've reached for her throat, had she not been trying to paddle to the surface; instead she made a sound like drowning would expect, a muffled pull of honey at the doe's crushed neck.

Movement came in the vocalized drip drop, and she was kicking her feet and fighting the tundra of waves when the water itself moved past her, billowing her clothes as it sloshed between her chest and legs in a downward vortex. All the water dropped beneath her, and air filled the panicked movement of her dummied throat as she hung above the surface of the fallen glass and its sea of blue, strapped into a surface of stars, light the only penetration of that sand which it hardens.

When Sarah kicked her feet, there was no resistance of water or floor or gravity, just a weightless confirmation that she was hanging. Blink hard. Scratch at throat, check the thing that hung you dry and find that you are floating. She swung from the pivot of a nothing and looked down, frightened she might be falling, but only the ceiling had. She was awash in sunshine above a pond, above a dock on the water and a man in an orange vest struggled at the place where everything met. The salt, Sarah's eyes, the wooden deck. A body.

She struggled again to find a common ground on which she could stand, to control her own position, but when the man with his six-barred star and bright-coloured vest pulled a girl from the water, Sarah froze to silence. A white dress splayed its paper boat catch out into the pond, letting the surface turn a reflection of snow and ice as the man pressed on the girl's chest, pumping up and down, rippling the clean water. Her hands splayed out beside her, her image caught between the fabrics in the pond and her noiseless blue on the dock. Her face a single image in the colour of the flock.

Her face. Pale.

A mirror?

Sarah's own face.

Sarah's own body.

Sarah's distorted image of where she had started and where the dock and water met.

The man in the vest continued to pummel her chest, bending over to kiss her with breath. He kept talking in between the two motions, saying, "Wake up, kid, wake up!" And Sarah knew what it was to speak fluently but never be asked what to say. To have so many titles of books line the lanes of your life and not know what they read. She felt it in everything as the letters and syllables with their sharp angles and black shapes and white spaces drove their cutting edges into her throat from her chest and just jammed up in the collapsed blockage that was her larynx. They piled up with the bile and throw-up until her throat distended and exploded a black rain that stained everything.

And Sarah watched as it dripped on her face.

She watched as the man picked up an apple that lay beside her, pocketed it, and then took her body, dragging it away from the dock. It left a streak of the black that came from her throat as her hair and clothes pulled the oily membrane away from her periphery, all the way into a van, closed the doors behind her.

Sarah hung there, gasping at lines that curved structures into Fibonacci and twirl into themselves. She hung and stared at where she had been pulled from the water outside the cabin… and at two gold coins that had fallen from her pocket, left in the oil.

She watched a raven come and snatch one of the coins from the dock, with its magic-trick beak.

A tentacle reached up from the water, fumble about the dock until it happened upon the other coin, and dragged it down into the still of the pond.

She hung; she watched the man turn and wipe his long black hair from his brow, looking up into the rain that Sarah spilled. He seemed to be praying for help as the wet washed away years of clay, and left the man beneath. He looked right into Sarah with sad, green eyes… and she knew them. She read the tag on his vest, 'Daniels,' and she knew him.

Part 28: Corduroy

"Do you think Daniel stood for something, like he was a representation of a specific event or idea that is important to you?"

Sarah said nothing in return to Dr. Pillapatti's question. She had pulled her knees up under the protection of her arms and hid her face behind both bodies.

"Sometimes the people in our dreams are directly related to an emotion or a sensation… a cultural identity. Is there something you've lost touch with lately?"

Cold radiated from the silhouette formed in the chair, it seeped in between the folds of her limbs and penetrated her castle's centre. With every hearth expired, the chill settled into the walls and brick, filling the mortar with a frost that slid and ventured to pull the structure in tighter, claustrophobia a statement of wearing thin.

"Come, Sarah, it's better to talk it out." The words, half wounded, split fractals of lonely umbrellas into Neptune's rings, its cold, its separate. "I know Daniel is important to you, but he is a *dream*. I want to say he might be there when you go back, but this is also a good chance to grow away from whatever Daniel meant—it's a hard pill, but it could have positive effects."

Two jagged knees unbuckled the stormbreaker's cowl and let the breeze in. "He wasn't a dream. He didn't act like a dream."

"I agree. I think he was a representation of something bigger."

"He wasn't. He wasn't a representation of suppressed emotions, he wasn't an archetype or a shadow self either. He was a friend," said Sarah slowly.

Dr. Pillapatti cocked her head to the side and Sarah could make out a scimitar of glistening, a place where tears decided to split, and which side. "Okay." She dropped her head back down and nodded with gestured sympathy. "What else was Daniel, aside from a friend?"

"It doesn't matter anymore."

"I think it matters to you." The doctor waited with a lack of crumbled shells beneath her feet. Sarah found their place on the floor and focused there. "I think you are very scared, Sarah."

Sarah gave up the Sphinx and looked Dr. Pillapatti in the eyes when she said 'scared.' The word entered her, slicking a tongue along her spine that made the jowls in her face tremble, trying to pull back her tear ducts so spinal fluid could seep out.

"I think you are scared because Daniel was the only realistic tie you had to the dreamworld—he's what made things seem plausible, and now there's a chance that the blinds are dropping. I think you're scared of facing the truth."

"That's not it." Sarah spoke to the floor.

"No? Then does something else scare you about his mortality in your dreams?" Dr. Pillapatti's eyes turned to palindromes, her question being asked in the same way from both sides. "What happened to Daniel?"

"I didn't see."

"But you know, don't you?"

"I don't."

"I'm sorry to hear that, it must make the situation even harder." She glanced and wrote something on the pad in her hands. "Tell me about the dream, then, that Daniel and you were in when you found him. When he—passed away."

"It docsn't matter."

"It does to you. If he's not just a figment of your inner works, if he's truly a person and he meant that much to you, then we should talk about grief and the best way to do that is go there. This is a safe place to do it. You know I won't judge you." Dr. Pillapatti smiled. "I just want to help you through it."

The warmth in 'help,' thawed the little bit of frost left in Sarah's joints, and she buckled to the pressure or slippage or faith. "I went to the dream tunnel."

"From which dream?" The question was flat, but Sarah couldn't see its horizon.

"I came in from the forest." The words entered the room and with them, a fine white powder shook itself from their consonants.

"Which forest?" asked Dr. Pillapatti, leaning into the words.

"My forest. Behind my house." Multiplying, the powder spread its spores across everything, leaving dust on the furniture and the people in the room.

"Which dream is that in, Sarah? I don't recall it. I'm sorry."

"None—I entered the dream tunnel from the forest." As Sarah spoke, dust entered her mouth and stuck to her tongue, making the new words into a paste on her lips. She struggled to form consonants and she couldn't see Dr. Pillapatti's pen scratching her words as her eyelashes tangled in the glue. All that showed through was her black eyes in contrast to a white room. "From the forest I went to the auditorium."

"The place with the woman in the ceiling?"

Sarah nodded. "I think she's me."

The doctor looked up. "Why do you think that?"

"Because I am her, and I saw what she sees." Black opals, split to red and left bloodshot and feigning to drip tears down Sarah's face, quiet tears, like an allergy.

"So you saw yourself from her eyes?"

"Yes, then I left to find Daniel. He was there too, in her eyes." The tears left streaks in the snow chalk of her skin.

"What was he doing?"

"Helping me. But I wanted to know more, so I left and went to his home." Sarah was aware of the streaks falling in single lines down her own face; she followed them as they cornered her chin and drove a thin line across her neck.

"You went directly to his home. At the opposite end of the tunnel."

"Yes. I entered the white door at the far end and walked into the back of the dream where he lives. It was bright going through the door; white panels had overwhelmed the tunnel, making it hard to see anything else, and when I left, the white had charred the sky, turning the dream monochrome."

"Monochrome... like black and white?"

As Sarah nodded, the powder exploded from her face, filling the room with fevers made of blind taste. She closed her eyes, wincing at the dusted sky that now overtook the room.

"So your dream lost all colour?" Dr. Pillapatti continued to write, scratches within the scratching white.

"It did... and there was a path, almost a trench from a massive worm or a snake; it wound through the dream to Daniel's house, and when I came to find him..." she heaved in breath. "He was broken, and he died." She swallowed a huge lump. "And he disappeared... "

Sarah put her hands out in front of her, grasping and clenching at the air, trying to find where her vision might be set out in front her. Her eyes, two lost stones in the snow, deep below the ice line, let the white squeeze the blood from the cores. Drip into sediment.

Dr. Pillapatti's touch on Sarah's shoulder was professional but it squeezed. "That's okay Sarah, you're safe. This is okay. I would never judge you for feeling this way." She pulled her hand away and waited.

Sarah had stopped talking. She let her hands fall into her orbit, bent over in the chair. For a while, only winter existed, in the same way it hung itself on the trees or stuck to the top layer of green, a glass layer from the cold. She let it hold her as she whimpered, to hide her emotions in the shivering of bones, waiting out the season.

Second hands passed. Stiff and empty, Sarah sat up in her chair. As she did, a thin stream of clear snot rolled out of her nose and formed a cleft on her lip. She sniffled and sucked it back in, pulling all the embarrassment in the room up her nose with it. Leaving the furniture and the people without dust. At night, it might settle in her brain.

"It's good to cry." Dr. Pillapatti feigned a smile before looking over her notes. "Was there anything else? Did the dream end there?"

"No... he told me that he kept it, and then he left an apple."

Dr. Pillapatti raised an eyebrow. "And you said there were huge ruts in your dream? Like, from a snake?"

"Yes." Sarah was back to looking away.

"And then when Daniel disappeared, he left an apple?"

Sarah nodded.

She thought a moment with her pen on her chin. "You know, in the Eden story, the snake talks Eve into eating an apple, and it gives her knowledge."

Following only the lines of shadows in the room, Sarah did not follow the lines of thought.

"Is there something maybe that you learned—and you regret learning it?"

All that white in her lungs became her skin and Sarah sank into the ghost on her chair.

"Is there something else you want to tell me?"

Her head shook back and forth.

The doctor made a quiet gesture, an unidentifiable sigh in her throat. She flipped the pages of her notebook back and forth a few times, then, placing her hands on top, closed it beneath her directed fingers. "I know we've talked about this before and… it's only an offer, I know one you are not keen on, but based on what happened last night, it might be a good option—just for a couple days."

Her head shook back and forth.

Dr. Pillapatti made a smile with her oil paints, one not specific to emotion, more like petting a cat. "I'm worried, Sarah, that something else might happen and you'll need someone right there, beside you."

"My mom is home," Sarah said, a blanket curled up in her throat.

"Yes. I know. But what if she needs help?"

"She won't." She let the blanket slip down into her chest, where it muffled her pulse.

"It would just be a night or two; you would sign yourself in so you could leave when you want."

Sarah hugged herself tight, making the blanket her warmth. "No, that's okay."

Dr. Pillapatti let out another sigh, this one recognizable. "Okay. May I phone your mom and let her know that you might need some extra help tonight?"

Sarah was hiding in amongst her bedcovers. "That's fine," she said, from behind thick, padded linings.

259

Part 29: Fire Upside Down

Sitting on her bed was the apple.

Red.

A beam of cut glass shone a slim, curving light across the fruit's surface, sparkling its ruby gloss, sugar coated.

Black swells billowed over her vision in slow motion, removing the apple's eye over and over while Sarah tried to piece it into the story. Where did it fit? Seeds? Worms? The glorious crowns that hold the sky for a century while the hands beneath are fed with sweet fruit? Flesh of knowledge. Harnessed wealth. It lay there, upright on her bed, begging questions of Daniel's motive, Sarah's hunger, and the way that nectar is harvested.

Darkness had wrapped its fingers around the windows of the house, and their curtains, unable to hold back the strong focus of the night, left all the room sat in long sunken ships. All the corners, where shadows hid by day, were now filled with eels whose eyes were caked in twilight, leaving luminous cuts that fell beyond the dark lines and lay in fractals on the ocean floor. A floor where sleeper sharks gathered round the ribs of daytime to feast and gorge, where from the lines left by sundials, the sand had come and filled the places round the bed with decay—with the deep filter of amphipods.

Creatures crawled amongst the abyssal plain as Sarah sat, a juvenile fish in the lantern light, face hugged by hands as she watched the apple. The only curiosity creating its own glow. A mechanism she could not place amongst all the pressure from a world above. She pushed it from the bed and let it fall into the silt; the crustaceans would have it. She sighed and lay on her back.

"Whatever you left me, Daniel, it's not enough."

In all the saltwater, her tears were obvious. The black settling in on her chest, the brine in her breath. Soon she would be a pool for fish to fall into and die.

A breeze rattled the storm windows on the house, its tantrum ran along the walls to the closet, where it shook the doors from their hinges and pushed a longtime reminder of the wound into the room. She turned her head and looked into the maw where the closet loomed, its facade all broken away, exposing an interior where sounds like beasts would come from in the night. There it remained, less black than the rest of her house—guidance would contract the light. She sighed again as the wind pushed harder and all the windows curved in the middle, shrinking the height of the ceiling and swelling the mouth of her closet, distending its teeth further into the room.

All she could feel was Daniel as she watched the room fall into a dark encompassing, while the closet only grew in hunger. All she could feel was Daniel as the apple lay in the corridor's scent lines to the bacteria-scavenging worms in the ground. Sarah shook from appetite lost and fed the ocean from beneath with her parasite, that which ate her in turn.

Her belly hollowing in size of her chest, she swung one hand off the bed absently, and it connected with the mouth of the nightstand. Once inside, the weight of gold called her fingers and she grasped a small metal object that stung her, a wasp in the ointment. But Sarah held it, clenching harder, helping the stinger press into her palm with such vigour that she was vinegar blood and all the air was sodium. It pulsed, and the reaction of spark and venom coursed its way to Sarah's heart; in it she felt for nothing and loved the feeling it brought.

Squeezing tighter, the outline presented itself as the coin. Sarah sat up and brought the disc to her folded lotus on the bed. She brought her hand beneath lighthouse eyes that penetrate egos in strange portraits and unfurled her now blood-dripped fist to see the coin in her palm. The wasp wriggled beneath the finish red, inserting its stinger from a crack in the papyrus into Sarah's flesh. In and out. Perforating violence, embedding venom and stingers like slivers made of rotted wood.

Sarah waited. She let the wasp finish pumping her body with its pollen, with its eggs. Soon they would hatch and wear her away. She waited, and when the insect had tired and lay itself into a sleep behind the currency of her skin, she rested and let her hand fall…

There on the bed was the apple again.

"The fuck?"

She lifted it and threw it against the wall, where it shattered into a million crustacea who crashed amongst the silt beneath her bed and scurried away. She waited, blinked her eyes. As they opened, the apple appeared again. On her bed. Perfect form.

With rage, Sarah again tried to move it, but it stayed. Her free hand beneath its pure red form could barely squeeze beneath and when she went to lift, it weighed a thousand pounds and she was very small, an insignificant scud in a swell of waves. It would not move.

So Sarah pulled back and squeezed upon the coin again; waking the wasp from its slumber, she let it sting her until she was only black, and fell into a paralyzed dream, gold ribbon whirling scene into faint, into white, on to the beach.

Where Sarah woke.

Looking down, she checked for the coin. On her feet were her converse sneakers, but black. She wore a trapeze dress with pockets, and inside them, she thumbed the coin.

Circling above her, a bird's silhouette passed over a still white body in the beach-red sand. Sarah saw herself beside her, laying in the mobile passage of the bird, her eyes opening to a mixture of consistent shadows as it crossed above a scattering of light-producing clouds. To the risen, the schedule may have been unexpected, but it was mechanized potential. Sarah turned her head to look at the propeller-type fashion of spinning, and then she was beneath the bird, squinting and shielding her eyes from the now expected.

Sitting up, the waves crashed on her chest, heavy, the sea currents exuding the same unrest as the colour of their wine-drunk surf. Across the tide and white roll clay of its water tips, was the endless—it swung a bat at her hips, swirling the sand around her body into a fervour that filled cavities with shells that cut all the fragile things before again, being washed out. Sarah was impermanence as she watched the angry tide and felt the weight of its patrons on her thighs; buckling under the pressure, she lay back down.

Toes to the horizon, head away from the moon's pull, the water started at her pointed feet and enveloped her in its translucent belly. Sea ran into her nose and traveled down her throat until her voice was calcified with brine and she could only speak in Atlantean, dead, mystic reach and drowning. She breathed out bubbles that broke the surface of layers of water no longer splashing in, just a surface like jelly above her, and their oxygen-rich corpses sizzled in the waterbug stream when they hit the air. Sarah breathed in more of the ocean, and it met the stream already trickling in, turning Sarah's lungs into an estuary, a breeding pool for crustaceans, a short place between two long stretches, her mouth a cup for broods of fishes fell dry for the lack of eggs.

Coughing on the ovum, the parts of Sarah's body that did not listen cried for air and began to convulse. The shaking back and forth shook her body so that she burrowed into the sand, filled her orifices with silt and became the bed on which she lay, for which the seaweed grew. Fertilize and be fertilized with brine. Become beneath the waves and sleep, and Sarah did, and she watched herself sleep below the sand, below the tide.

Dreams came beneath the ocean floor and in them, Sarah was pencil-hatch shadowed in every contour of her face. She checked over and over with her left hand as she worked, taking the fingers to her cheeks and dragging them until they were black with her pure white form.

She was searching the ground on her hands and knees. A pinpoint light rained wherever she moved and when she looked to view it, the black void of sky took a knife to dissect itself where the tiny stream of illumination came out and spilled its belly of snow into the air; huge, papery flakes of frost fell from inside. The small pieces, worth scribing, dropped in slow motion and built up on the ground. Sarah brushed it aside with her black fingers.

Beneath the snow was dirt, and Sarah dug it away too, pulling at the earth with her cold fingers now turning white from the soil as roots shrunk away from her claws like stones. She dug a long hole for bodies beneath the falling sky and when it was wide and shallow, the ghosts came in funeral parades and lay in the hole as the snow fell on their crossed arms. They rested until they became less than non-corporeal—from their final waste came the twice stone, a small gem, pink like an elephant. It waited in the shallow hole with its glass-cut shape of a thousand hexadecimals.

Sarah watched it in the carvings of her finger slate and guessed it had been there before the ghosts had come, before she dug the whole, before the sand had stifled her mouth and covered her in dark until she swallowed herself hole. She blinked and she watched herself, staring at the same stone from beside. She lifted it from the earth with her hands, and it was the size of her heart and weighed more than her chest could hold.

Blinking again, a great pedestal made of coloured rock thrust her upwards to above where the snow was snowing, and it was now beneath her and she fed the clouds with focus.

The stone sat on an anvil, and Sarah was a hammer, watching herself strike until it split with a great light, and two pieces off the dyadic whole formed.

One white.

One red.

Less silver, greater gold.

Sarah was herself again with the other stone and she watched herself with the other watching herself with the stone. The anvil disappeared, the pedestal crumbled, and a black curtain lay across all forms so that they became one, keeping the dust out for ages.

Sarah woke. Her eyelids, corked, lifted the drunken iris to walk on the water's surface so many ascensions above the dream. She met herself there on the beach and looked over to see that she was not the only one not alone. It breathed. It breathed and the taste was on the nape of her neck, crawling down her clavicle and settling an uncomfortable weight on her chest. So many fingers strong, it forced its way between the ribs of that protective breast, cracking the elephant tusk to split the head of the bull and dive into Sarah's fragility, her saturated lungs, her waterlogged heart gasping.

Even at such a young age, you could point to the night sky and she would know where Saturn shone, an obvious time mark in the clockwork of stars. Like Kronos, Sarah knew when she viewed a god, or a monster, the weight of each a balancing of those same stars.

It breathed again, the mass on the beach, a huge ovum-shaped blackness laying on its side in the sand, grains sticking to its body, its body sticking to the sand. Both making mirrors in the heat that Sarah watched herself gasp from, gawk at… be made whole within, from the pale white image of herself, pale as her heart was in the wake of such a being.

The count of breaths was centuries between where Sarah stood and where she tiptoed closer to the monster. At first it was the ovum, a fleshy sleeve that expanded in the middle where its egg would be accepted, but as Sarah adjusted to the vastness, the contours and shapes took readied form. A great mollusk sat there, a storey tall and three wide, so large that the obelisk shadow it cast could count the time of every star, every lengthening of its orbital rise… and it rose as Sarah came closer, or she shrank in its grand knowledge of gears as she watched the mural of years pass across its grandiose shell. Other mollusks, barnacles and skeletons of lamprey eels were scattered across the uneven terrain of its body where pustules full of mercury had popped and crystallized, leaving disfigured and bulbous outcroppings where the bodies of those creatures fell and hardened in a black wax sculpture of rest and death, frozen figures screaming in its murky calcite rasp. Sarah reached out to touch them, and in their falling she found the dolorous ribbon of the clam's mouth running across the entirety of its body. Its maw line rose and fell in ten-foot smooth trap jawline paces cut with a line of red furry algae, its lips pushing out against the backdrop of its centuries, thick with flat embalming protrusions that swelled and deflated in its respiration.

Sarah ran her fingers along its mouth, kissing it with blind hands and tasting the shape of its hinge, its trap, its appendage for which the fleshy centre would burst. Lightly, she nuzzled it with her face and grew from its sleeping a birth of wakefulness… and the clamshell creaked as muscles pulled back in the jaw and lifted the gates of Abaddon with slow, aching chains by slaves. In counting between the resuscitation of pretty drowning girls did the clamshell open; long throughout the day it pulled back to reveal its grey flesh, porous and rotten, lined with mucous that sprayed as Sarah reveled in its phlegm-sodden sinews and muscle. It reared back until all was exposed of its great body, its organs, essentials, appendages of swollen black tentacles that shot out from every corner and lifted the mollusk into the air. Tentacles full of eyes and welts and sores. Tentacles that had chased Sarah for miles, the Beast in its greatest form peeled back the layers of muscles and revealed a pearl, so large it could swallow Sarah with its gaze. Holy. White. Skinned back until its magnificent eye appeared. Majesty in ocular stone.

Poignant venom-steeped blink over a pinkwash eye exposed the sphere. Iris absorbed in a pupil for swimming, lakes deep and wide, it took focus and narrowed, contracted on Sarah's image: she, looking at her image in the Beast's plum, its pearl.

Its eye, huge and critical.

That which is served from sand.

Movement was separate from thought and neither came to mind; instead, Sarah sucked the sugar from her brain and tasted the cane. It stung. It stalled her mouth with shock and the Beast took her place. "Names," it said through heavy breath, from beneath the layers of its briny flesh.

"Sarah." Her name was stolen from her mouth with a honey-soaked paw.

The tentacles shivered at the word, spraying seawater from their riveting skin that splashed against Sarah's body and woke her from the hypnotism of insignificance.

"I've come, Beast… to deliver what you seek. To end the conflict." Her eyes could not focus, but strayed in minute flashes, miniature convulsions that left her gaze unsettled, constant vibration to her name. She felt the consistent blurring of her pupil's aperture turning the Beast, who stood twenty feet tall above her head on stilts of ooze, into a long slurring image that was always in or out of breath and forever growing in the shape of

Sarah's bagged-in eyes. She turned her head and rubbed her arms as if she were cold, trying to ignore the absence of her precision and continued. "It's what you want, isn't it?"

The eye, the glaze of pearl reeled back and all the flesh inside the clam quivered, pulling pores open in the stretch and spilling more black from its pouch of organs. "Given." It spoke blunt knives that penetrated Sarah's skin in long elastic wounds; she stepped back, only to have the Beast follow. It stretched its topside squid eye out on an arm of rotten meat that stank with fly larvae to get closer, to hang over Sarah's body and cast a shadow with its gaze. It strained down past its tentacles and frayed the long veins and nerves that pulled themselves thin with effort then swung up so that it might swallow her, her body the height of the eye. Its saline, inches from her breath.

Sarah didn't move.

Frozen or fearless, she couldn't tell, but her feet were wet with sweat and a heat at the bottom of her spine bloated to the point of cracking and spilling nerve ulcer blood into her belly. She swallowed a lump of coal that had drawn in where her mouth had tightened on a speck of dirt, but it only encouraged the warmth, so she spit it up and it got caught in her throat. Gagging on the sharp soot, she coughed and turned her head further away—but the eye followed, craning its broken pathways to look at her and when they met eyes again it was long into the pinky nucleus that Sarah fell, her back all shambles in the crux.

Each vein on the network of provisions was throbbing as the eye blinked yellow piss lubricant across the gloss. Every swiping of the lid left the eye, then the pearl, then the eye. It always blinked twice and each time, a miasma filled Sarah's nostrils and she gagged further, deeper into the retch of her reaction.

The Beast said nothing, waiting with an impatient focus like a child's, seemingly forever to one or the other.

Squinted so that her nostrils plugged under duress, Sarah reached into the pocket of her dress and withdrew the coin. She held it up between her thumb and pointer finger, exposing the squirming thorax of the wasp, its wild needle attempting to sew the dress to her hands to the coin. "Here. Have it," marked Sarah as her head lay further away still and her other hand guarded the flue smell from her throat.

A spark of light cast from the clouds hit the coin on its side and a prism of colours hit the Beast's eye. When faced with crayons, the pupil contracted to a tall, thin line and a noise, a dog kicked in the side, spilled out from everywhere as the tentacles sprang into convulsions.

"Got!" the Beast screamed, lifting its gargantuan body. It jumped; the legs of a horse kicked the great creature into the sky, where it hovered a moment to send its arms out like rays and take the centre of the sun before it closed its shell, tucked everything in and dropped onto its back, mouth up.

Shockwave sand came crashing from where the Beast had landed, a gust of hot water with it turned the projectiles into a wall of mud that hit Sarah hard enough to knock her over. She pulled the coin back, tight into her fist, into a fetal position as the clam shimmied and burrowed into the beach, shaking Sarah's soul enough that she thought it might escape, that she thought it might separate into the calamity.

Sifting the light from the dark and spitting out huge clumps of waste as it shuffled, the Beast buried everything but the winding path that was its mouth, deep into the silt. As a silent film's protagonist, Sarah rose in slow frames for the scene's unfolding, to watch the sea level rise, to shield her eyes from the clouds of sand that moved away in torpid waves, to fight for a chance to be filmed alone with the monster in her dreams.

"Got!" it cried again as the beach below Sarah's feet settled, and its great ochre-red seaweed mouth cracked open, exposing itself to the heavens for judgement. For sunburn. For Sarah's gift.

"Got!" It cried more, and Sarah found herself overtaken as she approached the gaping mollusk mouth. Her heart had been gripped with a jaw like lead, she felt weak and small in its insidious teeth… But most of all, she shook. With the wire already taut, her strength inside was dwindling to the last tremble of a rabbit in the snare. She swallowed hard and looked inside. Only the pearl showed where the eye had been; all the gamey meat was grey and throbbing, contracting its pores like puckering lips, hungry with salival sweat. It reeked, and Sarah reeled from the image and the waste and its smell, but her only divine intervention was self, and she hung her fist out over the pit of it, dangling the coin.

But her only divine intervention was self—and the coin remained, still tight in her palm, reminding her of all the walked through steps that had preceded this moment.

Pausing in reflection, Sarah questioned the motives of this relinquishing, shaking above the Beast, thinking on the words of Charon.

Sensing the lack of fallen coins, a dark tentacle sprang from the mound of the Beast and clasped Sarah's legs, jamming a line of razors into her thighs, pulling her knees tight and her skirt high. The force, unbraced, swung her flat backwards and her body tensed for the exorcism, anticipation of the sand that would wash her hair with scalp blood, but her neck hung and her brains fell out behind it. Another tendril had burst from the ground and it held her hands in a heart of vines that ribboned up around her throat and pushed her head into a bow. Sarah screamed, losing the thoughts of words as it was all surprise and no present given when the tentacles lifted her into the air above the beach. Her back arched, her muscles screeched, her hands pressed her spine and her feet shook to kick them all free but she was tiny in the arms of the Beast. She tried again to scream, but the tentacles dug tighter into her neck and crushed any echoing of noise back into her chest.

The Beast's call returned. "Names!" it cried, and Sarah convulsed above the waves, choking to blue glistened skin, suspended in Japanese wire that wound her so tight that the coil fractured in the heat and the back of her knees came and touched her hands. She looked down her torso like a horizon, her stomach pushed out to meet the climax of its arc as the tentacles wrapped her in half, fingers and toes to the ground, navel to the sky, head lost in the fray.

It was fire.

Just as the water had been fire in the lake, so was the weight of air not exhaled. It was fire, and Sarah's body charred from the inside, turning to black squares of wood in the stove of her dying. She cried, evaporating, as her head tore back further and she looked at the ground from snapping columns. Another tentacle rose from the beach and slung itself around her body so that its tapered head sat on pedestals above her. She felt the tendril enter her navel, pressing its black beak into her belly and engorging in her cavity where it searched as mice and rats and shrews through the empty pot of her stomach, hungry for what the internal fire cooked.

Lifting her higher in the air and burrowing further into her belly, the Beast had Sarah trying to shake and flee and writhe all at once. She felt one of her arms dislocate, the shock sending pins through her head that turned to light that blazed a line straight through her. Muffled noise emanated from her mouth as she cried and fought to position the knots so that they wouldn't crank her shoulder any further, but she was stupefied at Hercules' sword as it continued to bite at her clavicle, splintering further as her gimp arm, given in, fell further from its shape so that all the tendons tore.

"More!" screamed the Beast and the tendrils engorged twice, blunting Sarah's connectivity from normal senses to her brain and doubling the perception of touch. Penetrating further into pain, her body wailed at the hot column of tentacle inside her, swelling as it pushed her stomach lining out to her sides, finding its way into her esophagus and pushing at the cord wrapped around her throat.

She squeezed the coin hard in her useful hand, pain pressing her palms to dig into the metal, fear forcing the needle of the wasp into her tarot, but it was soft compared to the worm in her throat, the tendril like coals or pincers. Its proboscis probed her collapsing larynx just at the cusp of the other tentacle holding her throat from the outside. The two ends on each side of Sarah's thinning skin, shared a grinding salutation that caused one to loosen its grasp on the neck. Her eyes bulged at the decompression, and she readied to inhale, but the outside tentacle had only given way for the one inside, now wriggling from her navel all the way through her torso and neck, flattening her trachea twice as it folded over itself over and over again. Finally it passed the juncture, passed the ring of wrapped tendrils and clambered through her suffocated throat to protrude from her mouth. Sarah and the worm sprayed their halo of spit and blood across the empyrean of gore.

And it was fire to behold.

Two tendrils lifting the gated child, another passing through her body like a sword.

Sarah's body, hard tense from the radio static scream of pain it suffered before it loosened in her lost grip, wilted in her bed of arms and let her body fall to the slave. When her feet hung and the tentacles continued to shake and jostle, her heart gave way and everything turned towards black as she fell further from the dream, beyond death in the surreal place of pre-sleep.

Everything slowed—the arms, the breathing, her heart—all penny-drop into the well slow as Sarah eased her free hand and let the coin fall. It dropped forever. It dropped beside small beakers of blood that tangled her hair as the veins in her eyes split and bled. It dropped beside lashes of water from the tide splitting at the Beast's mad tendrils. It dropped and the darkness kept getting darker without ending.

It dropped until a spark of light bounced from its surface as it crashed into the sand, making a hollow sound, as if nothing was beneath its initial landing. Or wood. A driftwood bleach tone warbled up from where the coin landed, and even Sarah turned her head to watch the gold piece tumble away into the sea on its side, at a great pace.

Stilts gave no warning to the circus act just as Sarah watched her hair rise up on both sides of her face, beginning to trail vertically out in front of her. Brass whistled at her ear, and her arms were suddenly in front as well and she didn't feel the wrap of the Beast. She was free, falling at some pace that was through the belltop of stinging jellies, beyond their fabric body and getting tangled in the string line hooks so that she fell slow like an aerial silk artist, through miles of numbing venom.

Somewhere in her periphery, the Beast was storming the beach in reverse, throwing arms of water to the side, pushing a path through the wake and searching, angry and fast. Not like her, not like the hard paddle that broke her back and pushed the thick air from her lungs. She watched the rose-coloured mist spray up in fatty globules, in honey, their path as fast as it dripped from antennae. Viscous property in her eyes. It fell, eventually, and Sarah bathed in the ichor of her hard-earned golden nectar, covering herself in the weight of that exhalation, breathing into the sky.

One hand lay in disuse beside her body, while the other checked the evaporation of her chest, pulsing with the up and down of her breath before it fell off and landed on something hard and wooden. Eyebrows turned up, allowing light into her eyes so that she might illuminate thought and with some gesture, Sarah found panels beneath the sand. A hinge. A splinter pierced below her nail… she let it sink into her flesh and felt that it was oak and it was polished and it was good. She turned, then, to the water, rolling onto her good shoulder, leaving the other behind.

The Beast was still madly thrashing the surface of the ocean, making bubbles and hissing noises as it scoured the seabed in search of the coin. Sarah opened her mouth to call to it, but it was quiet, a squeak followed by more blood and sand. The light was bright above her head, and she tried to lever her bad arm up as cover—but it was useless, so she tried to roll onto her nauseous, uncomfortable belly and found resistance; the door's knob touched her navel and she spun back, once bitten, and looked again into the light.

The door.

…*A door*. Internal sigh. Sarah grabbed the knob with her good hand and turned it. The light fell away quickly this time, and everything was sand in her mouth.

Part 30: Where There is Blood, There are Sharks

With her body positioned for retching, Sarah's image stared at itself grieving from the puddle it laid upon. Eyes so wide and stretched that they absorbed more light than the wet auditorium floor provided and Sarah didn't return the favour of her mirror, she was sight blind. Pupils positioned with ghost fish who prey in the abyssal frozen in the embrace of anything less than dark, anything more than aware.

From the auditorium floor, the cold wrapped around her knuckles for as long as it had taken to have a thought beyond the tentacle on the dock, over and over she watched Daniel pull her from the water and cart her half dead body away. She watched him pick up the apple that fell from her chest. She watched the obols fall from her pocket, then she watched the raven and the tentacle steal them. The whole flurry of images played on in the cinema of her grave until the swelling in her knees grew so that they popped, and she collapsed under the loss of weight and the gain of new mass and gravity. Sarah then lay until a thought came that drove her from the floor and had her stumbling to the yellow door at the far side of the room.

"Of course that's where the fucking coin is." She held one closed eye in another bruised palm, letting the other fall to the ground as she dragged it along. "Why the fuck is Daniel hiding any of this? Why would he keep it from me?"

The doorknob, caked in layers of salt, cracked under her hand as she turned it, breaking the crusted-over entrance open and licking the mineral now in the air, in her hand, in her hair. Wounded, Sarah stepped over the threshold into the farthest end of her tunnels and began to trudge, marching the long way to a place where she could ballet the questions she now had the answers to. *How to get the coin. To bother getting the coin. How to sleep forever.*

Daniel must know—or at least hold close—the wound left from the shape of loose dress pockets; he owes me this.

Lights swung, synchronizing at random and then stopping, as rows and rows of water-washed books in their liquid-logged walls grew and faded and passed without ever giving away the secrets to their scrawls. The floor stretched in agony, its herringbone shape cutting into shoeless feet and clipping dangling toes that dragged below lazy, angry legs and hips and bellies. Doors, for miles, set in ceilings, walls and floors, all called for Sarah to enter, to walk here, fly there, drift in a lagoon forever while the scent of sea birds wore off, while the brine carried the wind away to die on a shore without a boat in the deep waves of Sarah's heart.

She walked. Not thinking of potions for portents that came at each turn she ignored. Not focusing on Dad's relentless jumble of those same strung together words. Not thinking of the reasons this all began, the cabin in the sand and the dock she was taken over and drowned. Sarah only focused on what was stolen from her pocket and the man that was there when it happened. The man who might know how to retrieve father's ticket, a man that owed her an explanation.

It was all the difference between running in her dreams and exploring them. The gold that kept the treasure buried. The light that kept the wolves at bay when nighttime fell and prey was stripped bare.

Daniel owes me this thing, thought Sarah as she carried on through the centipede's tunnel.

Across a span in which Sarah would have woken and fallen asleep again, where her eyes were long-thrown darts in dragged-out hours, the doors all fell in line behind her for miles and the auditorium became a place at the start of night, now mid-day. The tiptoe arrow stone of the floor steadily gave way to mirth, gave way to slipstreams of muddied water and foreshadowed earth, floors that pointed the right way turned to faded, even breaking up in some places and being overtaken by a long patch of dirt work.

Sarah's shoeless feet had changed from Blackfoot tribe to quicksand-walking when, further ahead, she made out the plain white paneled door at the end of her dirt path. It glistened under the swinging lights with smooth, seacliff white plaster that grew from throbbing waves beneath its veneer. A powdery mildew stretched from its timber, bicarbonate in water, woolly aphid eggs and larvae and full-grown chewing pests grew from the pulsing door and stretched across the walls and floor and ceiling. Every long angry step across the black beard algae grew further into the bleach white that engulfed it, and Sarah came close to not seeing as she clambered onto the bright white pad in front of the glowing door. She struggled for the knob, knocking her clumsy fist against the halo of white angel ebony that protruded from the first door in her tunnel; everything it touched was turned to static white and overtook the tunnel for miles behind her.

She stood in a wind tunnel of limp colour, and couldn't see. Pulling the entrance open, she fell into the dream.

Mad chrome.

Matted grass, the colour grey, pushed its bristles into her nose as she tumbled onto the other side of the door. Hands were under her chest fast and pushing up to relieve the soft needles that poked at the tunnels beneath her eyes, caused tears and snot to flow from her open nose, allergies high time in an always-spring world. She sat up, scratched her nose with a finger and looked back at the door, beyond its entrance, everything was starfire. Fusion-hot white mist emanated mist from the tunnel in Sarah's dream.

Vapours from the heat radiated up and formed one-dimensional metallic clouds in the sky, ready to rain glue, lacking birth and even colour, despite their constant grey. Blind fish whiskers came into contact with the camera and light, and Sarah noticed the sky behind the flat clouds was dark, ashen, monochrome. Following the pattern of soon to come rain stretched a membrane across the landscape and everything was without colour. First cut, low budget, black and white film.

She felt below her body, where the hard papercut grass was grey, too. The trees not green, a bird not red, the wind obvious and not clear itself; all was grey. Every shape a cutting, every colour bled and left without dimension in the dreamscape.

Hot metal bubbled in throat, leaving an electric voice to conquer the wits, and Sarah could not ask for clay. She rose to her feet and gazed across the field, towards the river that ran to Daniel's place: everything was one flat sheet of itself, sat one step over from its shadow. Her hands, when she checked, bled from something that had scraped her in the blinding light and it bled neutral, oozing old pastel horror effects. She put her hand away like a watch and started across the field.

Cutting feet into matte colours that left spores behind her, she soon found a rut in the ground that swelled out five times in front. Something had appeared from the sky and fell in this spot, multiplying in worms that writhed across the land, forming a large latitudinal trench that ran in the same direction she faced. Once followed, the ring-lined tracks fell off into a haze of white. Placing one foot into its path, her skin found glass—hot, red-lined glass that speared fire into her foot, and she reeled it back for safety.

"Shit!" Sarah remarked as she crossed it over her standing leg and checked her sole, still black but now smouldering "What is this?" she asked of the fuming line in the grass, all of it black, smoking in a billowing roll towards Daniel's home.

Spurred by sudden awareness, her feet became wings on speed of fear, and soon all the grey was a smooth subway tile, falling away in peripheries. The river rushed in quick, and Sarah fell sprinting into its water, papier maché thick with too much liquid as it split off around her fervid panic.

The willow tree appeared, and with it, the dock and the shed. Mermaids, slung together with scale-mail silver tails, clung to each other, hissing at Sarah as she dashed past them, bleeding their lips out into the water. Sarah drew closer and found the cabin's roof torn apart; the worming rut had followed alongside the river and turned into a crater of fiery ash that cleared out everything around the house. The tree bark singed, the windows crashed, the patio furniture and the little table full of glass smashed into pieces and strewn about still burning.

She pulled herself up onto the splintering dock, its boards torn apart and left at random shivs. She hustled across the open pit where a huge mechanism—or beast—had turned the area into the remnants of an exhausted volcano. The scorched land charred her feet as she fell across the well of violence that felt as big as the sky above.

In the centre lay Daniel, his stomach torn until his spine showed through the rough. What was left was discarded like a broken chime, and Sarah ran and fell beside it.

"Daniel!" she screamed as her kneeling leg's skin split and peeled in the heat, leaving her bones to cook alabaster bleach in the ash. "Daniel!" she screamed as she heaved his body over her kneeling stance and held his head up, cupping his face, gracing his silhouette with her trembling arms. "Daniel…" she cried.

And there was a tiny breath in the little place where his gentle face lay, broken. And Daniel said one thing.

"I kept it from him."

Then his eyes closed. His chest stopped, and in his hand appeared an apple.

Sarah screamed into blank. Inside her body, her diaphragm filled until she was rigid and seeping with pressure.

There bled what remained of Daniel.

He was rain beneath.

And when he wept into the earth, all that was left was the apple. Clean and red, like so many things are not.

Part 31: Nice White Suits

Coughing up sand was like scratching your throat with the same thing that made you itch, and it made things itch even more. Sarah itched. She tried to pull her hands through her throat from the inside, out, but she couldn't manoeuvre her dislocated arm to get it inside, so she resolved to shout as she choked, spitting up amoebae and hermit crabs that scuttled away to hide under her bed, avoiding the dry places of her room.

Once the bottom crawlers had tucked away, the questions came. Painful, itchy questions that washed through her head. *What had happened—how did my oblation not appease the beast? Why did it attack me and why does my arm feel like it is about to be pulled from its socket?*

She tried to form words, but they were just grainfed nonsense, and soon the pain from her shoulder took over as someone, unaware, continued to bend it.

"Sarah, please!" An unfamiliar voice was at her side, sounding ragged, long experiences in the dark night ragged. "Oh my god, your arm is dislocated! Okay, just relax, let's try not to aggravate it further." The man let go of her limp arm, and it slapped against Sarah's side, cramming a fist of glass into her shoulder's socket. Sarah screamed and writhed.

"Please relax, Sarah! We didn't mean to startle you—please let us help you with your arm." Another unclear voice, rasped and bent from weight, formed on her other side and Sarah felt pincers on her back. Two giant beetle mandibles held her body in check, crashing into her from both sides.

She screamed again, and more sand fell from her mouth, mixed with bile, hitting the familiar floor of her room, bubbling. She gagged, more cut glass in her throat, more debris, more guts.

How had so much of it penetrated my body? What was that arm looking for in my throat?

"Jesus!" yelled one of the voices, and Sarah opened her eyes.

Light pelted the left side of her head, pushing her focus sideways so that more beach sprayed and painted her walls sunny island beige. She coughed again; her other arm was free, so she kneeled down and put her one good hand up to quell the headache that was brewing. Her hips buckled. Her ass fell further to the ground. She was deep below the threshold realm.

"Sarah?" said the voice at her right, and she looked to find a man in a clean white suit who blinked at her, trying to make sense of a situation she didn't understand. "Sarah, what happened?" His bushy eyebrows pressed up his helmet's visor. White knight and shining, he looked down and the morning sun graced his shoulders. "Are you okay? Do you know where you are?"

Why are these men here?

Who sent you? she tried to say, but her mouth hung open as she sat back into submission and caught the tears that fell from her eyes.

"We're here to help." The man on her left was also in clean white; he too, was hunched over and looking valiant for a person who had just crash landed. "My name is Daniel." And he pointed at a name tag on his chest that was all swirls and inconceivable. A bunch of spheres dashing in and out in front of it. "And this is my associate—he's also named Daniel. It's easy to get confused. I'm sorry."

Sarah coloured in the white of her eyes with a black marker and turned back to the floor. *That's not Daniel.* Her back was full of thumbtacks and she had grown tired of twisting the pinpoints into her spine. The sand slowly cleared from her throat, but the pain lingered and she fought to form words while it presented itself in new places, like her thighs and her wrists, rising and heating, making fire of the wounds on her belly.

"Dr. Pillapatti sent us," said the Daniel on her left.

An image of tentacles raced through her mind again and she thought of her mutilated stomach, panicked. She leaned back and lifted her shirt to check her belly button, blinking several times, inspecting the size and the shape. Fingers splayed out in fives netted the outside of her navel, making a cat's cradle of her belly that she criss-crossed and double checked several times, but there was nothing. She dropped her shirt and checked her throat with her palms: it was sore, but not swollen. She coughed unrestricted.

"Where's her mom with that coffee?" asked the man on the right. "Everything was fine until she left."

Their voices were a spindle of thread, thinning as they spun away from her

"Did you see what happened?" said Left.

Then growing big as they returned.

"No. She was getting up fine and then just started throwing up sand."

But messier and tangled.

Sarah's senses fired in rows as every movement in the room became a rubber band that would not stop snapping. Footsteps treaded up the stairs and made their way down the hall but there was also the carpet beneath Sarah, rustling, and the jar in her nightstand that rattled, and the closet was making soft paddling sounds, all a crescendo that shook her, and she tried to slow the pour of glass...

"Sarah!" cried Edna. "What the hell happened?" Edna's sudden hand on her shoulder was a beam falling from the tunnel wall and Sarah flinched to cover herself from a cave-in or a hungry maw. "Oh my god your arm, what happened?" And Edna held her close for a second: more fire at Sarah's side.

Let go! Let go! Sarah tried to flinch, but the pain held her so tight.

Left piped up. "We don't know; she got up, she seemed fine but in a daze, and then she was throwing up sand."

"What?"

"It's all over the wall." He gestured behind Edna, and they looked at the painting Sarah had made with her belly-shaped beach. All except Sarah, who was trying to ignore the noise, the rattling in her nightstand, the breathing in the closet doors that stole all the air in the room—*Why was no one else struggling to breathe? It's so loud.*

"Sarah? Are you there?" asked her mother, but she wasn't. The jar kept turning itself side to side, stepping across the cheap pressboard wood and making echoing noises at Sarah in snipped letters that fell like snow from the thick syllables of air.

"Names." She could feel the word as it came from the nightstand's darkness, no longer cowering from the sun streaming in. So portentous that Edna's poking fingers in Sarah's chest and arms and hips as she checked for hurt were cast aside for the calling of the shadows. "Names," it called again and the words pushed themselves into her chest, lifting her from the ground.

"Whoa," steadied the right, and he placed a hand on Sarah's shoulder as her mother held her tight near the ground. "Don't get up just yet, Sarah. Just relax, okay?"

"Relax."

She tried to turn away, to cover her body in limp arms and stars from the shaking in her head, but the bleak took over then. A great mouth held court in her thoughts. Black bile wove the curvature of Sarah's cheeks and dipped in behind her head, following a line of spines and ribs where it made its way into her chest from behind and carved the tissue of her lungs into a woodwork of tides.

"No." The words came crisp with the last of the sand from Sarah's mouth, cutting the air where she was black and the room was white. "No, we have to leave." She spoke in wrangled tatter, shaking from the weight of her overcast shadow. "The Beast is coming."

As she spoke, a pattern of heavy feet crossing a waterlogged dock creaked at the closet behind them, and all but Sarah looked back to the doors that were distending. The breaking of the dam.

She stayed, faced away from the tragedy she was sure would spill into the room while Edna, Left, and Right stood jaw struck at the bending, warping wood that kept growing out until the screws on the hinges burst from their holes, red and hot and slinging lava across the room.

One screw bounced and hit the left; he wailed and grasped the arm where the heat embedded his flesh. He fell to the ground and Right left Sarah's side.

The room fell into a darkening under the mass of its acoustics and the turmoil began to push the sun away, slipping it behind false windows and Sarah's growing absence in the filling of her shadow. She could no longer see the colour of the floor as it dispersed in the contrast of missing light. Edna's hands dug tighter with their knotted frantic fingers. In the nightstand, shaking wildly with a storm's throw of stone, the jar spoke again but the words came clear to the space behind Sarah's eyes.

"Names!" it cried, and Edna dug her rebar hands into Sarah's concrete arm, forcing her upright.

"Sarah?" Edna cried at her daughter with loops in her eyes. "Sarah, what's happening?" she begged.

Another screw flung itself from the hinges and bounced into the nightstand, breaking the mason jar and crashing its shards into the room. The closet doors pushed until the metal turned white and the wood splintered, shooting tooth-sized spears across the floor. All sound gasped, the room was fading to dark, and the boards of the floor could be heard cracking as the closet doors gave in, fell, and let loose something inside.

The last pieces of natural light made for a single display of flashing before receding, letting the room fall into an absence of white. A strange, static quiet washed over the room, but from the closet, breath was heard—a churning kind of breath. Something that might macerate.

Nails tight in flesh.

"Sarah?" whispered Edna between footsteps on the floor that, when pressed, slithered like a snake. "Sarah, what's happe—"

"Sarah." Her name stretched across a long black tongue and hung in the air like so many apples in a tree. Bright. Red. Full of poison. "Sarah." Its voice was a bucket plunging into a dark well in search of water, deep and black and swelling with moisture. "Sarah?" It let the tail of her name inflect upwards as if the corners of the caller's mouth were rising, making room for teeth and flesh.

"Time to be given," it said.

And then the room flashed in black and white as the beast entered, holy and strobing, its tentacle-riddled body moving in stop-motion between the flashes, and dripping, pouring white sand upon the floor. "Sarah!" it screamed, and bodies began to move everywhere.

Sarah didn't remember it looking like this, but somehow it felt familiar. Familiar in the way a fear of spiders might be, like generations before you had embedded the terror deep within your marrow. Its body was simply a deep, dark mire of tentacles and mouths tucked inside a giant shell; Sarah had sunk in such darkness before. She feared it, yes, but it enveloped her and in it, she felt loved.

Left and Right rose, turned to try to dash, their feet slipping on the sand on the floor. Two tentacles lashed out and grabbed each one's leg, pulling them back and upside down to hang like the fools they screamed.

Edna grabbed her chest, fell to the ground, laying back as if she were about to meet God. Her eyes wide, her heart beveled and left bleeding.

Sarah pulled away. In the midst of frantic family and bodies and the sense of warmth from the well of limbs, she jumped behind the end of her bed to hide. Huddling in the corner between it and the wall.

Tendrils slapped the corners of the room, breaking the trim and drywall and setting frantic splashes of powder and paper to flurry throughout the room. The strobing lights increased, their frequency matching the pulses of every heart in the shape of their penumbra. Sarah's view of her hand, moving in blurs within the intermittent light… she felt sick, the fast-forward slowdown playing tricks on her eyes, making everything hot and sweaty.

"Sarah," called the Beast from its ripe, opening of mouths at the centre of the shell. "Sarah!" The drop growl overlapped the screaming of men, each syllable slipping out with wet, blood-streaked fluid. "Sarah!" it called, and her name stuck to the air like a tactile miasma, filling the room with the inevitable.

The Beast waded into the open area, swimming on its body of arms, and filled the bedroom to its corners with an ambergris resin that seeped into all the forgotten spaces. Once soaked, infested, the bile melted into one as a cordyceps fungus grew to occupy the pores of the house, blooming mushroom tops with white dusty caps that reached into the haze, bursting with more spores and mold and cluttering as they aged. Sarah felt an itching beneath her, an agitation on her skin. She looked down to find the floorboards overridden with the mushrooms, growing tall and lean, covering her body in a thick mycelium mat. She struggled to fend it off as it grew in heaps, gorging itself on everything.

Fearful and heavy with sweat, Sarah battled between being overgrown in fungus and peeking out from her space behind her bed. The curiosity of death was so close at her heels that she wasn't sure if she should be sitting or standing until the screams, the screams of Left and Right dragged her from uncertainty and she looked out from between the covers to watch the men be wrapped in wire.

Their bodies were churned to chum as their torsos were relieved of flesh by the tentacle's sucker teeth, while a single tentacle wormed into each of the men's navels. It was searching, pulsing, filling their bodies with an inescapable satiation. Sarah turned away when they stopped screaming, when their necks engorged and their eyes bulged in opposition to their organs making room, liquid pouring from their ears; blood from the womb.

The sick sound of bodily struggle stopped with a popping sound, as the Beast pulled an apple from each of the men's bellies on its tendril hooks. Sarah looked again and watched the retrieved apples fall into the Beast's flooded mouth, its jowls shivering with each bite, the flesh ruminating in its maw as it dropped each man limp and breathless to the ground. Swallowing sounds marked the Beast, delighted in the delicious cider, wiping its lips with Turkish barbs.

Edna screamed then, from her frozen fear, and it filled the room— and Sarah fell further to the floor to hide.

"Quiet!" howled the Beast, lifting Edna into the air by her arm, though she fought and kicked and screamed as the tentacles amassed from everywhere, writhing over her flailing body to make a pulsing worm of her flesh. They left purple marks on everything, bruises for the fruit of the room that loomed over Sarah's head. Bruises of the flesh on Edna's rabid body of insect. Bruises in the wet sloshing of their working tendrils, searching through a belly for a space to eat the bearing flower bloom. Bodies filled to bursting until the screaming stopped and the phosphorus dust of a matchstick struck, taking over the bones in Sarah's ears, rattling last rites into her brain.

There was a thump, then the crunching of teeth again, as the Beast fed another apple to the hole, to the well, to the swelling belly that left black marks on the floor and Sarah's mother's body made no more noise.

Sarah sat and shrank while the Beast grew larger, as it pressed all the furniture out with its body until all their legs could be heard scratching the floor. Moving the structure of the room with its great mass. Pushing the stars aside for the weight of its construction—its permanence in this life.

As it grew, another tension grew inside Sarah, like hot flesh expanding until her organs pushed out into the wet. She retched; she retched and rolled forward trying to expel these organs from her chest, dry heaving the humours stuck in her throat. Her mother's mouth curled wet, and she could hear the rest of the darting tentacles unwrapping the gift of her body. Sarah retched again and when her closed eyes were so full of tears that she couldn't hold the weight anymore, she opened them. Beneath her two outstretched arms was an apple.

Red.

Shining from the paper that wrapped its pulpy flesh. A single spire poking from its top with the fabric of a leaf.

The room turned to blur behind her focus, and it all stopped for a moment.

Sparkling red.

Perfect crown-shaped fruit.

Sarah took slow breaths, forgetting until later that she had just then remembered to breathe. Each inhaling chest brought in the aroma of the apple tree, the snake, the poison, and the knowledge of both of Eden's meals.

She remembered then. She remembered what Daniel had said: "I kept it from him." The apple, The knowledge of one's death; and suddenly it made a kind of sense. The boatman had said there needed to be an exchange between the two of them, for one to take control—and the knowledge of death seemed like the very thing that would balance it all.

As Sarah stared at the apple, everything moved in slow motion around her. She was finally in control of the real, despite her dreams sliding over, and in that moment she was calm because she was certain. She had made it to the other side of the great darkness. The long dark night of her soul was finally ending.

She reached out while everything else slipped into another door, or a hole or a tunnel longer than words, and became nothing important.

The Beast flipped her bed aside and leaned in to oppose her.

Sarah reached out and plucked the apple from its perch, its perfect shape fit to hold her hand in a mirror.

The Beast became the mouse, with a thousand eyes, all terrified. It screeched with its wide black opals full of the dirt that formed them and shuddered, every agitation a needle for the pupil.

Sarah brought the apple close, and the sun and the moon reflected from its surface as a single drop of perspiration fell from its bowing leaf, sliding across the red skin to not absorb along the surface.

The Beast reached out, every tentacle wild to the source, ringing, pulsing with emotions, to grab at Sarah's wrists. Lash her to bedlam. Free her from this.

But Sarah bit the apple.

And then the snow came.

All the slowed-down flashing came to a complete stop—the noise, the screaming, the fear… the tingling sensation in her neck—all ceased. All around her was black, but the two halves of herself, the twinned stones cast a grey light of half circles formed.

And snowing.

Snowing ash in the ring of the stage.

Sarah saw herself behind the bed, cowering atop the apple, her mouth full of juicy red. She was so small from the vantage point of the Beast, so far away from this great peak of madness that had come from the other side of her head that she felt sad for herself, looking as she did from the Beast's eyes, from its great owled eyes of yellowed coal, from the shadow of herself. And when she felt something for herself, the tide slipped out and all the seething began to wash away with it. All the fear and pain that had been building was weeping out the sides, clearing away the layers.

Underneath it, Sarah was herself.

The Beast and the body were all the same.

She looked up at the Beast from the ground where she had plucked the apple and ate it and she smiled—for the Beast was her, and she knew herself and she was no longer sad for either.

It was always two places, she thought. *It was never just one... it was always both of us.*

She leaned down to her other half on the floor, looking up into her shadow's heart. Sarah reached out to hold her own hand, twisted from the tentacle of the Beast that was her other self, and she embraced it.

"Sarah," was all she said.

Chapter Six

Between one realm and another, it's hard to catch the light that bounces from a claw or a tentacle or a hand. Difficult to distinguish the shape of man, especially when the light is behind him, or above... or when you're being shaken and the radiance of a witches' ball on your ceiling blinds you. It is hard to render the silhouette of a person or a father in your sleep-rolled eyes: they might be a monster or a Beast or a wicked thing that goes bump in your mind.

Every time Sarah was woken in such a manner, the lull of her father's gentle hand and voice on her shoulder were like the vicious tempests in her dreams. She would bounce from her bed screaming, maybe kicking, fearful that the black mold in her own corners would grow and entomb her, turning her into shadows, black places where her body would be torn apart.

No night was different, and neither was her father's response.

"Wake up, Sarah. It's time to start dreaming," he would say as he always said, and Sarah would respond in always the same way.

"But I am already dreaming."

"Are you sure?" he asked with such earnest, honest, steel-cut eyes. "You were screaming again. Are you alright?"

Sarah pushed the soft part of her palm into the hard part of her head and tried to blur the two worlds together like a pirate with an eye patch, stable dark below to sunny sky above. "Why do you say that?"

"Because you were screaming."

"No, no," she said as she pulled her soft clay face in smears and drawn-out shapes. "Why do you say it's time to start dreaming?"

He had pulled a small chair up from the corner desk and leaned back on it, as if to stretch the question out, testing its tensile strength, querying his answer before he spoke, to make sure it meant what he said. "You always say that your dreams feel more awake than your awake does. I figure I'm just acting accordingly." Her father smirked. "And if I do—act accordingly—maybe you'll be more comfortable slipping from one place to the other."

Pulling the hand from her vision, Sarah turned her father into speckles and floating orbs of light as he talked. Both his words and the images he'd become let her relax and even sent impulses to her cheeks, to redden them and draw her brightness out.

"Are you sure I was screaming?" she asked, well aware of the answer that would come, but never sure where her foot last left off; making ledges would seem important despite their consistency.

"I'm pretty sure, yes. You woke your mother up. You know she worries."

"And what about you?"

"What about me, kiddo?"

"Do you worry?"

Her father half kneeled on the bed, leaned over and gave her a hug, starting a fire with two sticks, warm and genuine. "Only if you think I should worry." He spoke those words to the wall, his eyes like telescopes, seated lenses on the mirror host. When he let go, he sat back, straight up, as Sarah adjusted her comforter and sat cross-legged, checking the balance of her spine.

"It's hard to tell anymore." A bundle of fabric had bunched up in her hands and she made a sandcastle of it over and over again, squeezing the cloth while she recollected the past happenings of every night since it had started. Never being different. The dreams, the melting barrier of her bed. The hard lemonade that is sunlight.

"What's hard to tell, kiddo?"

The clouds, mammatus textiles still lingering from the dream, hovered above her head near the ceiling, and she was distracted by their display. They rubbed away the roof and teased the night sky beneath only to set an overcast and block the stars, cutting the knowledge, refusing the way.

Sarah raised her Adam's hand and hung it near the clouds, half expecting an illuminated hand to reach back, half expecting she might extend her phalanx and accept the apple, but the clouds swirled and worsened into storms that raged until they again became the ceiling, returning the simple blank blanche above.

Her father blinked his eyes and waited. Patient. Man well-known of the fate of angels, watching his only creation flitter on the brink of something that she knew was gold, with no one else aware of the worth in lead.

Two eyes surfaced then from the bleak of it again. "What did you say?" She looked at him like she always had, in the way that worried her mom and her teachers and her friends, like she was somewhere else entirely… but he saw it as if she were almost there—or exactly where she should have been the whole time.

He chuckled.

"It's not funny." Sarah stammered, weighed down by the clouds disappeared above her head.

"I'm sorry. You're right." He choked down what was left and answered. "You were asking if I worried about you and I replied, 'should I?'" He looked close at his daughter, looking somewhere else… "Should I—worry about you?"

Beneath her, the bed and floor passed between a milky white vapour and a clear top plastic as the ground from the dream she'd just left reformed. Below her hands, the bedsheets changed into hardened black and asphalt, and a rainfall shatter slicked the flat pebbles, amalgamated in the roadwork and a sewer grate, swirling with latent storm water, sucked the grime of the alley away, along with all of Sarah's scattered eyes. "Everyone does," she replied, the whirling motion increasing when the grate sunk a few inches below grade, sitting as a hole in a hole.

He patted her back. "Well, I won't, then… unless of course you ask me to."

"Mom wants me to see a therapist." She muttered with her face towards the gutter on her bed.

He sucked in those words as if they were fire and all his limbs were frozen solid. "You heard her say that?" He breathed out, smoke and fume.

Sarah took her eyes to his heart for only a second, long enough for him to know that idle wasn't her desired chatter to follow the statement she'd made.

"Therapists aren't that bad, Sarah. Besides, I feel like you've got a lot of things that you want to talk about but are too scared to bring them to mine or your mother's attention."

From the corner of the bed, a flock of ant-sized humans started to pour into the alley that was Sarah's sheets. They bobbed and swarmed in bumblebee talk, amassing in a huge circle near the lip of the gutter, standing on the precipice of the fall.

"I'm not scared to talk about them, but I feel like everyone else is." Sarah said.

"It doesn't always have to be everyone else." He smiled. "I would be honoured to be grouped in with you instead of *everyone else.*" Sarah tried to hide a faint smile, and her father continued, feeling confident. "We could start right." He shrugged his shoulders and swung his arms up in a lackadaisical manner. "Tell me if you know why you scream when you wake up?"

Sarah's eyes widened and all the little people changed colour beneath her chin. They painted their vellum skins in turn of the other, most of them changing to the pitch-dark black of phantasm velvet. The few others turned bone white, wooden-tooth painted white, off-white but a perfect colour.

"I like the dreams," she said. "I don't know why I wake up screaming, in fact I rarely ever hear myself do it." She glanced at her dad, and he was intent on being quiet and listening. "But if I took a guess, I would say I wake up screaming because I hate being here." When he scrunched his face up, Sarah watched it through the puddle of liquid at the corner of her eye, and she felt oddly comfortable. "I love dreaming, I don't like leaving the places I go in my dreams, and I think when my mind figures out I'm back here, I get upset. And I yell out. I scream into the opposite of the void."

The shedding left Sarah feeling cold, surprised. And as she stared at the people in the alley in her bed, now forming a large black circle with a small white circle at the centre, she shivered and sniffled, giving up the last of her barriers to the necessity of hope.

It was quiet in the room, even the little people, as they formulated and accumulated, made little noise in the very naked wholeness of Sarah's bed. She startled when Dad had taken some of the bound-up sheets behind her from the bed and piled them onto her shoulders, trying to show that he wanted to keep the cold at bay. When she looked at him, he was smiling.

"That must have been hard to say."

A flick again at the corner of her mouth. She pulled the sheet up further onto her neck and continued to stare downwards.

"We're on a roll," he said, carefully, with steamy cocoa in his breath. "I'd love to know why your dreams are so much better than here. I'd love to know what makes my daughter happy."

In anxious vibration, the little people began to move in sacrosanct swirls. Their rows upon rows that formed the circles travelled in opposite directions and magnetised the current of their whereabouts. Pulsating at the centre, the white circle turned from a Euclidean shape into a bird. An outline of a bird. A pure white avian in the black of the cosmos. As Sarah watched, drawn by the electric hum of their phasing movements, the bird jumped from the black to land in the sewer, disappearing and then reappearing at the centre of the black again. Becoming a bird, flying and diving into the sewer, only to reappear.

"Here, when strange things happen," Sarah started, "It's like they aren't supposed to happen." She swallowed a lump in her throat. "It's like they aren't supposed to happen at all, and everyone panics if something is off. They fall into this state of alarm because normalcy has been interrupted—and it's choking me, the panic."

She poked her finger into the crowd of tiny painted humans, and they moved away from it but took no notice, continuing with their show as if that finger didn't exist at all. "It's as if the only things that should happen, already have, and no one is comfortable outside of that." Sarah drew her finger back and clutched the falling sheet from her shoulder, and held it tight to her chest.

"But here in my dreams, when something strange happens, it's fine. No one questions it or bats an eye. It's as if what's considered normal there is for the unexpected to happen." Sarah looked up at the foot of her bed, but it had disappeared into darkness and only she and the people and her father performed on a lit-up stage, floating in a forever night.

"I'm strange, Dad. I see weird things that no one else notices. And I don't fit in here because of that. But in my dreams, I'm the most normal person there is."

She wiped a storm that was leaking from the corner of her eye, then turned to her father.

"And I can breathe."

Again it was quiet. All the sweater vests and bad puns in the world could not outweigh the truth of her expression. No, he had to sit back a little. He had to puff a metaphorical pipe and take in the smoke, let it germinate in his chest so that he could better absorb the seriousness of its char. He had to be a father here, not just a dad.

"Well," he said as he stained his chin with the tobacco on his fingertips. "I can't say that I know how you feel, kiddo."

Sarah's shoulders dropped.

"But!" he blurted out, "I don't think that's the point. I'm probably not built to understand how you feel." The room softened at those words, and he grasped Sarah's shoulder, pulling her gently, as if to get a better picture of her emotion. "I can be here though. I *will* always be here. No matter how you feel or how strange you think that is, I won't leave your side, not for a second."

She looked at her dad and smirked. "You'll have to do a little better than that."

"Alright, not for a millisecond." He smiled a big camcorder smile.

Sarah looked back down at the cinema of her bedsheets and sighed. "I just want to stay there." The words were quiet hammers in her head, hungry for coffins, thirsty for nails.

He sighed too. "If I could find a way for you to stay in your dreams, I would do anything to make that happen. You're my daughter. I would do whatever it takes to make you happy... and if I can't, I'll just find a way anyway." He squeezed her shoulder again, reminding her that he wouldn't let go.

Sarah smiled. "You would do anything for me?"

"I would stare down death for you, if you asked me to. That's my job… so even though I don't understand, always know that I'll do whatever it takes to make it right."

She calmed in those words; and their weight would never leave her heart—she would always remember them, even when nothing else could be garnered from her thoughts. Sarah turned her attention from the little people to say, "Thank you."

In the show atop her bed, the little people, painted in white, had stopped making birds. Instead, in the centre of the black background, they formed a single, two-pillared castle that shimmered bright and beautiful in the night.

Part 32 B: The Meaning of Books

Sarah swallowed. "I don't know…" and closed the book.

The skull, as if attached to a drunken stick, swung in figure eight patterns out from the cloud of birds before stopping to speak down at Sarah. "Well, I can assume you know nothing at this point." Charon looked up and raised fleshless palms to the sky. "Humans—cut from what form, I ask?"

He waited. Nothing spoke, so he took the book from her hands and threw it into the river.

Gasping, Sarah reached out to grab the book but when the pages touched the river and all the ink bled out, she could see the chapters disappear into the water. It bubbled as it sank. *All things are fleeting*, she was reminded. Her heart calmed and she returned her hand to the seat of the boat.

Charon continued. "An unwelcome guest who travels the astral realm will always be pushed to another and another and another until they arrive in the realm in which they've been born. *You* are the unwelcome guest, travelling from place to place illegally, incorrectly, without permission from the door and therefore, always end up back in the Earth realm! Even from your tunnel it is not allowed without the allowance of the door! The door dictates all exchange for it is god, and god is alchemy."

The skull retracted and Charon's body went back to pushing the boat.

Sarah, from her retreated position knees deep in her chest on the only seat in the long wooden canoe, carefully ventured for more. "My tunnel?" She asked in mouse-squeak.

Charon nodded without looking back.

"My… tunnel allows me to travel to different dreams. Is that what you mean by realms?"

Charon spoke as if there was blood in his empty mouth. "Dreams are simple human things, miscalculations! You do not dream like a human, Sarah. Your father knew. You travel from realm to realm, child, not dream to dream. And if you want to stay, you must visit the door and pass its threshold like the winter cannot."

Sarah imbibed the information, letting herself be drunk in thought before continuing to poke the bear. "Does everyone go to the door?"

Charon hissed and let the fluid that might have been his tongue dribble through the gaps of his teeth. "Of course not! Most come by the river Lethe; you've come by the river Acheron, through a Hellmuth, I assume?" answered Charon.

Sarah nodded, wary of firing the chimney again.

He continued. "You had *forgotten* your death, child, whereas most are unaware of it and then, when they come by the river Lethe, souls drink its water in thirst and forget their lives too. All things are forgot in the River Lethe, coins or not. I must bring those forgotten souls to the afterlife but you, you have memories of death and life and know… now… where the coins belong. So I will take *you* where you ask."

"The door."

"I know."

Placing one elbow on the edge of the boat to prop up the boredom on her face, she let her other hand dip in the water. She swirled and turned it like a rudder, catching the stream on one side or the other, playing with the current like a fish, watching her hand appear and disappear in the black liquid. Funny how the shadow only exposes itself when agitated. "What of my father, Charon? Do you know where he is? Did he come by Lethe like so many others?"

"He did," said the boatman.

She blinked, trying to pierce his back with further questions. "Did he drink the water and go to the afterlife, or did he manage to take the door?"

"The door." The words came out in a fog, hushed and hidden as they slithered through the droplets with which they fell.

Sarah splashed the surface of the water with a feathered hand. "You know, you're far more cooperative now than you were before."

"Feels that way, doesn't it?"

The boat lurched to a stop, throwing Sarah halfway from her seat as a melody of rocks scraped the bottom of the boat. Dazed, she pulled herself upright with clumsy hands. The boat had bottomed out on a coastline of huge, white rectangular stones laid in a messy point, of which she was on the left-most side.

Her eyes got away from her as she scanned a shore that she had been unaware of, one that seemed to have appeared as the horizon rather than creeping up the way a landmass should. Her gaze followed the mislaid and carefree rock formation that was the coast, absorbing its faint white glow of water chilled and thrown at heated stone, an evaporative effect that shot rays of cool sun blades across the penumbra rise. It smelled of even mist. Of winter damp. Of air-pushed will-o-wisp. Sarah stood downwind and checked its scent for anything, but all was neutral.

Breathe out. Sarah opened her eyes wide as she circled back solely on her neck and checked the spiral ride up into the ceiling. The island, as it were, was isolate in black sky. It glowed and shone, but where it stopped was determined by the black of the cavern, the dark of the river and a thin red spectral line, faint enough to be wound metallic and confused in most light that would segregate the landmass in a lost, deep vellum night. A lighthouse bound by strings and the caution of rocks.

The boat tipped back and forth as Sarah noticed Charon stepping from his perch onto the rock. As his foot made contact with the ground, the storm of birds that fettered his ghastly effigy reflected away from his form, choosing the boat as a construct of winds rather than the bones of the death ferrier. Charon stepped forward with his other foot and all the birds slid off like a coat, so that he was naked on the shore.

There, in front of Sarah, the crop of his body grew: Charon became man, and Death was true to himself. The great enslaver, the possessor of host. DaVinci's greatest, never seen, halted naked on the stones, turning back with green eyes that cut his passenger in half. He beckoned to her to leave the boat.

"Where are we?" she asked.

"Questions!" Charon sucked his teeth and walked away in huge strides up the leg-length rocks. "Always questions, surprising from one who has travelled so many realms. How do you adventure," he asked to himself, "without the sense of it? One will never know."

Sarah stepped from the boat in her bow-legged form and followed the boatman up the shore, the two-storey rise of rocks. He summitted before her and stood, waiting, not looking back while Sarah sidestepped up the last of it and straightened beside Death, at the cusp of the coastline, overlooking the river Acheron.

Glory's price, she thought as she turned from the river and the boat to overlook the island. Long and flat, it held a lake of its own.

And across the lake there was a wooden dock. It reminded her of death in a way that Charon never could.

She shivered; Death grinned.

"Last words are often my own, so don't feel too miniscule in my grace, child. It's something everyone experiences," said Death.

Sarah didn't turn to look at him, didn't bother to reply. The weight of her lungs full of breath on her insides was too much to allot for words. She could not form them in such cramped quarters; instead, she just looked across the dock as a scarecrow might look to birds and let her eyes refine from the burn until they were as jewels that held many facets. In every reflection there was a hand or a foot, a bent nail and a cut, a throat full of water and a line of blood.

The boatman made his way to the dock, turned around and called. "Door is this way. Hurry up, child, I have other souls to ferry. Important tasks for which to bury bones in." He turned and continued on the wood planks, creaking the way Sarah's throat might. "Work to be done."

Each haunted stride squalled at her ears, their shape a conch shell for her own death. Listening in to the placement of steps made her wince, and she wished to abandon the shore, but the stern hand of her father's ghost lay on her shoulder, ready to push her on.

Nerves, taut bowstring-pulled, made twanging noises and Sarah soothed herself by pulling at the fabric of her dress. Her fingers moved back and forth in spider tracks before they caught the trace of a disc below the pocket, and she remembered the coins and the reason she stood anywhere. Her hand found its way into the pocket and a needle slip sharpness entered her fingers when she clenched tight around the coin. Hot entered her veins, its venom coursing; steam clouds entered her heart, the infection growing, until she saw the door again with its unmistakable symbol.

A circle, inside a square, inside a triangle again… inside the circle.

The boatman slipped into the growing fog several strides ahead and Sarah grimaced, shook off the hands on her back and put her two feet at the dock.

The first rotted board lay at her toes, black mold streaking through its grown splinters and cracks and a bent nail sticking out, one that had been slowly worked up over years of constant rocking. A line, an old scar on Sarah's arm, began to itch and she had to chew at her lip to deter the pain. Her foot reached out and hovered a moment, but the scar's inflammation grew and she considered stepping back.

The boatman's voice carried from the fog, overlapped the dock and nestled into her back.

"No point in going back now—I've already come too far."

When Sarah raised her eyes up to see him, she found the dock had been saturated in a thick fondant cloud of ash and paint that hadn't fully mixed, that left streaks of grey in the grey of her vision. His voice came again, but it was saturated with grainy images and Sarah could hear her father in his voice. *The door was the only way.*

She stepped down and she began across the dock, as water spilled up from beneath the sections of wood, rocking the posts in the mud so that silt rose into the gills of long-dead pike that wallowed somewhere as their bodies were picked away at by birds. Wading the fog, treading its thick cosmos of blindness and overcoming the sense of monsters in a breath of clouds.

Pieces of her memories doubled up, shooting back at her with hot lead. Her father, stuffing the coins in her dress as they were now; the dragging, the pulling at her shoulder as she stumbled along; the cut on her shoulder where she fell. Sarah saw a thin ice pad of her blood on the dock where her father had picked her up and hurried her along. She wanted to touch it, but everything behind her seemed to be under a thick plate of glass.

Eyes forward again, and a silhouette of a bench appeared in the snake's vapour walk. Then a man, Death, standing at the edge of the dock where her father had pulled her in. Where so many names were carved in rock and left to sink into the bottomless pond. She slowed, seeing mouths and throats in the fog ahead of her. Seeing blood and choking in the smoke. Feeling heat at the back of her throat, making her want to retch back like a pelican, open her jaws and force her spine out to cool in the fog. It was so hot.

Like fire.

Like she was stoking the fire.

"Come along," said Charon in his strong way of saying things and Sarah felt her feet pick up. She came up alongside him, looking into that which could not be pierced, a place where pareidolia flowers could bloom into vicious monsters. The fog at the edge of the dock where she had died. The fog: like a canvas for the imagination. A canvas for the shadows of self and in it, Sarah saw the Beast. It stood, as it always had, at the edge of that dock. Breathing slow and hungry.

"It's fine," said Charon. "Just a memory. The fog has your tendencies."

Sarah's breath matched the Beast's and it backed away into the cloud above the water.

Smooth silk wind cut the glass of their meeting there. It shaped a bottle from their meanings and filled it with water and cut flowers that bloomed with moonlight, calling the frogs and slugs to their nectar, to their pollen, to their seed that nightcrawlers would carry away in the meeting of Death and Sarah. At the dock.

"Well?" said Sarah as she stood unblinking above the smooth, unfettered surface of slate. "Now what?"

Charon turned to her. His face was smooth as a featureless marble stack, unreadable if not for the small chink at the top where the corner of his mouth twitched and the true face of Death could be learned.

"We are the only stewards to our souls," he said and reached out—pushing Sarah into the water.

Part 33: Part Thirty-Three

Ether surrounded her. Its long stems of late winter blueberry frost prickled every pore to static on Sarah's body. She tried to struggle against it, but it was vapourwave thin, so free of detritus that it was pure in its alcohol base and there was nothing to grip onto. In the cold, water thickens, but this was gaseous and when Sarah kicked her feet or threw her arms, the drowning waves separated and left spaces where her limbs had been, marooning nothing but empty void in the places where talons would ledge, so instead, she fell, her fledgling body a victim like any other, despite the wings on her back, the curve of her spine, the soak of her skin in the cold. She fell as so many shoreline rocks do, eroded from their families and left to saunter in the abyss, the tails of their asteroids docked at the breaching tide, slipping into dusk with not even a trail at their hide. Nothing to mark their loss by.

Deeper, she continued to fall; around her became the lack of colour in the water, the only pigments were her rosy cheeks and the slick of silver on the bubbles that sometimes formed where her extremities cut with planing blades, leaving slips of paper with her form drawn in the ink on the page. The lack of things in the water dragged more from Sarah than the inclusion of them and when she tried to scream, more than just breath escaped her lungs. Hope escaped as the steel peeled back and left profiles of air pockets, irregular shapes, tadpole throat envelopes that swarmed in the twilight above her frothing, flailing body.

Watching it leave her, the sense of soul from her breath and voice—simply effervescing in the liquid dark—pulled harder at the string that had tied to her spine, and it pulled her infinitely further into an upside-downed cosmos.

From afar, she was a folded comet in the Oort cloud, her hair and arms and legs splayed straight up as if her belly was made of watered ink and she dropped, spilling, leaving faded brushstroke tracks only visible in the sparse platinum spheres of her trailing song. The last song. The death cry. And from her eyes, the water became a well, only a scarce cylindrical beacon of light above, where ice blocks swirled at the top, leaving circling shadows to fall across her Milky Way eyes.

Clothes, now soaked, became heavy weights and the lack of traction in the water left her slipping and burdened with gravity. The lake was already dragging her further down, when a cold snap reached up from the abyss to grasp Sarah's leg, culling her from the top to drown in the undertow's wake. It took her from there, further, always further; and all sense of direction turned into her fleeting shape of courage, her shrinking sense of power, and Sarah knew the map of her nose was losing all the polarizing metals it had gathered. She was lost and the surface had fallen further away than she could ever bear, its length become the zipper on her chest. She reached up and grasped nothing. When she dropped her hand, it grabbed the zipper and she pulled her chest wide open to bleed into the water, and her heart slipped out into the nothing, frozen solid.

Breath leaving.

Lack of that pouring in.

Only when her fingers had become anchors and her spine had bent so that her sense was turned down and nothing could be seen above did the floor reach out and touch her. Her fingers touched first, then her toes. Her hair fell back around her face and made an Inuk burial of her cheeks before it too backed into the deep… Sarah's chakra line finally touched the bottom of the lake, and she stopped moving.

Breath had become an intermediary, a thin mucous that separated the molting egg from its shell. She neither performed it through force of will nor naturally as a part of function but when she reached the consummation of her descent into inferno she gasped, one hard inhalation of the liquid of the lake. And it was fire—it was pure and it was white and it was fire in her throat that burned so bad it left another hole—and when she breathed flames from her neck into the lake, the water boiled.

Crucible husk, Dante's soul.

Then dusk.

Calm seeped in, and the lake was empty of turmoil. And Sarah sat awake, awaiting whatever thing might be like death here.

But he would not come.

Instead, a sound crept up around her, a voice in the darkness, pleasant and speaking from beneath her. Buckle-swash movement and the water slurred as Sarah turned around to face the silt and found she lay on a glass ceiling. A cupola. A domed roof that held her and the water back. Beneath the glass was a room she knew well, a room at the end of her tunnel with an ice-laden floor where a girl stood, pale and familiar, mouthing something.

Sarah looked down at herself again, staring up at Persephone in the auditorium where the water dripped from a crack not far from her head. She looked at herself, smiling. And the glacier broke off.

Crashing along the entire lake's body, a split formed from the original crack, severing the ceiling in half. Sarah and her open chest and all the water she had swallowed and still meant to swallow spilled into the auditorium below, fertilizing the room with her ceremony of discharge. Sarah was a flood, and she meant it when she kissed the impact ice on the floor beneath the ceiling on the bottom of the lake. It spilled her lips into ribbons and left long streaks of red across her face, but she kissed it and she meant it and the floor was welcome to taste of her fluid.

There, breath came. It came hard like a slap on your back from the doctor after you were pulled from the plasma of your mother. It came hard like birth, and Sarah sucked it in, godly, hellspent, sower of earth seed mayhem dirt—breath came and she welcomed it as the water poured over her broken head and her hair made an inferior pocket to collect air in the fray. She engulfed it, encased the taste of oxygen on her axed lips and dribbling mouth.

When the well had emptied, Sarah kneeled in soak on the floor of the auditorium, impatient wobble in her exhausted neck. She looked out between the wet strands of her hair and there was anger there, a frustration, as all the snakes kept ending at their tails. She was hot, but not hot enough to eat herself, and it made her a furnace for those thoughts.

"Why am I here?" she seethed to herself, wet blood and mouth flesh dripping from her tongue. Sarah flung her head back and looked up where the lake had been, but there was only cosmos, black sky, endless nothing above a room at the end of her tunnels. "I've been here before!" She screamed, her arms shaking, her fists powdered lead hard.

"I've been here before," said whispered, as the branches of her eyelashes gripped the new dewdrops from her eyes and she sighed, dipping her head again in cycles of repeat and crestfall.

Water dripped somewhere behind her, the last remnants of the lake falling out of the room. With it, the ice beneath Sarah's praying knees was melting and Sarah sunk further in her place of worshipful weakness. Lowering into the layers of bottom. Allowing the dirt to call her its own when a hard surface was found beneath the melting snow.

Sarah stopped falling from her grace when she noticed the ice had disappeared and she was knelt upon something wooden: there was a door beneath the ice. A single, uncut piece of black wood in a black slate frame, with gilded edges and workings, hinges and hardware shaped by artisan hands. And where there should have been a knob, were two slots.

Emblazoned in the centre of the door was a symbol that Sarah traced with trembling fingers.

A circle. In a square. In a triangle. In a circle. The transmutation of man.

Inside, she was a flock of migrating birds.

With clumsy hands she reached into her pockets, not taking her eyes from the door while she grasped at the coins. She pulled them out and held them up to the slots. One for one. She fidgeted and smiled and dropped one coin in the right slot and it tumbled down, clanking through machinations of metal parts. Then the second coin, a similar sound, then nothing. Sarah waited with stars in her eyes on the edge of her entire universe… another clang, some mechanisms whirring and then a spring let go and twanged inside the door. Sarah smiled, huge and devious… and the door opened beneath her. Sarah dropped.

Knees crumbled up hard when they hit the ground again, several feet down into a room beneath the auditorium, beneath the lake, beneath the dock. It was bruise-hard and purple for Sarah and she rolled over after the initial impact, grasping her battered legs and muffling swears of agony as she rolled on a dusty tile floor.

"Does *everything* the universe create *have* to be a joke?" she moaned and rolled to her side, standing up, shaking, slowly.

She puckered her lips as she looked around a small room, a bare room of maybe twenty by twenty feet. Dirty white tiled floor, brown wallpapered walls with a flat roof that the closing Cartography Door had shut in. Sarah nodded and turned her bottom lip up and to the left, pushing her upper lip into a ledge of derisive belief. "Figures," she said, raising and dropping her hands.

In the centre of the room stood a rickety wooden table with a greasy, low wooden chair to match. Above it hung a triangular light fixture that illuminated the table's surface. On the table was a map and a book.

There were no sounds.

No other people or furniture.

"Practical, I guess?"

Sarah walked to the table and looked over the unfamiliar topography of the map in a single eye flash, then she picked up the book. Its leather-bound cover read, "*Territory 1*" in fat black letters. She sat down, and flipped open its tea-stained pages, flittering through the pages from back to front, across maps and strange hieroglyphics, drawings of foxes and birds until she fell to the very first page which read, "**Dear Sarah,**" in familiar red Garamond. And it gripped her heart like a cold fist.

Below, something new had appeared, a single sentence that drew all the air from the room.

I said I would do anything.

Something splattered on the words, a liquid, maybe, that turned the ink there to drizzle and the letters began to stream down the page and across the table.

She closed the book and held it so close to her chest that she might explode. Her eyes squeezed shut with sand and her throat wanted to cave in as she fought back the sense of wind in her chest. She sniffled and held the book even tighter… and her heart exploded in fireworks made of warm blankets and ash.

Realising she had been holding her breath, she gulped and made a quick gasp of the air before wiping "it's nothing" from her eye.

She stood back up and checked the room for something else, a reminder of a person or a clue of their being there, when something on the map drew her to single spot.

Without question of heart, it was immediate, and she pressed there on the paper without pause, confident in what she thought.

The Cartography Door clicked and opened above her.

www.ingramcontent.com/pod-product-compliance
Lightning Source LLC
Chambersburg PA
CBHW061518210726
48287CB00006B/1736